# Dearest Mother of Mine

## Book Six of the Overworld Chronicles

John Corwin

ISBN- 13 978-0-9850181-6-0

Printed in the U.S.A.

RAVEN
HOUSE

The characters and events in this book are fictitious. Any similarity to real persons, living or dead, is coincidental and not intended by the author.

# I Ain't No Mama's Boy

When Justin finds out Daelissa plans to use his mother, Alysea, to reopen the gateway between the mortal and Seraphim realms, he decides it's high time to mount a rescue operation. But she's being held by Jeremiah Conroy, the most dangerous and secretive Arcane in the Overworld.

Of course, Justin's got even more problems when he accidentally kills the brother of Maulin Kassus. Who happens to be the leader of the Black Robe Brotherhood, deadly expert battle mages. And Kassus wants revenge.

If Justin can't locate the Conroys and avoid the Arcane mafia, not only will he never see his mother again, but Daelissa will be one step closer to world domination.

**Connect with John Corwin online:**
Facebook: http://www.facebook.com/johnhcorwinauthor
Blog: http://blog.johncorwinauthor.com/
Twitter: http://twitter.com/#!/John_Corwin

**Books by John Corwin:**

**Overworld Chronicles:**
Sweet Blood of Mine
Dark Light of Mine
Fallen Angel of Mine
Dread Nemesis of Mine
Twisted Sister of Mine
Dearest Mother of Mine

**Stand Alone Novels:**

No Darker Fate
The Next Thing I Knew
Outsourced
Seventh

*To my wonderful support group:*

*Alana Rock, Kayla Moore, Patrick Yates, Karen Stansbury, Dana Prestridge, Karla Ileana, Keren Hall, Nicole Passante, Anino, and Pat Owens*

*My amazing editors:*
*Annetta Ribken and Jennifer Wingard*

*Thanks so much for all your help and input!*

# Chapter 1

The apocalypse was nigh.

Even so, I felt sickeningly optimistic as I walked to the mailbox and couldn't help but grin.

All was right in my universe—impending Seraphim invasion aside. I'd passed my fall semester classes. Nightliss was slowly recovering from the curse Daelissa tried to kill her with. My sister, Ivy, had cured me of the vampling virus. Life was wonderful. Now all I had to do was mail the invitations to my Christmas party and hope the world didn't end first.

Jeremiah Conroy had the Cyrinthian Rune. At any moment, he could use it to repair the Grand Nexus allowing Daelissa and her fellow angels to storm through it and enslave every last one of us in the mortal realm.

I, for one, wasn't about to let the apocalypse ruin the holidays.

Despite the hefty stack of invitations, I couldn't stop thinking about three missing names—Ivy, Mom, and Dad. Ivy still lived with the Conroys. Daelissa had locked Mom away in an astral prison to prevent her from interfering in the mad angel's plans for world domination. And Dad? He'd abandoned us to marry Kassallandra, a princess of House Assad, in the hopes of reuniting the Daemos for the war that would erupt the moment Daelissa repaired the Grand Nexus and led through a Seraphim army. I didn't buy his excuses for a minute.

I would bring Mom and Ivy home one way or the other. In fact, I planned to deliver their Christmas party invitations in person when I rescued them.

A flicker of movement drew my eye to the thicket of woods surrounding the mansion and separating it from the other houses on

Greek Row. Most students had gone home for the holidays, so I doubted a stray frat boy had wandered over from a neighboring house. Most people kept far away from this place anyway thanks to its haunted reputation.

The crackle of dry leaves and limbs came from all sides at once. I looked into the woods and saw flashes of gray passing between the skeletal trees. Before I could turn to run back to the house, something slammed into my back. Invitations scattered to the winds, fluttering everywhere as they burst from my grasp. My face slammed into the dirt. Despite the strength in the arms pinning mine to my sides, I roared, and broke free.

Another flash of gray came from my left. I dodged left, grabbed the man by his arm, and flung him into a tree so hard, I heard it crack. The man's head broke open, and a ball of sparkling energy floated out, miniature bolts of lightning erupting from it for a moment before it imploded with a little pop and vanished.

More men appeared from all sides. They wore gray business suits. Their skin looked pallid and gray. They each wore silvery hair slicked straight back. Oh, and they looked identical. In fact, they looked exactly like my friend, Cinder. They weren't the result of a crazy experiment with infertility drugs. No, I'd faced these things before. Technically, they weren't even alive. I called them gray men. Most people in the know referred to them as golems.

And they encircled me.

Each gray man was a killing machine. It had been a while since I'd seen them, but I should've known Mr. Gray would eventually come back for me. The worst part—I didn't even know why he wanted me dead.

"Can't we talk about this?" I asked.

The golems didn't so much as blink, but closed in from all sides, some of them pulling guns from inside their jackets. I'd faced a gaggle of these dudes before, but this time Mr. Gray had gone all out. I counted nearly a dozen. "This isn't exactly what I was hoping to get for the twelve days of Christmas," I said. I juked right, reversed course, and plowed through two golems blocking the path back to the mansion. Something whistled past my head and buried itself in the ground. Those weren't guns, I realized, but Lancers which fired darts used to incapacitate supernaturals. "Show some holiday spirit, you jackasses!"

A gray man grabbed my shirt as I passed. I ducked, raised my arms, and let the shirt slide off my torso, freeing me. As I blurred toward the mansion, another group of golems appeared from the sides of the building and converged on my spot. I'd never make it to the door in time, I realized. Since I couldn't run left or right, I made straight for the manor, planning to dive through a window, and make a run for the basement. The tunnels down there connected with the school. If I was fast enough, I could make it to safety.

Having unwillingly played football in high school, I knew my path would connect with at least two golems before I reached my destination. I blinked my eyes to activate my incubus sight, and reached for the magical energy, or aether, floating in the air around me, and pulsing like blood through the ground beneath me.

Swirling gray mist, streaking white comets, and pulsating black holes of ultraviolet energy appeared. I extended my senses, and drew in a breath—my way of absorbing aether. Ever since Ivy had healed me, something inside me had changed. Before, I couldn't sense how much aether I'd drawn inside me. When I drew it in now, I felt it coursing through my veins and filling my internal reservoir to the stretching point.

"I'm gonna use your heads for tree ornaments," I growled at the gray men rushing to block my path.

I brandished the practice wand Shelton had given me, focused my will, and a fireball coalesced around the end. I veered left so I'd intersect one of the golems before the other. "*Hadouken!*" I shouted, and flicked the wand. An orb of flame the size of my head streaked toward the gray man in my path. The golem dodged, but wasn't fast enough. The fireball blasted into him and hurled him in a lopsided spin to the side, charring his suit to ash.

The golem on my right altered trajectory. I focused on his legs. With another effort of will, I cried, "*Shoryuken!*" Web-like ropes of aetherial energy jetted from my hands like a bolo and wrapped around the golem's legs. The target crashed to earth in a heap. Rather than give up, it began crawling forward with its hands, eyes locked on me like some kind of terminator robot from the future.

The window lay ten feet ahead of me. I dove.

I hit the window hard enough to break through bricks. But it didn't break. It bent inward, stretching like rubber, and I suddenly remembered Shelton telling me how the windows on this place were enchanted to preserve them for centuries. I also suddenly realized why none of the windows in the place had been broken despite it sitting derelict for several years before my gang and I assumed control.

The rubbery glass pressed tight against my face. I saw the inside of the house. I saw a group of golems emerge from the kitchen in the back of the first floor. I realized they must have come in through the back door an instant before my forward momentum ran out. The enchanted glass made like a slingshot and hurled me backward at terrifying speed. I flew over the front yard, down the driveway, and finally met a tree.

Twisting to the side, I took the brunt of the blow on my side. The air exploded from my lungs, and I dropped to the ground in a heap, gasping for breath. My vision flickered back to normal. Fighting the oxygen deprivation, I scrambled to my feet, desperate to get my bearings. But the blow to my body left me off balance. I saw the mansion to one side through a blurry haze. Using it as a reference point of extreme danger, I ran the opposite way.

The driveway intersected the road just ahead. A cramp stabbed into my side. I sucked desperately for air, and finally managed to gulp a breath. I looked behind me. An army of gray men raced down the driveway toward me. Silver darts whistled past. I reached for my wand, and realized I'd dropped it somewhere between the window and the tree.

"Go bother Santa Claus!" I wheezed.

My absent wand left me only one alternative—my arcphone. I grabbed it and took a right where the road passed through Greek Row and looped back down toward the dormitories. As I ran, I flicked through defensive spells Shelton had given me in case of an emergency. They were ready made, kind of like scrolls, and all I had to do was activate them. I twisted my torso to look behind me as I ran, aimed my hand at the ground, and tapped the "run" command.

A glowing circular pattern flashed onto the ground and vanished. I activated the spell several more times before my phone flashed a battery warning. Even though it ran on magical energy, it had to recharge like every other gadget. I ran the spell once more, and Nookli—the name of my phone—desperately said, "Justin, please feed me," and promptly turned off.

A gray man hit the first trap.

Blue light burst from the ground, instantly gluing the golem in place like a fly trap. The other golems flowed around their trapped comrade without so much as a second glance. The ensnare spells flickered like flash bulbs as my pursuers triggered more traps. The traps snagged more and more golems, slowing them, and giving me a greater lead over my pursuers.

I saw the curve in the end of the road. Saw the last two houses on Greek Row. *I've got this*. The gray men were fast, but I was faster. Even if they dared follow me onto campus, I could run straight to security and let them deal with the golem menace.

Two platoons of gray men rushed out from behind the houses on either side of the road. They numbered far more than a dozen. I looked behind me and saw my pursuers fanned out across the road to prevent me from cutting left or right.

"What the hell do you want?" I said, my eyes desperately scanning the area for any method of escape. I saw no way out. It left me no choice but to fight dirty.

Reaching inside myself like my Aunt Vallaena had taught me, I opened the cage where the demon side of me stalked, always trying to break loose. Eager to consume, destroy, and basically do whatever the hell it wanted if I didn't control it. It flowed into me. I felt muscles coiling along my arms, my legs, and my back like snakes. Felt my skin press tight against my clothing as my body grew larger and taller. Felt a tail spring from my backside.

Sunlight glinted on silver in the air before me. I heard a whistling noise followed shortly by the sting of multiple projectiles piercing my skin. I looked down at tiny silver darts sprouting from my chest. One hit me in the nose with a painful *doing*. I heard more of them glance off the horns growing from my forehead.

I thought my demon form would protect me. Unfortunately, nothing could protect me from so many darts. I tried to walk. Tried to move forward. Intense pain coupled with lethargy crippled my muscles. All I could do was watch helplessly as the ground closed in on my face.

5

"Mr. Slade, I do hope you'll forgive this somewhat rude invitation."

I jerked awake. I peered through bleary eyes to find the source of the polite voice. My head felt as heavy as a bowling ball, mouth hanging open. I tried to lick my lips with a sandpaper tongue. Despite feeling the obvious presence of drool at the corners of my mouth, I was also so thirsty my mouth felt like a desert. "Wa-wa," I said, unable to properly form the word.

"Of course, Mr. Slade," said the voice of someone with an obvious nerd pedigree.

I felt a straw pressed into my mouth, and managed to suck sweet delicious water down my parched throat. I kept drinking until I thought I'd barf.

"Please don't overdo it, Mr. Slade," said the nasal voice.

I blinked a few times as my eyes focused on someone standing in front of me. A face resolved from the blob, and I tried to jump back but failed since I was sitting in a chair apparently attached to the floor.

A gray man looked back at me, smiling. The smile sent the feeling of spiders crawling up my spine, even though it looked amazingly genuine.

"Who are you?" I asked, and tried to stand, even though I fully expected restraints of some kind to hold me down. Much to my surprise, I rose to my feet, albeit with a bit of wobble in my knees.

"I am Lornicus," the golem said. "I apologize for the shoddy way you were treated, but it was imperative I bring you here to talk to my master." He clapped his hands, and the dim light in the room brightened perceptibly.

I felt another shock of confusion as I saw him clearly for the first time. Though he looked exactly like a gray man, his skin boasted a natural peach tone.

Lornicus seemed to sense my confusion, and held out a hand. "My skin is also warm, Mr. Slade, if you wish to see for yourself."

I backed away. "Are you real?"

His lips pursed in thought. "I am real in the sense that I am not illusion. However, the question you are asking is, 'Am I alive?'" He offered a slight smile. "I am not alive in the way you are, because I am a golem." Lornicus folded his hands behind his back. "However, I know you did not mean to engage in philosophy, and it is rather imperative you speak with my master while he's still here. Given that, would you please accompany me?" He motioned toward the door.

I could have played tough guy and refused or demanded more answers, but curiosity—as usual—got the best of me. I shrugged, and said, "After you."

We walked through a long hallway with white tile flooring and equally bland walls and ceiling. The light fixtures looked like ordinary fluorescents, and I noticed electrical outlets with a North American design interspersed along the wall. Evidently, I wasn't in Queens Gate anymore. We passed several closed doors and reached an elevator.

Lornicus pressed the call button. A moment later, it dinged, and the doors opened. The easy-listening version of a song I recognized drifted out. We stepped inside, and the golem pressed the topmost button.

"You're not like the other gray dudes," I said as the doors slid shut.

He shook his head. "No. I am either a success story, or a failure, depending upon the way one might look at it. My creator didn't intend me to appear or act as I do, though I take comfort in the fact he didn't destroy me upon realizing my defect."

I almost told him about Cinder, formerly a gray man who now possessed sentience, though he was completely ignorant of how to act like a real person, unlike Lornicus. The idea seemed like a bad one, though. Despite his friendliness, this golem served someone who'd tried to kill me on numerous occasions. On the bright side, I could ask all the burning questions I wanted once I came face-to-face with this special someone. Not that I anticipated solid answers.

"He is not expecting you," Lornicus said, clearing his throat nervously. "Please allow me to speak with him first in case he decides to kill you."

"Wait a minute," I said, fear gripping my bowels. "Why—what—"

I didn't have a chance to finish the question before the elevator opened into a spacious office overlooking a skyline crowded with skyscrapers. A man sat at a desk, fingers steepled, steely gray eyes staring pensively at the elevator.

He looked exactly like Lornicus and the gray men. More correctly, they looked exactly like him. His lips compressed into a thin line, and anger clouded his face. This man was Seraphim—an angel. He could kill me where I stood.

This man was Mr. Gray.

# Chapter 2

Mr. Gray's eyes switched to Lornicus. "I told you no," he said, his baritone voice deadly quiet. "I see my commands no longer hold sway over you, servant."

Lornicus bowed deep. "They do, master. But I am here to serve your greater good. Meeting the Cataclyst, in my estimation, serves you far better than ignoring or killing him."

"Explain," the angel said.

"Foreseeance four, three, one, one has come to pass, sir. The decision has been made. This makes the future uncertain, and I believe Mr. Slade is your best hope for determining what is to come." The golem bowed again. "I am only doing what you created me for, sir."

Mr. Gray regarded Lornicus silently for a moment before switching his unnerving gaze to me. He motioned toward a leather chair in front of his desk. "Please have a seat, Mr. Slade." He looked back at the golem. "Lornicus, leave us. I will decide what to do with you later."

"By your command, sir." The golem gave me a curious look before getting back into the elevator and disappearing behind the closing doors.

Deciding to see where this went and hoping desperately it didn't end with a horrible demise, I took the proffered seat and met Mr. Gray's eyes. "It's nice to finally meet the man who's been trying to kill me," I said, somehow managing to keep my voice friendly, and my lips from curling into a snarl. His gray men had attacked me and Elyssa in the Grotto as we tracked down an assassin who'd marked my father for death. His golems had tried to run me over with a garbage truck not long after. Seeing the puppeteer behind the attacks felt surreal. Controlling his surrogates in their attempts to kill me must have been like one big video game for this man. Except he had infinite lives to lose, and I had only one.

He regarded me for a moment more before speaking. "You are a dangerous force in any equation, Mr. Slade. Time and time again, you have outdone my greatest expectations, and lived up to my worst fears."

To hear that he, of all people, feared me bolstered me slightly, though it should have scared the ever-loving poo out of me. "You and your angel comrades want Armageddon," I said. "It sounds like a really bad deal for the billions of people in this world."

A smile crept over his face. "Your assumption is incorrect." He folded his hands atop the large executive desk. "True, I once enjoyed the fruits of enslaving the people of this world. I once commanded armies of humans, created legions of my minions, and reveled in the art of war." His eyes seemed to look into the past. "It was all a game. A meaningless way to pass the time." His unnerving gaze found me once more as he leaned forward. "I learned better."

I flinched in surprise. "Meaning, you don't want to take over the world again?"

He waved a hand toward the skyline visible through the huge windows. "In a way, I already have. I own businesses, which span the world. I employ thousands of humans, driving their daily lives with commerce. I revel in the battle of business, of outthinking my opponents and crushing them with wits." He flicked his hand, as if dismissing it. "I do not wish to see this mortal realm destroyed any more than you."

"Why try to kill me then?" I asked, even more puzzled. "It's not like I'm threatening your employees' health benefits."

He smiled and leaned back. "No. You represent chaos. You represent uncertainty. Quite simply, you are a force which could tip the precarious balance of the future."

I felt an eyebrow rise at his statement. "Um, and Daelissa doesn't? She's hell-bent on repairing the Grand Nexus and letting in the rest of your buddies. I'm just trying to stop her."

He seemed to mull that over for a moment, his figure growing still. "You have proven useful in delaying her plans. While her attempts at throwing the Overworld"—he paused, a corner of his

10

mouth lifting in obvious amusement—"into disarray have been childish and ill-considered, I have agents working to undo her feeble manipulations. Though you have done well in thwarting her, you are more like a bull in a china shop, wrecking everything with brute force. My subtle tugs on the threads would have been more than enough to undo her damage."

My nose wrinkled. "Wait a minute—are you blaming me for letting her get the rune?"

He lifted an eyebrow. "Your ignorance only compounds the problem, young man. She does not possess the rune and will not. At least not until I deem it time to set the wheels in motion which will create an absolute stalemate. I will create the balance I desire, and she will be undone."

The man was so full of himself he reminded me a lot of Underborn, the most notorious assassin in the Overworld and a great lover of manipulation. It raised a suspicion in me that Underborn might be the human version of Mr. Gray. Or maybe—"Do you employ Underborn?"

Surprise flickered across his face for the briefest second before disappearing into his poker face. "My business dealings are none of your concern—"

"Ah, so you do," I said, leaning forward with a grin. "It makes perfect sense for one big manipulator to use another." A smug feeling bolstered my grin. "Perfect balance between the dark and the light. I guess that's why they call you Mr. Gray."

"An apt description, Mr. Slade. You are, however, still woefully ignorant."

"Dude, I'm only eighteen. You're like eighteen-zillion years old. I would hope you know a lot more than me." I crossed a leg, attempting to give the impression I was more in control of the situation than I was. "Fill me in, then. Maybe I'll agree with you and let things with Daelissa and the Conroys go. I'd like nothing better than to relax without wondering when the next wave of creeps is about to beat the crap out of me."

He returned a level look, which seemed to bore into my very soul, as if deciding whether he should kill me now, or simply kick me out of his building. "There is an aura about you, Mr. Slade. A peculiar magnetism that makes me want to trust you."

11

I almost made a joke about my deodorant, but figured a being like this wouldn't particularly appreciate it. I took a deep breath and put on my best sincere look. "How can I stay out of your way if I don't know what to watch out for? Or are you afraid to tell me because you're really up to no good?"

"In truth, I see little disadvantage to informing you," he said. "Though I must deflate your sense of self-importance first." He stood, and walked to the window, staring out. "You have only a tiny notion of the scale of Daelissa's manipulations, or how many I have defused over the years. Your mind cannot even conceive the complexity of my operations. We are reaching a critical juncture. Others of my kind who survived the Desecration grow stronger with every passing day. Most of them wish a return to the old days. Others simply wish to return home to regain their dwindling sanity."

"Desecration? Are you talking about when the Grand Nexus blew up and husked everyone?"

He nodded.

"I've seen how crazy Daelissa is," I said, not giving him a chance to change the subject. "Are you losing your mind, too?"

"No. Balancing the light with the dark keeps me sane." He clasped his arms behind his back. "The others regard the dark as filthy and won't touch it. That is why they lose their grasp on reality. They refuse to draw upon both essences, even though it happens naturally in our home realm."

I felt myself slipping into confusion, as I usually did when trying to understand the difference between the dark and the light. In my world, it was cut and dry—good was light, and dark was evil. Not to the angels. "What's with the dark and the light with you guys? Darklings, Brightlings—what's it all mean?"

Mr. Gray turned from the window, an amused expression on his face. "Is that not always the question, Mr. Slade? I suppose I should make allowances for one such as you—an entity of three worlds. Part Seraphim, part Daemos, and raised as a human—you are unique. Your sister was raised to believe only in the word of Daelissa, and lacks the perspective you gained." He walked to a liquor cabinet and poured himself a glass of amber liquid. "Care for a drink, Mr. Slade?"

"I'm underage."

12

The Seraphim raised an eyebrow. "You see? Human perspective. It is, perhaps, one reason you're such an agent of chaos." He took a sip. "There are two primary essences in this universe: dark and light. Our souls are the containers of this essence, which gives us the true spark of life. Even though the aether in the air around us and in the ley lines beneath us roars with this lifeblood, there is something about the soul that transforms it into rarified form. As aether, we use it to wield magic. As part of a soul, it is something quite different."

I'd made a tenuous connection between aether and the two spectrums. After all, I'd seen plenty of ultraviolet, white, and even gray clouds of aether floating in the air when I switched to my incubus sight. I'd also wondered if it had anything to do with soul essence, given the little I knew about how angels fed. Daelissa had fed on Elyssa once, drawing light essence from her. But I'd seen Meghan feed Nightliss glowing white soul essence as well.

"I'm following you," I said, only partly lying.

He nodded. "Neither the dark nor the light is evil, in and of itself. All of my kind are capable of feeding from either spectrum, but as we age, our bodies naturally take on an affinity for one or the other."

I waited, expecting a shocking revelation. His matter-of-fact explanation left me feeling disappointed. "That's it? Why do Brightlings think Darklings are evil? Why did the Brightlings treat the Darklings like slaves?"

"Quite simply, prejudice," he said.

I thought back to everything I'd been through. To the strange visions I'd suffered, demanding I choose either the light or the dark. His explanation made no sense in that context. In other words, Mr. Gray was hiding something from me. I waffled, uncertain if I should call him out on this. Even if he knew the true meaning behind the whole Dark-versus-Light thing, would he tell me?

Mr. Gray took another sip of his drink. "There is, however, a much grander scale to this, as I'm sure you've realized." His eyes met mine. "The choice in Foreseeance Forty-Three Eleven pointed to a choice between the dark and the light. As Lornicus stated, it is my belief the conditions for the foreseeance have been met. The decision was made. You were not the one who decided."

This was something I already knew, or at least those of us in my extended family had surmised. I'd had a chance to betray Ivy. She'd

13

had a chance to let me die. In both cases, we'd chosen each other. Whether that meant our choices were a wash or not, I had no idea.

He paused, as if letting the import of his words sink in. I wanted to hear what he thought before I said anything.

"Which side did she choose?" I asked.

"As with any foreseeance, it is rather unclear." Mr. Gray finished his drink, and set the glass down on the granite bar countertop. "Though the universe has long waxed and waned between periods where one essence was slightly more powerful than the other, it has enjoyed a remarkable period of relative neutrality."

"Between good and bad?" I asked.

"Good and bad are moral absolutes, Mr. Slade. I thought you understood they bear no connection to the Murk and the Brilliance." Despite his rebuff, his face held no disappointment. "Darklings bear the mark of the Murk. Their wings are ultraviolet. Their magic utilizes the dark spectrum of aether more easily than the light. The Brightlings are the opposite."

"So, we're not talking Yin and Yang here," I said, confused.

He traced the air with a finger, forming a perfect circle of pale light. He drew a line down the center, flicked a hand. One side filled in ultraviolet, the other pure white. "Is this what you imagine the balance to look like?" he said.

I almost blurted out a resounding yes but, miraculously, managed to keep my mouth shut to allow my brain a few extra seconds of processing. I only needed to consider the speaker to realize what he thought the balance looked like. "Everyone carries a bit of the Murk and Brilliance in them," I said. "That would mean we're all mostly gray."

He looked almost as pleased as one of my professors when I managed to say something smart. "Precisely. Too much of one or the other causes imbalance. This causes actions which one might judge as good or evil. Imbalance is imperfection."

"What you're saying is the universe is fifty shades of gray?"

"What I am saying, Mr. Slade, is an oversimplification. These two colors are simply the way our eyes translate the two most primordial forces in the universe." He folded his arms across his chest. "Creation and Destruction."

I almost made a quip about the good versus evil analogy being spot-on, though technically, neither of those forces was good or bad within themselves. "So, which is what?" I asked.

"The Murk creates. The Brilliance destroys," he said in a matter-of-fact tone. "The Murk is cold like space, the Brilliance burns like the sun."

"Considering what you and your Brightling pals did when you were in control, I suppose I could see that," I said. They'd nearly wiped out human civilization with their war games. "If the Brightlings are so big into destruction, how'd they manage to build the arches and the Grand Nexus?"

"The Brightlings did not build the arches," he said.

I raised an eyebrow. "The Darklings did?"

He shook his head. "The Grand Nexus already existed. We merely found it."

I felt my mouth drop open. "But that would mean…"

"We are not alone in this universe, Mr. Slade."

# Chapter 3

Mr. Gray checked his watch. "I'm afraid we've run out of time."

I gulped, and wondered if this was it for me. Then again, why would he go through the trouble of educating me if he only meant to kill me? "I still have questions," I said, deciding to press my luck.

"I'm sure you do. I am undecided about your future." He pressed a button on a phone.

"Yes, Mr. Gray?" asked a woman on the other end.

"Please inform the pilots I will be up to the helipad in five minutes."

"Immediately, Mr. Gray," she said.

"Another reason I'm letting you stay free, Mr. Slade, is this: Though the foreseeance seems to have concluded, it does not mean your presence is inconsequential. You may yet have a role to play. Until I determine what that role is, I am unwilling to cut your thread short or obstruct it."

"Gee, thanks, Methuselah," I said, heaping scorn into my words. During a conversation with Mr. Bigglesworth, Ivy's deceased shape-shifting pal, I'd figured out Mr. Gray's real name. If I'd expected a big reaction from him, he left me disappointed.

"I haven't heard that name for a very long time," he said, without putting any particular emphasis or surprise into his tone. He touched a button on his desk phone. "Lornicus, our guest is ready to depart. Please collect him, and return him home."

"At once, sir," came the golem's nasal voice.

"What's in this for you?" I asked, trying to glean a little more information before Lornicus collected me. "Are you really happy playing human? Or do you enjoy playing the role of fate more?" His talk of snipping threads and manipulating events to suit his purpose struck me as awfully conceited.

"As I said, Mr. Slade, our time has run out. Until I know more, I see little value informing you further."

Someone knocked on the double doors. A woman opened them. "The pilots are ready, sir."

"Very good." He looked at me. "Until the next time, Mr. Slade." Mr. Gray left, closing the doors behind him.

A split second later, the elevator dinged, and an anxious-looking Lornicus emerged. He raised an eyebrow. "You are still alive. I suppose it's a sign things went better than expected."

"What, did you really think he'd kill me?" I said, anger flaring. I was tempted to throw him out the plate glass window.

"I determined the possibility of his killing you to be very slight— no more than a thirty percent probability."

"You call that slight?" I said. "Maybe you need to take math again."

"I've learned a great deal from observing my creator," the golem said. "Though he has a keen eye when it comes to the big picture, I believe he leaves cards unused, avenues unexplored. As the Cataclyst, you have great power to effect change."

"Why do you keep calling me that?"

The golem tilted his head slightly. "You are a catalyst, a prime reactive in events leading to a possible cataclysm. I have heard others refer to you in this way, and believe it's an apt descriptor."

"What others?" I asked.

"Why, the others controlling the game," he said, as if it should make all the sense in the world.

"Names, Lornicus. I want to know names."

"Daelissa, Jeremiah Conroy, Underborn, and some leaders of the primary supernatural factions." He tapped his chin in thought. "I am certain there are more, though knowing their names will make no difference."

"I'm nobody's pawn," I said, slashing the air with a hand, even though I knew full well I'd been played time and time again by people like Underborn, assassin and master manipulator.

"You are a reactant," Lornicus said. "When something affects you, your response tilts the balance. Because you are the Cataclyst, your decisions impact the future in interesting ways."

"I don't want to deal with this crap," I said. "I'm a simple kind of guy. Give me my family, my friends, and leave me alone."

"And to hell with the world, Mr. Slade?"

I clenched my teeth. "Obviously, if angels enslave the human race it's going to affect my happy place. If Mr. Gray really wants to keep Daelissa from completing her diabolical plans, then he can handle it so I don't have to."

"You're still posed with rather serious obstacles when it comes to your family, however." The golem seemed quite smug at this statement. He motioned me into the elevator. "I have arranged transportation for you to a destination of your choosing."

"Queens Gate is fine." I stepped into the elevator with him, my insides roiling at his statement about my family. The golem sure had a way of spoiling my holiday cheer, especially since I knew he was right. What information did he have? Could he help me rescue my mother and Ivy? I sure as hell didn't have a plan. I didn't even know where the Conroys lived, or if they kept my mother in the same location as Ivy.

I remained silent as the elevator descended. Lornicus seemed content to leave me to my thoughts. Fantasies of having Mom and Ivy home for the holidays swirled in my head, warm fuzzy feelings mingling with ice cold reality. The golem probably had information that could lead me directly to them. Why would he have gone through all the trouble to kidnap me unless he wanted to use me in some way?

The doors dinged open to a tunnel stretching into the distance. A sleek, floating platform of some shiny metallic substance hovered a few feet off the ground.

"Where are we?" I asked.

"Not far from an arch which will return you to Queens Gate. Never worry, you are quite safe." Lornicus motioned for me to board the craft.

I stepped aboard, keeping a wary eye out, but saw no other doors in the tunnel from which gray men might spring. The shuttle whisked us down the tunnel, during which time Lornicus busied himself checking an arcphone, tapping out what looked like emails until we stopped at a cavernous room with an Obsidian Arch dominating the center.

The Obsidian Arch network provided nearly instantaneous travel for citizens of the Overworld. Hundreds of them dotted the globe, most located in way stations near the entrances to what could only be described as pocket dimensions—places like the Grotto or Queens Gate, which existed in a place other than the mortal realm, enclosed by an impenetrable barrier to whatever lay beyond. If Mr. Gray wasn't lying and the angels hadn't built the arches or the pocket dimensions, then who had? Did giants watch us from outside the barriers, tiny ants in detailed snow globes?

"Which way station is this?" I asked, looking around the empty space. Most way stations were packed with travelers much like an airport. Each usually had a stable for the menagerie of animals visitors used to transport themselves.

"It has no name. Mr. Gray knew of its existence and uses it for himself." Lornicus ushered me toward the arch.

*Mom. Ivy.*

I had to ask the golem for information. If I stepped through the arch, I might not have another chance. But would he help me, or rub it in my face?

The arch hummed to life as we walked toward it, the center flickering between ultraviolet, white, and gray, the thrum of energy vibrating the air around us.

Lornicus had mentioned my family on purpose. *He's manipulating me.* He wanted me to ask for help with my family. If I did, I'd be stepping right into his trap. My friends and I had overcome obstacles before. We could find Mom and Ivy without the help of a conniving golem. *I hope.*

"This will take you to Queens Gate," Lornicus said.

"Thanks," I said, and headed for it without another word as the center of the arch flashed faster and faster. *Did I really just thank the jackass who kidnapped me?* Each step felt leaden as my desire to turn and ask the golem about my mom threatened to overwhelm my self-control. *Would just asking him hurt?* I knew from experience with the assassin, Underborn, how easy it was to be manipulated.

"Mr. Slade, may I have one more moment of your time?"

I held back a sigh of relief. "Yes?" I asked, facing the golem and trying to look impatient.

He regarded me with a neutral expression. "As you are aware, the Cyrinthian Rune will restore the Grand Nexus to functionality."

"Yes, and then the Alabaster Arch network will reconnect to the angel home world. Daelissa will raise her army, and mankind will suffer an eternity of slavery and oppression." I raised an eyebrow. "What's your point?"

"It is not quite as simple as replacing the Cyrinthian Rune," he said. "There is another vital element to the process."

"She has to be capable of putting the circle in the circular hole, and the square in the square hole? We'd better make sure she doesn't kidnap any kindergarteners to help her out."

He offered a smile. "It is a bit more complicated than that."

"No way, really?"

My sarcasm failed to erase Lornicus's smile. "The first angel to activate the arch somehow attuned the Cyrinthian Rune so only they could remove or replace it."

I didn't bother to ask him how he knew this. "I assume this angel was Daelissa?"

He shook his head. "No. In order to repair the Grand Nexus, Daelissa will need this angel or risk another Desecration."

"Is that what happened during the angel war?" I asked.

He paused. "No one is certain who actually removed the rune during the Battle of the Nexus, but it most assuredly was not the angel who attuned the rune. Mr. Gray believes this caused the backlash which husked every living creature within range of any Alabaster Arch."

I tried not to think about the shadow creatures or infantile cherubs haunting the way stations with Alabaster Arches. "Can you skip forward to the part that concerns me?" I asked, suddenly realizing where he was going with this. "Do you want me to find this person for you? Kidnap them?" I blew out a breath of disgust. "Do it yourself." I turned and headed toward the arch as an image of Queens Gate appeared in the center.

"I cannot," Lornicus said. "Mr. Gray is sworn to remain neutral in these affairs lest Daelissa and others turn their hostilities upon him."

"Not my problem," I said without turning around. I reached the arch and stepped forward.

"The angel in question is Alysea, your mother."

I jumped back from the portal just before my foot made contact with the image of Queens Gate, and spun to face him. "My mom? But she's only forty!"

He shook his head, a grave look on his face. "I'm afraid she's much older than you think."

I felt a little faint. "She's the first?"

"Daelissa needs your mother to place the Cyrinthian Rune. As of yet, she does not possess the rune."

"Jeremiah Conroy has it," I said.

He nodded. "Indeed."

"But she does have my mom."

"Correct again."

"Well, do you plan to help me get her?"

"Perhaps."

I gripped him by the shirt. "What the hell do you mean, 'perhaps'? Daelissa has everything she needs to repair the Grand Nexus. The minute Jeremiah gives her the rune—" I shuddered. "Game over, man. Game over."

"Reopening the nexus is not necessarily bad, Mr. Slade."

"It's horrible, you heartless hunk of wood!"

"I am not constructed of wood."

"Yeah, you're constructed of goat crap if you think letting the angels take over the planet isn't a bad thing." I clamped my mouth shut before anything worse escaped. This was just as I'd feared. Lornicus was setting me up for something. Why else would he even tell me all of this?

"I believe I said 'not necessarily.'" The golem smiled. "I, however, believe it is in our best interests to delay Daelissa."

Hope tried to bubble up. "Then you'll help me rescue my mother."

"In a limited way. As of yet, I do not know her location since Daelissa and the Conroys have done a remarkable job hiding her."

I narrowed my eyes. "What's the catch?"

"There is no catch. I would simply ask you to look into something—"

"That's called a catch, Lornicus." I huffed out a breath. "Fine, what is it?"

He held out a tiny micro card which would fit into my arcphone.

I regarded it with suspicion. "What's that? Something to infect my phone so you can spy on me?"

The golem smiled. "I have no desire to spy on your text messaging, Mr. Slade. Consider looking into this a favor to me."

I stared at the card. No question the golem was manipulating me. But if it meant I could save my mother, I had no choice. "Find me useful information and I'll look into this." *No sense doing it for free.*

"What you find on this card will change everything," he said.

"You sound like a used car salesman." I took the card. "I'm not looking at anything until you find out where my mother is."

Lornicus shrugged. "Very well, though I think you'll only be depriving yourself. Safe travels, Mr. Slade."

I jogged to the arch, peering through once more to make sure my destination looked like Queens Gate, and stepped through. The scene stretched as if looking through a warped lens, snapped back into place, and I was there. I peered at the doors leading into the pocket dimension and recognized the guards with the big puffy hats like they wore at Buckingham Palace in London above. At least the golem hadn't been lying about this.

On the way back to the mansion, I noticed my invitations weren't lying on the ground where I'd left them. I opened the mailbox to find them neatly stacked inside. I guessed Lornicus must have had his golems clean up the mess. Thoughtful, or just creepy? I shuddered. No telling with that guy.

I waited until I was securely inside the mansion before looking at the memory card he'd given me, wondering if I should open it or not. Nobody else was home. I didn't want to risk frying my phone, Nookli, so I dug up a spare arcphone Shelton kept around for experiments.

The card fit into the slot on the side. I directed the spare phone to project a three-dimensional hologram of the contents, which turned out to be a single file. I opened it. Instructions for activating one of the small arches in an Obsidian Arch control room appeared, complete with the Cyrinthian symbol to press on the world map for the destination. Up until a few months ago, arches like this one hadn't worked properly. Daelissa and the Conroys had employed an Arcane

22

company called Darkwater along with arch operators to make them functional.

I flicked the image and a map appeared, entitled *El Dorado Subterranean Map.*

"El Dorado?" I muttered in disbelief. That fool expected me to step foot in the dead city where I'd almost died a hundred times?

I located the huge cavern where my crew and I had fought Vadaemos, been chased by hundreds of light-sucking cherubs, and was nearly devoured by giant leyworms. I remembered watching as the leyworms inadvertently sucked dozens of cherubs into their mouths while trundling after me and Elyssa, apparently drawn to the portable arch she'd held. If I went back now, I wondered if I'd find husked leyworms, drained of all light by the ravenous cherubs.

A numbered legend on the side of the map indicated points of interest, one of which was in the center of the cavern. It claimed the room was supposed to house an Obsidian Arch. If I scrolled to the control room on the three-dimensional map, I could touch each arch and see a description of the destination, though most of them listed "Unknown." A large arch in the middle of the control room caught my eye, and caused my breath to hitch in my throat.

It was an Alabaster Arch.

From what I knew, there were at least five Alabaster Arches in the world, one of which was the prime arch the Seraphim called the Grand Nexus. As far as I knew, the Alabaster Arches connected only to the angel realm, though each supposedly also connected to the Grand Nexus. I had no idea if the white-striped design of these particular arches held any significance. Maybe the creators wanted a little pizzazz. Maybe they really like zebras. Most likely, the material made opening a gateway between two realms easier. The Obsidian Arches—black and shiny as their namesake—only connected to other Obsidian Arches, but didn't seem to have the ability to connect to other realms. Not unless someone counted the accidental fractures in reality, which could suck someone into a dreary dimension called the Gloom.

Rebel Darklings, Arcanes, Daemos, and humans had banded together to drive the angels from this world by destroying the Grand Nexus. They hadn't destroyed the nexus, but instead removed the Cyrinthian Rune, a vital component. But removing it had caused a massive shockwave which reverberated through every Alabaster Arch in the network, and drained the light from any nearby entity.

The husked remains of angels, humans, and even shape-shifting Flarks now haunted places like Thunder Rock and El Dorado. So far as I knew, the Grand Nexus remained inoperable. I had to hope Mr. Gray wasn't lying when he said Daelissa didn't have the rune.

All the same, any Alabaster Arch would supposedly take someone dumb enough to use it back to the Grand Nexus, wherever it was.

In other words, Lornicus had just given me a map which might lead me to the portal Daelissa would have to repair if she hoped to bring across an army. Maybe there was a way to destroy that arch once and for all. I'd seen the broken remains of the smaller black arches. If the Obsidian Arch in El Dorado had been destroyed, why couldn't we do the same to an Alabaster Arch? Even if it caused another backlash, everything within range of them was already husked.

*This is so tempting.*

That golem really knew how to push my buttons.

A glowing line on the map led past the Alabaster Arch and into the main cavern where the Obsidian Arch would be. There, the line terminated in an "X". I suspected it didn't indicate pirate booty.

I touched the "X", but no description rewarded me for the effort. What waited in that dread cavern?

Curiosity joined arms with irritation, urging me to investigate. I just had to know despite the obvious fact that Lornicus was manipulating me.

*Resist!*

*Why don't I just take a quick peek?*

"Off," I said, flicking my hand at the arcphone. The image vanished. I wouldn't go. No way, no how. *The only thing waiting in that cavern is death.* I thought back to my expedition through the caverns beneath El Dorado. Our first encounter had been with shadow people, the husked remains of humans. Shadows drifted off them like ultraviolet smoke, and they used those wisps to snare people and drain them. Their weakness was light of any kind. One of them had been overexposed and crumbled to dust.

The cherubs, on the other hand, didn't seem to care about light. I'd kicked them, batted them around, and abused them mercilessly, but nothing seemed to harm them. Hardly surprising since they'd once been angels. Their only weaknesses were lack of speed, and ungainly infantile bodies.

The most dangerous husk of all, however, might be the one I'd encountered at Thunder Rock—a Flark. Bigglesworth was the only Flark I'd ever seen. He'd been immune to direct magic attacks, and virtually impossible to kill with physical attacks, especially since his skin burned like acid when it touched a victim. When Kassallandra, Elyssa, and I had been swimming the depths of the quarry lake at Thunder Rock in a bid to escape the interdiction spell around the area, an oily tentacle had grabbed me and flung me into the caverns beneath the lake. I suspected it had been a husked Flark. I'd witnessed the thing kill several hellhounds before it had taken me. Why it hadn't killed me outright, I didn't know.

I knew how to kill shadow people, and I knew how to avoid cherubs unless they swarmed in overwhelming numbers like the last time. I had no idea how to avoid or contain a husked Flark. We hadn't seen one in El Dorado, but that meant nothing.

If I took another expedition for a quick look at whatever Lornicus evidently wanted me to see, we could probably get in and out without much trouble unless something like that made an appearance.

The front door opened, and Elyssa walked in, a black dog the size of a toy poodle scampering after her, and panting with excitement. The dog was, in fact, a hellhound—the very first one I'd ever summoned. Though he wasn't much to look at, he was pretty popular with the women.

I blurred across the room and kissed my girlfriend before she had a chance to speak. When I pulled away, her eyes were bright with amusement.

"Missed me, huh?"

"Not a bit," I said, leaning down to pat the hellhound. "How did your parents like Cutsauce?"

"I'm pretty sure Dad hated him, but Mom finally gave in to his cute factor." She laughed. "He's irresistible."

Cutsauce made a growl of agreement. Sometimes, I'd catch glimpses of images or words from him, something completely normal according to my Aunt Vallaena. The longer a hellhound stayed with a Daemos, the better the communication became, though some souls in the demon plane were more mature and easier to understand right away.

Elyssa's gaze narrowed as she looked at me. "Where did you get those clothes?"

The new slacks and button-up shirt Lornicus had put me in were a far notch above the cargo shorts and t-shirts I usually wore. I realized I should have phoned Elyssa the minute I had a chance to tell her about my encounter, but I'd let the map distract me.

"You look hot," she said, running a finger along my shirt collar. "Did I forget a date we're supposed to have tonight?" she said, her dark eyebrow arching with concern.

"I had a bit of a run-in with some gray men this morning," I said, trying to figure out the best way to start the story.

Elyssa's forehead pinched with confusion. "And they dressed you up like a doll?"

"That came a little later," I said, motioning her to the red leather couch. "Want some popcorn?"

"Stop kidding around, and tell me what happened," she said, squeezing my hands tight.

I winced at the pressure of her grip and gave her the details. When I finished, I showed her the map.

"You're right," she said. "Either Mr. Gray is manipulating you, or Lornicus is doing it on his own."

"Exactly," I said. "I'm not even gonna try to keep up with people like them or Underborn. Every time I tried, I came out on the losing end."

"Like Michael," Elyssa said, referring to her big brother who'd worked for Underborn in the hopes of keeping Elyssa out of the master assassin's games, only to end up manipulated into a position where his sister thought he was a traitor. Thankfully, they'd worked through their issues.

"Exactly," I said. "Which is why going to El Dorado would be a terrible idea."

A slow grin spread over Elyssa's face. "I agree. We should go right away."

# Chapter 4

I did a double-take. "Wait a minute. Did you just say we should return to the bowels of hell?"

"Drama queen," Elyssa said, shaking her head. "Think about it. There's an Alabaster Arch, a mystery prize, and possibly access to our own arch control room. You remember those omnidirectional arches you discovered? What if we can get those working?"

"That's a big if," I replied. "And what if the mystery prize is a gruesome death?"

"It's not," she said with certainty. "This is totally worth the risk. If we take a look, Lornicus will help us save your mom."

"Mom and Ivy," I clarified. "Once we have them, we won't need to take the rune from Jeremiah since Daelissa can't do squat without my mom."

Elyssa nodded. "The golem called you the Cataclyst. You're no pawn in a chess game. You're a queen."

"I guess it's time I came out of the closet."

She rolled her eyes. "He wouldn't send you to your death if he thinks he has a chance of controlling you."

"Yeah, but what if he doesn't think he can control me and this is a convenient way to have me dispose of myself?"

She quirked her lips. "Sure, he might get rid of you then. But so far, I don't think he's determined if he can control you or not. If you go, he'll think he has you." Elyssa tapped her chin. "We also have another unused resource in the dungeons."

"Rusty chains?" I said.

"No, silly, the arch."

Ezzek Moore and the original Arcane Council had used the arch in question to hide the Cyrinthian Rune from Daelissa by placing the rune into the arch here beneath Ezzek's mansion, and closing off both ends with shields to keep it from coming out either end. Unfortunately, the result of the rune pinging back and forth between each end of the traversion tunnel over the centuries had caused a pulsar of malignant aether to build up which might have eventually gone nuclear and husked everyone in Queens Gate.

We'd stopped it, but Jeremiah Conroy had stolen the rune right out from under our noses.

"Cinder calculated that the arch's destination is in Antarctica or the North Pole," I said, giving her a confused look. "Why would we want to go there?"

"We never actually explored it," she said. "What if it goes to another control room?"

She brought up a good point. After surviving another close call, we'd all been busy enjoying life instead of carelessly throwing our bodies into the unknown. "I hadn't thought about it." My mind ran through the possibilities. "We'd have our own private control room full of gateways."

"Exactly."

I pursed my lips and regarded her. "Since when did you become the instigator of dangerous adventures? Usually, I'm the one ready to lead us off the cliff."

"You've been slacking lately," she said, poking a finger in my ribs. "It's time to spice things up."

"Oh, yeah?" I tickled her tummy, causing her to giggle and guard it with her arms. "I know how to spice things up."

"I know you do," she said, and disarmed me with a kiss. Her smile faded. "In all seriousness, I think we should check out the arch in the cellar. I also think we should talk to Bella about putting together a small group to look at El Dorado."

"You're just as curious as I am, aren't you?" I said.

A smirk lifted the corner of her mouth. "Maybe."

"You've been hanging out with me too long."

Cutsauce yipped in agreement.

I dispatched an email to my inner circle—Shelton, Bella, Nightliss, and others who'd been with my through thick and thicker— requesting a meeting for that evening. Nightliss was the first to show.

She still looked a bit wan and pale from her ordeal with Daelissa's deadly curse despite Ivy healing her.

I gave the petite angel a hug, and even Elyssa seemed glad to see her feeling better.

"Have you felt any different since Ivy removed the vampling curse?" Nightliss asked me.

I shook my head. "Aside from sprouting wings in front of the Lady of the Pond, I haven't noticed anything else to indicate my angels powers are ready to shine."

She sighed. "It's frustrating. Instinct has guided me all this time, but made me a poor teacher. And even if I wanted to teach you, I am still too weak."

"I feel fully recovered since Ivy healed me," I said. "Did the curse permanently damage you?"

"Perhaps not permanently, though it may have set back my recovery from the Desecration by a few years." Her brow crinkled.

I touched her hand. "You'll bounce back. Nobody comes that close to death and makes a complete recovery in a couple of months." Truthfully, though, I'd expected her to be back to full power by now. The Desecration had severely weakened her just as it had Daelissa, and it had taken them centuries to recover. Even half strength for an angel was like double strength for most Arcanes, and Daelissa only seemed to get stronger while my side lost powerful allies like Nightliss.

Bella and Shelton walked through the front door, Cinder close behind. Adam Nosti and his girlfriend, Meghan Andretti, showed up shortly thereafter. Neither Katie nor Stacey could make the meeting so I decided to go ahead and start with the current group. I filled them in on my meeting with Mr. Gray, including his assertion that the Seraphim had not created the arches, and the importance of my mother.

"This is unbelievable, Justin," Nightliss said.

"You didn't know?" Bella asked.

She shook her head. "The Desecration damaged my memory. I remember some things with uncanny clarity while others only seem to return with time."

"Who built the arches if the angels didn't?" Meghan asked.

I met Shelton's eyes. "Remember the omnidirectional arches?"

"Yeah." A shrug. "It looked like the angels added them on later because they didn't fit with the original design of the room."

"Right. What if the angels figured out how to build arches, or tried to make versions of their own?"

He nodded. "Makes sense they'd try."

"But the Grand Nexus leads from our world to the angel realm," Bella said. "What if there are arches leading to the realm of their creators?"

"Or what if they created other artifacts that are even more powerful?" I said.

Elyssa's gaze flicked to me. "The Map and Key of Juranthemon," she said.

"Exactly." The key could be used to open a door to just about any location so long as a person used the map to activate the portal. Underborn had sparingly informed me about the ancient relics, but I had no doubt he'd omitted critical facts. The key changed its appearance depending on the expectations of the wielder. The map looked like old parchment but scrolled like the map on an arcphone or arctablet.

"You mean the key you used to go from Bogota, Colombia back to Atlanta?" Bella said.

I nodded. "The same. What if the beings who made the arches also made the key and map?"

"What if there are more than just those two relics?" Shelton added.

Several competing conversations broke out at once. I clapped my hands together. The room went silent. "Look, it doesn't matter right now. I've tried searching for information on those relics and found nothing. What we do have is a way to access an Alabaster Arch in El Dorado." I held up the memory card Lornicus had given me. "I say we go check it out."

"You're insane," Shelton said, his face a mask of disbelief. "You need to toss that memory card in the fire and forget you ever saw it."

"That would be stupid," Elyssa said. "We should let Lornicus think he's controlling our actions. Once we figure out what he's up to, we spring a trap of our own."

30

"Terrible idea," Shelton said. "I think Michael proved you can't outthink these people, or have you forgotten how Underborn schooled him?"

"I disagree, Harry," Bella said, raising an eyebrow at her boyfriend. "I agree with Elyssa. This merits investigation."

"With extreme caution," Adam said. "After reading Cinder's account of what you went through in those caves last time, I suggest we take plenty of flashlights, batteries, and glowballs."

Cinder nodded. Even though he'd improved with his gestures, he came nowhere near to Lornicus's mastery. "Justin, do you think these creatures could affect me?"

I felt my mouth drop open slightly. I hadn't even considered such a question. "Can husks feed on a golem's spark?" I asked, looking at Nightliss.

She shrugged. "I do not know."

"A golem's spark isn't a soul," Shelton said, giving Cinder an apologetic look. "Sorry, buddy, but it ain't like soul essence. So I don't think those little freaks could do anything to you."

"In other words," I said, a revelation coming into my mind, "Lornicus probably sent in gray men to scout the area. That's how he knows what's in there."

"It is possible," Cinder replied. "If you ask, Justin, I will go to El Dorado alone and confirm this without putting any of you at risk."

I shook my head without hesitation. "No, I'm not risking a friend like that. We'll go together or not at all." I gazed around the room. "So, who's with me?"

Shelton was the only one who didn't raise his hand until Bella elbowed him in the ribs. "I'm gonna string Christmas lights around my body," he said.

"Better yet," I said, "how about I glue glow sticks to a leotard and you wear that?"

Adam snickered.

Shelton glared at him. "Laugh it up, fur ball."

"What about the arch in the cellar?" Meghan asked. "Is there a safe way to find out where it goes?"

"After Justin banished the demon guardian from the arch, it apparently disconnected the arch from its destination," Cinder said. "There are no obvious controls in the room."

The arch in the cellar looked like a miniature version of an Obsidian Arch. Instead of being large enough to admit a jumbo jet, it was maybe ten feet tall and twice as wide. Every arch I'd seen had a circle of silver embedded in the floor around it—a magically closed circuit which prevented accidental Gloom fractures from forming outside the ring. "I once activated an arch by closing the circle around it," I said. "Maybe this one works the same way."

"Or maybe Jeremiah Conroy did something to hide the controls," Shelton said. "He seemed to know a hell of a lot about this mansion."

"Well, there's only one way to find out," I said, and stood up.

"Now?" Shelton said, aghast.

I shrugged. "Why wait?"

"You need to take up scrapbooking," Shelton said. "Because I don't like it when you get bored."

I led the group into the cellar, down another set of stairs, through a tunnel, and into the room where the arch sat. It stood on a polished circle of obsidian bordered by a silver ring. There were no markings on it or the floor around it.

Shelton ran his hand up the twisting ebony material. "Look at the design of the columns," he said giving me a look. "Remind you of something?"

I thought back to the time we'd inspected arches in the control room at Queens Gate, and the answer occurred almost immediately. "The geometry is as complicated as the omniarches," I said.

"Yep."

"Mind explaining what you're talking about?" Adam asked.

I knelt next to the arch and pointed to the triangular base. "A normal arch has a three-sided column which twists as it runs the span."

Adam traced his eyes up the column. "Whoa, it makes my eyes go crazy trying to follow it, but it looks like it changes from three-sided to a lot more than that."

Shelton retrieved a picture comparing the two arches from his arcphone and displayed it as a hologram. "This arch looks like an omniarch," he said. "Question is, will it work right, or dump you in an alternate dimension?"

"I concur with Harry's identification," Cinder said, looking at the pictures.

The only time I'd taken an omniarch, it had sent me on a joyride through hell, and finally deposited me in El Dorado. Omniarches, from what we'd determined, had no set destination, but could open anywhere.

"According to your theory, these arches could send you to locations even without an arch at the other end," Cinder said. "But how do you control where you want to go?"

"I just told it I wanted to go home," I said. "And it took me to Elyssa."

She smiled.

"But then it sucked me back in and tossed me in El Dorado," I finished.

"I suggest we grab an ASE and send it through to video the area," Adam said. "That way we don't risk anyone."

"That's a great idea," I said. ASEs, or all-seeing-eyes, were orbs which could record everything around them.

Adam ran upstairs to retrieve some ASEs, while Shelton and I thought up a place to send it first.

"I say we send it through to Thunder Rock," Shelton said. "That way we can see what Daelissa has been up to."

"If she's there and sees us, we're done for," Meghan said.

"How about El Dorado?" Bella said.

Elyssa shook her head. "We should try somewhere safe first."

I listened to them argue over destinations and finally threw in my own two cents. "Let's just send it to the room over yonder." I indicated the chamber beyond the arch. "Then we can worry about complicated stuff later."

"Uh, that's actually a good idea," Shelton said, pulling off his wide-brimmed hat to run a hand through his hair.

"Baby steps," I said. "Baby steps."

Adam returned with a handful of the marble-sized ASEs. He took one, flicked it between forefinger and thumb, and released it. The sphere dropped an inch before spinning and hovering in mid-air. He looked at me. "See if you can get the arch connected, and I'll set the ASE to record mode."

"Why record anything if you're just gonna send it one room over?" Shelton asked.

"In case it goes on an intergalactic joy ride," I said as I stepped inside the silver circle around the arch.

"Wait!" Elyssa said, appearing with a coil of normal rope. She wrapped one end around me, tying a loop around my waist, and secured the other end to a metal ring embedded in the stone wall.

"What's this for?" I asked.

"In case you open a Gloom fracture," she said, securing another length of rope to her waist and an iron ring next to the first. "If you do, I'll save you." She grinned.

I didn't dare tell her to let me do this alone. She'd probably punch me in the throat if I tried.

Adam set the ASE to record mode, and sent it drifting inside the circle with me and Elyssa. I knelt, pressed a finger to the ring, and willed it closed. The ensuing rush of aether as it filled the enclosed magical container made my ears pop. This place was right over a major ley line. I wondered what would happen if a circle was too full of energy. Would it explode? Or would it just fill up and not allow any more inside?

Elyssa made a little gasp, her eyes flaring as the magic closed all around us. "That felt…weird," she said, rubbing her arms. "I have goose bumps."

"Me too," I said, though it was more from hearing her gasp of surprise than anything else. That sound reminded me of something else entirely.

Pushing such thoughts from my filthy mind, I turned to the destination room, and imprinted an image of it in my brain. Even with it in my sight, it was difficult to maintain a crystal clear image especially with the butterflies in my stomach. What if I opened the arch into a void and it sucked me in? What if I triggered a fracture into the Gloom?

*Elyssa will save you.*

She seemed to sense my unease, and touched my arm.

*Everything will be okay.*

The myriad thoughts pinging around in my mind vanished. I found focus, and willed the arch to open a portal in the room beyond. *Go there*, I thought. *Now!* My vision flickered, and the world vanished in a puff of shadow only to appear a second later. I heard cries of surprise from my friends sounding much further behind me than they should have been. I felt disoriented. Dizzy. My legs wobbled, and I went down on my knees.

I looked around, blinking dark spots from my eyes, trying to figure out what the hell I'd done. Where was Elyssa? Where was the arch? I looked at my waist and saw the rope was gone, too. It was then I recognized the room I was in—the destination I'd envisioned the arch opening to. Had I somehow used the arch and not realized it?

"Justin?" Elyssa said, touching my shoulder. "Are you okay?"

I opened my mouth to say I was fine, when my last meal made an unexpected return trip up my esophagus. Only Elyssa's supernatural reflexes allowed her to dodge the spew. When I finished emptying my stomach, I looked up to see the others around me, looks of awe on their faces. Even Nightliss looked impressed.

"How in the hell did you do that?" Shelton asked, looking back and forth between the arch and me.

"What happened?" I asked.

He stared at me, mouth open. "I don't believe it. Holy butt-cakes in a meat grinder, man! You teleported."

# Chapter 5

"I what?" I asked, shock jolting my heart.

"You freaking teleported yourself," he said. "One minute you were over there, and the next, a puff of black smoke, and you were over here."

"I believe I am flabbergasted," Cinder said attempting to modulate his usually deadpan tone to match the word.

I accepted a wet wipe from Elyssa—*where in the world do women keep this stuff?*—and cleaned my lips. She helped me to my feet as I considered Shelton's question. I'd done something I'd only seen Ivy do. She called it *blinking*—instantly moving from one point to another. She said it didn't work for long distance, only for a place I could see.

I explained the concept to the others.

"How did you do it?" Nightliss asked, a look of wonder on her face.

I shrugged. "I dunno. It just kind of happened. I focused on where I wanted the arch to open, and the next thing I knew, I was there."

"Doesn't look like something you want to do on a full stomach," Shelton commented, pinching his nose and backing away from the puddle of upchuck on the floor.

Equilibrium returned to my disoriented brain, and I was able to stop leaning on Elyssa for support. "That is so cool," I said under my breath, looking at the distance I'd covered. True, it wasn't a huge distance, but it was pretty freaking awesome. I just hoped the barfing part went away eventually.

"Dork," Elyssa said in an affectionate tone. "Maybe we should wait before trying the arch."

I shook my head. "No, I'm fine, really. At least my stomach is empty in case I do it again."

She sighed. "A stubborn dork."

"Ha, ha." After walking back to the arch, I found the loose coil of rope I'd blinked out of, and fastened it back around my waist. Elyssa did the same. Apparently, my blink had opened the circle and released the aether within, so I had to close it again. I turned back to the arch, keeping the destination in mind, and imagined a tunnel from the arch to the next room. *Connect*, I commanded, visualizing a scene of the room beyond appearing within the columns of the arch.

The center of the arch flickered ultraviolet and white for a split second before an image of the room clarified into focus. I looked through the arch, and then around it to the next room. An open portal hovered in the air, shimmering like a window made of liquid glass.

"Whoa," Adam said, jogging to the portal. He reached for it.

"You're gonna lose a hand," Shelton said, as though castigating a kid about to stick his limb in the garbage disposal.

"I want to see if it's solid," Adam replied. He made a motion with his hand, and the ASE floated through the arch, appearing from the other one. "Looks safe."

I gave Elyssa a look. She raised an eyebrow.

"On three?" she said, unfastening the rope from her waist.

I nodded, removing my rope.

She took my hand. "One, Two, Three."

We stepped inside. The world warped like a fishbowl for the barest instant, hardly enough to even register, and then we stood next to Adam.

"Well, you're still alive," he said, and touched the edge of the portal. The image didn't shift or ripple. "I feel a slight resistance on the outer edge, but it's not solid."

"Fascinating," Shelton said, walking over to touch the portal. "Now, how do we turn the thing off?"

"I'm guessing it stays open until you close the connection," I said. "Otherwise you might strand yourself."

He grunted. "Good point."

"Maybe we should leave it open for now," Adam suggested as he walked around the arch. "Just to be sure your theory is correct."

"Considering the Cyrinthian Rune bounced between the two ends of this arch for so long, I believe it would stay open indefinitely," Cinder said.

I examined both sides of the portal to see the same image of the arch room. Apparently, it was possible to walk in from either side and end up in the same place. Excitement rushed through me. "You know what this means?" I said. "We have a blank ticket to go anywhere."

"I can go to Colombia and visit my friends whenever I want," Bella said, a smile brightening her face. "I've really missed my pink house."

"Everyone can come straight here," I said, thinking about my other friends. All I had to do was open a portal at their end.

"How would that work?" Adam said. "Do you need to visualize where you want the arch to open? What if you've never been there before?"

"Good question," Shelton said, eyeing the thing.

"We should test that next," Bella said.

"Agreed," I added. "It won't do us much good if we haven't been somewhere before."

"And what if the places look almost identical, like control rooms?" Shelton said.

I felt a frown tug on my lips. That was a really good question. "Maybe minor details would help," Elyssa said. "Like the stable looks different at the Grotto than the one in Queens Gate."

"Yeah, but we don't want to open a portal in plain view of people who aren't in on our little secret," Shelton said.

"Let's figure out if we can open a portal somewhere we haven't been," I said.

Shelton grunted. "Let's see if you can turn this one off first."

I looked at the arch and thought, *Disconnect.* It folded in on itself like an accordion, seemingly disassembling itself at the molecular level before vanishing. I made duck lips and gave Shelton a *top-that!* look.

He rolled his eyes.

"Mind if I give it a try?" Adam said as we walked back to the arch.

Meghan gave him an alarmed look. "I don't know if you should."

"I'll be his arch buddy," Shelton said.

She raised an eyebrow. Her lips trembled as if she really wanted to say something, but held it back. "Fine."

"Let's try to replicate Justin's feat," Adam said, fastening the rope around his waist.

Shelton nodded, and closed the circle.

I explained how I'd imagined the connection between rooms to Adam. After staring at the arch for a moment, the destination portal appeared in roughly the same spot mine had. Adam and Shelton high-fived before stepping through and emerging at the other end.

It took Adam a few seconds to shut down the portal. He and Shelton walked back, talking excitedly.

"Would someone need Arcane abilities to use the omniarch?" Cinder said.

"Probably," I said. "Then again, if you can close a circle, maybe that's all there is to it." I felt certain a golem couldn't do even that, but didn't want to voice my opinion to Cinder. It might hurt his feelings.

And so began the experimentation. Several hours and a few pizzas later, we figured out a few things. If we visualized a specific location, the portal would open there. Sometimes, though, it would open in a place that looked similar but was actually someplace completely different. Bella opened a portal in the front yard of her Colombian home, gave an excited squeak, and retrieved her favorite teacups. I taught Elyssa how to close a magical circle and she opened a gateway in front of her parents' house, much to the surprise of a patrolling Templar who nearly nailed me with a Lancer dart.

We even let Cinder take a stab at it, but he couldn't close the circle or cause the arch to do anything. I felt really bad for him as he stepped back outside the circle, his face betraying no emotion, but his voice sounding glum.

"It appears you were right, Harry," the golem said, looking at the omniarch. "My spark is not a soul."

Shelton patted the golem on the back. "Nothing to be ashamed of, man."

"I do not feel shame," Cinder said, tilting his head slightly. "Although, I do feel an overwhelming sense of disappointment at my inadequacy."

Next, we tried opening the portal in places we hadn't been. In one case, it opened into a black void. Thankfully, it didn't seem to be a vacuum, because the air didn't rush out of the room and sweep us to our doom, but Shelton and Adam nearly crapped their pants. Bella told them to send a globe of light through.

"This is freaking me out," Shelton said as a glowing ball floated from his wand and into the void.

Something growled in a tone so deep, the air vibrated.

"Disconnect!" Adam shouted in unison with Shelton.

The omniarch flicked off.

The two men wiped sweat from their foreheads and staggered out of the circle on weak knees. Shelton, the whites of his eyes still showing, pointed back at the arch. "I will never use that thing again without knowing the destination."

Nobody disagreed.

"Would a picture of a location be adequate?" Cinder asked.

"I ain't gonna test it," Shelton said.

Elyssa and I took places inside the circle, making sure to firmly fasten the rope to our waists.

"Try this one," Adam said, showing me the picture of a snowy mountain top. "It's the top of Mount Everest."

I stared at the picture, noting the permanent landmarks as opposed to the snow and other fluid elements which could change. If, for example, I imagined a grassy field, the arch might open in any of a zillion places. If I knew of a grassy field with a red fence, that might cut it down to a few thousand. But a grassy field with a particular boulder in it might land me in the right spot. Unique landmarks seemed necessary.

I concentrated on the arch, envisioning the destination. It hummed and flickered. Snow swirled through the opening and freezing air stung my cheeks. A man in a yellow parka stood outside a domed tent, staring at us open-mouthed. He yelled in another language, and someone else poked their head out of the tent.

*Disconnect!*

The arch blinked off.

"I'd say it works," Shelton said, "Although it's kind of cheating to get to the top that way."

"Those noms are gonna be scarred for life," Adam said with a chuckle.

Elyssa gave him a disapproving look. "It's not funny. Now I'll probably have to let the Custodians know so they can bring them in for rehabilitation."

"Nah, they'll be fine," Shelton said. "There ain't much oxygen up there, so he'll probably chalk it up to hallucination or something."

"That's true," Bella said.

Elyssa mulled it over for a moment before nodding. "I hope so."

As they continued to discuss the merits of nom rehabilitation, I opened the file Lornicus had given me—this time using my phone—and scrolled through the map. "Nookli, zoom into first person view," I told my phone.

"Justin, there are three Indian restaurants nearby. At which one would you like me to schedule a reservation?"

I took a deep breath, holding back a choice curse word, and repeated myself in concise tones. This time, Nookli got it right. The first-person perspective allowed me to view the control room at El Dorado in much better detail. Even better, the imagery had apparently been taken with a camera, or the magical equivalent—an ASE perhaps?—so it was as good as having a picture. Unfortunately, the control room looked identical to the other two I'd seen at Queens Gate and the Grotto.

The Alabaster Arch wasn't a good reference either since the control room at Thunder Rock had one. On the other hand, it narrowed our odds to one in five of landing the right one, provided there weren't more Alabaster Arches than we'd calculated.

"Project image," I told Nookli. The phone complied, creating a holographic image of the control room for all to view.

"I see what you're doing there," Shelton said. "Good idea."

"Gotta find a unique marker," I said. "Otherwise, we'll end up at the wrong city of doom."

Adam shuddered. "Or a monster void."

"What was that dark place?" Elyssa asked.

Nobody answered.

"Imagine if we let something loose," Bella said. "What if that growly thing came through?"

"New rule," Shelton said, "No using the arch unless you're absolutely sure you can picture the location."

"Or using the arch without a companion," Elyssa said, giving me a pointed look.

"I believe I see something," Cinder said, pointing toward the upper right corner of the world map on the wall in the front of the control room.

I zoomed in on the area, and found a symbol. "That's not Cyrinthian," I said. "At least not a symbol I recognize." By now, I'd memorized the alphabet and could read a little bit of the language, though I understood very little.

"I don't recognize it either," Nightliss said.

I looked at my companions, but everyone seemed mystified. The symbol looked simple enough, a thin vertical line with a vertical wavy line running back and forth through it, each end terminating with a dot.

"Maybe it's not supposed to be a letter or number but like those icons you see on road signs," Adam said, peering closely at it.

"Then this one means watch out for snakes," Shelton said with a snort.

"It might be the landmark we need," I said.

Adam shrugged. "Give it a try."

Elyssa and I took our positions. I visualized the world map in the control room as if looking up at the symbol. The arch hummed. Images flickered past, each one with a world map in it. I caught a glimpse of symbols in the corner of the map walls, but they flashed past too quickly for me to determine if they were all the same. The slideshow halted before a world map with the exact symbol in the corner. I looked through the arch and noted with some alarm the exit was just to the side of the white-veined columns of an Alabaster Arch.

"We did it!" Elyssa said, clapping her hands together and peering through. She took an ASE, spun it in mid-air, and motioned for it to go through. It proceeded onward, drifting around the room.

I stuck my hand through the arch. When nothing severed it, I poked my head through. The control room looked just like the one at Thunder Rock. I wondered if all of the control rooms with Alabaster Arches had the strange symbol on the world map. I scoured the room with my eyes, looking for any nasties that might be lurking nearby, but the place looked empty. I noticed the exit door was closed, so I couldn't send the ASE outside to be sure we had the right place—at least not without stepping into the room and opening it.

"Should we?" I asked.

Elyssa twisted her lips, giving the room a thorough visual examination. "I think we need more preparation. We need food, water, flashlights, and other survival supplies before we risk setting foot in there."

"But it's already lit," I said. A yellow glow suffused the room, much as it did in the other arch control rooms I'd been to.

"The cavern area in El Dorado wasn't well-lit," she reminded me.

"We could look through the door," I said. "Just a little peek."

"No," she said, setting her arms akimbo. "Not until we're prepared for anything. I'm not willing to take one more step. If you try, I will knock you out and drag you up the cellar stairs by your feet."

I gulped. My girlfriend was a grade-A certified badass with a litany of ways to take down even the biggest supernatural. "Sure thing, honey. Whatever you say."

I heard Shelton snicker behind me.

"Let's call it a day," I said, noticing it was nearly two in the morning. Man, had it been a long day. Kidnapped, returned, and now this.

"First thing in the morning?" Adam said, eyes bright with excitement.

"Make it after eleven," Shelton said with a groan and a stretch. "I gotta get my beauty sleep."

"I'm sure that's all you need," Adam said, winking and looking at Bella.

Bella laughed as Shelton turned a shade of red.

I reluctantly shut down the arch after giving the ASE instructions to record every inch of the room just in case there were hidden dangers. Even though I desperately wanted to go through, I knew Elyssa was right. Tomorrow we would be ready. Tomorrow we would find the secret Lornicus wanted us to find. Tomorrow I would be one step closer to saving my Mom and bringing her and Ivy home.

# Chapter 6

Despite my excitement, I slept like a baby and woke up ready to go. Shelton joined me in the large dining area a few minutes after I'd arrived. Elyssa entered, sweat glistening on her body, twin sai swords sheathed across her back. She leaned over the table and pecked me on the lips.

"I just finished morning practice. I'm gonna shower, and I'll be ready." I couldn't take my eyes off her limber form as she jogged up the stairs in her tight-fitting yoga pants and sports bra.

"You're drooling," Shelton said, and took a sip of coffee.

The corners of my mouth twitched up in a smile. "That's a good thing, right?"

He snorted. "Yeah. Guess so."

By ten a.m., everyone was gathered in the den. Adam lugged in a duffel bag full of lighting gear, some of it powered by aether, some of it by battery.

Cinder watched the proceedings with great interest as he usually did from a seat with a view of the entire room. The golem did his best to mimic facial expressions, and even had a room of mirrors upstairs so he could judge his performance.

*Maybe I should send him to acting school.*

Once everyone was assembled, we double-checked our supplies, and made sure each person was outfitted with a miner's headlight, a magical glow stick, and a vest with bright LED lights all along it in case of an emergency. I noticed Nightliss sitting at the table, eyes pensive.

"Are you coming?" I asked.

She shook her head sadly. "You told me Daelissa could not go near the cherubs without becoming extremely weak. I'm afraid they will have the same effect on me, and I don't wish to burden you." Her lips twisted. "I am also not quite up to fighting anything yet."

"I understand," I said, giving her an understanding smile. "Unless we all die, we'll be back soon."

"Don't say that," Elyssa said, batting me playfully on the shoulder.

We went downstairs to the omniarch. Using the same precautions as before, I connected the arch to the control room with the weird symbol. The image of what we supposed was the El Dorado control room flickered into view between the columns. Elyssa recalled the ASE from the other side, and told it to show her the activity log. It had nothing to report.

"That's one of those special ASEs the Templars use, right?" Shelton said.

"Yeah," Elyssa replied.

"So, if it even caught a hint of movement, it would have noted it in the activity log."

Elyssa nodded.

"Ain't it kind of strange there's nothing on it? Not even a cockroach?" He took a sip from his travel mug. "I'd expect there to be something living down there."

"Lots and lots of cherubs," I said. "I doubt they all moved out after we captured Vadaemos."

"I don't think even bugs want to be near husks," Adam said. "Insects and animals sense when there's something wrong and flee on instinct."

Shelton didn't look convinced. "Glad I'm wearing my adult diapers today," he muttered darkly.

Elyssa and I stepped through at the same time—that was the deal we'd made the night before. I sniffed the air. Took in a breath. It was a bit musty, but otherwise seemed normal.

The control room looked virtually identical to the others I'd visited, a huge rectangular room carved from the surrounding stone. A dull yellow glow suffused the room, its source as much a mystery as the creators of this place. A world map ran the length and height of the large front wall, a slightly raised platform situated before it. At the front of the platform, a gray sphere sat atop a pedestal. Arch operators—Arcanes who were tasked with the daily operations of

Obsidian Arches—called the sphere a modulus. It would rise from the pedestal and allow them to select the destination for the Obsidian Arch. On the right side of the world map was a rather plain-looking metal door which led to the cavernous way station where an Obsidian Arch usually sat, though I didn't remember seeing one the last time I'd been in El Dorado.

We stood in an aisle just behind the control platform and between rows of smaller arches, each one of identical size—roughly ten feet tall by twenty wide. Cyrinthian symbols to the left of the world map corresponded to symbols on the floor in front of these smaller arches, each one presumably linked to a specific location. The main difference between this control room and the ones I'd seen in the Grotto and Queens Gate stood to our right—a large black arch veined with white. An Alabaster Arch. If Daelissa repaired the Grand Nexus, this arch would open to the angel realm.

Elyssa and I waited a moment, ready to retreat through the arch in an instant should anything attack. Elyssa dispatched sentry wisps, little balls of light that would flit around the room and emit alarms if they noticed hostiles. She'd obviously raided the Templar armory for a rainy day.

After touring the room and determining it was safe, we signaled the others to come through. Adam and Shelton, staffs held at the ready, walked over to the exit door and inspected it.

"Many of these arches appear damaged," Cinder said, surveying the room.

I joined his gaze and saw broken structures just as I had in Thunder Rock. Only a handful of the numbered arches remained standing. The row of omniarches to the side of the room seemed mostly intact.

Shelton pulled the lever on the door, and opened it a crack. Beyond lay pitch black. He gulped, and shut the door. "I haven't felt like this since the first time I went to a haunted house," he said.

Adam unpacked a couple of industrial-sized magical glowballs, and activated them. They hovered in the air, casting bright white light in all directions.

"Before we step into the unknown," I said, "maybe we should look at the arches in here. Maybe activate the Alabaster Arch and see if it works."

"Hey, anything to delay going out there," Shelton said, jabbing a finger toward the control room door.

I ran a finger along the surface of the spherical modulus on the pedestal in front of the world map. Stars located all across the map—each one indicating the location of an Obsidian Arch, lit in succession. If I wanted to request a connection to a particular arch, I would flick my finger once the appropriate star lit, and wait for the arch operator on the other end to verify.

"I don't see a star for El Dorado," Shelton said. He pointed to the star indicating Bogota, Colombia where the La Casona way station was located. "I see all the known arches like the Grotto and La Casona, but not El Dorado or Thunder Rock."

I removed my finger from the modulus. "I wonder what would happen if I requested a connection."

"I don't think we want to find out," he said. "We don't want to risk Gloom fractures."

I didn't want to bear responsibility for killing anyone in a freak Gloom rift accident. "Without a star to mark this place on the map, we don't even know if we're in El Dorado or one of the other abandoned way stations like Thunder Rock."

"This appears to be the symbol for the Alabaster Arch," Cinder said, pointing out a large icon consisting of a solid circle with an upside-down "V" in it. In Cyrinthian, it was the symbol for zero. A line of symbols ran down the left side of the map, each one a number corresponding to the rows of small black arches behind me. Touching one of the symbols should light one of the arches, provided the device still worked. Unfortunately, it wouldn't light a corresponding star at this location.

Shelton stared at the symbol for activating the Alabaster Arch. "Should we turn it on and send through an ASE?"

I met eyes with Elyssa. She shrugged. "Sure," I told him. I pressed my hand against the symbol. A deep klaxon bellowed throughout the room. Meghan jumped and shrieked.

Elyssa's arms blurred, reaching for the swords strapped across her back. She stopped with them halfway out. Shoved them back in and gave me a dirty look. "Next time you scare me like that, I might take off one of your fingers."

I smirked. "Sorry, couldn't resist."

47

The black-and-white-striped arch pulsed with ultraviolet and white energy, jagged bolts arcing from the twisted columns to the silver circle bordering it. The klaxon thrummed again as the arch continued sparking massive amounts of energy into the circle around it. We waited for several minutes, but no destination appeared within.

"Can I have an ASE?" I said, holding out my hand to Elyssa. She deposited one of the marble-like spheres in my hand. I walked to within a few feet of the silver circle, not daring to get another step close to the deadly looking storm of lightning bolts dancing across its surface, spun the ASE, and directed it to go through the arch.

The ASE obediently hovered across the circle and made it to within twenty feet or so of the arch before exploding in a cloud of sparks as a flash of ultraviolet nailed it.

"Holy Zeus on a tricycle," Shelton cried out in surprise. "That thing is broken as hell."

I jogged back to the control button and touched it again. The klaxon wound down as the Alabaster Arch de-energized .

"Perhaps there is another button to access the Grand Nexus," Cinder suggested, looking the rows up and down.

"I ain't going near that thing," Shelton said.

I looked toward the exit and shuddered. "Then I guess it's time to go out there."

Shelton flicked off and on his glow vest a few times. The rest of us took his cue and tested ours to be sure. Now was not the time to rush blindly. The Arcanes took out their staffs, eyes set in concentration for whatever lay outside. Bella brandished a wand in addition to hers. Elyssa retrieved a compact pole from a pocket on her side, and at first I thought she'd brought her own staff. I gave her a puzzled look. She grinned and snapped out a quarterstaff.

"Swords won't do much against cherubs," she said. "But if I can knock 'em across the cavern, that'll keep them out of the way."

"Smart thinking," I said.

She kissed my cheek. "Naturally. I'm a girl."

Shelton and Adam took up positions on either side of the door. I twisted the handle, and pulled it open. The industrial sized glowballs drifted outside, lighting the immediate vicinity outside the control room. I checked the map on my arcphone. The cavern was as large as the way station in the Grotto, which meant the "X" on the map was a couple hundred yards away in the center.

"I don't suppose anyone can cast one of those light burst spells like Curtis did?" I asked, looking at Bella. Curtis had come along on our expedition through El Dorado during our mission to apprehend Vadaemos. He'd scoffed at my suggestion to take along flashlights, and screamed like a little girl when a drain rune sucked us dry of aether and nearly left us helpless against shadow people.

"It's a waste of energy," Bella said. "Curtis is a bit of a showboat."

"Talk about blowing your entire load for one spell," Shelton said with a chuckle. "Amateur."

Adam sent the glowballs drifting higher until we had a clear view in a hundred-foot radius. I led the group forward until the door remained barely visible at the back edge of light, held up my hand for everyone to be quiet, and listened. Elyssa closed her eyes, presumably doing the same thing. I heard shuffling noises. Low groans from giant throats somewhere ahead. And then I heard the sound that sent a pant-wetting chill down my back.

"Dah nah," croaked an infantile voice.

A whistling gurgle answered. Cherubs were ahead of us, but not by far. I assumed the things could see us highlighted in the middle of the light, or maybe they just sensed our delicious, creamy souls.

Shelton's staff burst into a roiling inferno. "Maybe I should do that light spell after all," he said.

Elyssa threw out a handful of tiny glowing orbs which swept through the area around us. The last time we'd been here, cherubs literally carpeted the cavern floor. Elyssa had used them like stepping stones. Light glistened off shiny pitch-colored skin as the orbs drifted along the path toward the center. Each time one spotted a cherub, it took up a position directly over their heads. By the time the path was scanned, wisps of light bobbed above at least twenty cherubs. On the bright side, we had a fairly clear path.

Bella pointed ahead. "Do you see a light?"

"I see light everywhere," Shelton replied, waving a hand at the glowballs above.

"No, it's yellow, not white." She squinted. "I think the light we're putting out makes it hard to see."

Adam spoke a word, and the huge glowballs winked out. Shelton flicked off the roiling fireball above his staff, leaving us in nearly pitch black aside from the wisp markers over the cherubs.

"What the hell?" Shelton said in a harsh whisper.

My eyes adjusted, and I saw what Bella had pointed out. A yellow glow, like a campfire, flickered ahead. If I was any judge of distance, that put it about where Lornicus had marked the map.

"That's where we're going," I said. I heard another cherub cry out and my teeth chattered in response. "Can we get the lights back on, Adam?"

The glowballs burst into light. I noticed Shelton huddled tight against Bella. The petite dhampyr wore an amused smile.

"Don't worry, dear, I'll keep you safe."

Shelton growled.

We moved ahead. As we drew closer to the wisps marking the cherubs, they began to move toward us in a wobbling motion. The first cherub waddled in, the white light reflecting off the glossy black flesh. A circular orifice lined opened in the featureless face. "Dah nah," it cried, holding nubby little hands out to us. "Dah nah!"

My butt cheeks clenched tight as a bank vault. "Don't let that thing touch you."

Elyssa sprang into motion, spinning her quarterstaff so fast, it blurred like a propeller. She connected with the cherubs head. There was a meaty *THWACK* and the creature flew into parts unknown, vanishing into the dark. Two more cherubs walked into the circle of light. My ninja girl handled them with equal aplomb, sending their bodies careening away, their tortured cries vanishing into the dark.

"Justin, I see something," Cinder said, pointing to the side.

We sent a glowball that way and found a still form in a gray suit. The body was crushed.

"One of my kind," Cinder said, kneeling to inspect the motionless form. "Something very large ran him over."

"Leyworms," I said.

"Maybe we should run away," Shelton said.

"We're almost there." Adam gazed toward our destination. "Besides, Elyssa is pretty handy with that staff."

"I don't know about a staff versus a leyworm," Elyssa said.

50

"We've come this far," Meghan said. She hadn't said much, choosing to remain in the center, her staff held ready.

"Fine, fine," Shelton grumbled. "Lead on, Pocahontas."

Elyssa narrowed her eyes at him.

We pressed forward. The low groans I'd heard grew louder. While they weren't quite monstrous bellows of anger, they still made my stomach clench. After clearing the path of a few more stray cherubs, we finally found the source of the light. A slab of polished obsidian took over from the stone cavern floor, and a yellow nimbus provided a dim light by which to see. Giant scaled forms lay in the center. Parietal eyes big as boulders blinked at us. A long narrow muzzle opened wide, revealing jagged black shards and a dull yellow glow deep in its maw.

The leyworm hissed.

Ruby red slits appeared in the dark to the side of the first creature, opening wider, regarding us. The earth dragon rumbled. The first one seemed to reply with a low groan and hiss.

"We should probably keep a safe distance," Adam said, sending the glowballs higher, bolstering the yellow light suffusing the air.

The first leyworm suddenly threw its head back and let out a shrieking roar as if it were in intense pain. The creature loomed as tall as a two-story building. A person could drive a monster truck down its throat and it probably wouldn't notice. What could cause something so huge such pain?

I shifted to my incubus sight. What I saw made me gasp. A river of aether flowed through the ground beneath the obsidian slab. The leyworm was funneling nearly all of it into its body. A flash of brilliant white exploded from the creature's mouth, and it made a horrible gagging noise. Something very small jettisoned from the giant's maw, landed, and rolled on the floor to stop a little more than a hundred feet away. The tiny figure opened its mouth and cried. I felt my mouth drop open as I looked at what appeared to be a baby. As it continued to wail, tiny puffs of white blazed on its back, fluttering. This was no ordinary baby.

It was an angel.

# Chapter 7

"You gotta be kidding me!" Shelton said.

"We can't just leave it there," Elyssa said, already running toward the infant.

I heard a slithering noise from ahead, and two smaller red eyes coming straight for us. A much smaller leyworm appeared, mouth open as it roared. Elyssa snatched the infant from the floor, and ran.

"Defensive circle!" I shouted.

Elyssa blurred to the side as jaws snapped at her. She tossed the baby in an underhanded motion toward Bella.

"Don't throw the baby!" Shelton yelled at the top of his lungs.

Bella caught the small form without trouble, cushioning the momentum by swinging her arms with it. Since the baby had survived being shot from the mouth of a dragon, I highly doubted landing on the floor would have hurt it.

The leyworm chasing Elyssa wasn't much larger than a car. Which still made it more than we could handle. Shelton growled a word, and a shield sprang up around us. The leyworm smacked into it, coiling in on itself like an insanely large snake. It hissed and roared, snapping at the barrier.

The baby, for its part, continued to cry at the top of its lungs.

I figured the leyworm was a baby itself, judging from the size. I watched as it slithered the perimeter of the shield, as though probing for the way in.

"It's intelligent," Adam said. "Look at it. Like it knows what it's doing."

I noticed two puckered scars where scales had inadequately covered some old injury, and wondered what could have hurt the leyworm like that. The only time I'd seen an injured leyworm had been—I gasped. I'd seen this creature before. I'd rescued it from the clutches of Dash Armstrong, Maximus's pet Arcane. He'd been using the creature to power an arch along with some kind of funky Tesla coil, using cruel barbs which he'd stabbed into the leyworm's scaly side. I'd freed it, and it had promptly eaten Dash.

"Can we move with this shield with us?" I asked.

Shelton shook his head. "Not easily. This is a lot bigger than what I'm used to. If I tried to maintain it while we move, I might lose it, and junior there gets a full meal deal."

"Options?" I asked.

"I have Lancers," Elyssa said, adjusting something strapped on her wrist. "They might knock it out."

I watched the leyworm snake around, its glowing red eyes fixed on Shelton. It seemed to know the Arcane was straining to maintain the shield. Noticing the beads of sweat gathering on my friend's forehead, I knew he had to be giving it his all.

"Elyssa, be ready just in case," I said, and took a gamble. I walked to the edge of the shield, and waved my arms to attract the leyworm. Red orbs narrowed to slits. "Remember me?" I said. "I saved you from Dash Armstrong? The crazy guy using you for experiments?"

The leyworm roared in my face. The shield saved me from a face full of dragon breath and spittle.

"Don't you have any gratitude?" I said. "I saved your life."

The "little" dragon made a low growling noise, and regarded me for a moment.

"We're not here to hurt little babies," I said. "But we want to know what's going on, and how in the world your, uh, parents are making angel babies."

The leyworm tilted its head ever so slightly, as if trying to judge my character.

"I can't...hold much longer," Shelton said, his face glowing red.

"I'm ready," Elyssa said, quarterstaff spinning.

The leyworm looked at Shelton. It looked at Elyssa. Then it let out a hiss that sounded more like a sigh, and motioned with its head.

"Promise me you won't attack," I said to it.

It made another hissing noise.

"Lower the shield," I told Shelton.

The hum of the shield faded, and Shelton bent over, panting. Bella and the others held their staffs in defensive positions, various hues of deadly energy glowing atop them. The leyworm simply turned and trundled away, straight toward the giant dragons in the center.

"Maybe we should take the baby and run," Adam said, glancing curiously at the little bundle of joy.

Bella had calmed it down, stroking its cheek affectionately as it stared at her with wide eyes. "She's adorable."

"Something ain't right about dragons upchucking angels," Shelton said. He looked tired, but seemed to have caught his breath.

"That's not our biggest problem," Elyssa said. "It's Seraphim. If Daelissa is somehow making angel whoopee down here, she won't even need to fix the Grand Nexus."

"Somehow, I doubt she's getting it on with leyworms," I said.

"That does seem improbable considering the size differential and other physical incompatibilities," Cinder said. "Provided, of course, female Seraphim do not have extremely flexible—"

"I'm going to stop you right there," Bella said, giving him a warning look.

The small leyworm hissed and growled at the leviathans. The other two dragons regarded us before making low rumbling noises, which I prayed were assent.

"They look exhausted," Meghan said. Her eyes widened as she caught sight of something beyond.

I followed her gaze and my stomach flip-flopped.

"You've got to be kidding me," Adam said.

Beyond the two leyworms were more babies than any mother could survive. At least a dozen angel infants crawled, bawled, wriggled, and drooled. The scaly red coils of the dragon which had spit out the baby formed one half of a protective semi-circle, with the purple hide of the other dragon completing it. Several younger leyworms formed a loose inner perimeter, preventing the babies from wandering outside.

"What beautiful scales," Bella said, admiring purple dragon's diamond-shaped plating.

"Dah nah," cried out a cherub as it wandered in from the dark, making a beeline for the babies who began wailing at the tops of their lungs.

The small leyworm streaked for the creature, and using its long snout like a club, batted the cherub toward the purple dragon. The creature opened its gaping maw and swallowed the disgusting form whole.

"What the hell is going on down here?" Shelton said, staring aghast at the monstrous dragon.

"If I am correct, a baby angel will eventually emerge from the gullet of the dragon," Cinder said.

Heads turned toward the golem.

"Explain," I said.

"In your account of the Vadaemos incident, leyworms swallowed a great number of the cherubs." Cinder took out his arcphone, and projected simple three-dimensional image of a leyworm swallowing a cherub. "As you know, leyworms seem to feed directly from ley lines."

"We don't know exactly what they do to it," Meghan said. "The prevailing theory is they help keep the planet healthy by managing the flow of aether. Kind of like earthworms do for soil."

"Perhaps," Cinder said. "Inside a leyworm, the aether takes on different properties. You once mentioned the incident of a Templar swallowed by a leyworm, being irradiated by something like malaether."

Meghan tapped a finger to her chin. "That's right. Aether in its natural form isn't harmful, but whatever a leyworm does with the energy makes it dangerous, at least to most of us." She shrugged. "Whether it's identical to the malaether thrown off by the Cyrinthian Rune when it was trapped inside the arch, I don't know."

"I see where you're going with this," Shelton said. "And I don't like it."

I stared at the image of the leyworm swallowing the cherub. At the sheer volume of aether suffusing the beast. It didn't take much of a leap to see what Cinder thought might be happening.

"You're saying there's enough light essence in the leyworms to reverse the husks. To turn them back into angels."

"Precisely," Cinder said. "It must have started happening after you left."

"I witnessed leyworms swallowing dozens of cherubs," I said. "And I don't see nearly that many babies."

The young leyworm blinked at me, and rumbled. It led us into the space between the giants. We followed it far back to the opposite side of the obsidian slab. Bones the size of shipwrecks jutted from the floor. Adam directed the glowballs higher. I noticed small infantile forms littering the area. I jumped back, expecting them to attack, but they lay motionless. I walked closer, knelt next to the body of a cherub. Shelton prodded it with his staff. It clinked.

I ventured a careful hand and touched it. It was petrified. I looked up at the leyworm bones. I saw bits and pieces of internal organs. The area around the carcass was blackened, as if something had exploded.

"I estimate hundreds of bodies," Meghan said in a whisper. "Maybe more."

"It must have overloaded," Cinder said. "Perhaps the sheer number of cherubs caused a chain reaction. The pattern appears to have started as an implosion which sucked both light and dark aether from everything, and then exploded outward after petrifying the creature and the husks within it."

The young leyworm blinked and rumbled.

"The leyworm that spit out the first baby was drawing so much aether from the ley line beneath this place, it was literally absorbing the entire flow," I said. "And that was for one cherub."

"How many are left?" Elyssa asked. She blew out a breath. "If only we could light this whole place up instead of running around in the dark."

"Perhaps there is a way to do that in the control room," Cinder said.

I looked at the baby Bella carried then turned to the leyworm. "Why are you helping the angels?" I asked. "What do you plan to do with the babies?"

It simply stared at me for a moment, before slithering back toward the nursery. Following the creature, I switched back to incubus sight. Tendrils of gray energy drifted from the young leyworms nearby, swirling like miniature vortexes into the outstretched hands of the babies.

I told the others what I saw. "They're somehow converting aether into essence."

"It's gray, so it must be neutral essence," Adam said. "Maybe that'll keep the babies from aligning with Brightlings or Darklings."

"I don't get how these dragons know what they're doing," Shelton said. "They're a lot smarter than they look."

The young leyworm made a low rumbling noise.

Shelton gave it a nervous glance. "How do they know how to feed angels?"

"They've combed theses depths for probably thousands of years," Adam said. "I'm sure they knew all about the Seraphim. Maybe they even know who originally built this place."

At this, the leyworm's gaze flicked to me.

"Do you know?" I asked it.

It simply stared back.

"Guess you'd better brush up on your language skills," Shelton said with a chuckle. "Who'd have thought it? Leyworms, the dolphins of the underground."

The small dragon snorted.

"I should leave the baby here, then," Bella said reluctantly. "I'm afraid of upsetting its diet." She walked to the cluster of babes and set it down. "This goes against every motherly instinct in my body."

"I don't like it either," Meghan said, eyes locked onto the seemingly helpless bundles of joy. She looked to Adam. "Maybe we should take them. I can probably gather enough soul essence."

The leyworm made a harsh growling noise.

"I don't think they'll let us do that, honey," Adam replied, pulling her away from the temptation.

I heard a noise like the roar of a lion mixed with the braying of a donkey. All heads turned toward the sound. Shelton held a white-knuckled grip on his staff.

"What in the hell is coming now?"

I glanced at Elyssa. "Sound familiar?"

She nodded. "I don't think it's anything to worry about."

"I'll be the judge of that," Shelton said.

Bella patted him on the back. "I'm still here to protect you."

I spotted a glowing shape approaching from the darkness. It broke into a galloping lope, coming straight for us.

"Uh, can the leyworm help out?" Shelton said, placing himself squarely behind the reptilian creature.

Shaggy hair hung thick from the glowing creature. Tall, thin ears flopped from the top of its feline head. A long thin tongue lolled from the side of its mouth. It made another bray-roar noise, and skidded to a stop when it neared us, stopping to rub its body against the leyworm like a cat.

"Yolo?" I said.

The creature trotted up to me, and sniffed. I reached out a tentative hand, and scratched behind its ear. It made a soft noise, something between a bray and a purr.

"Wait a minute," Shelton said. "Is that the thing that chased you when you came down here the first time?"

"Yeah," I said. "Scared the crap out of us."

"Wasn't it Vadaemos's pet?"

I shrugged. "I think it just wanted attention."

Yolo brayed and licked my hand.

"Aw, he's sweet," Bella said, leaning over and scratching the beast.

Cinder appeared from the dim surroundings. "Justin, I took the liberty of surveying the area. I found several more crushed golems. It would appear Lornicus sent them to investigate, but the leyworms attacked."

As if in answer, the small dragon rumbled.

"Ah," Elyssa said. "I think I know Lornicus's game now."

I looked at her expectantly. "And that is?"

"He knows you have a powerful influence on beings around you. He obviously couldn't infiltrate the leyworm perimeter, so he figured you could do it." She pointed out a gray-suited shape at the fringe of the white light from the glowballs. "I'll bet he sent golems to take some of the babies."

"I estimate there are nearly a hundred destroyed golems around this area," Cinder said. "It would appear he had no success."

Shelton whistled. "That's a lot of dead golems. It can't be easy to replace them."

"Makes sense," I said, mulling it over. "Does he expect me to take a baby so he can steal it from me?" *Is that what he wants in exchange for help with saving Mom?*

58

"He wants information," Elyssa said. "Think about it. The golems didn't get close enough to see much. They may not even know these are angels."

"Wittle baby angels," Bella said in a coochie coo voice, while staring adoringly at one making eyes at her.

I looked at Cinder. "Do gray men share a consciousness of any kind? Or would an individual scout have to report the information?"

Cinder made a stiff shrug. "I do not remember. I would surmise a shared consciousness and the instant sharing of information is possible."

"They still didn't get close enough," Elyssa said. "So unless they spit out a baby at a golem's feet, I doubt they know much. Maybe they didn't even see the babies and only saw the leyworms acting weird."

"You still aren't asking the important questions," Shelton said. "Why are the leyworms doing this, and who are they helping? Because if they're helping Daelissa, we're in a world of trouble."

# Chapter 8

Nobody had an answer for Shelton's questions, and the young leyworm remained silent, giving nothing away. Judging from the brutal demises the gray men had suffered, I knew we'd be no more successful removing a baby from here than they had. One thing was certain—I had to find out everything I could about this situation before agreeing to anything with Lornicus.

"I just thought of another question," I said. "Supposedly, even being near the cherubs would weaken Daelissa. How are these babies not affected?"

"The leyworms," Adam said. "If they're feeding the infants constantly, that might mitigate the effects of the cherubs. Or it could simply be the leyworms are keeping the cherubs far enough away."

This was certainly a wrinkle in the greater scheme of things. If just one angel was powerful enough to end the world, what did it mean to have a few dozen? How long would it take for them to grow up and wreak havoc? Those questions would have to wait. Since we had access to a control room with an Alabaster Arch, it was time to branch into other avenues of exploration.

"I think we should figure out how to work the control room," I said. "Maybe see if we can get the lights on in here for starters."

"And the Alabaster Arch?" Elyssa asked, eyes worried.

"That too." I ran a hand through my hair. "If we can get through to the Grand Nexus, maybe we can ward it, set up booby traps to keep Jeremiah Conroy and Daelissa from using it." Taking Mom away from them would delay them, but that would only create the constant threat of Daelissa trying to steal her back. Destroying the nexus would remove the threat.

"I say we get a bunch of plastic explosives and blow it to hell," Shelton said.

I raised an eyebrow. "You think it'll work?"

He shrugged. "It's worth a try. That way we can set a timer and be far away before it blows."

"But if it causes another backlash," Bella said, eyes horrified. "What will happen to the babies? What if it husks them again?"

Shelton opened his mouth, probably to offer some heartless comment, but shut it again. "We'll figure something out," he said after a pause. "Maybe our reptilian pals here will see clear to let us evacuate them."

Bella gave Shelton a stern eye. "No blowing things up until the babies are safe."

He put up his hands in surrender. "Hey, I ain't no baby killer, woman. Sheesh."

"I don't think this place ever had an Obsidian Arch," Elyssa told me, returning from a walkabout. "I looked for rubble, or even the broken remains of a column, but the slab is smooth."

"So the creators relied on the smaller arches," I said. I sighed. "I'd really like to know who made this place. What if they're worse than the angels?"

"Then they're worse," Elyssa said. "For now, we have to worry about the clear and present danger."

"And learn how to speak leywormese," I added.

She smiled. "That too."

We herded everyone back to the control room, with Elyssa batting away any stray cherubs wandering across our path.

Shelton glanced back at the yellow glow in the center. "I wonder how long it takes to process a cherub. The one that thing ate earlier still hasn't come out."

"I find the entire process extremely disturbing," Meghan said. "Eating those disgusting husks and regurgitating a baby seems incredibly unnatural."

Nobody disagreed.

Once back inside the control room, we studied every inch of the place, but came no closer to finding out how to turn on the lights in the main cavern, or how to make the Alabaster Arch do what we wanted.

"Maybe we should recruit an operator," Adam said. "At the very least, they could tell us how to turn on the lights."

"Sounds like a plan to me," Shelton said. "Jeremiah Conroy was using the operators at Queens Gate and the Grotto to figure out how to use the smaller arches." He looked at me. "Maybe our Darkwater creds will still hold water with them."

I raised an eyebrow. Jeremiah was using an Arcane company named Darkwater to explore dangerous relics like Thunder Rock. Shelton and I had masqueraded as employees to glean information from arch operators. "I dunno. Sounds risky."

He shrugged. "Hey, what's the worst that can happen?"

"An awful lot," I said.

Adam chuckled. "Are we going to kidnap one? Or go through the process of vetting someone so we can trust them." He motioned around us. "True, they may know about these control rooms, but the babies out there are complete game changers."

"Of course we'll vet them," Shelton said, blowing out a breath. "It's about time we brought in an expert, for crying out loud. I don't know jack about traversion theory."

Adam raised an eyebrow. "How do you suggest we go about it?"

"I dunno yet." Shelton pursed his lips. "Let me think about it."

I looked at the still-open portal back to the mansion. "I wonder if the omniarches here work, just in case we lose the connection back home."

"I'll put that on a list of things to test," Adam said, pulling out an arctablet and tapping on it.

Cinder, who'd been inspecting the Alabaster Arch, approached as we discussed plans. "Justin, I think I will remain here and survey the cavern. Perhaps I should also attempt to establish communications with the leyworms."

"Be careful," I told him. "I don't want them to mistake you for a hostile gray man."

"I believe the smaller leyworm now recognizes me," he said. "Hopefully this will prevent an attack."

"Okay. I'll close the portal behind us. If you need us to open it, call, okay?" Arcphones used ley lines for a wireless signal, so contacting us shouldn't be an issue.

"I will, Justin."

The rest of us stepped back through the portal to the mansion.

After disconnecting the arch, I walked upstairs after the others. My mind still reeled from the discovery of angel babies. Even though the leyworm I'd rescued from Dash Armstrong had vouched for me, did that mean we were on their safe list? Or would things be different the next time I walked in there?

*And who are they really helping?*

So much made so little sense. True, I'd only known leyworms in the most terrifying sense, when they'd chased our small group through dark tunnels deep in the earth during our expedition to apprehend Vadaemos. I wondered if Yolo could communicate with the leyworms. They seemed pretty cozy.

Elyssa and I took a flying carpet down into Queens Gate that night. The bustling city looked like London from the Victorian Era. A huge clock tower rose from the center, flanked on either side by domed buildings used for official Arcane Council meetings, among other things. We grabbed dinner at the Copper Swan, a popular Chinese restaurant.

"I think Shelton is right," Elyssa said as we discussed his plan to question an arch operator about the control room beneath El Dorado. "You obviously can't tell the operator this is about El Dorado unless he still believes your Darkwater story."

"If the arch operators don't help, what then?" I asked.

Elyssa shrugged. "Kidnap one? Torture him for information?"

I felt my forehead pinch. "What?"

Elyssa laughed. "I'm kidding, babe." She put a hand atop mine. "Do we even know where this Darkwater organization is based? Maybe we could break into their headquarters and find more useful information than the operators know."

"Now, that's a good idea," I said.

"Probably because a woman thought of it," she said.

I snorted. "I think we should start with the operators. Infiltrating Darkwater sounds risky." I narrowed my eyes in thought, remembering a conversation I'd once had with Bella. "Although…back in the day, Bella and Stacey used to be cat burglars. Maybe they could help with something on that scale."

Elyssa's violet eyes widened. "They were thieves?"

I nodded. "Bella told me stories about the two of them. Maybe they'd be willing to come out of retirement."

"It could be fun," she said, pursing her lips.

"Now you're scaring me again," I said with a smirk.

After dinner, we went back to the mansion and found Bella playing Scrabble with a grumpy-looking Shelton.

"You clearly don't have a life," he said, as she placed a long word I'd never seen before across the board. "What do you do, read dictionaries all day? Is that even a word?"

"Of course," the petite Arcane said with a bright smile.

"What the hell does it mean?" he said.

"It means I won." She stuck out her tongue.

Shelton's grumpy façade vanished in a burst of laughter.

"We've been discussing plans," I told them as Bella cleared the board.

Shelton gave us a suspicious look. "As in plans for new bedroom furniture or plans for something that'll make me wish I didn't know you?"

I took a seat at the table. "We figured grilling one of the arch operators might be a good starting point, but Elyssa thinks infiltrating Darkwater is a good backup plan in case the operators don't have answers." I chewed on my inner lip. "We need to know how to operate the Alabaster Arch so we find out where the Grand Nexus is. We need to know how to turn on the lights. We need information to bargain with Lornicus so he'll help me rescue Mom."

Shelton's forehead wrinkled into an incredulous look. "Just so happens I know where Darkwater is located," he said.

My eyebrows pinched. "You do? How?"

He shrugged. "When we were pretending to work for Darkwater, I did a little extra research. I don't like impersonating employees of a company I know nothing about. I also wondered what kind of people the Conroys were hiring."

"Tell us more," Elyssa said, taking a seat next to Bella.

"Jarrod Sager originally owned the company when it was known as Arcane Enterprises," he said, speaking of his adoptive father, the former Arcanus Primus, now dead thanks to the late Bigglesworth. Shelton flinched, but soldiered on. "He hired them for the Gloom Initiative, even though using his own company for a public contract was an obvious conflict of interest. Cyphanis Rax, his primary opponent for the Primus election, dug up the dirt and called him out on it. Everyone figured Sager's political career was over, but then I caught the Pinkerton Gang, and dear old dad took the credit for it."

"You caught the Pinkertons?" Elyssa said, an amazed look on her face. "They remained at the top of the Templar Most Wanted for years."

He gave a modest shrug. "I was getting pretty good at the bounty hunting biz."

"They weren't political enemies of your father, were they?" Bella asked.

A scowl twisted his lips. "Nah, they were legit bad guys. Not the ones Aerianas sent me after."

Aerianas, Vadaemos's daughter, had used Shelton to carry out bounty contracts on Sager's political enemies in a twisted deal with Daelissa to push funding for the Gloom Initiative through the Overworld Conclave. Sager needed political cover to fund the project and Shelton had unwittingly helped him by bringing in his opponents on fake charges. We still didn't know much about the Gloom Initiative or its purpose.

"Taking credit for their capture was enough to rescue Sager's career?" I asked.

Shelton nodded. "Once Aerianas got her claws into me and had me hunting down political enemies of Dad's, Cyphanis's name came up."

"Did you arrest him?" I asked.

"No. He was too rich and powerful for me to go after. I tried a couple of times, but the man was untouchable." Shelton shrugged. "Plus, he moved around a lot, so it was hard to get a fix on him. Most of the time, I ended up tracking one of his doubles instead of the real deal." He leaned back in his chair. "So, Sager sold the company to a shell corporation owned by the Conroys, and the name changed from Arcane Enterprises to Darkwater."

"Where are the headquarters?" I asked.

"The tech sector of the Grotto, right next to MagicSoft and Orange." He sighed, ran a hand through his hair. "They probably have a mix of tech and magic protecting the place, so infiltrating it ain't gonna be easy."

"That's where Bella comes in," Elyssa said. "And maybe even Stacey."

Bella gave her a shrewd look. "Did Justin tell you about my nefarious past?"

Elyssa nodded. "Yep. If anyone could get in, it would be you two. I'd like to help as well, maybe learn a thing or two along the way."

"Whoa, whoa, whoa!" Shelton said. "I know about your thieving youth, woman, but you haven't done it for a century at least."

"You make me sound awfully old when you put it like that," Bella said.

"I'm not kidding. Their defenses ain't gonna be kiddie stuff. You could get killed."

"Maybe it's not such a good idea," I said, not liking the idea of Elyssa going along.

The two women gave us sharp looks.

"Harry Shelton, you know I can take care of myself," Bella said. "Elyssa and I saw a lot of action in the streets of Bogota, so I know we can handle this."

"And you think Stacey is gonna just jump on board with this insanity?" Shelton said.

A grin spread Bella's lips. "I think she'll enjoy it."

"Let's hope the arch operators can tell us what we need," I said.

"They might have more than just information about the arch control rooms," Elyssa said. "If Jeremiah Conroy owns the company, maybe they have information about where he lives."

"Don't count on it," Shelton said. "The old man is trickier than the devil."

Elyssa flicked his comment away with the back of her hand. "We can't overlook the possibility. We find your mother's location, and Lornicus is out of the loop."

"I'm going to call Stacey right now," Bella said, her eyes bright with excitement.

"I can't wait to test out the new Templar stealth pack," Elyssa said, matching the other dhampyr's excitement.

Shelton and I exchanged distressed looks. Stopping these two would be an uphill battle.

"That reminds me," Elyssa said. "This Saturday is my initiation, and I want to invite everyone."

I'd already known about it, but had kind of forgotten to bring it up with the others.

"What do they do for initiations these days?" Bella asked. "Since you can't use the torches anymore." Templars formerly used torches to call the Templar Divinity to bless newly minted soldier with immunities to certain curses, super strength, etc. But since discovering Daelissa was the Divinity and that she'd used her magic to blank out each initiate's memory of the proceedings, a major portion of the Templars had broken away from the organization. Christian Salazar, the commander of Templar forces in Colombia had called for an Imperator Concilium to replace the Synod. The vote had passed, but forces loyal to the Synod threatened war if the others tried to replace them.

"It's a simpler ceremony now," Elyssa said. "Although Arcanes who don't already have supernatural strength, won't get it."

"We'll be there," Bella said. "I'm very proud of you."

Elyssa's lips spread into a smile. "Thanks, Bella. It means a lot to me."


The next morning, Adam, Shelton, and I took a shuttle down to the Queens Gate way station to see what information we could glean from the operators there. I took along my practice staff just in case we ran into trouble. Oh, who was I kidding? Trouble would find us. As with most Obsidian Arch way stations, a large parking lot took up a generous portion of the massive cavern while a huge, enclosed stable spanned the opposite wall. Between the back of the stable and the wall ran a narrow alley. Shelton and I had discovered each way station had a door concealed by illusion in this narrow alley and through it sat the control room.

Slipping along the aforementioned narrow alley behind the stables, we found the hidden door and stepped inside. Two of the operators glanced up with confused looks, their black-and-yellow-striped robes adding a mild comedic air to their expressions.

I recognized one of them as someone Shelton had questioned before.

"Got some questions," Shelton said, walking in like he owned the place.

"About?" the man said, looking at us, and then looking down the aisle running between the smaller arches in the control room. The control room looked identical to the one beneath El Dorado aside from a gap where no Alabaster Arch stood.

"We're looking into some other arch control rooms, and need to know how to activate the lights in the main cavern."

The operator's face changed. "Oh, well that's rather simple." He walked up to the modulus, a gray sphere sitting atop a pedestal in the floor like the one in El Dorado. "You need to trace the Cyrinthian symbol for light across the modulus. To indicate which area you wish to light, you can spread your fingers across it for everything, or simply flick a finger like so"—he demonstrated the motion—"to light parts of the cavern."

"Looks simple enough," Shelton said. "Thanks, that'll help a lot."

"Of course." The man looked back down the long center aisle, forehead wrinkling, then back to us. "Have you found other hidden way stations?"

"That's classified," Shelton said, then with a conspiratorial glance around, leaned forward and said, "Two of them." He winked. "Don't tell anyone."

The operator returned the wink. "How exciting."

"Yeah. The problem we're having is one of the Alabaster Arches is blowing everything up that gets near it."

The operator's brow furrowed. "I thought we'd solved that issue." He narrowed his eyes at Shelton. "Surely, you drew the pattern on the modulus—"

"Who are you people?" said a stocky man flanked by two others as he strode down the center aisle. Each man wore black Arcane robes, the material fitting snugly down to the beltline before flaring out like a trench coat.

"I might ask you the same question," Shelton said. "We're with Darkwater."

The man raised an eyebrow, and looked at his companions. "That's funny," he said with a smirk. "Because I'm with Darkwater, and I sure as hell haven't seen you before."

# Chapter 9

A cold feeling clenched my bowels. Out of the corner of my eye I noticed Adam and Shelton tense.

The stocky man pulled out an ebony rod, flicking it to full staff length, his smirk never wavering as his companions followed suit. Without warning, he whirled his staff. Silver bolts of light flew from them. The arch operator yelped and threw himself out of the way as energy shards pinged against a support column inches from me.

Shelton cursed, stabbing his rod into the floor. The azure blue nimbus of a shield sprang into place. A flurry of purple orbs from the staff of another Darkwater man blasted against the shield, ricocheting in all directions with a buzzing whine. The third man held his staff straight out as a white light gathered at the end.

"He's charging a wave," Adam said, his own staff glowing green as he leveled it at the attackers.

"I see that," Shelton muttered, pulling out a wand, and flicking it.

An invisible force yanked the end of the man's staff up just as a column of ghostly figures charged from the end of the rod, screaming like banshees. They roared up at an angle, missing us, but cutting a gouge in the dark stone of the support column.

I looked behind us. Only the open platform before the world map lay there, offering no cover from there to the door. I grabbed my staff as another flock of silver projectiles smashed against Shelton's shield.

"It's not gonna hold," he groaned, sweat glistening on his forehead.

Adam released the charge of green light even as another wave of the white energy leapt from the end of the third man's staff. They met in the middle, pushing against each other, coalescing into a ball of energy. Shelton growled something, motioning us to fall back behind the column. His shield flickered out, just as the ball of raw energy between Adam and the other man exploded. The deafening roar echoed through the large space. A purple orb blurred toward me even as I brought up my staff, desperately thinking of some spell to use. The orb shattered the end of the staff. Another one slammed into my chest, throwing me back.

I thudded against the floor as my staff clattered away. All I heard was a high-pitched whine. My chest felt as if it was on fire. I tried to move, but my legs wouldn't respond. I attempted to suck in a breath, but failed. I looked to the column and saw Shelton and Adam taking cover behind it. Adam gave me a horrified look. Silver bolts pinged against the floor all around me. I looked up in time to see another death wave screaming my way.

I tried to roll, but my body failed to respond. "No!" I cried out, throwing my arm straight out as if that would do anything to stop it. The heat in my chest seemed to expand outward. It burned up the length of my arm, concentrating in my hand. A bolt of ultraviolet energy burst from my palm, crashing through the deadly force coming at me, splitting it down the middle and meeting the end of the attacker's staff. The wooden rod splintered, spraying shards. My attack blasted the man in the arm. He spun in two full circles before dropping like a rag doll.

The stocky man's eyes went wide. "Everyone get out here now!" he snarled, spinning his staff, and hurling another onslaught of silver bolts at me. "Kill these sons of bitches!"

My body finally responded to my commands. I rolled away from his attacks as silver bolts gouged the stone around me, peppering me with shrapnel. The pain receded even as I felt the brief sting of impact. I rolled to my feet. Blurred from the path of more purple orbs. Leapt high, and crashed down atop the Arcane firing them, my fist cracking the stone next to his head.

I heard shouts, and looked up in time to see another dozen men in similar robes racing down the aisles from the back of the control room. The stocky man swung his staff at me. I caught the blow on my arm, gripped him by the front of his robe, and flung him down the aisle to crash into the other men.

Another man appeared, a protective barrier glowing in the air before him. He threw back the hood to his robe, revealing a bald head and a chiseled face with a black goatee. Strange tattoos curved beneath his eyes. They almost seemed to glow. The man's lips pulled back in a snarl. A staff in each hand, he slammed the butts against the ground. Roiling red energy gathered between the ends, glowing brighter and brighter.

"Run!" Shelton shouted. "Run your damned ass off!"

I snapped from whatever trance held me and raced back toward the exit even as a high-pitched whine split the air.

"Jump!" Shelton said.

I jumped high as a red beam tore through the stone floor beneath me. Still in the air, I saw the beam angling upward. I flung out a hand, and cried "*Shoryuken*!" A rope of magical energy shot from my hand and coiled around the nearest support column. I jerked, snapping myself out of the line of fire at the last minute. I hit the ground, rolling behind a nearby arch and glanced back as Shelton sent a scorching orange meteor whooshing down the aisle. The bald Arcane dove out of the way as it shot past.

Shelton and Adam raced for the exit. I blurred after them, deadly bolts, rays, orbs, and spheres raining down all around me.

I saw the arch operators huddled in the far corner of the room, the whites of their eyes showing. What pattern on the modulus had the man been talking about? The answer to finding the Grand Nexus had been so close. Now we definitely couldn't return to find out. I ran out the exit, slamming the door shut behind me. Adam aimed his staff at the door, invisible behind an illusion, and a thin beam of red light struck where the seam would be.

"That should weld it shut for a few minutes," he said.

We ran down the narrow alley, through the way station, and left via the doors to the pocket dimension housing Queens Gate.

Shelton and Adam were panting by the time we reached the shuttle station. Luckily, the sky car to the university was nearly ready to depart when we rushed inside. Most students were away on holiday break, so only a few curious eyes regarded us when we stumbled into our seats.

"Mother of sheep farts," Shelton said, breathing heavily, a sheen of sweat glistening on his forehead beneath the wide-brimmed hat. "Those people aren't playing around."

71

"Battle mages," Adam said in a dark mutter as the sky car lurched upward. "Mercenaries."

"Who do they think they are attacking like that?" Shelton said.

"I guess they figure working for the Conroys gives them free license," Adam said, inspecting a burn mark on the sleeve of his shirt.

Shelton glared down at black smudges on his leather duster. "Good thing I just refreshed the armor charm on this baby." He reached beneath, pressing a hand to his chest and winced. "Still hurts like hell."

My shirt was charred in various places where I'd been hit, leaving raw, burned skin beneath. As my adrenalin receded, pain grew. The puckered skin where one of the silver bolts had sliced me looked like a knife wound. My supernatural healing seemed to be mending the wound much slower than usual.

"Magical injuries can take longer to heal," Adam said, noticing my discomfort. "At least that's what Meghan once told a lycan after his bar fight with an Arcane."

I caught Shelton looking at me with undisguised confusion. "Mind telling me what you did in there?" he said. "You've never demonstrated that kind of raw firepower before."

I shrugged. Winced at the pain in my shoulders. "It just kind of happened." I described the feel of the heat flowing from my chest to my hand. "It felt like it came from my heart."

Adam and Shelton traded looks.

"Angel magic?" Adam offered with a quizzical look.

Shelton grimaced. "I think so." His face brightened. "Hey, at least you learned something."

"Not to mention stayed alive," I said. "I don't know if I can reproduce it though."

"Obviously a byproduct of my teaching." He shivered. "Whew! What an adrenalin rush." Shelton flicked his staff back to compact form and slid it into a holster on his side.

"Those men have some serious battle mage training," Adam said. "Did you notice all the high-level Arcane attack forms they used?"

"I'd have to be blind to miss them," Shelton said, again wiping away sweat from his forehead. "I took battle mage training, but some of the forms they used were above my level of control."

"Forms?" I asked Shelton as the sky car bumped down atop the landing zone.

We stepped outside into the cool air and headed down the path toward Greek Row and the mansion.

"That's what we call them in battle mage training," Shelton said as we walked. "Just like kung-fu masters use forms."

"Like the crane kick?" I asked demonstrating by standing on one leg and then kicking with the other.

He rolled his eyes. "If you can pull off magic like you did today, maybe I'll show you a few forms."

"Shelton, he pulled off an arc with his bare hand," Adam said with wonder in his voice. "I can list on one hand the Arcanes I've seen do that."

"Angel magic," Shelton said again, as if he knew all about it. "They can use their hands as a focus."

"My hand would be a bloody stump if I tried that," Adam said. "Human flesh just isn't made to handle that kind of energy."

"Tell me about it," Shelton said.

"I have a stupid question," I said.

Shelton snorted. "Never heard one of those from you before."

I gave him a sideways glance. "Why does a staff make for a more powerful focus than a wand?"

"He hasn't learned that yet?" Adam said. "I thought you were teaching him."

"I kind of explained it," Shelton said, flicking away Adam's comment with the back of his hand. "Anyway, it has to do with complicated stuff you haven't learned, like runes and enchantments and design elements. It's tough fitting amplifiers on wands, and if you use arcane generators like I do, you can't fit them in wands without a lot of effort." He pulled out his staff, flicked it out to full length, and ran his finger along the designs, some of them Cyrinthian symbols, others odd designs I hadn't seen. "When you make your staff, you can enchant it all sorts of different ways. Some designs give you finer control, others are meant for raw power."

"That's why some of us have more than one staff," Adam said.

"And wands?" I asked.

"Wands are generally geared toward fine control," Shelton said.

"Are they always wood?"

He shrugged. "I've seen other materials, but wood won't heat up like branding iron while you're channeling through it like metal will."

"And stone is fragile," Adam added.

"What about diamond fiber?" I asked. "That stuff seems indestructible."

Shelton shook his head. "It won't conduct magic since it's made to resist magic."

When we arrived at the mansion, Elyssa, Bella, and Stacey sat huddled at the table, engaged in what looked like a super-serious discussion. Elyssa looked up at me, smiled. Her eyes widened as she saw the state of my clothes. In an instant, she stood in front of me, hands pulling away the charred shirt to inspect my wounds.

"Oh my god!" She ripped the shirt down the middle and gasped. Her eyes went to Shelton. "What happened?" she said, tone low and dangerous.

Shelton backed off, holding up his hands. "Darkwater didn't like us poking around in their business."

Bella already stood next to him, looking at his duster. "Did you call them names?"

"No," I said, responding before Shelton could. "They attacked for no reason."

Elyssa's lips curled back in a snarl. "Let's see how they like having the Templars all over their case."

"You know Arcane politics won't allow the Templars to do anything," Shelton said. "Especially since these people are working for the Conroys."

"Nobody has the right to attempt murder," Elyssa said in a low growl.

Shelton's eyes widened at her ferocity. "Look, we're fine. Justin here nearly charbroiled the bastards." He told them about my feat.

"Your angel side is emerging," Bella said, wonder in her eyes. "This is good. This is very good." She looked at me like a proud mother.

"Where's Meghan?" Adam asked.

"In town for supplies," Bella said.

"How very vexing," Stacey said, standing with a hand on her curved hip. "I would enjoy teaching those Arcanes some manners."

She growled like a cat, an accurate description, given she was a felycan and could turn into various feline forms.

"We need to treat these wounds," Elyssa said, eyes softening as she inspected each cut and burn.

The next thing I knew, three women were doting over me while the other two men stood idly by in the den. Elyssa pulled out a chair and grabbed wet cloths to wash my wounds while Bella applied one of Meghan's healing salves. Stacey cooed, seeming to enjoy the exercise.

Within minutes, I was bandaged up and feeling much better, especially since the salves assisted my supernatural healing. I made a mental note to avoid magical damage in the future, if at all possible.

*Fat chance of that.*

"We're devising a plan to raid the Darkwater facilities," Stacey said. "Ah, it reminds me of the fun Bella and I used to have."

"What do you want us to do?" I asked, indicating myself and the other guys.

"This is *our* mission," Elyssa said. "No boys allowed."

"It will be quick and covert," Stacey added with a smug grin. "Not loud and messy like you lot."

"Not our fault," Shelton said, enjoying some attention from Bella as she looked at his bruises.

"You're still going to need some hacking tools to break into their systems," Adam said. "Just so happens I can help with that." He glanced at me. "I'll need all the specifics you're looking for."

"Information about the arch control rooms and the Alabaster Arch is important," I said. "But the most important thing is finding out where my Mom is being held."

"You think Darkwater has access to that information?" Adam said.

"It's a long shot, but if the Conroys own them, it makes sense they'd use them for containing powerful people."

"They're most likely keeping her close," Elyssa said.

Meaning Mom and Ivy were probably both in the last place any sane person would want to invade. "Yeah. At the Conroy residence."

# Chapter 10

"What?" Shelton said, eyes wide. "You want to charge into the lion's den? We don't have the power to fight Jeremiah Conroy, much less your sister."

"I hope we won't have to fight Ivy," I said. "If anything, I hope she'll help us free my mother." Meeting Elyssa's eyes, I said, "There's a slim chance Darkwater knows where the Conroys live. But I happen to know a person who's found plenty of people who didn't want to be found." At this, I turned my gaze to Shelton. "So, how about we use those mad skills of yours to find the Conroys?"

Shelton worked his jaw for a moment, as if chewing a particularly rancid mouthful of tough beef. "Well, it would be a challenge. If nothing else, we could find them, maybe home in on your mom."

"My primary concern is how, exactly, one goes about breaking a person out of an astral prison," Bella said. "I have never encountered one."

"How exactly does an astral prison work?" I asked.

"Traps a person in between here and another reality," Shelton said.

"Do they still have to eat?"

He gave a slow nod. "But you don't pop someone as powerful as your mom in and out of the astral prison just to feed her." He chuckled. "There ain't no food slot. I'd bet good money they put her under a sleeping spell to slow her metabolism so she doesn't have to eat often. I'd also wager they haven't fed her much soul essence to keep her weak."

I hated to think of Mom slowly wasting away, caught between the walls of two dimensions.

Meghan walked in carrying bags. Adam crossed the room and relieved her burden. "Thanks," she said, and locked eyes on my bandaged form. "What in the world happened?"

We brought her up to speed while she checked the handiwork of Elyssa and the others. My wounds were mostly healed, pink skin already replacing the cuts and burns.

"To answer your question about a preservation spell, a person could go months without sustenance if the spell is powerful." She chewed on her lower lip. "If Daelissa had a hand in it, there's no telling. Plus, angel physiology is very hardy. Your mother might go even longer."

"We need to figure out how to crack the prison," I said. "Ivy might be able to help."

"Your sister might have played nice the last time we saw her," Shelton said, "but that's no guarantee she'll be happy to help you with this."

I shrugged. "Couldn't hurt to ask."

Shelton barked a laugh. "I disagree. It could hurt a lot."

Everyone started speaking at once, mostly about just how stable my little sister was after years of brainwashing by the Conroys.

I waved them off. "Hold on, people. Let's find my mother and Ivy first, and figure out the prison problem afterward." I looked at Shelton. "You with me?"

He groaned. "Fine. I'll track them down. But no promises on the jailbreak."

"That's all I ask," I said.

"You ask an awful lot," he said, scrunching his forehead.

"I'm in," Adam said. "I've studied spell decryption in my spare time, so maybe we could use the same kind of scanning spell we used to open a hole in the shield around the Cyrinthian Rune. It's at least worth a shot."

"Maybe," Shelton said.

"Justin, I don't like the idea of you approaching your sister." Concern filled Elyssa's eyes. "I have a terrible feeling about it."

Truth was, I didn't know what to expect. Ivy seemed to have come around, saving my life and Nightliss's, but it didn't make this a slam-dunk. Jeremiah Conroy had his hooks in her impressionable mind, and I knew I couldn't change that overnight.

Stacey clapped her hands gleefully. "I've missed your adventures, Justin. This will be so much fun."

Nobody else seemed to share her enthusiasm.

After dinner, Elyssa and I went through the cellar, past the arch room, and into the dungeons beneath Arcane University. An abandoned gauntlet room, formerly used by Arcanes to practice their skills, seemed a good place to attempt a replication of my earlier feat against the Darkwater battle mages.

"It felt like my chest caught fire," I explained as we stood before a target practice range.

"Tell me what happened leading up to it," Elyssa said.

I thought for a moment. "I got hit by magical damage, and then it was like my body reacted to it. Maybe it was a defense mechanism?"

"Hmm," she said, tapping a finger against her chin. "Most of the hits you took were centered on your chest. Maybe it had something to do with that."

"Or else, it was pure instinct, like what happens with my demonic side." I pursed my lips, trying to recall the exact feeling. "I felt powerful. Like nothing could stop me."

Elyssa rummaged through a satchel she'd brought along with her practice swords, among other interesting-looking knick-knacks. She slapped my hand away as I tried to grab a silvery sphere and removed a scroll. "This is a low level spell intended to stun supers that are immune to Lancers," she explained. "It's not too strong, just enough to knock someone on their butt."

I raised an eyebrow. "And what do you intend to do with it?"

She smiled. "Hit you with it."

I backed away. "Hang on. I've been hit with magic before, not to mention shrapnel, and a bunch of other bad stuff. Why would this do anything?"

"I don't know," she said with a shrug. "Maybe it'll just knock you senseless."

I knew Elyssa would never do anything intentionally to harm me, so I sighed, steeling myself. "Will it hurt?"

"A little." She pecked my cheek. "Think my big boy can handle it?"

"I guess." I walked a few feet away from her. "Ready when—"

She said a word, and a zap of lightning struck me in the chest. I made a gurgling noise as my body went into spasms, and stumbled over backwards. My butt hit the floor, causing the breath to explode from me. As I sat there gibbering like a madman, sudden warmth spread from my chest, spreading to my left arm. I felt a tingle of power itch the palms. Ultraviolet light gathered in my hand. I aimed toward the low wall separating me from the target dummy and focused.

*Fire!*

A thin beam sputtered from my hand, crackling for an instant before dying in a shower of sparks.

The warmth in my chest faded back to the usual temperature. No matter how hard I tried to repeat the pitiful success, my palm remained woefully normal.

"It worked!" Elyssa said, eyes alight. She rummaged in her bag. "Maybe I have something more powerful—"

"Whoa, hold on," I said, gaining my feet, shaking the fuzz from my brain. "I don't think I want you hitting me with something more powerful. That hurt."

She laughed. "You looked funny."

I sighed. "Yeah, a real barrel of laughs."

"Now you sound like Shelton." She smirked. "If anything, we know how to trigger your power."

"Yeah, but I don't want to take blunt force trauma to the chest every time I need to defend myself," I said. "It seems a bit self-defeating."

She touched my chest, closing her eyes, and holding the palm of her hand there as if listening to my heart beat. I felt a wave of heat that had nothing to do with angel magic radiate from her touch. Elyssa raised an eyebrow, opening an eye to look at me.

"Don't you ever think about anything else?" she said, the tone of her voice indicating she didn't mind.

"Sorry, you have that effect on me."

She removed her hand, regarding me like a lab rat she wanted to experiment on. "Can you remember the feeling? Maybe reproduce it?"

I closed my eyes and focused on my heartbeat. I could hear it beating away, probably wondering what other horrible things I planned to do to it. I thought of the heat. Tried to will the furnace to light and spread to my limbs. Nothing happened. I idly wondered if I could shoot magic beams from my feet or other appendages, and decided aiming would be awkward.

"You've lost your train of thought, haven't you?" Elyssa asked, amusement in her voice.

"How do you know?" I asked, eyes still closed.

"Because your eyebrows start moving like a nerd trying to figure out an obscure physics problem."

I sighed and gave up, opening my eyes to give her a hopeless look. "Yeah. Can't get the feeling back." It sucked not having a teacher.

Elyssa offered to zap me again, but I declined, and decided to practice the normal magic I knew while she practiced her ninja moves on a combat dummy.

"You really should join me sometime," Elyssa said, wiping sweat from her forehead as she cleaned her weapons and packed her gear.

"Join you?" I asked with a quizzical look.

"Practice," she said, nodding her head toward the combat dummy. "Magic is a great tool, but knowing how to defend yourself with finesse would definitely increase your survivability."

"Vallaena kind of taught me a little," I said, referring to my aunt's penchant for physically attacking me in her succubus form, teaching me to defend myself and manifest my demonic side without spawning into full-out beast mode.

Elyssa blurred. I felt my feet fly from beneath me and my back smacked the ground. She held a wooden practice knife to my throat. "'Kind of' isn't the same thing, Justin." She gripped my forearm and pulled me to my feet. "You used to practice with me all the time. You've gotten rusty."

"You've been doing this all your life," I said, feeling foolish and unprepared. "Plus, that wasn't even fair. Why would I be on the defensive against you?"

She raised an eyebrow. "Challenge accepted."

"What challenge?" I asked, backing away.

"Best of three takedowns," she said, shoving her duffel bag out of the way with a foot.

The center of the gauntlet room resembled a circular arena. I threw up my hands. "Wait, I can't beat you hand-to-hand."

"Use magic then," she said. "Do whatever it takes to beat me."

"But I might hurt you," I said. The only offensive spells I knew involved fireballs.

She grinned. "I doubt it."

I gulped. "Fine." I took a defensive posture, the very same Elyssa had taught me a few months ago. "Let's do thi—"

She blurred. I dodged to the side. My feet left the ground, and a hand closed around my neck, pressing me to the ground.

"That's one," Elyssa said.

I growled. Jumped up. Fine. If she wanted to prove something, I'd make her work for it.

We backed to opposite sides of the circle again. This time, I charged Elyssa, flashing toward her. She moved at the last instant, her leg sweeping low. I'd anticipated another leg sweep, and leapt over it, planning to drop behind her, and put her in a hold. Her arm jutted out and clothes-lined me in mid-air. I whumped to the ground and felt the breath fly from me.

"Two," she said, pulling me to my feet. "I win."

"Best of five," I muttered, feeling anger boiling in my stomach.

"Is someone getting angry?" she asked, batting her eyelashes innocently.

I didn't answer as I stalked to the other side of the ring. When I turned, I switched to incubus sight, enabling me to see the aether floating in the air around us. I drew it in through the thin tendrils of my incubus senses, which I typically used to feed from humans. Focusing my will, I assumed my defensive stance. Elyssa recognized my positioning instantly and came for me. This time, I threw out my hands, as if to ward her off, but instead yelled, "*Shoryuken!*"

Strands of webbed energy shot from my hands, wrapping around Elyssa's legs and tripping her. I jerked the strands, flipped her on her back, and straddled her.

"Two to one," I said, dismissing the spell and standing.

"Well played, babe," she said with a wink. "I like to see you think on your toes."

I didn't answer, trying to hold onto the anger that seemed to help me focus when it came to magic and demonic abilities. I had one more trick up my sleeve, but I wasn't sure I wanted to ruin my clothes to use it.

"I guess one win isn't too bad," she said, assuming her position. "Against a girl."

Suddenly, I didn't care about my T-shirt and cargo pants. I let the anger teeter on the edge of the cliff as Elyssa approached, her stance warier than before. I flung strands of energy at her, but she seemed to sense them even if she couldn't see them, and flashed out of the way.

"Not gonna work twice, hon," she said with a confident grin. She lunged.

I let the anger fall off the cliff and opened the door to my inner beast. My body swelled, muscles coiling like serpents beneath my skin, hands and feet expanding, and horns curling up from my forehead. A tail sprouted from my backside, whipping back and forth. I'd felt the pain of manifestation so many times, it hardly made me flinch anymore. Vallaena had taught me how to do it within seconds. Elyssa's hands met my huge hands. Her sweep kick couldn't dislodge my wide feet. I gripped her hands and pinned them together.

Her face went red with the effort to break free. Her foot smashed against my head, but I caught it on a horn, used my other hand to bind her feet together. She was strong and slippery as an eel, but I managed to lay her down flat on her back. I grinned, feeling my sharpened teeth against the insides of my lips.

"I win."

She slapped the ground with the palm of her hand when I let her go, growling, eyes blazing. "I'm happy you can actually defend yourself," she said, her expression clearly anything but happy. "But now you're pissing me off."

I laughed, low and guttural. "Looks like we're tied two-two."

"Not for long." She sprang to her feet, looking me up and down as she walked back to her side of the ring.

I had a sneaking suspicion she had a dozen ways to take me down in this form, but decided I could use the extra strength and stability it afforded me. As we prepared for the last round, I heard running footsteps in the hallway outside. Shelton rounded the corner, huffing and puffing.

"I just found out something really bad," he said, leaning over to catch his breath. "We've got a more serious situation than I thought."

# Chapter 11

I let my demon form slip away, melting back to my usual size. "What is it?"

"Adam and I were talking about the battle mages we fought earlier." He drew in a deep breath and continued. "Remember the guy who was walking up the aisle near the end?"

"The one who looked like he owned the place?" I said, thinking it would be hard to forget a bald man who wielded dual staffs and had bizarre eye tattoos. "What about him?"

"He ain't no ordinary battle mage," Shelton said, motioning us to follow him. We went upstairs and found Adam looking at the three-dimensional image of the man as it hovered above his arctablet. Stacey and Bella stood behind him.

"Meet Maulin Kassus," Adam said without preamble. "Head honcho of the Black Robe Brotherhood."

"No girls allowed?" Elyssa said, narrowing her eyes at him.

"They have female members," Adam said. "But they never changed their name like the Assassins Guild."

"These people are the Arcane mafia," Shelton said. "They don't play by the rules."

"Okay, so he's dangerous," I said. "It's not like we haven't faced scary supers before. Why the rush to tell me about him?"

Shelton exchanged a glance with Adam. Looked back to me. "Because they will find out who we are. They will watch us for an opportune moment. And then they will kill us."

"Still nothing new," I said.

"I disagree," Elyssa said. "This is completely new. We usually have to hunt down our targets. These people are hunting us."

"And we'll never see them coming," Shelton said.

"So let's find them first," I said.

Shelton gave me a crazy look. "How do you propose we do that?"

"Don't they work for Darkwater?"

"Well, yeah—"

"And you know where they're headquartered," I said. "Now we have one more reason to go after them."

"You ain't ready to go up against Kassus's level of badassery yet, kid." Shelton stared at the man's image. "You remember when I told you there were very few battle mages who'd mastered all the Arcane attack forms?"

I nodded.

"Yeah, well he's one of them."

My confidence crumbled like a dry biscuit. "Maybe we should ward the perimeter and build a really tall wall."

"Another thing," Shelton said. "I used to train under Kassus. He knows who I am."

That sent a shock of apprehension through me. "Did he see you?"

"I don't think so," Shelton said, rubbing his jaw. "Adam and I were behind the column when he appeared, and he was focused on you when I attacked with the meteor."

"It's not like they know our names then," I said. "Not a lot of people know about us being here."

"Lornicus sure did," Adam said. "If he does, who else might?"

"I'll put up some ASE sentries," Elyssa said, rummaging through her duffel bag. "I have access to a number of other defensive devices that should be helpful."

"I've had a lot of practice at hiding," Adam said. "I'll put down some diversion wards around the perimeter. Unless they know for sure we're here, those ought to fend off anyone cruising the area."

"Let's not forget we have an arch that can take us anywhere and an underground tunnel to the school," Elyssa said. "We don't have to use the front door all the time."

"Excellent point," Adam said, grabbing his staff. "I'll get started with warding."

"Me too," Elyssa said, following him out.

Shelton gave me a knowing look. "How do you do it?" he asked.

My eyebrows pinched. "Do what?"

"Take us from zero to 'we're all gonna die' in less than a week?"

I sighed. "I dunno. Practice, I guess." My phone chimed with an unknown number. I excused myself and walked into another room to take it. My heart constricted with dread. Had Kassus already found me? Should I answer? Hoping for once it might actually be a telemarketer, I answered.

"Hello, Mr. Slade," said the nasal voice of Lornicus. "I hope you found the visit to El Dorado worth the effort."

"What makes you think I went?" I asked.

"Your desire to save your mother and simply curiosity." He paused. "Did you find the trip enlightening?"

The golem sounded awfully sure of himself. Was he going entirely off calculations about my personality, or did he have another means of knowing I'd been? He'd also couched his words in generalities. I had to assume he didn't know anything and try to give away nothing.

"Why did you want me to go in the first place?" I asked, deciding to neither confirm nor deny his allegations.

"You saw them, didn't you?" he replied, seeming to ignore my statement.

"What, the stress pimples on my nose?" I asked. "I get those when an army of gray men chases me from my own house."

The golem sighed. "You're being obstinate."

"You're manipulating me, and I'm not falling for it," I said, feeling a tiny bit smug.

"Of course I am," he said. "But it is for your benefit and the greater good."

His admission caught me off guard. "Then you'll understand if I don't tell you anything. For all I know, you're waiting for me to give something away."

"Understandable. Very well, I will give you information in return."

"The location of my mother?"

"Unfortunately, I still do not possess such information." The golem cleared his throat. "This information is, nonetheless, quite valuable." He seemed to pause for dramatic effect. "My master has created other golems who look as alive as I do. They blend into crowds and spy for him. This was how I found your residence."

A wave of cold shivered down my spine. "Are they as convincing as you?" I asked.

"They do not have personalities, no," he said. "They can talk and mimic very specific behaviors, if necessary, but they are nothing like me. I feel this information is quite valuable, Mr. Slade. Do you agree?"

Valuable? It was crushing. If Mr. Gray really had such lifelike spies everywhere, how could I trust anyone? Lornicus was right, though. He'd just given me a very valuable bit of intel. Now I knew, and knowing was half the battle.

"What do you want to know?" I asked.

"What did you see in the El Dorado way station?"

He asked it as if he didn't know. Then again, he could be testing me to see if I'd play tit-for-tat on the information sharing game. But if he didn't know about the baby angels, sharing what I knew could be very dangerous. If Mr. Gray found out his kin were being resurrected by leyworms, what would he do? Kill potential rivals before they grew up, or raise his own Seraphim army?

"If you're wondering, Mr. Slade, I already know about the infant Seraphim, and can understand why you would hesitate to enlighten me."

"Then what possible use could you have for any information I give you?" I asked. "If you know, that makes it worthless."

Lornicus chuckled. "Despite my knowledge of what lies beneath the city, I do not know the particulars. Please enlighten me."

I realized I already had. Now he knew I'd been there. He knew I'd seen the babies. *Man, I suck at intrigue.* "There are about a dozen babies," I said. "The leyworms eat the cherubs and spit out resurrected angels."

"Anything else of note?" he asked.

"There was a dead leyworm," I said. "I think it swallowed too many cherubs. The overload killed it, and the reaction petrified the cherubs, killing them as well." I heard a slight intake of breath on his end, almost as if he'd stifled a gasp. I wondered if the golem had practiced human emotions for so long he reacted automatically, or if this was feigned.

"I did not realize husks could die," Lornicus said. "How interesting."

I knew for a fact he found it more than interesting. I'd seen cherubs take all sorts of abuse, and nothing seemed to faze them. Now we knew they could die or be reborn. Something about that gave Lornicus pause. "It surprised you," I said. "Why?"

The golem didn't answer for a moment. "Perhaps it is knowing my master can die. Seraphim have died before, but I have never witnessed it."

"Are they more vulnerable in angel land?" I asked.

"No," Lornicus said without pause. "They do not die of old age. They do not reproduce without permission of their leadership. They simply exist for eons."

I paused at this new bit of information. "Leadership? They have a government?"

"Indeed. It is quite different than mortal governments. I sense a great opportunity to trade information, Mr. Slade. Perhaps you would be interested in—"

"No," I said. "Anything you tell me about the Seraphim is for entertainment purposes only. So what if they have a nifty government? That's not going to help me. I need to find my mother, and this banter isn't getting me any closer."

"You never know," he said in a cautionary tone.

This dude was pulling me into deep waters. I had to get off the phone with him before I gave up the family cow for magical beans. "I don't think we can do business," I said. "I get the feeling you're just toying with me, and talking with you is very dangerous."

"I can also help you with the Black Robe Brotherhood," Lornicus said as if it were an afterthought.

I couldn't speak for a moment. How in the hell did he already know about that?

As if sensing my question, he said, "My spies reported members of the brotherhood asking about a young man fitting your description. I also had spies question the arch operators. If you like, I can have my assets watch out for you and send warning."

"For what price?" I asked.

"Free share of information," he replied.

I gritted my teeth. "I can't do that without asking my friends."

"They won't like it, I suspect."

"I don't like it either," I said. "We can defend ourselves."

"Can you spare enough people to track members of the brotherhood? To find out how close they are to discovering your location?" Lornicus pressed his attack. "Defensive measures are all well and good, Mr. Slade, but I have an army at my disposal. If you need them for a fight, I will help. These people stand between you and your mother. If they kill you or your friends, nothing else matters."

My heart skipped a beat at the thought of losing my friends. Much as I hated to admit it, his point was valid. Unfortunately, his leverage over me had just ballooned. "You obviously just want us to help you get the baby angels out of El Dorado," I said. "You want them for some reason."

"Indeed," the golem said. "They should be rescued."

"I won't agree to hand them over to you," I said. "They're either staying in El Dorado or coming home with me." I shuddered at the idea of caring for a bunch of whiny babies, but leaving them in a cavern of eternal darkness seemed awfully cruel. Maybe if they were raised right, they wouldn't turn out like a bunch of spoiled buttholes who wanted to rule the world.

"What if I discover your mother's location? Would that be worth the price of one Seraphim child?"

*Yes!* "Absolutely not," I said after a slight hesitation. *Of course it would be.* I just couldn't let him know that without bargaining the price down. "Like I said, they stay in El Dorado or with me."

"I suppose I could agree to that," Lornicus said.

My eyes narrowed as a thought crossed my mind. "You keep talking about you, but what about your boss?"

"I am acting in his best interests," Lornicus said.

"And he knows what you're doing?"

"I keep him well informed," the golem replied.

I decided not to press the issue. Obviously, the golem wasn't beyond ignoring his master's commands if he thought it was for the best. I really didn't care if he hid this information from Mr. Gray or not. "Let me talk this over with my friends. I'll let you know."

"Very good, Mr. Slade. Until then." The golem disconnected.

"I think it's a good idea," Shelton said the minute I finished telling everyone about the golem's offer.

Elyssa squinted. Nodded. "I agree. We can't trust him as a complete ally, but more eyes would be good. And he's right, Justin. We have no hope of saving your mother if the brotherhood finds us."

"Does anyone else find this idea questionable?" Bella asked. "What if the brotherhood makes him a better offer? What if they agree to help Lornicus remove the babies and he decides to get rid of us?"

"Lornicus sees Justin as the Cataclyst," Shelton said. "He wants to use him, not kill him."

"A warded perimeter will help to an extent against surprises," Adam added, "but if someone of the brotherhood's caliber takes a close look and sees all those wards, they might get suspicious, especially since this house is supposedly abandoned." He shrugged. "They could de-ward the place and slip in without us being any wiser."

"The ASEs are hard to spot," Elyssa said. "I think they'd give us advance warning, but for now, we should accept the help." She drew in a breath. "Besides, Lornicus agreed to let us do what we want with the angels."

"Yeah, but the leyworms haven't," I said with a grim note. "I don't know what would be best for them."

"They're in a dark disgusting cave," Bella said. "It might be dangerous moving them, but I think we have to consider it."

I didn't sleep well that night with dreams of little angels toddling around and wreaking havoc while golems tried fruitlessly to breastfeed them. The next morning Elyssa and I opened the arch back to El Dorado and found Cinder sitting cross-legged near the front of the control room. He stood, brushing off his pants, and approached.

"Justin, I have made a number of interesting discoveries," he said without so much as a "Hello". "The cherubs do not affect me, nor do they seem interested in devouring my essence. I believe this means I have no soul for them to consume." His voice sounded almost wistful, as if the most wonderful thing would be for a cherub to want his soul.

"Good to know," I said. "Anything else?"

"Yes," he said with a nod. "I believe the babies are dying."

# Chapter 12

"Dying?" Elyssa said in a shocked tone. "How?"

Cinder tilted his head. "The leyworm Justin befriended allowed me to approach and observe. It seemed intent on communicating something I could not at first understand."

"It tried to talk?" I asked.

"I believe so, if hissing and growling is a method of communication."

"Oh, brother," Elyssa said. "What did you find out?"

"It carved an image in the floor using its boring abilities in a very interesting fashion—"

"Stay on target," I said, not wanting him to go off on a tangent.

"Perhaps I should show you," he said, and walked for the exit.

"Hang on," I said, and went to the modulus on the control platform. Tracing the pattern the arch operator had shown me, I activated the ambient lighting in the cavern outside.

"Interesting," Cinder said, looking out the door as the dim yellow light suffused the cavern. "I will disable the glowballs since they are no longer necessary."

"What were you going to show us?" I asked him.

"This way, please." The golem left the room.

We followed. I noted a trench carved in the stone floor to our right. Several cherubs whined inside, trying futilely to climb the side as we walked past, their screeching cries like nails on a chalkboard.

"Where did the trench come from?" I asked, unable to repress a shudder at the horrific cries of the husks.

"I asked the leyworm to set up a perimeter," Cinder said. "It carved the trench across the room and knocked wandering cherubs inside. We patrolled the area and determined this side is now free of them."

"Good job," I said, patting him on the shoulder. "I never would have thought of that."

Cinder paused a moment. "Thank you, Justin."

"Can we keep moving?" Elyssa asked, casting uneasy glances at the nubby hands of cherubs as they opened and closed, straining to reach us.

The golem continued without comment. I spotted a glowing, shaggy form racing toward us and braced for impact as Yolo skidded to a halt a few feet away, his tongue lolling while he panted musty breath. The glow from his body seemed just a little brighter than the yellow light.

Elyssa scratched his ears. Yolo purred. "I can't believe he would help Vadaemos," she said. "He must be awfully lonely down here."

"An interesting creature," Cinder said. "He seems quite intelligent, but is prone to disappearing regularly."

"Maybe he has ADD," Elyssa said, giving Yolo one last pat on his furry mane.

We continued onward, Yolo tagging along behind us for a bit before huffing, legs going rigid as he stared into the distance, and abruptly streaked away for parts unknown.

"Wonder if he saw a squirrel," I said, peering after him.

The small leyworm approached, its parietal eyes blinking at me. It hissed and slithered into a U-turn to precede us. We came to the carving Cinder had mentioned, and I knew almost immediately what the problem was. It was the image of a calf sucking the teat of a cow. How the leyworm knew what a cow was, I had no idea, but didn't feel like playing Pictionary with it to find out.

"They need milk?" I said.

The leyworm hissed, stopped, and seemed to sigh. Then it nodded.

"What the—" Elyssa's mouth dropped open.

"I taught it elementary methods of human communication," Cinder said. "Yes-no questions should be a feasible form of discovery."

"Baby angels need milk?" I said in a wondering tone, trying to imagine Daelissa breastfeeding. "How is that going to work?"

"Uh, this is getting a little ridiculous," Elyssa said. "We can't run a nursery."

"The leyworms already are," I said. "They feed them soul essence, somehow pulling it from ley lines. I guess they need a supplement." I turned to the leyworm, decided I was tired of referring to it in the generic, and thought up a name. "Can I call you Slitheren?" I asked, figuring it was an accurate if not equally generic description of the creature.

It tilted its head, eyes blinking several times. If it had shoulders, it might have shrugged. Instead, it nodded.

"Okay, great, Slitheren." I paused, wondering what to say next when Elyssa spoke.

"Can we take the babies back to Queens Gate?" she asked.

Slitheren shook his elongated head, forked tongue working in and out.

"How are we supposed to feed them?" she asked.

The dragon offered no response.

"We'll have to set up shop down here, I suppose," I said, not seeing an alternative, and dreading the idea of bringing the little tykes back. "Besides, what if the little tykes try to feed off our souls? I wouldn't know how to deal with that." Not to mention the impossibility of kidnapping a bunch of babies with Slitheren and his gargantuan pals ready to give chase the minute we tried anything of the sort.

Elyssa tapped her chin. "I wonder if they can handle formula or regular milk."

Slitheren didn't offer an opinion.

"We will have to experiment," Cinder said.

"Maybe Meghan can help," I offered. "She's a healer after all."

"Good idea," Elyssa said. "Let's ask her."

I called Meghan and reached her on the second ring. I told her our idea.

"How interesting," she said. "I'd be delighted to help."

I didn't bother to ask the details because I wasn't ready to play doting parent just yet. We walked to the nursery. I could tell the babies weren't having a good time of things with their constant wailing. Some of them looked pale and gaunt. I figured their hardy angel physiology, as Meghan had put it, might be the only thing keeping them from starving to death.

Meghan showed up an hour later, Adam in tow, with a flying carpet laden with supplies.

"I'll test different forms of milk," she said. "I asked Nightliss her opinion, and she said angels eat food much the same way humans do, though the memory of her home is still fuzzy."

I told Meghan about the trench. "I wonder if Nightliss can come down here with the cherubs out of the way."

"Speaking of which," Elyssa said, "aren't these babies more like real cherubs than the husks?"

I shrugged. "It'd be confusing to change things up and start referring to them as cherubs. Maybe we can come up with a better name."

"Cupids?" Meghan asked.

"I love it," Elyssa said, eyes soft as she regarded the starving little Seraphim. "Itsy bitsy little cupids."

Adam and I looked at each other and rolled our eyes.

Meghan produced some bottles, filling some of them from cans of infant formula and others with what she said was goat milk. "My childhood friend, Netta, was allergic to everything but goat milk," Meghan said. "Hopefully the cupids will find it palatable." She handed Cinder a bottle. "You know how to feed a baby?"

Cinder regarded the rubber nipple for a moment. "From the informational films Harry watches, I have seen how men enjoy—"

"Enough!" Meghan said, alarm in her eyes. "Just put the nipple in the baby's mouth, okay?"

"Of course," he replied, head tilted with curiosity while Adam and I giggled like school girls.

"Educational films," Adam said with a snort.

Cinder gingerly picked up a baby from the floor, and cradled it in his arms. He offered it the nipple and the infant sucked greedily. Meghan did likewise with one of the other babies. After the bottles were empty, she waited a couple of minutes, observing the two infants who now cooed happily.

"It looks like either formula or milk works," she said. "We'll have to keep an eye out for diarrhea or vomiting, to be sure."

"Can't wait," I said, wondering if she'd brought nose plugs and a plastic coverall for protection.

She handed bottles to each of us. "Let's feed them."

I walked up to one particularly gaunt little baby, and picked it up. It stank to high heaven. I wondered if it had been peeing or pooping itself despite the lack of food. My supernatural sense of smell certainly didn't help matters, bringing forth the odor in all its glory. *Nose plugs, please!* The baby sucked the bottle dry in seconds.

"Should I give it another?" I asked.

"Give it a minute to digest," Meghan said. "In the meantime, you and Adam can unpack the cribs and baths."

Adam indicated several tightly packed bundles. He set one down, and untied the bow on top. The bundle sprang open, forming a hammock lined with soft fur and glinting like diamond fiber. We did the same with the other bundles, lining them in two rows while Meghan and Elyssa fed the other babies.

"Coochie-coo," Elyssa said as one baby smiled up at her, its little tummy round and full. "You are just adorable."

"I'll need water," Meghan said to Slitheren.

The dragon slithered away about a hundred feet and abruptly dove straight down, burrowing into the obsidian slab as if it were butter. A moment later, he returned to the surface, his body writhing through the stone, leaving a shallow channel behind. Once close to the cupids, he spun in a circle, carving out a bowl. He resumed his handiwork, creating another aqueduct on the opposite side before burrowing straight down. Water gurgled from the new hole he'd made, trickled into the channel, and pooled in the bowl, filling it and flowing into the other shallow canal where it drained down the first hole.

"Have you ever considered a career in construction?" I asked the dragon.

Slitheren tilted his head and blinked at me.

"Wonderful," Meghan said. "I won't even need to use the portable bathtubs I brought." She took the baby in her arms and lowered it into the water. "Oh, it's warm," she said, smiling at Slitheren. "Thank you."

The leyworm almost seemed to smile back, his tongue snaking in and out a bit faster than usual.

Adam and I watched as the women bathed each infant in turn while the little buggers cooed happily. Elyssa set the clean cupids in the cribs until all thirteen were processed. The giant purple leyworm hawked up another sparkling new cupid as we looked at the nursery. Cinder picked it up by the feet, and gave it a gentle spank on its bare bottom. The baby burst into tears.

"Coochie-coo," he said in his monotone voice, and held a bottle to the newborn's mouth.

Adam and I snickered.

"How interesting," Cinder said, watching the little life form drain the bottle. "Watching them feed has an almost soothing side effect."

Adam barked a laugh, which he quickly covered with his hand, while Elyssa and Meghan looked on in surprise.

"Can you remain and be responsible for feeding them?" Meghan asked. "I would stay, but have other pressing matters to attend."

"Yes," Cinder said. "It will be interesting to learn how one should interact with babies."

"Heaven help us," Elyssa said.

"Did you find out anything about the arches in the control room?" I asked Cinder. "Like maybe how to work the Alabaster Arch?"

"Unfortunately, I was unable to determine how to safely reactivate the Alabaster Arch," he said. "Some of the other arches seem to work, though I lacked the resources to test them."

I didn't really see a need to spend time testing the mini-arches just yet, so long as the omniarch at the mansion worked. It might be handy having an extra omniarch here in El Dorado in case someone became stranded, but with the other problems heaped on our plates, I wasn't sure when we'd have a chance to mess with them. I told Cinder goodbye, and we left.

"Thanks for the help, Slitheren," I told my new dragon buddy as we walked back to the control room.

He looked at me for a long moment, almost as if he wanted to say something, nodded, and slithered back into the cavern.

"I wish he could talk," I said, wondering what was going on in that reptilian brain of his. I cast a glance at Meghan. "Know of any good animal speech spells?"

She smiled. "Novelty spells, perhaps, but nothing that truly translates."

"Give Cinder enough time and he'll have them all talking," Adam said with a snort.

"I hate to admit it, but he kind of rubs off on you," Elyssa said. "Don't get me wrong, he's still a creepy golem, but he seems to have a heart."

"Our very own Tin Man," Adam said.

As we walked to the open portal leading back to the mansion cellar, I gave the Alabaster Arch a wistful look. The arch operator in Queens Gate had mentioned tracing a pattern on the modulus to unlock it. Without specifics, it might be impossible to guess, and I didn't dare go back with Kassus or his people waiting. We stepped through the portal, back into the mansion cellar. I deactivated the omniarch, and we headed upstairs.

"I guess I should call Lornicus and tell him we accept his help," I told Elyssa.

She nodded. "Waiting won't help, especially if the BRB is hunting us."

I shuddered. This was not a good situation. Cutsauce greeted us with a happy bark as we appeared at the top of the stairs. I scratched behind his ears and idly thought of Yolo, wondering if the shaggy beast was lonely or best buds with the leyworms. Maybe he and Cutsauce could be best buds.

"I could ask for help from Vallaena," I said. "Surrounding this place with hellhounds might be super effective."

"The university won't allow it," Meghan said. "Plus, hellhounds would be very conspicuous."

I hated to admit she was right. On the other hand, I could summon hellhounds if the going got rough. I'd have to do it well in advance since it took me a while to find a suitable spirit on the demon plane and manifest it on this side.

It looked like Lornicus was our best bet. I called him.

"Have you reached a decision, Mr. Slade?" he asked.

"We'll partner with you," I said. "But the minute I get wind of treachery, we're out."

"Quite reasonable," he said. "Have you anything else to report on the infants?"

I fought back the urge to lie and told him about the day's activities.

"I wondered if they require food," he said. "It greatly concerned me."

"Really? Then why didn't you mention it before?" I said. "Don't blow smoke up my butt, Lornicus. The only reason you care about the babies is so you can use them."

"Regardless of my reasoning, Mr. Slade, I do have concern for the welfare of the infants."

*I'm sure you do.* "Fine. You have your information. Do you have anything for me?"

"Indeed," he said. "I discovered something rather troubling for you."

My stomach clenched. "And that is?"

"During your encounter with the brotherhood, you struck one of the attackers."

I decided not to tell him it had been an accidental discharge. "Yes."

"He's dead."

A shock of cold froze my chest. "He—he's dead?" Everything had happened so fast I hadn't had time to see the results of my strike.

"Yes, from what I have determined, he died upon impact."

I didn't exactly go around killing people, and even though the man had been trying to kill me, I still felt sick to my stomach. I'd accepted killing in self-defense as something necessary, but hoped I would never cross the line to cold-hearted lack of concern for life.

Lornicus resumed after a brief pause. "Unfortunately, this man also happened to be Victor Kassus."

"Kassus?" I said, my dread deepening. "You mean—"

"Yes. The man was Maulin Kassus's brother."

# Chapter 13

*His brother?* "Now it's personal." A nauseating feeling turned my stomach. I'd seen enough mafia movies to know gangsters never gave up. It might be ten years later or a hundred, but a bullet to the brain was inevitable.

"Indeed," Lornicus said. "I must admit Kassus surprised me with the sheer manpower he devoted to finding you, and determined there must be some other factor in play. True, he would still want you dead for the insult of attacking any of the brotherhood, but would typically content himself using an outside contractor."

"Like an assassin?" I said, trying not to gulp.

"Precisely." Lornicus paused a beat. "Once I discovered the death and the deceased's relationship to Kassus, I immediately understood why this was a personal vendetta."

"They tried to kill us!" I said. "Doesn't he understand we're going to defend ourselves?"

"He only cares that you die, I'm afraid." Lornicus sighed. "Men like that are rather stubborn. He and his people will come after you until either they or you are dead."

"All of them?" I said, my voice sounding weak.

"Quite likely," he said.

I ran a hand down my face and groaned. This had gone from worst to most worsterest. "Anything else I need to know?"

"My assets are now actively patrolling and keeping a wary eye out for you," he said. "If you happen to notice anyone following you, it could be one of them."

"Uh, Elyssa might cut one of your golems to pieces if she thinks it's a member of the brotherhood," I said.

"Point well taken," he replied. "If you are unsure about someone's affiliation, simply tap your forehead twice. If it is one of my assets, they will respond by scratching their head."

"How do you tell them what to do?" I asked. "Is it a shared consciousness?"

"Not precisely," he said. "I can, however, send commands to multiple units at once."

"Sounds really complicated," I said. "Especially considering how many you have under your command."

"Not as complicated as one might think," he said. "Arcphones are rather handy."

I imagined using a program to command thousands of golems. Even that sounded unwieldy.

"I'm glad you decided to partner with me," Lornicus said. "I see a bright future ahead, Mr. Slade."

With mafiosos stalking me I didn't see how such a thing was possible. I disconnected and updated the others.

"We're even more screwed than I thought," Shelton said, shaking his head.

"Now, Harry, don't be so glum." Bella patted him on the back. "After all, we have an army of golems watching out for us now."

"An army that was, until recently, trying to kill Justin," he said.

"We need to be proactive," Adam said. "Let's track them down first."

"Already working on it," Bella said. "Speaking of which, it's time for another planning session." She, Elyssa, and Stacey left, heading to the war room.

"By the way," Shelton said after the women left. "We figured out how Jeremiah Conroy was spying on us."

"You did?" I asked, thinking back to how he'd stolen the Cyrinthian Rune right out from under our noses.

"Yeah, he was using nom equipment."

"Hidden mics?" I asked.

"Yep." Shelton sighed. "It's easy to overlook the ordinary when you're living inside a magical pocket dimension."

"The place is clean of bugs now?"

"If it ain't, we're screwed," he said with full confidence.

"I'm not entirely confident Darkwater will have the location of the Conroys," I said. "And I sure as hell don't want to pay Lornicus's price for finding Mom and Ivy. Have you made any progress using your bounty hunter contacts?"

He nodded. "Remember Oliver over at the Grotto?"

I pictured the stable boy who was one of Shelton's assets. "Yes."

"He's going to sneak a tracker onto the Conroy limo before it splits into illusions."

I felt my eyes go wide. "Are you sure using a kid like that is smart? What if you get him killed?"

Shelton held up a hand. "Relax, he knows what he's doing."

"Won't the limo be warded against trackers?"

Shelton shrugged. "Probably. Doesn't hurt to try though."

"Coming from you, that's pretty optimistic." I stood and paced restlessly. Even with golems watching out for our wellbeing and the other precautions we'd taken, sitting around felt too defensive. It seemed like we were always reacting to evildoers instead of whatever the opposite was—proacting? Elyssa's plan to break into Darkwater— much as it scared me—was a positive first step. But placing all our eggs in that basket was risky. We needed to split push on several fronts until something gave.

Shelton took his leather duster from the coat rack and shrugged into it. "Doesn't look like you're any better at waiting than I am."

I sighed. "It makes me feel like we're just sitting around waiting for the axe to fall."

"I know the feeling," he said. "But jumping into a fight with the brotherhood will only get us killed faster."

"Then why did you put on your coat?" I asked.

He chuckled and placed his favorite wide-brimmed hat on his head. "I just realized that not every problem needs a complicated solution."

"Oh?"

He motioned me down the stairs toward the arch. "I got to thinking about how Jeremiah bugged us with simple nom tech that Bella and I didn't think to search for. Using a magical tracker is just the sort of thing the Conroys ward against."

"But if they use nom tech for spying, wouldn't they also think to have countermeasures to it?"

"Of course," he said, walking through the cellar and toward the staircase to the arch room. "So we go even simpler."

"We steal a variety of bird eggs and train the hatchlings from birth to follow the Conroys, leaving a trail of bird poo along the way?"

He stopped in his tracks to give me a look. "You and that mouth of yours." He resumed walking. "What I have in mind is stupid simple."

"Lead the way. I can't wait to see you do something stupid."

We traveled via the omniarch to a dingy alley on the west side of Atlanta, and closed the portal behind us. Shelton said a word, and a nearby brick wall vanished to reveal a non-descript blue sedan, quite a departure from his pickup truck. The inside of the car smelled like stale sandwiches and old coffee. Brown stains on the upholstery confirmed my suspicion that he'd used this car for stakeouts.

"Ever heard of a car wash?" I asked, wrinkling my nose since my supernatural olfactory senses launched background smells into nauseating hyper-drive. I noticed an old fast-food wrapper in the floorboard, and realized with disgust mold had overgrown it. Using my fingers like pincers, I tossed the long-dead remains into a trash heap in the alley, figuring nobody would notice the addition.

"Don't want it too clean," he said. "Sparkling clean cars draw attention even if the model is common."

"I'm talking about cleaning the interior," I said, noticing even more discarded food wrappers in the back. "It's like a rat's nest in here, man."

He waved away my complaints. "Ah, you'll get used to it." He drove us to Phipps Plaza in Buckhead, a ritzy place in North Atlanta. We entered the parking garage through the back entrance, and drove straight through a concrete wall—rather, the insubstantial illusion of one. A winding ramp led deep underground to the Grotto way station where an Obsidian Arch allowed Overworld citizens to travel across the extensive network. Before we reached the way station, Shelton stopped near the base of the ramp. He put on his hazard lights, threw the car into park, and got out. He walked across the driveway holding what looked like the kind of colorful handlebar streamers one might see on a kid's bike. Removing some duct tape from his duster, he attached the streamers to the wall.

I stared at him as he slid back into the car and drove inside the cavern housing the Obsidian Arch. A large parking lot spanned nearly half of the massive space.

"Not only stupid simple," I said, "but also plain stupid. What the heck are handlebar streamers gonna do?"

Shelton sighed. "Think about it. What's the difference between an illusion and the real thing?"

I thought about it a moment before his meaning clicked. "Illusions are immaterial. They go through physical objects. They also don't make a breeze when they go past."

"Exactly."

"But what about solid illusions?" I asked, thinking about the barrier illusions we'd used in the past to block off places we didn't want people wandering. They were solid.

He shrugged. "Spells don't come free. They cost aether. An illusion spell is already pretty expensive to cast, even if you have arcane generators helping. Illusion plus solidity doubles the cost. Now imagine casting that spell times a dozen illusions. We're talking astronomical aether usage." He nodded toward the streamers. "So the Conroys hop into their car as usual. It duplicates into illusions, and they drive out of here in a line, right?"

I thought back to the last time I'd seen their car split into illusions to confuse any would-be stalkers. "Yeah."

He nodded. "So when the duplicate illusions of the Conroys' car drive past the streamers, they won't make a breeze. We just sit back and make note of the car that does."

"I guess it's not quite as stupid as it sounds," I said. "Are we just gonna sit here and wait until we see them?"

Shelton drove up and down the rows of parked cars, eyes roving. "Nah. I'm checking to see if their limo is even here."

My eyes caught on a leopard-print Hummer with dark-tinted windows and chrome spinner wheels. I saw no sign of a black limousine. "Is there any guarantee they're still using the same car?"

"The illusion spells are charmed into the limo," he said. "It's not a spell someone casts every time they get in." He stopped to inspect a black car. Grunted, and eased off the brake. "They either bought it or leased it from Overworld Security, a company that provides protection to celebrities and politicians. Even if they got another one, it'll look the same."

We finished a circuit of the parking lot without spotting the limo.

"Don't they have a driver?" I asked. "I doubt it would be parked out here."

"It'd usually be waiting in the motor pool," he said, pointing to a line of other cars, stagecoaches, and even elephants waiting to pick up VIPs as they emerged from the Grotto. "But it never hurts to be thorough." He parked the sedan, got out.

We walked to the stables and found Oliver shoveling a massive pile of steaming poo into a dung wagon.

"G'day, guvnahs!" he said brightly.

"Hey, Oliver," Shelton said, patting the boy fondly on the head. "You seen the Conroys around here lately?"

"No, Harry. I saw Miss Ivy and Mrs. Conroy just two days ago, but not since." He heaved a shovelful of poop into the wagon.

"Don't worry about the tracker," Shelton said. "I don't think it'll work on their limo."

"Did they take their car when they were here last time?" I asked Oliver.

The boy nodded. "They came from the arch and went straight to the limousine. I think they were coming from Queens Gate."

That would've been a day or so after school let out for the holiday break, I realized. "They might not come back until school starts again in January," I said.

"Any Darkwater people lurking around here?" Shelton asked.

"Yes, there were several looking for people who match your descriptions," he said, tilting his head slightly. A few brown clods dropped from his shovel as he contemplated something. "Did you do something horrible again, Harry?"

Shelton looked offended. "Why would you ask that, kid?"

"Oh, please tell me about it," Oliver said. "I would so love to hear another of your stories."

Shelton sighed. "Stay away from those bruisers." He waggled his thumb to indicate the two of us. "They want our hides."

"You don't need to tell me that," the boy said brightly. "The one named Kassus sounded very upset."

My stomach clenched. "Did it sound like they had any idea where we were?" I asked.

He shook his head. "I saw several of the brotherhood taking the arch to different locations. I would say they're casting a wide net."

"How did you know they're with the brotherhood?" Shelton asked.

"I hear a lot," Oliver said with a grin. "Most people ignore the stable boy."

Shelton passed him a wad of tinsel, Overworld currency. "Stay out of trouble, kid. And let me know if you see or hear anything else."

"You got it, Harry!"

We walked back to the car, Shelton muttering to himself along the way. "I don't know if we should stake this place out, or leave," he said. "Man, I could really use a donut right now."

I didn't like the idea of sitting for hours in a smelly car with Shelton, but going back home would only make me feel powerless again. On the bright side, it didn't sound like Darkwater had any reason to suspect where we lived if Oliver's assumptions were true.

"Darkwater is headquartered inside the Grotto?" I asked as we climbed in the car.

He nodded. "Don't even think about going near the place. Their security probably flagged our images."

"It doesn't sound like they have pictures of us," I said.

"Nah, but they probably have drawings which will be close enough to tag us."

"I don't want to go home," I told him. "We've got to figure out something."

Shelton pursed his lips. Started the car and backed out of the parking lot. "I've got some ideas. They may not pan out, but it won't hurt to try."

I didn't argue with him.

He drove up the ramp and down Peachtree Street to a two-story building with stretched Hummers, limos, and even an elongated Lamborghini on display in a glassed-in showroom. A sign proclaimed the place as Luxury Transportation. Shelton drove to the back, parked the car, and led me toward an outbuilding without any signage to indicate what lay inside. I saw a simple service bay and gas pump to the rear of the complex.

Shelton went inside the small building and up to a counter. He dinged the bell. A short man with glasses came to the front. His eyes narrowed when he saw us.

"Harry Shelton," he said in a neutral tone after a moment's pause. "I haven't seen you in a while."

"Yeah, took a break from the bounty-hunting biz." Shelton shrugged. "This is my friend, Justin. Justin, this is Walter Lerner."

"Justin Slade," the man said.

"You know my last name?" I asked.

He nodded. "The security business has been good with everyone scared to death of you and your gang."

"My gang?" I asked. "What kind of things have you been hearing about me?"

Walter shrugged. "The vampires have their PR people going all-out to portray you as a dangerous lunatic. There are some on the Arcane Council trying to blame you for the Grand Melee incident."

"They're lying," I said in protest. "We saved their lives."

"You don't have to convince me," Walter said, propping his elbows on the counter. "That's just politics. Right now, it's good business."

I looked around the room at the blank walls, the lack of furniture. "What exactly do you do here?" I glanced at Shelton. "Isn't this a nom business?"

"I cater to noms as well as supers," Walter said. "Wouldn't be enough money in this business otherwise."

"Walter here provides secure transportation to the high muckety-mucks in the Overworld and for the noms," Shelton explained. "He sends his vehicles to places like Overworld Security and has them add other enchantments."

"Even for noms?" I asked.

"Oh, sure," Walter said. "But only things they'll never notice." His eyes met Shelton. "Why are you here? I know it isn't to socialize."

"Fair enough," Shelton said. "I need some information on the concealment illusions like they use on the high-end limos."

"Like what?" Walter asked suspiciously.

"How long do the illusions last? What kind of scripted behavior do they have?"

Walter dug behind the counter and tossed Shelton a folded brochure. "It's all in there."

"Is it accurate?" Shelton said.

"Yeah, by the Overworld truth in advertising standards."

"I need it to be accurate," Shelton said, not moving to pick it up.

Walter sighed. "It is. Anything else?"

Shelton took the brochure and looked it over for a minute. He nodded. "Yeah, does Bruce still work at the OTA?"

"I wouldn't advise talking to him," Walter said. "Not after the little stunt you pulled. He almost lost his job over that."

"It wasn't me," Shelton said. "Someone there must have overheard him talking to me and blabbed."

Walter held up his hands. "Don't tell it to me," he said. "We done here?"

Shelton stared at the man. "What the hell is going on with you? Last time we did business you seemed plenty happy, especially when I steered clients your way. Now you're treating me like I'm diseased."

The other man chewed on his inner cheek. "It's Cyphanis Rax," he said after a moment of consideration. "He's still upset about you trying to hunt him down, and now that your old man isn't around to protect you, he's put out the word that it's bad for business to do business with Harry Shelton."

"He's threatening you," Shelton said.

"Of course he is," Walter replied. "He knows who helped you track him, and he's made sure to let each and every one of us know that."

"How in the hell could he possibly know who helped me?"

Walter shrugged. "All I know is if he catches wind that you were here, it could spell trouble for me."

"Maybe we should go," I told Shelton.

He growled. "The man is dirty, Walter. I should have finished the job I started."

"You never had enough proof to lock him away," Walter said. "With your father gone, he'll probably be the next Arcanus Primus."

"Is that bad?" I asked.

Walter snorted. "Rax makes Sager look like the poster boy for ethical behavior," Walter said.

"Hey now, that's my father you're talking about," Shelton said.

The other man looked surprised. "Since when did you develop a love for your old man?"

Shelton clamped his mouth shut.

"Kind of a sensitive subject," I said.

"Thanks for the info," Shelton said, and headed for the door.

"Keep my involvement to yourself," Walter called after us.

We left and ventured a few miles to a section of town with rolling terrain and residential houses. Nestled in an industrial stretch of road sat a squat windowless building with what looked like totem poles arrayed in a circle outside. The sign proclaimed it as Antique Emporium. A smaller sign on the door indicated it was closed. Shelton rapped on the door.

Seconds trickled by as we waited. I took a closer look at the poles and recognized Cyrinthian symbols etched into the dark wood. I hoped they didn't represent a deadly trap for trespassers, and edged closer to the building, as if it might offer more protection. Shelton pounded on the door, his patience clearly running low.

"Open up, Bruce. I know you're in there!" Shelton shouted.

The door jerked open. A balding man with a sizeable paunch stood there, face contorted with anger. I looked down and saw the metallic gleam of a large pistol in his hand.

# Chapter 14

"Holy cornballs in paradise," Shelton said, backing away, hands held in surrender. "Take it easy, Bruce."

"Take it easy?" the man said in a growl. "You nearly cost me my job, and they cut my pay thanks to you talking to the authorities."

"Not me," Shelton said, one of his hands lowering toward the compact staff he kept in a holster on his side. "You know me. Why would I ruin a good thing?"

"Because you're scum," Bruce said, grip tightening on the gun.

Shelton's hand went back up. "Look, Walter told me Cyphanis was stirring up trouble. Saying I was bad for business. You know I wouldn't jeopardize my network of informants." He sighed. "Remember what I did for your cousin? How I got him out of the trouble he was in with those loan sharks? I put myself on the line for you. Think about it, man."

Bruce stared at him, the snarl fading from his face. He blew out an explosive breath and lowered the firearm. "I still don't like the fact Cyphanis is all up in your business, Shelton. If I'm seen talking to you—"

"Then let us inside before someone notices," Shelton said.

"I should make you and whoever the hell this kid is leave."

"This is Justin Slade," Shelton said.

"Oh, now you're really trying to get me in trouble," Bruce said. "Isn't this the same kid who wrecked the Grand Melee?"

"I didn't wreck anything!" I protested.

"Forget all that," Shelton said with a sigh. "Bruce, what if I told you I could get that nephew of yours out of Russian prison?"

Bruce's forehead crinkled. "How in the hell could you do that?"

Shelton shrugged. "I have my methods. You help us with this, and I'll deliver him to your doorstep."

I felt my own forehead wrinkle at Shelton's boast. What nephew? What Russian jail? I didn't want him getting off track and pulling a crazy stunt that could get him noticed by noms.

Bruce considered it for a long moment before waving us inside. He closed the door behind us, and led us down a hallway to a large room with an array of holographic images of the city and a number of orbs hovering above a console.

"What is this place?" I asked.

"Overworld Transportation Authority," Bruce said, a proud note in his voice. "We enforce restrictions on magical transportation. This," he said with a grand wave, "monitors traffic to make sure nobody breaks the ban on flying carpets, flying cars, and other obvious magical means."

"And you're the only one who monitors all this?" I asked incredulously.

He made a noncommittal shrug. "I rotate shifts with a few others." His eyes locked onto Shelton. "You'd better not be lying about my nephew."

"I'm not," Shelton said. "Just give me a picture of his prison cell."

"I don't have a picture of his cell," Bruce said. "How in the hell would I get that?"

"It's a nom facility," Shelton said. "Can your brother get an ASE inside?"

Bruce gave him a dubious look. "I'll ask him."

"Get me a picture, and I'll get him out."

"How is a picture going to do you any good? Don't you need a layout of the place?" Bruce narrowed his eyes. "And don't think you can go blasting in with magic. The Overworld will have your butt in a sling for interfering with noms before you can count to three."

Shelton held up a hand. "Let me worry about that. Get me the image."

Bruce twisted his lips. "Fine. I hope it isn't a mistake trusting you."

"You know my word is good."

The other man grudgingly nodded. "What do you want in return?"

"I need the tracking data from Overworld Security limos leaving the Grotto two days ago."

"You need what?" Bruce's eyebrows rose in unison. "If you're tracking Cyphanis again, you'd better think twice. Even getting my nephew out of a gulag isn't worth having that tyrant breathing down my neck."

"I'm not tracking him," Shelton said.

"Then who?"

"Best you don't know," Shelton replied. He looked around the room. "So, can you get it for me?"

Bruce nodded. "I'll need a few minutes to copy the footage onto an ASE."

We took seats in the back of the room and waited. I leaned toward Shelton. "What in the world are you promising this man?" I asked in a low whisper. "We can't break a felon out of jail, especially not in Russia."

"Sure we can," he said with a confident grin. "Especially if they get us an ASE with all the details of the cell."

"How is a picture—" The flow of words cut off as I realized what he intended to do. "You want to use our omniarch to get this man out?"

His grin widened. "I'm a genius, right?"

"You're insane," I said. "What if someone sees a magic portal materialize in his prison cell? What if we open it in the wrong place?"

"That's why we need a detailed image. If his brother can get an ASE in there, we're gold."

My stomach twisted. I didn't like his idea at all. On the other hand, it made me realize we could use the omniarch to infiltrate the Conroy residence. If we used the OTA tracking system to track their limo, we had a good chance to find out where they lived. I just had to hope they were keeping Mom and Ivy there. The omniarch might even help us overcome the hardcore security sure to be guarding the house.

Bruce returned with a marble-shaped ASE, and dropped it into Shelton's outstretched hand. "I don't know too many people in the Atlanta area who use those limos," he said. "I don't need to know specifics to know you're hunting dangerous game, Shelton. Make sure

I don't end up exposed again, or I'll pull the trigger next time I see you."

Shelton flicked his hand as if knocking away the threat. "Get me detailed images of your nephew's cell, and I'll hold up my end of the bargain."

"I'll be in touch." Bruce motioned us toward the exit. "Now, get out of here before my shift relief shows up."

We left, Shelton chortling all the way to the car.

"You really enjoy this, don't you?" I asked.

"Man, I didn't realize how much I missed the hunt," he said, eyes sparkling. "We're gonna find old man Conroy and show the girls how it's done."

"This isn't a contest," I reminded him sternly. "It's a team effort."

Shelton rolled his eyes and guided the car onto the road.

"What now?" I asked as he drove.

Shelton mulled it over for a moment. "Well, we need to get back home to look over the footage. I say we go park my car back at the hideout, send a picture to Bella, and ask her to open a portal so we can return to the mansion."

I felt relieved to be going home. "Sounds like a plan to me."

He called Bella, but she and the others had apparently gone into Queens Gate to eat and wouldn't be back to the mansion for a while. Shelton nodded a lot as Bella's voice went on in muffled tones I couldn't understand thanks to a spell Adam had put on our phones to prevent eavesdropping. Shelton made a talking mouth with his thumb and fingers as he tried to get in a word edgewise.

"How long?" he asked in a loud voice. He nodded. "Fine, just call me. We've got other things we can do." He hung up. "I love that woman, but man, can she talk your ear off."

I chuckled. "What do we do in the meantime?"

He sighed. "Depends on how adventurous you're feeling."

My grin vanished. "Nothing that will get us killed."

"We can use the extra time to stake out the Grotto way station in case, by some random chance, the Conroys show up." He gave me a sideways look. "Is that low risk enough for you?"

"I suppose," I said, feeling weight lift from my chest.

He nodded. "Maybe we'll get lucky and post the limo. The girls should be back at the mansion in a couple of hours."

We worked our way through traffic and made it back to Phipps Plaza. Shelton drove down the ramp, his pace slowed by a vintage car creeping ahead of us.

"Sunday drivers," Shelton growled. We reached the bottom of the ramp.

The driver of the car ahead turned his head sharply to the left, drawing mine and Shelton's attention with it. A man in the dark robe of the brotherhood stood against the wall, his eyes meeting ours. He glanced down at a sheet of parchment and back to us, eyes flaring with recognition.

"Son of a—" Shelton jammed on the brakes. Hit reverse, and nearly slammed into a car coming up behind us. He veered out of the way, the rear bumper crunching against the wall. Jammed the car in drive, and peeled out, completing a U-turn.

I watched as the man charged toward us, staff held out.

"Go!" I yelled as a bolt of energy splashed across the trunk, spreading out and dissipating.

Tires squealed as the sedan lurched forward, up the ramp.

"I got this thing charmed against offensive magic," Shelton said. "But it won't hold out if we take too many direct hits."

"I wish this was your pickup truck," I said, suddenly missing the extra horsepower.

"You and me both," he grumbled, steering the car up the ramp.

Another car appeared ahead. Shelton swerved to miss it as the front end of a car going the opposite way appeared in our path. He swung the wheel back, narrowly missing the vehicle. A warning light on the car's dash blinked.

"Crap," Shelton said. "They hit us with a tracker."

"Isn't the car protected against them?" I asked.

"It was," he said. "I haven't used this car in ages. Some of the wards must have worn off."

"Are you sure this thing can hold up against more hits?" I glanced behind us.

He suddenly didn't look too sure. "I doubt they'll try anything with noms around." Two black-and-white police cars roared from the garage about a hundred yards behind us. Shelton looked in the rear-view mirror. "Those bastards," he growled.

"Where did the cops come from?" I hadn't seen them in the mall parking garage.

"It's Darkwater," he said. "They're using illusions."

I watched as our pursuers gained. "Can this heap go any faster?"

"I've got the pedal to the floor already."

"I can run faster than this," I said, patting my jacket pockets and realizing I hadn't grabbed another staff to replace the one destroyed in our first encounter with Darkwater.

Cars swerved out of the way of the fake police cruisers, clearing a path. Shelton swung the steering wheel right and took us down a ramp onto a highway. The road ahead held only a smattering of traffic, but the small engine in Shelton's car screamed like it was ready to give out while the Darkwater cars gained on us effortlessly.

As if emboldened by the lack of traffic, a man in the black robe of the brotherhood leaned his upper body out of the passenger window, extending a wand our way. A beam of energy speared into the trunk. At first, the beam simply dispersed across the metal. Another warning light on the car's dash blinked.

Shelton swerved right. The beam speared into the road, gouging it.

"Can you take the wheel?" he asked.

"Right now?" I ducked as another death ray speared from the man's wand and dispersed across the rear window.

"I need to shoot back at them!" Shelton said. "Hold the wheel. I'm gonna slide out backwards." He leaned the seat all the way back and set the cruise control to whatever insane speed we were travelling.

I grabbed the wheel as he shimmied into the back seat, and slid over the center console into the driver's side, somehow managing not to jerk the wheel into a ninety-degree turn that would have flipped it like a blueberry pancake. My foot found the accelerator, and I discovered, much to my dismay, it really was pegged to the floor. The speedometer crept slowly but surely past a hundred.

Shelton pulled out his staff. Flicked it to full length. The ends smacked against the door panels. He cursed, rolling down the manual windows, arms pumping furiously. By the time he rolled a window down, the Darkwater vehicles had pulled nearly even. He jerked on his staff, but it was too cumbersome to maneuver in the confines of the car, so he flicked it back to compact size, and withdrew his wand.

The man leaning from the passenger window of the fake cruiser to our left aimed his wand at Shelton. I hit the brakes. Tires screeched and the odor of burnt rubber hit my nose. Shelton *oofed*. I felt his face smack into the back of my seat. A wicked ray of red light shot across the hood of the car and nailed the other Darkwater sedan, splashing across it without damage.

"They have defensive charms on their cars, too," I said, eyes casting about for escape. My supernaturally quick reflexes examined the scene in an instant. Time seemed to slow to a crawl as the pursuers hit their brakes to match our speed.

This was a controlled access freeway. No nearby exits for escape. A tall, concrete median blocked a U-turn. Only a handful of other cars populated the road. A quick glance in the rearview mirror revealed traffic falling far behind to avoid the conflict.

*We're so screwed.*

Time seemed to resume its normal flow.

"Ouch," Shelton said. I saw him shaking his head in the rear-view mirror.

A flicker of movement to my left caught my attention. "Hang on!" I veered sharply, crashing the nose of the car into the rear quarter panel of the attacker's vehicle. The rear end lurched left. Sparks sprayed as metal met the concrete divider. Their car ground to a halt.

Shelton grunted as he bounced off the door. "Take it easy!" he said. "I don't exactly have a seatbelt on back here."

The car to our right swung away to avoid a slow-moving compact car in the center lane. I saw a blonde head poke over the roof of the car as a woman slid her torso out of the passenger window. Hair billowing in the wind, she flicked open a full-length staff. A ball of brilliant yellow blurred from it, exploding into the road. I had no time to avoid the sudden pothole, and the car slammed into it, the shock absorbers bottoming out.

Shelton cried out as his head hit the ceiling. Cursing like a sailor as he aimed his wand, he fired a return shot at the other car. The beam narrowly missed the woman's head. He aimed it lower, tracing it down the side of the car. As before, the light seemed to refract, but within seconds, the energy overcame the protective spells, and left a ragged streak of scorched paint down the side.

The woman released another fireball. I anticipated it this time and veered to avoid it. My eyes flicked to the rear-view mirror and saw the other car racing to catch up. This terrain favored Darkwater. We couldn't outrun them. We couldn't outfight them for long. I spotted an exit sign ahead. The other driver seemed to sense my intentions, and blocked access to the lane while the blonde woman shot fireballs into the road, trying to disable us. I had a feeling they didn't want to outright kill us. That privilege was probably reserved for their boss, Kassus.

The car rattled. The wheels thumped as though one might already be going flat. I smelled the distinct odor of burning oil. I had a feeling this contraption wouldn't last much longer. The exit ramp loomed a hundred yards away. I had to make a move.

"We need to make the exit," I shouted. "Get them out of the way."

He took another shot at the woman, but I could tell he wasn't trying to hit her, just scare her. She seemed to figure that out pretty fast. I saw the grin spread across her pretty face.

"Hit their tires!" I said.

"I tried," he said. "I think they're made of diamond fiber."

I growled. Diamond fiber was made to resist magic, and it was nearly indestructible. "I guess we'll do it the hard way." I jerked the wheel toward the ramp. The other car blocked. I slammed against them, but their tires were too solid, their car too heavy. The other car came up from behind, and slammed into our trunk. The car blocking the ramp pulled away to the right just enough to let me move over another few feet.

The minute, I did, I realized my mistake. A crash barrier with yellow drums lay right in my path. I tried to steer away, but white lines of energy from the woman's staff suddenly gripped the car, holding it on course. The car behind us crashed into the trunk again.

No way out.

# Chapter 15

I hit the brakes, desperate to avoid slamming into the barrier. Metal screeched on metal as the brakes tried to stop our forward momentum. I could already see this rolling pile of junk wouldn't stop in time. Colliding with the water-filled drums wouldn't kill us, but we'd be sitting ducks for the Darkwater agents.

Shelton roared like a wild beast. I saw him aim his staff out the right window. A white wave exploded from the end, slamming into the side of the blocking sedan, and shoving it sideways. Tires screeched and smoked as the car jetted sideways even as momentum carried it forward at the same time. I twisted the steering wheel right. The car clipped a barrel. The front end sparked against the concrete barrier. And then we zoomed up the exit ramp. The car riding our tail slammed on the brakes too late. Water exploded as it plowed into the crash barrels.

"Yes!" Shelton shouted as we whizzed past the car to our right. I took a right off the ramp since the light was red, and took the next left. I wasn't sure where we were, exactly, but kept going, checking the rear-view mirror for pursuit.

"We need to dump the car," Shelton said. "The tracker."

I pulled down a road where a giant warehouse store had gone out of business and now stood empty and boarded. A loud pop preceded the thumping noise of a flat tire. I urged the car further. As if in answer, the tire made one last squealing noise before the metal rim rasped atop the asphalt.

I hit the brakes. The car slid a few feet and skidded to a halt sideways across the road. I got out while Shelton wrestled with his staff as he slid out of the other side. A steep hill on the side of the road opposite the warehouse led to an apartment complex. Since I didn't feel like hiding in an abandoned warehouse-sized building with angry Arcanes after me, I scrambled toward the hill.

The screech of rubber on road caught my attention as the two poser police cars rounded the corner and roared toward us like dogs on the scent of a fox. Shelton sent a meteor flying at the lead car. It swerved as the sphere cratered into the asphalt. The nose of the second car dived into the hole. The rear flipped up. The car teetered for a moment before toppling over onto its roof with a crunch.

I saw the driver of the lead car snarl. He hit the gas, and the sedan lurched forward. The blonde woman sat on the window sill firing blasts of energy at us. Shelton and I dove behind the cover of his ruined car. He poked up his head and ducked as another crackling strand of lightning flickered past. Another blast rocked the car. My teeth clenched tight and anger boiled through me. *I've had enough of these clowns.*

My demonic side surged through the cage door, flooding through my veins, swelling my muscles and causing my skin to strain against my clothes. I felt my tail punch through the back of my pants. I stopped the demon from taking over at the last second as a roar burst from my throat.

When I stood up, all seven feet of me, muscles bulging like some obscene steroid user, the blonde woman's eyes went wide. She aimed at me. I tore the rear passenger door off Shelton's car and flung it like a Frisbee at the sedan. The woman screamed. The door smashed into the hood, shattered the windshield, and bounced off the roof as the car veered out of control. The tire caught the curb and the car flipped, catapulting the woman from her perch.

I saw her body fly through the air, a scream trailing from her wide mouth as she sailed toward a future as a blood smear on the asphalt. I knew she would die. I knew she'd been trying to capture us so her leader could kill us. But a part of me couldn't take the guilt of seeing her splatter all over the road. I blurred, the scene slowing as my supernatural reflexes kicked in. I caught the woman, swinging my arms to lessen the impact.

The car rolled toward me, glass flying everywhere, metal sparking. I jumped, felt the car clip my feet from beneath me as I failed to avoid it. I landed with a thud on my back. The woman lay atop me, her eyes wide with fear and loathing as she looked into my demonic face.

I scrambled to my feet, leaving her on the ground with a look of astonishment on her face. She suddenly crawled on hands and knees toward something—her staff. I snatched it, and broke it into four pieces. I looked at the flipped car and saw the driver woozily pulling himself out while the other two Darkwater people did the same from the second car.

"Let's go!" Shelton said.

I ran to him, scooping him up beneath an arm.

"Wait," he said, aiming his staff at the blue sedan. He said a word, and the vehicle burst into unnatural flames, melting the vehicle down to slag in seconds.

I clambered up the hill and leapt the fence into the apartment complex where trees hid my monstrous form. I put Shelton down, suppressed my demon essence. Thankfully, my clothes hadn't torn completely, but they were definitely ruined. I kicked off my now useless shoes and cursed. "How many clothes am I gonna go through if this keeps up?"

"Think about it later," Shelton said, motioning me on. We entered the parking garage. He walked down the row of vehicles and chose an identical make and model to the car he'd just blown up, though this one wore a disgusting shade of mint green. He aimed his wand at the lock, and made a flicking motion. The handle sprang up. The inside of the car reeked of pine air freshener as we slid inside, though it was infinitely better than the stale food odor from the last vehicle. Shelton aimed the wand at the ignition. After a few false starts, the car thrummed to life, sounding more like a cheap lawnmower than a car.

"Couldn't you have chosen something a little faster?" I asked.

"It might take me too long to steal a car I'm not familiar with," he said, backing it out of the spot and steering it from the parking deck. "If you think magically hotwiring a car is easy, maybe you should give it a try sometime." His brow furrowed. "On second thought, don't do that. You might blow it up."

"Ha, ha," I said, taking a deep breath to calm my frayed nerves. I felt weak with relief for a moment before realizing something. "They know I'm Daemos now," I said.

Shelton nodded. "Yep, their search list just got a lot smaller." He waved a hand dismissively. "Nothing else you could've done."

"If I could master my damned magic," I said. "Hell, even throwing standard fireballs would've been better than giving away the one thing that makes me different."

"They'll probably figure out your name," Shelton said. "I don't know of too many other Daemos who hang with us regular folk." He took a left to avoid going back past the road we'd just come from.

"As if you're regular," I said, keeping an eye on the back window in case Darkwater had magically repairing cars.

Shelton's phone rang, and we both nearly jumped out of our seats. He answered. I heard Bella's cheerful voice on the other end for several seconds before Shelton interrupted and told her we would be at the hideout in fifteen minutes and send her a picture so she could open a portal for us. He parked the car in an alley when we arrived, and ran a simple cleansing spell to wipe down the interior of fingerprints. We walked a few blocks back to the spot where Shelton had stored the blue sedan, and opened a hidden staircase.

I recognized the hideout as one of the few we'd circulated through while on the run from the numerous jackasses who wouldn't leave me alone. Bella was already waiting inside, standing outside the portal. She looked from Shelton's rumpled state to my stretched clothes and groaned.

"Oh, dear. You two did something terrible, didn't you?" she said.

Shelton held up a hand to stop her. "I don't want to hear it now. I'm starving, and I want a beer."

She pressed her lips together, as if it was an effort not to say something, and nodded. "I brought you some potion beer from town. It's in the cooler."

He sighed, bent down, and kissed her on the lips. "You're the best."

She giggled.

I went through the portal back to the mansion cellar and ran upstairs to find Elyssa and Stacey hunched over a game of Scrabble. A third spot at the table—presumably Bella's—remained empty while she and Shelton smooched downstairs and a thousand miles away on the other side of the omniarch. From what I could tell, Bella was beating the other women handily.

John Corwin

"I've never cared for these board games," Stacy said, her British accent loading the sentence with disdain. She looked up at me, and a sensual smirk drew up her lips. "I see someone has been naughty as usual."

Elyssa's forehead scrunched. She rose from her chair and inspected me. I told her what had happened before she could ask.

"If they figure out your name, they'll know you're going to school here," she said. "That narrows down the search parameters by several million people."

"Survival was higher on my priority list at the time," I said.

She rubbed my arm. "I know. I'm not blaming you, but we need to be even more on guard now." Her eyes lost focus. "Posting sentries to watch the way station entrance was a smart move on their part, though I would have put people at the entrance to the pocket dimension instead of at the bottom of the parking ramp."

"We didn't see them until the last minute," I said. "For all we know there were others waiting at the door, too."

"I doubt it," she said. "Unless they have more manpower than we thought." She kissed my cheek. "For what it's worth, I'm glad you saved that woman even if she was trying to catch you."

I shuddered. "I'm already responsible for one death. Plus, I don't think I could stand the sight of seeing her hit the asphalt at fifty miles an hour."

"You've seen worse."

I'd cut vamplings to bloody chunks before. Crushed a man's skull with my bare hands after a drug lord had taken me captive. I'd seen Maximus blow his master's head off with a gun. Yeah, I'd seen worse, but that didn't mean I wanted to see it ever again. I knew with absolute certainty my wish was an impossibility.

Shelton and Bella appeared from the cellar. Bella looked concerned. She locked eyes with Elyssa, probably communicating something in girl code. Women had a knack for saying more in a silent look than most guys did shouting what they wanted in everyone's faces.

"Justin, let me grab a potion beer, and we'll go over the footage on this ASE," Shelton said, heading toward the kitchen.

"Need help?" Elyssa asked me.

"Always," I said with a smile. I leaned in and whispered in her ear. "You can sit in my lap."

Bella laughed, her supernatural hearing obviously picking up my words.

Elyssa blushed and pecked my lips.

"How adorable," Stacey purred, her hearing no worse than Bella's.

It was my turn to blush. I still had trouble remembering to keep certain things to myself if I didn't want every super in the vicinity to overhear me. Or maybe I just needed to learn how to craft a muffling spell.

We gathered in the briefing room slash war room, presumably the safest place to discuss super-secret things. Cutsauce followed the crowd, growling and yipping at anyone that didn't bend over to scratch his ears. He snuggled into Bella's lap as the meeting commenced.

Shelton copied the ASE by waving his wand at it, and directing four streams of aether to blank ASEs so everyone would have one to look at.

"We're looking for a specific limo," he explained. "According to the informational brochure Walter gave me, the illusions last for up to twenty minutes. Each illusion is spelled to drive a random route and find a good spot to pull off the road, like a parking garage, before vanishing." He pulled up the images, and showed an overhead view of Phipps Plaza. "We need to eliminate the limos that vanish in plain sight. The ones that vanish into parking garages make things a little more difficult because we won't know if they disappeared or not."

"A bloody needle in a haystack," Stacey said.

"Let's count the limos as they exit the garage," Elyssa said, zooming the image of her ASE on one limo, and slashing her finger across it to number it. "That way we can eliminate the fakes."

"How do we even know this is the right set of cars?" I asked. "I don't remember Oliver giving a specific time."

Shelton grunted. "I called him a minute ago. He told me he doesn't remember the exact time because he was in the stable. He also said there were four limos using similar illusions that day."

A brilliant idea suddenly occurred to me. "Hey, if Overworld Transportation Administration tracking system monitors magical

121

transportation, why don't we just find the residences where the limos originated? That would pinpoint the exact house, right?"

"Nice thinking," Shelton said, "Except we'll have to look at every magical limo in the city no matter where they're coming from."

"There could have been fifty other limos driving around the city that day," Elyssa said. "The number leaving the Grotto should be a lot smaller, so tracking them will be a lot easier. Using the common point of origin of those vehicles eliminates work."

"What if the Conroys have some kind of charm to prevent the OTA tracking system from following them?" I asked.

"Then we're screwed, and everything we went through today was for nothing."

# Chapter 16

"Dramatic much?" I asked. "Maybe you could have mentioned the possibility of a blocking spell *before* we almost died in a car chase."

Shelton raised an eyebrow. "It would be too aether-intensive to cast blocking spells on all the illusions, so the tracking system should follow them. But the original limo could have a blocking spell preventing the system from picking up on it." He shrugged. "There's still a good chance we'll find something useful."

"The tracking system is basically a network of sentry ASEs," Elyssa explained. "After several close calls with idiots on flying brooms or carpets nearly hitting nom aircraft, the Templar Custodians asked the Overworld Conclave for a system to find out who the lawbreakers were."

I remembered the Custodians from my conflict with Maximus in Bogota, Colombia. They cleaned up supernatural messes to keep the noms from finding out about the Overworld. I wouldn't want their job for all the peanuts in China.

Shelton clapped his hands together. "Let's get to work, then."

We assigned numbers to each of the limos and watched the first group leave the Grotto. The illusionary vehicles only lasted ten minutes, and we figured out the real one by a process of elimination, following it to an affluent Dunwoody neighborhood. Unfortunately, the trackers wouldn't identify the people in the video unless they'd violated the law, so we marked down the address to look up later.

It took us nearly three hours to track the next two limos and mark down their destinations. Despite our fears that we wouldn't know which cars were illusions if they went inside a parking garage or other covered structure, the ASE trackers swooped inside the decks to maintain a line of sight. I wondered if the tiny marble-like devices interfered with aircraft, or if noms ever saw the little things flitting around. They were probably charmed with diversion spells to make noms and supers alike ignore them without even knowing about it.

I wondered what prevented someone from hijacking such an extensive system and spying on anyone they wished but didn't voice the concern for fear it would derail our mission. The OTA's network of little spy bots made the NSA look like small fries.

"We've got a problem," Elyssa said about forty minutes into tracking the fourth limo.

Shelton looked at the three-dimensional holograph hovering above her part of the table. "What's the issue?"

"Who has a limo that didn't vanish?" she asked.

Nobody raised their hands.

"I counted ten illusions," Shelton said. "There are five of us, which means we each tracked two."

"One of my cars was not tracked," Stacey said, rewinding the footage, and pointing to car number seven. As the image played forward, the limo simply drove off, vanishing down the road without a tracker following it.

"That's the original," Shelton said. "And it has an anti-tracking spell on it."

"One of the illusions is following it," Elyssa said, pointing to car number four, one that I'd tracked.

We watched it for a few minutes, until the original limo turned left at an intersection while the illusion continued on straight.

"Any idea if it's the Conroys?" I asked.

"Dollars to donuts it is," Shelton said, pulling up a map on his arcphone and looking at the intersection. "That's a wealthy part of town. I'd bet they're going somewhere within a few miles' radius of there."

"Too wide a net to cast," Elyssa said, shaking her head. "Let's move on to the next limo for now."

Shelton stared at the map for a long moment before nodding. "Yeah. Maybe it wasn't the Conroys." He didn't sound convinced.

The next limo used five illusions, each of which vanished after ten minutes, though the original limo went to a high rise building just down the street from the Grotto. We felt pretty certain the Conroys didn't own that one due to the paltry number of illusions it cast.

Shelton ran the addresses we'd gathered through a database he used for bounty hunting. He gave a low whistle. "Wow, there were some heavy hitters at the Grotto that day."

"Like who?" Elyssa asked, leaning back in her chair, one hand clasping mine.

"Otto Strassman and Bara Nagal, for starters," he said, bringing up images of the two.

Elyssa gasped at the second name. "Bara Nagal?" she said. "The Grand Master of the Templar Synod?"

"The one and the same," Shelton said.

I looked at the images. Otto was a tall, thin man with spectacles perched on a narrow nose. Bara Nagal's graying hair and the fine lines on his face marked him as middle-aged. Both men were obviously very wealthy, judging from the numbers indicating net worth listed beneath the bios.

"Otto is the head of the Red Syndicate," Shelton explained.

I blinked at him. "Wait, he's the head vampire?"

"This is too strange to be coincidence," Elyssa said.

"Bloody peculiar," Stacey said, raising an eyebrow.

Shelton flicked the image to that of an ordinary looking man. "This is William Hodges, a power broker who works as a mediator for companies and individuals."

"Who were in the other two limos?" I asked.

"I ran a search in my address database, but the residences they went to are titled by shell corporations." Shelton stared at the large house in Dunwoody. "I gotta say, this one looks really familiar, though." He snapped his fingers. "Now I remember. When I was tracking Cyphanis Rax, this was one of several houses his fake corporations owned to keep his holdings secret."

"I don't like the sound of this," Bella said. "If I had to guess, I'd say a high-powered meeting just took place in the Grotto. For the actual leaders of factions to meet is unheard of, though. Ambassadors and elected officials are the usual proxies."

Shelton's jaw tightened. "I heard Cyphanis is running in the special election to take the Arcanus Primus spot."

Bigglesworth had killed Jarrod Sager, the former Arcanus Primus, a couple of months ago, but the man's death had been covered up until after the Grand Melee massacre during which a titanic golem, modified by one of Daelissa's underlings, had attempted to kill the Arcane Council. Several spectators and two council members had been killed as a result.

"Did we ever find a solid reason for Daelissa attempting to murder the Arcane Council?" I asked.

"I'm forming a theory," Shelton said, eyes narrowing. "If Cyphanis is meeting with these other bigwigs like he's already part of the club, it makes me wonder if he didn't have a part in her plan." He sat down. "My old man, Sager, was tired of playing ball with Daelissa. Maybe she decided it was best to clean the slate and sent Bigglesworth to kill him."

"Two of Cyphanis's cronies are vying to replace the murdered council members," Bella said. "If they win, Daelissa will have even more control."

"Then why are the factions meeting?" I asked. "Daelissa wants to break the alliance apart, not strengthen it."

"I can only think of one reason," Shelton said, his face grim. "The Seraphim created the vampires, right?"

I nodded. "Yeah, it was the way angels awarded immortality to their best human servants. You think Daelissa is trying to reignite the love?"

"She ain't stopping with the vampires," Shelton said with a grimace. "I think she's working to create an alliance of her own. If Cyphanis takes over as Arcanus Primus, you can bet he'll throw his support behind her when the crap hits the fan."

"That would explain why the Conroys were there," I said. "But why would they choose the Grotto as a meeting spot? Wouldn't so many VIPs attract attention?"

"I think I know," Elyssa said.

Everyone turned their attention on her.

"The repaired mini-arches," she said.

Shelton tapped a finger to his chin. "You think Daelissa is showing them how she can access Thunder Rock and the Alabaster Arch?"

A shrug. "It's possible. Maybe she wants them to know her army will be marching through any day now, using fear to forge an alliance."

Bella made a thoughtful sound. "Couldn't those factions stop her plans, though?"

"True," Shelton said. "Tipping her hand now would be premature unless she already has an agreement."

"In other words," I said, "we don't have a clue what's going on, just that something really bad is afoot, as usual."

"More or less sums it up," Shelton said, and blew out a breath.

"We should refocus on the original objective," Elyssa said. She winked at me. "Baby steps."

I chuckled. "You're right."

"In case you don't remember," Shelton said, folding his arms across his chest, and leaning back in his chair, "we don't know where that other limo went."

Silence ensued, presumably as everyone went into deep thought. I wondered if Shelton had connections with the people who controlled nom traffic cams and the like so we could cobble together a route using nom technology. Provided we could access the footage, it might be the best way to go. If he didn't know anyone, maybe we could somehow get an image of the inside of the traffic control building and use the omniarch to get inside. I thought up all sorts of crazy schemes to get us that picture, when a much simpler solution presented itself.

"We know the general area the limousine went to," I said. "And you said we can track other vehicles from their points of origin."

"Yeah," Shelton said. His eyes brightened. "We could search that area for morning traffic and find out where it came from."

"Great idea," Elyssa said. "I was trying to figure out how to break into the nom traffic control buildings downtown so we could look at all their footage." She sighed. "I wasn't looking forward to that chore."

I grinned. "Read my mind, babe."

Shelton combed through the footage. Thankfully, Bruce had given us all the footage from one day, and the ASEs didn't record unless there was a magical vehicle present. He spotted a flying carpet zooming far above the city which the ASEs flagged red. We watched as a Templar slider, their version of magical aircraft, intercepted the violator and hauled them away. Shelton pinched his fingers to widen the view of the map and panned by, waving his hands across it until we saw the area where the possible Conroy limo had vanished. We counted three total limos departing in a ten-mile radius. One of them went to an expensive country club. The other went north along the interstate until it vanished from the Atlanta OTA tracking zone, and was picked up by another authority.

Once we eliminated the illusions on the remaining limousine, we followed the original to the Grotto.

"Bingo!" I whooped, meeting Elyssa's high-five as we celebrated a minor victory.

Stacey hugged Bella. "Bloody fabulous!" she said with a grin.

"Hold on," Shelton said. "I don't want to rain on your parade, but we won't know for sure if this one came from the Conroy residence until we scout it."

Our celebrations subsided as his sobering words sank in. He was right. And what was to guarantee this was the only house the Conroys owned?

Shelton toyed around with the map application on his arcphone. "The house is on Riverside Drive," he said. "It has a steep driveway, and a wooded area around it. That means it'll be hard as hell to stake out using conventional methods."

"Or magical," Bella added. "I'm sure they have a substantial number of wards on the property."

"We have an omniarch," I said, an idea springing to mind. "What if we used it to leapfrog across their property until we get where we want to go?"

Shelton looked impressed. "Way to go, kid. That's a great idea."

Cutsauce yipped.

I felt so pleased with myself, I didn't bother correcting his use of the word "kid". "I figure if we get a detailed image of the front yard and surrounding areas, we can open a portal there, then find another point somewhere further in, close the arch, and reopen it on that spot."

"You'll need to exercise caution," Bella said. "If you open the portal in the middle of a tree, it will probably sever the trunk. Not to mention what might happen if you open it inside of something living."

I made a face, imagining the results. "Are you sure opening the portal will destroy anything in its path?"

Shelton shrugged. "I'm a bounty hunter, not a magic arch specialist."

"Shall we experiment?" Bella asked, standing. Cutsauce leapt from her lap as she stood, perking his ears at her as if wondering what was so important it warranted disrupting his nap. Bella motioned toward the door.

I rubbed my hands together. "I love experimenting."

We made our way down to the arch room with the little hellhound dogging our steps. Bella continued through it to the gauntlet room. After a few minutes, she returned. "I set up rows of bricks. When I open the portal, it should open up in the middle of the stacks. I'm curious to see if it will sever the bricks, or merely pulverize them."

"I'll go watch the bricks," I said, taking Elyssa's hand and walking to the gauntlet room. On the other side of the low wall in the practice range, I saw several rows of the large cinder blocks we used for levitation practice arrayed in such a way that no matter where Bella opened the portal it would intersect with the bricks.

"You realize we never finished our match, don't you?" Elyssa said, giving my hand a squeeze.

I smirked. "Pretty sure I had it in the bag."

"Oh, really?" She punched me in the shoulder with her free hand. "Maybe we should settle that right now."

The air above the center of the cinder blocks shimmered, flickered, and split into a portal right in the middle of a stack. The bricks bent around the portal as if suddenly rendered insubstantial, clearing a space for the portal. Cutsauce yipped at the portal, hopping around on his little legs. The portal flickered shut a few seconds later, and the bricks snapped back to their former shape. The hellhound whined, tilting his head.

"Calm down," Elyssa said, picking him up.

He licked her face.

"Attention whore," I said.

Our little contest forgotten for the moment, I walked to the formerly warped blocks and inspected them. They seemed no worse for the wear. It was as if the portal temporarily transmuted them from solid to something else. Bella joined us for a repeat of the experiment. I touched the warped cinder blocks. They felt solid as ever.

"How bizarre," Bella said, obviously as puzzled as the rest of us.

We repeated the experiment using the wooden melee dummy, chairs, and even a pool of water. In all cases, the portal merely warped the objects in its physical space, displacing anything there. Nobody volunteered to let Bella open a portal on top of them, but we felt confident it wouldn't kill anyone. Shelton wanted to test it on Cutsauce since the little hellhound kept following us everywhere, yipping excitedly whenever the portal opened. Bella gave him a horrified look.

"One thing I'm concerned about would be Gloom cracks," Elyssa said after we finished experimenting. "The silver circles around the Obsidian Arches and the smaller arches in the control rooms prevent Gloom cracks from spreading outside the magical circuit. There's no circle at the destination portal, so what's to prevent cracks from opening and spreading?"

"It might create a temporary invisible circle around the area it opens in," Shelton said. "I guess we'll have to experiment more."

At that point, though, it was late, and I wanted to go to bed. We opened the omniarch back to Stacey's residence, and saw Ryland, Stacey's lycan boyfriend, on the other side wearing a chef's apron and not much else. She let out a sensual growl and raced through the arch and into his burly arms.

Bella shut the portal in record time.

# Chapter 17

The next day was Saturday, so we got up extra early to go to Elyssa's initiation ceremony for the Templars. Bella, Shelton, Elyssa and I used the omniarch, opening the portal in a room inside the Templar compound and leaving it open for our later return.

"Where has Nightliss been lately?" I asked as we walked outside to the large lawn behind the house where the ceremony was to take place.

"Meghan said she was going to practice and recover, but I haven't seen her for a few days," Bella said.

"Justin!" said a familiar voice. I turned in time to receive a hug from Katie. She squeezed me so tight I couldn't breathe for a minute.

"Hey, Katie," I wheezed as she released me. "Geez, you been working out?"

She squeezed Elyssa with a hug, eliciting an *oof* from my girlfriend.

Katie gave a sheepish grin. "Um, kind of, I guess."

I'd once had a huge crush on the pretty blonde. By the time she'd reciprocated the feelings, I'd already moved on and fallen in love with Elyssa. Unfortunately for Katie, that had been about the time hellhounds decided to chase me out of my childhood home, leading to her terrifying initiation into the Overworld.

"How's college?" I asked.

She shrugged. "It's okay, but it's so boring going to a nom school when you know about all the cool stuff at Arcane University and Science Academy."

I chuckled, though a sobering thought flattened my smile as I remembered the last time she'd seen action with us and mowed down a gang of armed vampires with an assault rifle. She'd saved our lives, but at the cost of emotional trauma.

Katie turned to my girlfriend. "I'm really happy for you, Elyssa." She held out a wrapped package. "It's not much, but I figured graduating to a full-fledged Templar means you deserve a gift."

Elyssa's eyes softened. "Thanks, Katie. It means a lot to me."

My stomach clenched. *Should I have bought her a gift, too?*

Shelton's eyes caught mine. He smirked, probably knowing exactly what I was thinking.

Other members of my extended family were also there, including Felicia Nosti and her nom boyfriend, Larry. I was happy to see them still together after a few months, since she wasn't usually one to stay committed to anything or anyone. After her and Adam's parents had died, she'd gone off the deep end, doing drugs, and abusing her body in all sorts of other ways, culminating in her becoming a vampire and doing dirty work for Maximus. He'd nearly killed her, allowing her to be infected by vamplings, but Nightliss had cured the curse somehow by purging Felicia with the blood of the vampire who had turned her.

I spoke with her for a while, moving on to other friends, Ash and Nyte, former schoolmates from Edenfield High School.

"Justin!" Ash shook my hand with bone-crushing force.

I winced. "Easy, dude. You're gonna break somebody's hand if you're not careful."

Ash smiled sheepishly. "Sorry. I got excited when I saw you."

Nyte snorted. "Life has been an adjustment ever since the Maximus ordeal."

The rogue vampire had used my blood to make a potion that turned noms into vampires. Ash and Nyte had taken the potion and joined the blood-sucking crowd. But when I altered a spell intended to kill all the vampires in Maximus's Atlanta compound, the alteration removed the vampirism from the vampires present, instead. Even though my intervention had taken the fangs and desire for blood from my two friends, they'd retained supernatural strength and crystal-blue eyes—a side effect of my blood having been used in the vampire potion.

"I'll bet," I said.

Nyte grinned. "So we decided to join the Templars."

Ash nodded. "Mr. Borathen—"

"*Commander*," Nyte said with a sigh. "He isn't the dad of your best friend anymore; he's your leader."

"I know," Ash said, grinning at Elyssa. He and Nyte had been her besties before I'd stumbled into their lives.

I spotted Elyssa's father walking from the house and flinched in surprise at the woman walking by his side.

"Nightliss?" I said.

Elyssa's forehead furrowed at the sight. Ash and Nyte both went silent with awe, their mouths dropping open in unison.

"Dude, that's the angel?" Nyte said. "She is so hot."

"Is she single?" Ash asked.

"I'll be right back," I said, and made my way through the crowd, Elyssa following close behind.

Thomas Borathen, leader of the Atlanta Templars and father of my girlfriend, regarded me with his cool blue eyes. "Mr. Slade," he said in a professional tone.

"Hello, sir," I said, giving Nightliss a quizzical look. She smiled.

"Hello, Dad," Elyssa said, and went in for a hug.

In the past, her father had spurned such things, but after his son Jack's death, things had changed. He embraced her in a firm, albeit brief hug, and stepped back. "I'm proud of you, Elyssa."

"Thanks, Dad" she said, unable to repress a beautiful smile.

He checked the time. "Cadet, you should be joining the others for the march. I'm calling this to order."

She offered him a smart salute, kissed me on the cheek, and went inside the compound to join the procession.

"What's going on, Nightliss?" I asked.

She took my hands. "I've found a new calling, Justin. I hope you'll be pleased."

I looked to Thomas, but his stony expression gave nothing away. "Are you going to become a Templar, too?"

She smiled. "Not exactly."

I narrowed my eyes at her. "What's going on?"

Katie wandered up to our group, grinning brightly. "Did you tell him?" she said to Nightliss.

"Not yet."

John Corwin

Katie looped her arm through mine. "You're gonna be so surprised," she said, and led me to the front row where most of my friends sat.

I cast a glance back at Nightliss, confused and a little worried. She hadn't been at full strength since Ivy had healed her from Daelissa's curse. I hoped she wasn't about to do something she wasn't ready for.

We took our seats and waited for the procession. Katie released my arm. I couldn't help but notice her glancing down the row at Ash. He looked at her, and quickly turned away, his face red.

"Are you two still seeing each other?" I asked.

She shook her head. "No. After they went vampire, I just couldn't look at him the same. I mean, I'm glad you took away the vampire part, but I guess we never reconnected, you know?"

I nodded. "Looks like he still has feelings for you."

A sad smile clouded her face. "Yeah. I just don't feel like I'm ready for another relationship. They all end badly."

I didn't even want to remind her of Brad Nichols. He'd been a recruit of Maximus's, but since Maximus hadn't been mature enough to properly turn a nom into a vampire, he'd infected Brad with the vampling curse, turning him into a member of the blood-sucking walking dead. He'd promptly massacred half a dozen corrupted high school officials who were trying to blackmail me. The incident remained a dark stain in my memories, but Katie had lost her virginity to the guy, so I couldn't imagine how brutal his death had been for her.

"Ash and Nyte have been training with Templar initiates," Katie said. "I think they're really serious about using the abilities you gave them. Maybe if Ash applies himself and proves himself to me, we can try again." She sighed, her hand brushing against mine. "Elyssa is so lucky to have you, Justin. We all are."

I tugged on my collar, feeling a bit embarrassed by the sudden praise. "You're all lucky to still be alive," I said. "I think I've nearly gotten you killed on two or three occasions."

Her laugh echoed across the crowd right when everyone stopped talking. She clamped a hand over her mouth, looking mortified.

A trumpet blared, and a drum punctuated the air with a precise military beat. A rank of Templars in shining armor, red crosses atop

134

white shields emblazoned on their chest plates appeared from the direction of the old stone church to the side of the house. They wore no helmets, and I recognized one of the people in the line as Christian Salazar, the commander of Templars in Colombia. Templars bearing flags with the same symbols marched behind the commanders, followed by drummers and trumpeters.

The commanders stopped before Thomas Borathen. The drums and trumpets sounded a final cadence and stopped playing, leaving a sudden silence hanging in the air.

Christian saluted Thomas, and said in a loud clear voice, "My legion is at your command, sir knight." He gave a short bow and backed into line. Each commander followed suit. I counted thirteen in all, and wondered how many had gone over to the dark side of Bara Nagal and the Synod.

After Thomas accepted each of their offerings, he shouted a command. The drums rapped a complex series of beats, and the trumpets blared a somewhat familiar melody. I heard a gasp of awe and followed other's gazes to see an army of Templars marching from the church. Ranks upon ranks appeared, marching to the military cadence in perfect unison. I had never seen so many Templars in one place, and wondered if each commander had brought every unit under his command, or if this was just a sample of the entire army.

For nearly half an hour, the drums rat-a-tatted as the Templars filled the pasture where horses normally grazed. With a final beat, the drums ceased, their final strikes punctuating the air.

A sense of awe and anticipation hung heavy in the air as Thomas Borathen walked up the stairs of a tall gray podium. An Arcane Templar made a motion with his wand, probably casting a voice amplification spell, and stepped aside as the Templar leader stood atop the platform. It seemed this was something much larger than an initiation ceremony.

"It has been a trying last several months for the order of the Knights Templar," Thomas said, his voice sounding almost as if he were right beside me. "The revelation of the Divinity's origin fractured our order. Former brothers in arms are now enemies."

"And sisters in arms," Katie whispered, obviously trying to keep things equal opportunity.

"Because of this rift, we have lost the ability to protect our initiates against certain curses, and to grant them enhancements they need in the war against chaos. We have lost the solidarity that makes Templars a barrier against evil. This threatens law and order."

Murmurs of agreement sounded in the crowd.

"The Synod, for all practical purposes, has fallen into chaos and ruin." He paused, looking around as if to emphasize the point. "Those of us who have remained united for the cause say, no more!" Thomas pounded a fist into his palm.

At this, a great cheer went up from the assembly, and the ranks of Templars sounded a single solid roar echoing in the chill air.

After the noise faded, Thomas continued. "Today we bring not only new initiates into the fold, but we also gain a new weapon in the battle against chaos."

The air became absolutely still as everyone waited with bated breath to hear the next words.

"I give you Nightliss, Seraphim, and the Clarion of the Knights Templar!" he shouted.

The crowd roared as Nightliss ascended the podium, looking fragile, petite, and cute—certainly not what one would expect of the new Divinity, although they'd obviously opted for a new, less pretentious title.

I sat open-mouthed as Katie beamed at me, gripping my arm and cheering.

The angel moved to the podium while Thomas stepped back. "I am honored to accept the responsibilities granted me by the Templar order," she said in her peculiar accent. She smiled, looking toward me for a moment. She seemed to steel herself, fists clenched, eyes closed. Ethereal ultraviolet wings fanned from her back, bathing her body in a halo of dark light. She opened her eyes to reveal glowing orbs, opened her hands and held them high. "The Templars will be a mighty force," she cried out in a voice that sounded like several voices speaking at once. "Order will be restored!"

Everyone leapt to their feet, cheering and roaring while the Templar army raised silver swords high in the air. As one, they swept the swords, point-down to the earth, and knelt, foreheads resting on the hilts.

I had to admit, I was pretty awed by the spectacle, and found myself kneeling with the others in the crowd.

"You!" Nightliss called out.

I looked up and saw her pointing toward me. I pointed uncertainly at my chest. "Me?" I said in a small voice.

"Justin Slade, please rise."

I did, feeling my face grow warm as all eyes settled on me.

"Without you, none of this would be possible. Without you, I would have died." She floated down from the podium, ultraviolet wings stretched wide, shimmering like black smoke, and landed in front of it. "Please come forward."

Glad we were near the front, I stepped toward her, legs feeling like jelly as everyone watched me. I'd never much liked the attention of the crowd. In high school it generally meant people were making fun of me. But this was different—so much different.

Nightliss smiled, looking cute and scary as hell at the same time as she took my hand. Despite the glow, her hand felt no warmer than usual. She stepped to my side and raised our hands high as cheers erupted.

"*Slade! Slade! Slade!*" the crowd chanted.

I managed an uneasy grin, but couldn't move my mouth to speak.

"Today, a new alliance is forged, and we go forth to victory!" Nightliss cried.

The cheers nearly overwhelmed my supernatural hearing.

Nightliss led me up the podium stairs where Thomas joined us. He gave me an almost smug look, as if happy to see me suffering stage fright.

"Today," he said, "marks a new chapter in the Templar order. No longer will the Blessings be given in secret. Let us begin the ceremony."

I wasn't sure what to do, so I stood with Nightliss and Thomas as initiates came up to the podium and were introduced. Nightliss pressed her hand to the chest of each one, speaking a few words of encouragement, and apparently imbuing them with supernatural gifts. I shook hands with each person as they passed by. Some regarded me with awe. Or maybe my deodorant had failed thanks to the cold sweat of stage fright.

It made me wonder what in the world these people knew about me, or if my sudden fame was because I got to hang with Nightliss.

Elyssa's beaming face appeared at the top. She already had a blessing from Daelissa which protected her from vampling curses and a host of other things, so I didn't know if Nightliss gave her a gift or not, though she pressed a hand to my girlfriend the same as she had the others. Thomas shook her hand, and pinned a Templar cross to her outfit. I could tell he was fighting to maintain a stern look while pride threatened to burst from his chest.

Elyssa reached me, and held out her hand. Since I wasn't exactly a Templar and didn't feel bound to be all strict and stuff, I pulled her to me and planted a big kiss on her right in front of everyone.

A collective gasp went up from the crowd, followed by a cheer. When I let Elyssa go, she seemed a little dizzy, as if she couldn't believe I'd just done that. I winked at her.

"Congratulations, Templar Borathen."

Her lips curved into a smirk. "Thank you, Mr. Slade."

My blood caught fire.

The next cadet approached, a lean, muscular guy. When I shook his hand, he gave me a disappointed look. "Don't I get a kiss?"

As the next initiate came up the stairs, something in the back of the seated crowd caught my attention. A young girl frantically waved her hands at me. Not just any girl.

It was Ivy.

# Chapter 18

For some reason, neither Nightliss nor Thomas seemed to see my sister. I looked and saw two more initiates remaining. I couldn't just leave until the ceremony was over, but something had to be terribly wrong for Ivy to be here. This couldn't wait. I really had to talk to her. I stared at her, wishing I could just pause time and find out what was going on.

The last two initiates finally passed by. I leaned to Nightliss. "I have an emergency to take care of."

She gave me an uncertain look but nodded.

I descended the podium as Thomas gave a speech, and made my way down the center aisle, feeling eyes on me the entire way. I reached the house and went to the corner.

"Justin, something terrible is about to happen," Ivy said.

I reached out a tentative hand, and felt warm skin. "You're not projecting," I said. You're actually here." I went to hug her.

"I couldn't project here. The perimeter is warded." She pushed me away before I could embrace her. "We don't have time," she said. "You have to warn Thomas Borathen that the Synod wants him dead."

"The old Templar leadership? I think he knows that," I said.

"He's a good man," Ivy said. "Bigdaddy said so a lot of times, and I heard him arguing with Daelissa not to do this. He said for her not to let vengeance control her."

"What? I don't understand."

Ivy gripped my hands. "Tell him now. Please."

"Why do you care?" I asked.

She bit her lower lip. "Bigdaddy said it's wrong. And I got to thinking about the things you told me about Daelissa, Justin. She can

139

be mean. I followed her one time and saw her do bad things to people because they wouldn't obey her."

"Has she repaired the Grand Nexus?" I asked.

"No," Ivy said. "We don't have time to talk. I have to leave."

"Wait," I said. "I'm trying to save Mom. Can you tell me where she is?"

Ivy made a frustrated sound. "In the basement of the house. But you can't get to her. Not even I can." She scrunched her face and *blinked* away in a puff of shadows.

"Damn it," I said, pounding a fist into my hand. I looked up at the podium as Thomas spoke, and considered Ivy's warning. What if—I saw a shadowy figure positioning what looked like a rifle on the crenelated walls atop the flat church roof. Everyone seemed too intent on Thomas's speech, even the patrolling Templar sentries.

I raced around the front of the house to keep myself hidden from view, and down the path to the church. I spotted a Templar standing guard at the front of the church and ran to him.

"I think there are people on top of the church," I said.

"Please, go back to the assembly," he said. "We have people positioned on the church standing guard."

"I need to be sure they're supposed to be there," I said.

The man seemed to reach a decision. "Of course. I'll go with you."

"Thanks," I said, and turned toward the church.

A flash of blinding pain struck me in the lower back. I twisted, felt the sting of metal tear my flesh, saw the man thrusting a knife at me. My hand flashed to his wrist. Gripped it and squeezed until I heard bones crack and a scream of pain. His foot flashed out. I somehow dodged, letting my demonic instincts take hold as I had when fighting against Thomas Borathen when he wanted nothing more than to take my head clean off for daring to date his daughter.

One of his fists slammed into my chest. I dodged the next blow directed at my throat, and lashed out with my hand. Heard his arm break. Then I slugged him in the face. He dropped like a rock. The people on the church roof had to be with this guy. *Assassins.*

I wanted to shout an alarm, but the crowd burst into loud cheers. I saw the other commanders lining up in front of the podium, and realized with sudden horror why the assassins hadn't struck at Thomas yet. They didn't want just him. They wanted to kill as many leaders as possible. I ran to the church doors. Locked. I kicked them with all my strength and nearly broke my foot. *Magically reinforced, those bastards!*

Running to the side of the building, I jumped, my hands seeking purchase on the stone blocks so I could scale the building. My hands slipped as though the building were coated with grease. *How in the hell am I supposed to get on top of this place?* I had no choice but to run for the front of the assembly and warn them. Then I saw a dark figure positioning himself. Saw several others rise from behind the parapet, aiming more guns. I might be able to stop one of them with magic, but not all of them.

If only I could—I pause mid-thought and remembered my accidental blink across the arch room. I could do it again. I *had* to. I looked at the nearest assassin. I focused on that spot with all my might, and imagined opening a portal there. The world vanished in a puff of black. When it reappeared, I saw blue sky for an instant before I fell, crashing on top of someone who let out a muffled cry of surprise.

Dizziness washed over me, and I felt my gorge rising. I looked and saw several masked figures staring at me, each one holding a sniper rifle that could probably stop a charging rhino.

*I am so screwed.*

The figure closest to me slammed the butt of his gun into the side of my head. I saw stars, and felt the stone roof smack my face.

"Execute your orders!" one of the men shouted. "Kill Slade afterward."

I heard the guns cock. Heard the man say something in a calm voice, though my ears felt as if they were stuffed with cotton. I gritted my teeth, fought off the fog. Opened my eyes, and saw fingers pulling on triggers.

I raised my hand, and shouted, "No!"

A brilliant fireball burst from my hand, detonating above the heads of the assassins. Shots exploded. I heard the sound of ricocheting bullets and a cry go up from the crowd. Then I saw one of the figures aiming the huge barrel of a gun at my head. A brilliant bolt of ultraviolet light speared through his chest. His mouth opened wide as if trying to scream though his lungs had charred to ash.

I crawled, watching other bodies crumpling nearby, some full of the silver Lancer darts used to incapacitate. One of the figures ducked low, tugging a lever on his gun, apparently trying to fix it. Templars raced from the door on the roof toward him. I managed to gain my feet, sucking in deep breaths to ward off the dizziness and nausea threatening to overwhelm me.

The masked figure looked at the Templars. He snatched a device with a switch from the belt at his side. It was then I noticed the large backpack at his feet, and even more importantly, the bricks of explosives and wires spilling out of it. He had a detonator!

"Die you demonic son of a bitch," the man behind the mask said, and flicked the switch on the detonator.

I didn't think. I acted by pure instinct, and threw myself off the building.

A tremendous boom went up from the roof. Heat washed over my skin as a shockwave flipped me through the air, end over end. I bounced off the roof of the house. Rolled over the peak, and slid down the other side. My fingers caught on the gutter before I plummeted three stories to hard concrete and the promise of broken legs and agony. I shimmied to the side and gripped a sturdy downspout, braced my feet to the sides, and slid down.

The Templars had formed ranks around the podium, and I saw the bluish tint of a shield in place. Other Templars herded guests into an underground bunker facility, while teams of black-clad soldiers fanned across the area, probably looking for more intruders. Still choking back the urge to vomit and staggering, I weaved through the crowd to the front. Two grim-faced Templars parted ranks to let me inside the protective circle. What I saw made me even sicker.

Two of the commanders lay dead, a fact made more obvious by the complete mess the huge sniper rifles had made of their heads. I saw Thomas Borathen on the ground nearby, a gaping hole in his shoulder being tended by healers. Christian Salazar looked unhurt, as did the other commanders.

Arms wrapped tight around me. I looked into Elyssa's worried eyes. She kissed my cheek, my lips, my forehead. "Oh, god, I saw you up there. I tried to get to you but there were too many people in the way."

"It's okay," I said, brushing back her hair with my hand. "I'm okay." I looked at Thomas. "How's your father?"

"He'll be fine," she said, relaxing her embrace. "Whatever you did up there saved his life."

*I must have distracted the shooters enough to hurt their aim.* But what if Ivy hadn't warned me? Would I have still been up on the podium? Would my head look like a pulverized tomato? I felt relief and, despite the terrible circumstance, happiness my sister had risked so much to help me.

It only reinforced my determination to rescue Mom and get Ivy out of there. If she was starting to see Daelissa's bad side, maybe it wouldn't be hard to convince her. On the other hand, she still adored Jeremiah Conroy, and his argument with Daelissa over attacking the Templars might have only reinforced her feelings for the crotchety old bastard. She wouldn't betray the people she thought were her grandparents, even though I knew by now they had no relation to us at all.

I watched Nightliss as she helped with a wounded initiate. Anger flared in her eyes. She looked at me, lips pressed tight. I knew she wanted to punch Daelissa in the throat as badly as I did. Unfortunately, during her last confrontation with the other angel, she'd nearly died. Despite her recovery, she couldn't solo Daelissa—not a chance.

Thomas held a meeting with the surviving commanders in his underground war room despite the healer's recommendation he rest for the remainder of the day. Even with the supernatural protection granted him by Daelissa centuries ago, it would take time for the large wound in his shoulder to heal. The only reason I knew about the meeting was because, for some unknown reason, Thomas had invited me. Elyssa and her brother, Michael, were also present, along with Nightliss.

I took Nightliss aside before things got underway and asked her, "Are you sure you're up to being the new Divinity—err Clarion? You don't look like you're back to full strength yet."

"I'm much better, Justin," she said, touching my arm with a dainty hand. "It isn't easy, but I need this. I need to feel useful."

"Have you remembered enough to teach me how to unlock my angel abilities?" At this point I was desperate to make my angel magic more reliable instead of something I couldn't count on.

"I only know how I feel when I want something to happen," she said. "I don't know how to teach it."

"You need to figure it out," I said, a little testily. "If you hadn't noticed, I need the help." I looked away and sighed. Met her eyes again. "Just try. It's all I ask."

"Please don't be angry, Justin," she said. "I will do my best. How, exactly, I do not know."

"At this point, anything would be useful." I ran a hand down my face as if it would wash away the fatigue plaguing me from the earlier fights and injuries. "When?"

"I will make time," she said. Her hand pressed against my chest. "Everything you need is locked in your heart, Justin. You must simply discover how to ignite it."

Relying on Elyssa's shock scrolls certainly wasn't the answer I needed. Neither was waiting until I was in a dangerous situation and relying on instinct. "I'll be by soon," I said. "This can't wait any longer."

Thomas called the meeting to order a few minutes later and asked for reports from the Templars investigating the crime scene atop the church. Even the building's magical protection hadn't been enough to prevent part of the sanctuary from collapsing, and the Templar Chapel where Daelissa had once given initiates their "gifts" and then wiped their minds of the entire incident, was in ruins.

"The remains were difficult to identify, sir," the Templar in charge of cleanup said. "We believe this was a suicide mission from the start. They each planned to fire a round into a commander, and then blow the church. We believe the destruction of the chapel was intentional. Probably a message from Daelissa."

Thomas frowned. "Comb the ruins. I want to know who these assassins were."

"I'm almost certain they were Synod Templars, sir," the young man replied.

"Almost isn't good enough, lieutenant," Thomas said. "Collect blood and have the healers reconstruct images."

144

"The bodies were all but vaporized, sir," the man said, sounding a little nervous now. "The bomb was of nom design. It charred tissue and blood to ash. There may be nothing for the healers to find. The perpetrators weren't wearing armor, just black outfits which resembled nightingale armor, making it easier to destroy all forensic evidence."

I shuddered at the thought someone's body parts reduced to mere evidence. Those assassins had been insane. Then again, Daelissa might have controlled them somehow.

The arcphone in a case on the lieutenant's side buzzed. He flicked on the screen and looked at it for a moment. "Sir, they've found something."

"What is it?" Thomas said.

"The healers found bone fragments with undamaged marrow inside belonging to a human Templar." He projected a holographic image from his phone, depicting a young man with brown hair. "This is what the man probably looked like. We're running his image through our records to see if there's a match."

"Anything else?" Thomas asked.

The man's face grew pensive. "I'm afraid the second finding is even more troubling." The image of a yellowed tooth popped from the phone. He didn't have to explain why the image might give us cause for concern.

The tooth was quite clearly a vampire fang.

# Chapter 19

"Oh, crap," I said.

Elyssa gripped my arm. "The covert meeting at the Grotto between the leaders must have been about this," she said.

"Earlier, I thought we were jumping to conclusions about there even being a meeting," I said. "But in this case, I think you're spot on."

"Commander, we have more information," Elyssa said to her father. She told him about the suspected meeting and the attendees.

"What an unholy alliance," Christian Salazar said, lips peeled back in a grimace. "Renegade Templars, Vampires, and possibly Arcanes?"

"If Cyphanis wins the Arcanus Primus special election, there's no telling what he'll direct the Arcane Council to do," said one of the other commanders.

"The council doesn't have nearly the kind of control over Arcanes that the Red Syndicate has over vampires," Thomas said.

"If they declare us outlaws, it won't exactly be helpful," Christian said.

I raised my hand, forgetting for a moment I wasn't in class, and spoke. "How many Templars do we have compared to the Synod?"

"There are twenty-seven legions worldwide," Christian said. "Thirteen joined with us. Ten remained loyal to the Synod and Daelissa. The smallest four legions took neutral stances with no indication which way they might eventually swing."

"There are many individuals from both sides who have left their legions to stand with the side they believe is right in this," Thomas said. "Unfortunately, the Synod received the majority of those defectors."

"So they have the numbers advantage," I said.

He nodded. "But I highly doubt it will come down to a battle of legions," he said. "The Templars have drastically changed over the centuries from a military institution specializing in large-scale battles to smaller units dedicated to quick response and covert action."

"What they did today is a perfect example of Templar evolution," Christian said. "It means we'll have to be even more vigilant."

"How did those men get into the church?" Thomas asked the lieutenant.

The man flicked his arcphone off. "We believe they infiltrated one of our legions by posing as defectors a month or so ago. This made it easy for them to be assigned guard duty to the church."

Thomas cursed. "We can't even trust our own people?"

"We haven't had time to vet them," one of the other commanders said. "We don't have enough Arcanes in our ranks, especially those with truth-saying abilities."

"We need to make vetting a priority," Thomas said. "Outsource if you must."

"Can we trust non-Templar Arcanes?" the man asked.

"I can help with that, sir," Meghan Andretti said. She was the chief Arcane healer in Thomas's legion. "I know several truthsayers we can rely on."

"Thank you, Healer Andretti," Thomas said, some of the tension in his face easing. "We *will* get through this crisis, people."

"Commander, we thought this could wait," Christian said. "But it's obvious it can't any longer. We"—he indicated the other with his hand commanders—"have voted unanimously to elect you as Supreme Commander of the Templar forces."

Thomas regarded them with his trademark stony face. Some of the younger commanders actually gulped under his glare. Finally, he responded. "I am, unfortunately, the most qualified here to lead our combined forces. I will serve in this capacity until unable to do so." He regarded the commanders for a moment. "We have rewritten the rules, people, but this doesn't make us any less Templars than we were before the Synod abandoned the rule of law. Speak with Healer Andretti about truthsayers, and start vetting your people immediately. I'm sure we'll find out soon enough who the other traitors are."

"We should do the same to them," said one of the younger commanders. "Assassinate their leaders, and let them see how it feels. We should go after Bara Nagal first."

Thomas shook his head. "Retaliation is warranted, but not yet. They've shown their hand, perhaps squandered the ace in their deck on this failed assassination attempt." He motioned vaguely at me. "Thanks, yet again, to Mr. Slade, most of us survived."

"My sister warned me," I said. "If not for her, we might all be dead."

Thomas spoke about a few more internal matters, doling out responsibilities to the other commanders, and dismissed everyone. I was on the way out, when he motioned to me. Elyssa paused, but a look from her father sent her from the room as well. This man had nearly taken my head off in a sword fight once. Later, he'd actually apologized to me. Regardless, he still made me very uneasy.

"You impressed me, Justin," he said, his rare use of my first name falling strangely on my ears. "I saw the commotion before the first shot was fired. I believe the bullet which hit me was aimed for Nightliss, because it hit me when I dove for her."

"They were going for a clean sweep," I said, feeling sick to my stomach over the idea of Nightliss's head exploding like a watermelon.

He nodded. "You usually act in an unorthodox capacity with very little planning, sowing nearly as much chaos as you do order."

"It's not like I do this for a living," I said, trying not to sound too defensive.

"I understand. I would ask you to sit in on officer training so you could learn the value of discipline and solid planning, but I have a sense such classes would only hinder you."

I felt my eyes widen at this admission. "You think I should rush in willy-nilly?"

"No." He winced as he tried to move his injured shoulder. "You have the makings of a natural-born leader. You have good instincts and intuition. I've discovered when people with your skillset try to overthink matters, they botch it. I've been around long enough to know. I've seen natural leaders in action. I've learned much from them." He took in a deep breath. "I was not born a leader," he said. "I had to learn the hard way. Even now, I still struggle to see the best path despite all my experience." His eyes seemed to focus on the past for a moment. "Experience will serve you well, but for now, follow your gut and your heart."

"Um, maybe I should go to officer training," I said, not as confident about my abilities as he was.

He offered me the barest hint of a rare smile. "I haven't seen someone with such raw potential since the Revolutionary War," he said. "I think your time would be better spent honing other abilities." He motioned me toward the door. Apparently, the pep talk was over.

"Thanks," I said, and left, feeling a little weirded out by the whole thing. Thomas Borathen wasn't a man I'd heard praise people. Considering our rough history, such high compliments from him made me wonder if I'd somehow crossed into an alternate dimension, or if maybe my deodorant was doing a bang-up job.

Elyssa met me outside, her eyes worried. When I told her about the conversation, her face brightened. "I'm so happy," she said, her eyes misting. "I think he's finally accepted you."

"I thought he already had," I said.

"I think he was tolerating you more than anything," she said, peppering my face with kisses. "And the recognition they gave you at the ceremony was amazing."

I still didn't know what to say about that. "They surprised the heck out of me," I said. "It felt nice to be recognized, but what does it mean?"

Elyssa took my hand and led me down the hall toward the mess hall where the much-delayed lunch was being served. Her eyes narrowed in concentration. "I think my father is setting you up as a leader," she said. "The recognition was one thing, but his talk with you indicates he has bigger plans."

"So he's manipulating me," I said.

She shrugged. "He's positioning a future asset."

I sighed. "You military people make it all sound so impersonal."

Elyssa shoved me against a wall and pressed her lips to mine, kissing me until I had to come up for air. "Was that personal enough?" she breathed.

"Oh, yes," I panted, partly from lack of oxygen, but mostly from desire.

149

Her face turned serious. "Did your sister tell you anything else while she was here?"

I nodded. "Told me Mom is being held in the basement of the Conroy's house, but even she can't get to her." A groan emerged from my throat. "There has to be some way."

"We'll find it," Elyssa said, gripping my hand tight. "Don't lose faith."

"Yeah, I know," I said, trying to melt the frustration away with a healthy dose of optimism. "Should we tell your dad about the cupids?" I asked. It was something I'd mulled over, but I didn't want a Templar invasion of El Dorado if he saw them as either a threat or another "future asset."

Elyssa pursed her lips, eyes distant. "It's possible he might see them as dangerous variables. I don't know if he'd try to exfil them from the cave or leave them there in the hopes they're currently contained."

"Exfil?" I asked.

"Sorry, another military thing. It means to sneak them out."

"Opposite of infiltrate," I said, filing the jargon deep into the recesses of my mind. "So, I guess that's a 'no' to telling him."

She sighed. "I hate to say it, but I think there's a high certainty he'd go after them, if for no other reason than to remove uncertainty. Let's keep it quiet for now."

I nodded. "I just hope he isn't pissed later when and if we tell him."

"We should tell him about your mother, though."

My gut instinct was to say no to Elyssa's suggestion. Then again, it couldn't hurt. Thomas might even throw in a helping hand if the Templars added another angel to their arsenal. "Do you plan to tell him about breaking into Darkwater?"

Her lips parted a fraction. "On the other hand, maybe we shouldn't tell him just yet. Let's see how our plans pan out."

I spotted Katie coming down the hallway. Her eyes brightened when she saw me. "I'm so glad you're okay," she said. "The explosion—I don't know how you survived."

"Same way as usual," I said. "Blind luck and Axe Body Wash."

She laughed but sobered quickly. "It isn't luck. No matter how hopeless things look, you never give up. If anyone can beat the odds, it's you."

"Why didn't you or Nightliss tell me about her becoming the new Divinity, or whatever you call her?" I leaned back against the wall with Elyssa to my right. "She's still way below a hundred percent."

"She didn't want to tell you. She thought you'd discourage her." Katie's eyes looked worried. "You're not mad at us are you?"

"No." I sighed. "I just don't want her falling into a relapse. I don't know how much stress giving 'gifts' causes, but it's a risk, and we need her full strength for what's to come." I remembered how strong Katie's grip had been earlier. Something about her had changed, and it wasn't from working out. The answer hit me. "Did she give you a gift?"

Katie offered a sheepish grin. "I let her try it out on me to see how the strain would be. She can't protect us against the Brightling curses or make us as strong and fast as Daelissa made other Templars, but there's a huge difference." She flexed her hand. "Now I know how Ash and Nyte feel."

"You're not indestructible," I said. "Don't go playing superhero."

"Pot, meet kettle." She grinned. "I won't. I will be training with the initiates, though. Maybe I can learn some karate." She made a chopping motion with her hand.

Elyssa laughed. "I think it's amazing what Nightliss is doing. I hope you go far."

"Thanks," Katie said, her eyes softening. "I want to make a difference. It's boring being a nom."

"Will you keep going to school?" I asked.

"Yeah," she said wistfully. "I'll train when I'm not working. My parents made me get a job. They told me I need to learn responsibility."

"I don't think that'll be a problem with training," Elyssa said. She motioned toward the kitchen. "Let's eat. I'm starving."

My stomach rumbled in agreement.

The three of us sat at the table with Thomas and Leia, Elyssa's mother. The woman's attitude toward me was positively rosy compared to the last time I'd seen her. Even so, the conversation consisted mainly about Templar stuff, so I mostly listened and tried to keep the wise cracks to a minimum.

By the end of the day, I was more than ready to be out of there. Templars kept coming up to me to shake my hand. Embarrassingly enough, some even asked for autographs. When we got back to the mansion, I felt dead on my feet.

Lornicus, of course, chose that time to call. "It appears the brotherhood has homed in on Queens Gate," he said. "I'm not entirely clear on the details, but it has something to do with you and Harry Shelton."

I groaned. "Let me sleep. I'll tell you about it tomorrow."

"I'm sure it will only take a moment for you to tell me," he said. "It's important I know if I'm to keep you protected."

I grumbled some dirty words and told him about the car chase. And since I figured he would find out soon enough, I also told him about the assassination attempts.

"Goodness," he said. "Daelissa wishes to clear the table of opposition, it would seem."

"Obviously," I said, stifling a yawn. "Can I go to bed now?"

"I have more information for you," the golem said. "Information you may be very interested in—if you can remain conscious."

I almost nodded off, and jerked awake just in time to keep the phone from slipping from my fingers. "Wha—huh?"

He chuckled. "I believe this will wake you up."

I shook my head to clear it of sleep. "Just spit it out."

"It's about your mother."

Adrenalin shocked me wide awake. "Really? Tell me."

"As a matter of security, the Conroys rarely stay in one place for very long. They own a network of houses, all fully furnished, and move from place to place to prevent anyone from discovering where they live."

My heart sank. *We just found out where they live!* "Did they just move?" I asked.

"No, but according to my spies, they will be moving in two days."

*Two days? Oh, crap.* "How did you find out?" I asked.

"It appears they have a bit of a logistics problem," he said, voice sounding amused. "One which they did not have the last time."

"Stop beating around the bush," I groaned. "This is important."

"In two days they will relocate to another home. In addition, they will move your mother. If you wish to rescue her, it will probably be your last chance."

# Chapter 20

Adrenalin made sleep a distant memory. *They're moving Mom in two days?* I considered it for a moment. "You're sure about this?"

"I am," he said. "The semi-trucks used to move very dangerous supernatural criminals are a rare resource. Every time one of these vehicles is employed, I'm notified."

"Daelissa can't teleport her to the new location?" I asked.

"Seraphim have limits," Lornicus said. "Their ability to blink is based on line of sight. If they cannot see through an object like the back of a semi-trailer, they cannot escape from it. And Daelissa would be hard-pressed to keep your mother contained during such a move by herself, even if she is much stronger."

"I take it they can't put her in an astral prison while moving her?"

"To my understanding, it would be impossible."

When he didn't elaborate, I asked, "Is it possible to break someone from an astral prison?"

"Every cell has a key, yes?" he said laconically.

"Of course."

"The creator of the micro-dimension, which houses the prisoner, creates the key when they create the prison. But the key is not something physical. Rather, it is more like a word or thought which must be sent by the creator." He sighed. "Otherwise, an astral prison is somewhat impenetrable."

"If the person who casts it dies…" Horror at the idea choked off the rest of the question.

"There is literally almost no way to free the prisoner," Lornicus finished.

"You said 'almost'. That leaves the possibility of breaking someone out," I said.

"Indeed. Someone of your particular persuasion might manage it, or a skilled summoner." He paused, as if letting the suspense build. I kept my mouth shut. "To penetrate such a prison, the use of a powerful demon would be a necessity."

I had no skills in that area, so I didn't know what he meant by his "persuasion" comment. On the other hand, rescuing Mom in transit sounded like our best bet. "Do you know the details of her transport?" I asked. "Will Daelissa or the Conroys be present?"

"I believe I can safely say no to both of those questions," he replied. "I do not know for sure, of course, but judging from the way the Conroys operate by hiding in plain sight, they will secure your mother, go about their usual business, and secure her at the new residence. It is possible they may even move her to a more permanent holding facility. I've heard rumors Darkwater has been working on such a place."

"Their own personal prison?" I blew out a breath and fought back more questions. *Mom first.* "What else do you know about the truck?"

"The transport was leased by the Templars—those loyal to the Synod, of course. They listed it for transporting a dangerous Arcane."

His mention of the Synod helping the Conroys reminded me of the meeting at the Grotto. While Daelissa was out making best buds with the vampires, the Synod Templars, and probably other higher-ups in supernatural nations, our side had been diddling its collective thumbs.

"Unfortunately," Lornicus said, "I have no further details. I do not know the route, or who will be guarding it, though Darkwater will almost certainly be involved."

"They're definitely moving her in two days?" I asked.

"That is when the truck is scheduled to leave the facility, yes."

"You have a destination address?"

"I can secure such information for a price, Mr. Slade."

Even though I already knew the answer, I asked anyway. "What's the price?"

"Why, a Seraphim infant, of course."

"As in just one?"

"I believe that would be fair compensation." Lornicus made a pleased noise. "This can be highly profitable for both of us, and all

155

you need do is remove one infant and bring it to me. I promise the child will never want for anything."

True, the baby might be well-tended, but what kind of psycho would Lornicus raise? In the short term, I might rescue my mother, but in the long term, we might have an even more dangerous adversary than Daelissa to worry about. "Tell me exactly what you intend to do with the baby," I said.

"Feed him, teach him, clothe him—"

I felt my jaw tighten. "I mean in the long run, smartass."

"I will expose him to various stimuli and raise him to suit my needs," Lornicus said in a matter-of-fact tone.

"Brainwash."

"A rather crude term."

"Absolutely not," I said. "You'd have to promise—"

"Mr. Slade, I will not negotiate the rearing of the child. Do you wish me to find the destination and route for your mother, or not?"

"You'll need to do more than that to deserve an angel baby," I said. "You'll need to directly help us rescue her."

"Unfortunately, I cannot. If Daelissa sees my master's golems helping you in any way, she'll think he's abandoned his neutral stance and come out against her. This would make him very angry, and I'm afraid he would destroy me."

"He *should* oppose her," I said. "What she wants is wrong. It's bad for us, and it's bad for him if he's telling the truth about enjoying this life."

"I believe he is sincere in his desire to preserve this place," Lornicus said. "But he believes balance and moderation is the key."

I groaned. "Moderation? *Moderation?* There is no moderation when it comes to world domination and invasion."

"He has events well in hand," Lornicus said tartly, as if I'd just insulted him directly. "Do not expect him to choose one side over the other."

"Because he's on the third side," I said. "His side."

"These are very interesting times, Mr. Slade," Lornicus said. "A great split in former alliances. The harbingers have aligned themselves with the Templar factions. Daelissa has already spent her best assets on a failed assassination attempt."

"Why don't you make some popcorn and enjoy the show?" I asked emphasizing a tone of disgust. "And just sit by while good people die."

"Now, now, Mr. Slade. I believe our information sharing has already proven to be quite helpful in your endeavors. Don't ruin a good thing." He made a tutting noise. "Perhaps you should sleep on it and decide about my price tomorrow." The line went dead.

I growled and resisted throwing the phone on the floor. Elyssa entered the bedroom, smiling and humming something to herself. She noticed my face and frowned. "What's wrong?"

"We have two days to plan a prison transport jailbreak," I said.

Her eyes widened. "Is that all?"

I nodded, and filled her in on the details.

"We definitely can't let Lornicus have a cupid," she said. "Besides, Stacey, Bella, and I are breaking into Darkwater tomorrow night."

"Tomorrow?" I said, a shock of panic racing through me.

"Calm down," she said, and kissed me on the cheek. "The timing of Lornicus's new information is perfect. If Darkwater is handling the transport, maybe they'll have information on the route and destination. We don't need to give up a cupid to Lornicus. Our original mission was to search for the location of the Conroys, but if breaking someone out of an astral prison is really as hard as Lornicus claims, then rescuing your mother en route really might be our best hope."

"Unless Lornicus somehow already knows about our plans to break into Darkwater and gave us this information to trick us into doing something else."

"Justin, don't try to second-guess him." Elyssa squeezed my hand. "Let's move forward with the plan—"

"I'm coming," I said. "I'm not letting you do this alone."

"No, Justin," she said, steel in her voice. "This requires finesse and stealth. Any more than three people will be too many."

"I can watch the outside. Warn you if anyone is coming in."

Her eyes hardened. "I said no, and I meant it. We've spent a lot of time planning this. We know what we're doing. So help me, if I find out you've gone anyway, I will flay you with my katana and move back in with my parents."

I felt my mouth drop open and my eyes go wide with hurt. "If you don't want me helping just say so," I said sarcastically. "I don't want to get in the way."

She rolled her eyes. "How many times have you run off without letting me come along, or without even telling me?" She took my hands. "Justin, I love you, but you have to believe in me and my team. We can do this."

I felt the wind go out of my sails as my shoulders slumped in defeat. "Fine."

"There is one thing you can do," she said, as if something had just occurred to her. "Since Kassus wants you so badly, maybe you could put in an appearance somewhere far away and draw him and his gang out of the Grotto. Maybe even the Atlanta area altogether."

Playing bait wasn't usually my idea of a good time, but if it made Elyssa's task any easier, it was a no-brainer. "I'll make sure I get his attention," I said with a confident grin.

She purred, sounding almost like Stacey as she nipped my ear. She'd obviously been hanging out with the felycan too much.

"Let's go to bed." Her lips worked down my neck, sending electric waves of pleasure tingling through my skin.

I took her in my arms and fell onto the soft bed with her.


The next morning, I told Shelton and Adam about Mom. I also told them about Elyssa and her gang infiltrating Darkwater that night.

"I know all about it," Shelton said, looking worried and miserable. "Bella told me if I tried to interfere, she'd leave me because it meant I didn't trust her."

I chuckled, remembering how similar Elyssa's words had been.

"It ain't funny," Shelton said. "What if something happens to her, man? I don't know what I'd do." He seemed to suddenly remember Adam was there and covered his worry with his poker face.

The attempt obviously didn't slip under Adam's radar. "You need to stop repressing," he said, rolling his eyes. "Bella, Elyssa, and Stacey are more than capable taking care of themselves. If there's anyone I'd be worried about, it's the poor saps that get in their way."

"Yeah, well what if Meghan was going?" Shelton said.

Adam shrugged. "She knows how to handle herself. These women are more than capable."

I knew he was right. "I hope they can get the route information and times for moving Mom," I said. "Otherwise, I don't know what else to do."

Shelton pulled up the schematic of a semi-truck on his arcphone. "Special transport trucks are about as secure as they get," he said. "The trailer is made almost entirely of diamond fiber, and the doors are sealed with blood so only the person who closed them can open them."

I remembered my time as a captive in Maximus's Colombian compound. He'd used his blood to seal the diamond fiber straps around me, and only quick thinking by Felicia had gotten me out of that when she dug in his garbage and found a bloody tissue he'd used after cutting himself while shaving.

"So, even if we take out the guards and take control of the truck we're screwed," I said. "Because there's no way to break it open."

"Can we use the arch to get inside?" Adam asked.

Shelton shook his head. "The trailer is identical to every other one like it. You remember what happened last time we didn't have a precise location." He looked to me. "What about that blink thing you do?"

"Similar issue. I have to see my destination," I said. "Otherwise, my mom could probably escape on her own."

"Once the Conroys move to the new house, we should be able to raid their old one," Adam said. "Maybe dig through the garbage and find traces of blood."

"But, whose blood will they use?" I asked.

"I'd be willing to bet Jeremiah's," Shelton said. "But Arcanes like him don't just leave bodily fluids lying around for his rivals to get hold of. You can do some nasty stuff with someone's blood, even if it's old. He probably uses magic disposal to get rid of loose hairs and that kind of stuff."

"Back to square one," I grumbled.

"I disagree," Adam said. "Nobody's perfect. With enough planning, we can get the blood. First, though, we need to know whose blood."

Shelton pursed his lips. "Yeah, I suppose you're right." He threw up his hands. "I'm gonna hate waiting while the girls are off on their little mission."

"We don't have to wait," I said. "Elyssa asked me to help with a diversion to draw the Darkwater people away from their HQ."

"Good idea," Shelton said, face brightening. "I assume we'll use the omniarch to travel somewhere?"

"I'm thinking Bogota." I said.

"Why there?" Adam asked.

"If we appear in Bogota, Kassus's people will have to use the Obsidian Arch in La Casona to get there," I said. "As the Templar commander in Colombia, Christian Salazar has the authority to shut down the arch and keep the Darkwater people from returning to Atlanta anytime soon."

"Oh, I see." Shelton clapped me on the shoulder. "Good thinking, man."

"Elyssa and her crew will need to use the omniarch tonight to open a portal inside Darkwater," I continued, trying not to smile to broadly at Shelton's compliment. "We'll need Meghan here to reopen a portal for us so we can get the hell out of Bogota once Kassus and his crew show up."

Adam took out his phone and tapped on the screen. "I'll text her about it."

"This is gonna be fun." Shelton pursed his lips. "Why don't we use this opportunity to ambush Kassus and get him off our case for good?"

Adam's eyebrows shot up. "You really want to ambush that monster? He isn't some hack, Shelton. You're strong, but this guy knows all the tricks."

"And my magic is unpredictable at best," I added. "Do you really think we can catch this guy off guard? Besides, he won't be alone if we do our job right."

Shelton made a back-handed motion. "Yeah, you're right. It'd just be nice to have this monkey off my back."

"Agreed," I said. "But we aren't ready to take him on just yet."

He nodded. "True." Stretched, and stood. "Well, at least we won't have to storm the Conroy stronghold to rescue your mom after all. I'm gonna study these semi-trucks and see if I can figure out a weak point."

Adam left to meet with Meghan, so I contacted Christian and asked for his help in shutting down the Obsidian Arch in La Casona once I drew threw Kassus's men.

"I can do that," he said after I explained the situation.

"Any tips for hijacking an arcane prison truck?" I asked.

"Templars usually escort them, so I have a little inside knowledge," he said. "Your best bet is to disable the escorts first, and use them to block the truck. Don't let the size of the semi-truck fool you, either. It may look like a typical nom tractor-trailer, but the engines are magically enhanced for extra speed if it needs to escape."

"Anything else I should know?"

Christian paused a moment. "The doors are always blood sealed. Protocol demands the sealer not accompany the convoy, but proceed to the destination, leaving a vial of blood in another secure location should something happen to him. Since you're dealing with a rogue operation, I doubt they'll follow protocol and set aside a blood vial. This means you'll need to secure the blood from the person who sealed it."

"Isn't there some way to open the trailer in case of emergency?" I asked. "Like a magic word?"

There was no hesitation in Christian's answer. "Without the sealer's blood, no, I'm afraid not."

I thanked him and hung up feeling even more discouraged about the entire thing. I saw two major problems. One, we'd never done anything like this before, and two, we didn't have nearly as many people as Darkwater, if it came down to a fight. We'd need to neutralize the escorts instantly, leaving only the semi-truck to deal with.

I sketched scenarios on an arctablet, straining my imagination to come up with some way we could incapacitate highly-skilled battle mages without killing them. I didn't even know what kind of escorts to expect. Would they be in normal vehicles, or might they utilize aircraft? Templars commonly used sliders disguised as helicopters, and I had no doubts Darkwater had access to all sorts of gadgets, magical and tech-based alike.

*Part of being a good leader is knowing when you don't know jack.*

My next vital steps involved grabbing donuts and a monster-sized energy drink from the kitchen, and placing a phone call to Thomas Borathen. I called the compound—the old man had never given me his digits—and after a few minutes of waiting, someone put him on the line. Leaving out Elyssa's plans for Darkwater, I explained the transport situation. "I don't know what the hell I'm doing."

"And you want my help," Thomas said, voice neutral.

I laid out more facts about a possible ambush. "There aren't nearly enough of us to fight a battle if it comes to that. I think overwhelming force will allow us to take the transport without incident. That's where you can help."

He grunted. "I want you to think about this carefully. Darkwater is comprised of Arcanes. The transport is ostensibly being used to transport a dangerous Arcane."

"Right," I said, trying to see where he was headed with this.

"So, you see the problem."

I pulled away from my phone and gave it a confused look as if Thomas could see my face. *What's he getting at?* I opened my mouth to ask for clarification when I suddenly saw his point. "To observers, this is an internal Arcane affair."

"Precisely," Thomas said.

"A force of Templars interfering in an Arcane matter would look pretty bad."

"The political situation is already dire," he replied. "The Synod retained its position on the Overworld Conclave even though the Templars split. Bara Nagal and his political advisors are attempting to cast us as dangerous rebels who should be put down. If we're seen attacking an Arcane convoy, it will give Cyphanis Rax extra ammunition for the council to side with the Synod Templars should he win the special election."

I sank into a chair. It was all so complicated. I'd never had to worry about politics, but things had changed. Thomas's decision to acknowledge me during the initiation ceremony made a lot more sense now. I wasn't just some upstart kid anymore, I was a political symbol right along with him and Nightliss thanks to my constant meddling.

"My mother is Seraphim," I said, grasping at straws. "That makes this an inter-super conflict which gives the Templars jurisdiction."

162

"Do you have proof your mother is actually onboard?"

I had no proof aside from the word of Lornicus.

Thomas apparently took my silence as an answer. "You grasp the situation better now, don't you?"

"My mother would make a powerful ally," I said, trying to think in military terms. "Isn't it worth the gamble?"

"That's a good question," he said. "Does the risk outweigh the reward?"

"I think so." Or was I thinking with my heart instead of my head?

"Let me give you more information," Thomas said, not a hint of condescension in his voice. "The Synod moved a legion to the west side of Atlanta. They're constructing a compound and dispersing units into the region my forces patrol."

"Can't you stop them?" I asked.

"Only if I want a war we're not prepared to fight," he said.

"They started a war yesterday."

"Even if that's true, it doesn't mean we're ready to fight them."

I blew out a frustrated breath. *Screw it. He's not going to help.* "I guess we'll just have to make do." I wasn't going to beg for help.

"I will intercede if you request it," Thomas said.

"Intercede? As in, troops and everything?"

"Overwhelming force or whatever suits the situation." Thomas's voice was firm. "I've given you the facts. I've explained the possible consequences. Now that you are informed, I am placing the final decision in your hands, Mr. Slade."

"Let's say we hijack the transport," I said. "Can we claim jurisdiction and demand the sealer open the vessel?"

"They will likely show a false manifest, and claim the Templars acted without proof or jurisdiction. Political pressure would be applied. It's also possible the Synod would step in and ally itself with the Arcane Council to force us to return the transport."

As my mind considered the political ramifications of involving the Templars, especially when we needed to win the hearts and minds of Arcanes and other supers if we had any hope of forming an anti-Daelissa alliance, it made me wonder if this was Thomas's way of testing me. Was he truly offering help, or just seeing how stupid I really was?

My mind ran in circles before I finally said, "Are you serious about helping me if I give you the go-ahead?"

"Do I sound serious?" he replied.

"Always," I said.

"Then you have your answer."

I knew the decision was too complicated to make without conferring with the others. "Let me consider all the options," I said, quoting a military movie I'd seen before. "Maybe there's a better way to handle this."

"Very well." Thomas disconnected without another word.

# Chapter 21

That afternoon, our group of six conspirators met for a late lunch and to prepare for Operation Clearwater, a nickname Bella had given our scheme. I explained my plan to use Christian to trap Darkwater people in Colombia so Elyssa and crew could infiltrate their corporate headquarters and search for information regarding my mother's transportation route, discover whose blood would seal her transport, and, last but not least, dig up any useful information on the research Darkwater was doing on the arches and control rooms. We would need the information if we had any hope of using the Alabaster Arch in El Dorado to find the Grand Nexus and, if possible, destroy it.

Adam had written a script to search the magic-based computer system Darkwater employed. Such systems were called Arcsys datacenters and used spells similar to what ASEs used to store data. All Elyssa had to do was attach her arcphone to an Arcsys node and run the script—at least in theory.

I also mentioned my conversation with Thomas. Elyssa and the others furrowed their brows in almost perfect unison when I told them he'd left the decision up to me.

"I knew he was setting you up for leadership," Elyssa said, "but this is unheard of."

"Thomas Borathen really said he'd give you the final decision?" Shelton said, sounding baffled. "The old man is losing it."

"Thanks," I replied, voice heavy with sarcasm. "I'm not sure what to do."

"We don't have enough intel," Elyssa said. "We need the schedule, the identity of the person sealing the doors, and the route. Then we can plan how to handle it."

"I realize that," I said. "At least we have another option on the table, and that's good."

"It's bloody wonderful," Stacey said, her eyes narrowed to contented slits as she regarded me like a cat might regard a bowl of milk.

"How do you plan to let Kassus know you're in Bogota?" Elyssa asked.

I offered her a knowing smile. "You just let me worry about that, okay?"

She gripped me by the front of the shirt and pulled me close. "Fine," she whispered with a grin, and pecked me on the lips. "I love you. Good luck."

Shelton said his goodbyes to Bella while Adam did the same to Meghan. It felt like we were going on a long trip and wouldn't be back for a week, though if everything went well, we'd be back in town the minute Kassus fell for our ploy. Ryland sauntered into the room, prowling like a wolf on the hunt. I noticed he wore his sideburns in the mutton-chop look he'd favored the first time I met him.

"You guys need a fourth?" he asked, running a hand through his short thick hair. "I'd be happy to run with you."

"Kassus might add you to his lists of targets," I said. "It might not be a good idea."

He shrugged. "I ain't worried about that."

"My wolfy will make sure nothing bad happens," Stacey said, her eyes examining Ryland's posterior.

"Won't find me turning away help," Shelton said.

Ryland was a Templar, and he could turn into a really big wolf, so he might be handy in case things went from bad to worse. In my book, that was always a possibility. "Let's go, then."

"We set up a long-range ASE to keep an eye on Darkwater headquarters," Elyssa said. "If it spots any commotion, we'll let you know."

"We'll leave the portal open for our return from Bogota," I said. "But if we see an opportunity to lead the Darkwater people on a longer chase we will, especially if Christian is delayed in shutting down access to the Obsidian Arch so they can't return."

"Sounds like a remarkably well-considered plan," Stacey said with a wink.

We went downstairs to the omniarch. Christian had sent me the picture of an empty room in a Templar safe house near La Casona for the portal exit. I concentrated on the image, and the image of the room appeared in the center of the omniarch. When we stepped inside, I noticed the portal had opened in the middle of a wall. As we'd seen before, the physical world seemed to warp around the shimmering gateway, unaffected in any other way. Through the thin gap between the wall and the outer edge of the portal I saw another room.

"That thing isn't gonna bring the house down, is it?" Shelton asked, looking uneasily at the way the wall bent around the opening like rubber, even though it remained solid as ever to the touch.

"The wall would have already collapsed by now," I said.

"Peculiar," Ryland said, pressing a hand against it. "I wonder what would happen if you opened it on a person."

"Nobody had the guts to be the guinea pig for that little experiment," Shelton said.

We left the room, walked down a hallway, and into a large foyer. A Templar sitting at a desk looked up. "Justin Slade and company, I presume?"

"That would be us," I said.

"The La Casona way station is just down the road. We sent a couple of scouts to check it out, and they reported two suspicious individuals watching the door to the pocket dimension."

*Perfect.*

Unlike the Grotto, the Obsidian Arch at the La Casona way station was above ground and covered by a large warehouse around which jellyfish-like creatures called minders patrolled to keep out the noms. The door leading inside the pocket dimension was inside a courtyard.

"Thanks," I said. "You have the image of Maulin Kassus?"

"Of course," he said. "The minute you give the word, we'll lock down the arch and tell everyone it's because of Gloom fractures."

"Thanks," I said. We left the nondescript house, part of a connected row of houses lining a winding street, and headed toward the La Casona way station. A minder approached us when we went to the gate guarding the entrance to the warehouse grounds, but a Templar waved it off, and let us through. Once inside, we headed toward the door leading into the La Casona pocket dimension.

"I'll watch your backs," Ryland said, slipping away into the crowd and vanishing.

As we approached the simple wooden doors disguising the entrance into the pocket dimension, I spotted Black Robe Brotherhood thugs examining the crowd. One of them locked gazes with me. His gaze flicked to a piece of parchment in his hand and back to me. I pretended not to notice, watching him out of the corner of my eye.

There were only two of them from what I could tell. If they charged us, we could handle it.

"They're calling someone," Adam said as we walked toward the stables.

My phone rang seconds later. It was Elyssa.

"At least thirty men plus Kassus just ran out of Darkwater like their asses were on fire," Elyssa said. "You're going to have company any minute."

"Thanks, babe," I said, and disconnected. "Looks like the diversion worked," I said to the others.

"We have a problem," Ryland said, suddenly appearing at my shoulder.

I nearly jumped out of my skin.

"What is it?" Shelton asked.

"Every minder patrolling the perimeter just changed course."

"Where are they going?" I asked.

"Right here," Ryland said pointing at the ground.

"Can't the Templars hold them off?" I asked.

"The Templars on duty tried, but the minders ain't listening." He looked over his shoulder.

Shelton's lip curled into a grimace. "I should have remembered, dammit. Darkwater is the contractor that finds minders in the Gloom and brings them here. I'll bet they have some agreement with the friggin monsters."

"Let's go before they surround us," I said.

"Too late for that," Ryland said. "All the exits are blocked."

"If one of those things even touches you, you won't be able to move," Adam said, his eyes searching the area. "We'll be dead meat."

I scowled and cursed. "There's got to be some way—" my eyes settled on the stable. "The control room, hurry!"

I saw the brotherhood members pacing us as we headed for the stables. Rather than circle around the wooden structure, we dashed through. A long aisle ran between stalls holding all sorts of beasts. Ryland and I pressed our backs flat against the wall on either side of the door. Our two admirers entered. They locked eyes on Shelton and Adam ahead, never once glancing to the sides. I karate-chopped my man on the back of the neck, and sent him sprawling into a pile of steaming dung. Ryland's target hit the floor a second later. I took their wands and staffs, broke them to useless splinters. I grabbed their arcphones but passwords foiled my attempts to access them. I flung them into a heaping pile of elephant manure.

We raced across the stable, out the other door, and took a left around the corner into the narrow alley between the stable and the wall. The setup was identical to the other way stations and Shelton located the hidden door within seconds. He opened the door. Two arch operators looked up in surprise. I ran across the control platform and looked down the center aisle. It appeared free of Darkwater employees.

"You can't just come in here," one of the operators said, pulling out a phone.

"Templar business," Ryland said, pulling a badge on a lanyard from within his shirt. "Go about your business."

The man eyed us warily, but tucked his phone away.

We jogged toward the back and found a row of omniarches on the right side in an alcove, exactly where they'd been in the other control rooms. They looked intact, but that didn't guarantee anything. We stepped inside the silver circle. I pressed a finger to it and willed it closed. The static feel of aether filled the air around us. I imagined the omniarch room beneath the mansion, picturing every detail the best I could, and willed the portal open.

The omniarch flickered with static. A jagged bolt of energy flashed against the silver circle, narrowly missing Shelton. He cried out in surprise. I was about to tell everyone to abandon ship when the space between the columns flashed into an image of the mansion arch room.

"Yes!" Adam said.

I heard shouts and looked down the aisle to see a line of minders heading our way, their tentacles waving eagerly, hungry to feed on our thoughts while the arch operators recoiled with horror.

"Go, dammit!" Shelton said, pushing me.

I stumbled through. The world warped, snapped back into place, and I stood feet away from the omniarch beneath the mansion, the image of the room in the Templar house still visible through it since we'd never closed the connection. Everyone else entered right on my heels. My phone dinged. I looked to see a text message from Christian.

*The Obsidian Arch is shut down. The Darkwater people will be stuck at the La Casona way station for as long as I can manage.*

"We did it!" I said.

"Thank god," Shelton said, taking a step toward the room exit. An invisible force seemed to push him back. The air around us warped and bent like a bubble.

*Disconnect*, I thought to the portal we'd just come through. The image of the control room at La Casona flickered away, but a shimmering portal remained. Jagged bolts of energy flashed between the gateway behind us and the mansion's omniarch.

"Close the other portal," Shelton said. "They're reacting off each other!"

"I'm trying!" I willed the portal we'd just used closed again. Energy arced, popping and crackling off an invisible barrier around us. I tried to deactivate the mansion omniarch. The image between the columns flickered to a silvery sheen. With a loud pop, the two portals suddenly shut down. The bubble of energy around us warped into an oblong shape and snapped back into a sphere. The world flickered.

We stood in utter darkness even my supernatural sight couldn't penetrate. Freezing cold stabbed into my lungs. I heard someone suck in a harsh breath.

I realized, with horror, this was the same way I'd ended up in El Dorado the first time.

*Flicker.*

We stood in a large square tiled with giant slabs of stone. A monolithic pyramid stood in the background. I had no trouble recognizing the place. It was the city of death, El Dorado. I didn't want to be here. *Anywhere but here.*

*Flicker.*

We stood on a rocky plain of shining obsidian. Twin moons hovered on opposite sides of the horizon, one dark and shadowy, the other brilliant white. Two feminine figures stood a hundred feet distant, the thick hair on their heads writhing like snakes. They stood with legs spread shoulder width, hands reaching for the sky. Their heads tilted back, mouths gaping inhumanly wide. An eerie chorus reverberated in my skull. I clamped hands to my ears, but the song filled me up, vibrating my body like a tuning fork. Pressure built from the inside. The song wouldn't stop. It wouldn't stop! My teeth clamped together.

*Quiet!*

"Look at the stone," Adam said in a halting voice, his hands also pressed tight to his ears. A grimace contorted his face.

Two thick columns of rock spaced a hundred or more feet apart grew from the stony terrain, twisting into glittering vortexes. As they grew, a vein of white laced through the obsidian.

*They're growing an Alabaster Arch!*

These might be the people who made the Grand Nexus. Who made the Obsidian Arches.

*Flicker.*

We stood in a control room, though it looked double the size of the others I'd seen before. The agonizing song vanished from my head, the pressure abating from my skull. I slumped and heard sighs of relief from the others. A monstrous Alabaster Arch, rivaling the size of the Obsidian Arches, stood before us, a dim white glow emanating from the white veins. Hordes of cherubs stood frozen around us. The nearest one twitched. Its featureless black head jerked toward us, arms jutting out.

"Dah nah!" it screeched.

The room burst to life as every cherub responded, wobbling toward us on infantile legs.

"Holy mother of baked ham!" Shelton shouted. "Get us out of here!"

Why was this happening to us?

*I just want to go home!*

*Flicker.*

We stood in a carpeted room. A leather couch sat in front of a television. A man biting into a slice of pizza screamed. Pizza still in hand, he flipped backward over the couch and scuttled on his butt toward the kitchen. Déjà vu smacked me in the face. I recognized this place.

*It's home.*

My childhood home.

The furniture had changed, but not the layout. Why were we here? I looked around in confusion before an idea clicked into place. I'd wanted to go home, and the bubble had taken us here. Now all I had to do was turn this infernal portal off!

*Disconnect! Turn off! Deactivate! Stop!*

The bubble winked out. A woman in a T-shirt and loose-fitting pajama bottoms patterned with pink cats screamed and dropped a glass of water. The glass shattered on the tile floor even as the gibbering man with pizza scooted through the spilled water.

"We're free!" I said. "Let's get out of here."

The new homeowners ran shrieking down the hall, slamming a door shut. I was admittedly curious to snoop around my former digs, but now wasn't the time.

The four of us ran out the front door. I motioned them down the street, and we made our way to a strip mall near a laundry mat where my father had first taught me to feed as an incubus. We stood outside, panting. I wondered if the look of horror on Shelton's face mirrored my own.

"How did we get out of the bubble?" Adam asked.

I caught my panicked breath, gathering my thoughts. "Somehow, it took us to places we thought of, though I'm not sure how we actually got there."

"Who the hell were those god-awful singing women?" Ryland asked.

"They were growing an arch," Shelton said. "Singing the thing from the freaking rock."

"Where were we?" Adam asked.

"No idea," I said. "When we ended up in that black void, I realized what was happening to us was the same thing that happened to me when I ended up in El Dorado the first time."

"And then we showed up in El Dorado," Adam said. "I recognized it immediately."

I nodded. "Same here. I just wanted to be anywhere but there."

"And it took us to freak land." Shelton rubbed his jaw. "Those people didn't look like Seraphim," he said. "What if they're really the ones responsible for creating all the arches?"

"They looked like sirens," Adam said, his tone a mix of wonder and terror. "Did you see their hair? It looked alive."

"Nothing good comes from a woman with living hair," Ryland said, picking up a loose stone and tossing it into the woods on the side of the parking lot.

"I was wondering if they were the ones who made the Grand Nexus," I said. "Next thing I knew, we appeared next to that huge Alabaster Arch."

"You think that was the Grand Nexus?" Shelton said.

I nodded. "It seems the likeliest explanation. But we've never seen it before, so how did the portal know to take us there?"

"Maybe because there's only one Grand Nexus, so you don't need a specific image in your mind?" Adam said in an unsure tone.

Shelton's face looked grim. "Well, we know why Daelissa hasn't fixed the arch. The control room is chock-full of cherubs. I ain't stepping foot in there again, that's for damned sure."

"It was ground zero for the Desecration," Adam said.

The control room at the Grand Nexus had been terrifying, but it didn't trouble me nearly as much as knowing the Seraphim might not be the worst thing in the universe we had to worry about.

# Chapter 22

*Elyssa*

Elyssa watched the live feed from the ASE she'd positioned outside the Darkwater HQ from the mansion strategy room. At least thirty black-robed figures plunged through the liquid glass on the front of the Darkwater corporate building, their bodies phasing through the rippling material in lieu of a door. Elyssa felt her heartbeat quicken as a bald man led the group to a levitating transport, his every motion filled with violence and anger.

"That's Kassus," Stacey said, pointing to the man's holographic image as projected by Elyssa's arctablet. Elyssa repressed a shudder. Kassus was probably ordering his minions to trap Justin like a rabbit. She wouldn't let that happen. She called to warn him.

"Thanks, babe," he said, and hung up.

She shook her head at his cavalier tone, but knew with the combined skills of the other men in his party, they should be able to get away easily.

Bella set a timer on her arcphone. "They should be back in the mansion in twenty minutes. Let's get make sure we're ready to go when they arrive."

As the time ticked by, Elyssa loaded her compact satchel with supplies, checked, and rechecked her gear, and tried her best not to worry. Even so, her mind calculated the time it should take Justin and the others to run out of the La Casona way station, cross the road to the safe house, and come back through the portal. Christian Salazar would order the Obsidian Arch shut down at the way station, and trap the Darkwater people in Bogota for several hours.

Even at a non-supernatural pace, it shouldn't take Justin and the others more than ten minutes to return through the portal. But what if the perimeter had somehow been closed?

*Don't worry so much!* Her stomach tightened anyway.

Elyssa huffed, and looked over her gear again.

"It's time," Bella said, the petite dhampyr somehow giving off a commanding aura in the black nightingale armor Elyssa had provided her.

Stacey wore her own set of nightingale armor, the flexible material clinging to her curvy frame and accentuating the movement of her hips as she prowled about the room, obviously as restless as Elyssa. "About bloody time," she said, her British accent thick with tension.

The three women went down to the arch room. The arch appeared inactive, but the men weren't there. She exchanged glances with Bella and Stacey.

"The portal is closed. Shouldn't the boys be back?" Elyssa asked.

"Justin did say they might stay there if they needed to keep the Darkwater people occupied longer," Bella said.

"Yes, but the portal would still be open, right?" Elyssa asked.

"Maybe they came back through, and used it to go somewhere else," Bella replied.

Elyssa called Justin. Her call went straight to voicemail.

"I'm sure they're doing their job," Stacey said. "Probably leading Kassus and his blokes on a merry chase. Let's not dawdle and waste their effort."

Despite the dread clinging to her heart, Elyssa knew the felycan was right. She nodded to Bella. "Let's do this."

Bella flicked on her arcphone and accessed the image of an office. She'd posed as a potential client for Darkwater and toured the offices, taking pictures as she went. They'd determined this particular office as the best point of insertion. The dhampyr concentrated on the image for a long moment. Nothing happened.

"Strange," Bella said. "The omniarch isn't activating." She studied the structure for a moment. "Do you hear that hum? It seems to be coming from the center of the arch."

Stacey walked the perimeter of the silver circle banding the base of the arch. "I hear a faint buzz."

"Me too," Elyssa said.

The portal abruptly flickered on. A man with a slice of pizza clenched in his hand screamed and flipped over the back of a couch. The image winked out before Elyssa could process anything else. The three women looked at each other, confusion wrinkling their foreheads.

"What in the bloody hell was that?" Stacey asked.

"Did I imagine that?" Bella asked.

Elyssa shook her head. "Maybe the office picture isn't working like we thought it would."

"I know it works," Bella said. "I opened a portal there the evening after I made the pictures to be sure it worked."

"Are you jonesing for pizza?" Elyssa asked.

Bella raised an eyebrow. "No, I'm not. Let me try again." She concentrated on the image again.

The inside of the omniarch flickered, and an office with a large oak desk appeared. Bookcases lined the wall behind it, awards, plaques, and even an occasional book populating it.

"I told you it works," she said, shrugging. "I just hope Harry didn't decide to use the portal for a pizza break after they escaped. Especially without calling me."

"Bloody men," Stacey said with a languid smile. "They don't communicate very well."

"No, they don't," Elyssa said, checking her phone again to see if Justin had returned her call and she'd somehow missed it. He hadn't.

Meghan appeared at the bottom of the stairs cellar, breathing heavily. "Sorry I'm late. I was held up at the clinic."

"Thank goodness," Bella said. "I was worried you might not show up."

"So, you just want me to hang around in case the portal closes?" Meghan said.

"If you see anyone besides us coming to the portal, close it," Bella said. "And use the image of this office I gave you to reopen it on our signal, should it be necessary."

"If we need to evac from anywhere else, we'll send you a new picture," Elyssa said.

"Got it," Meghan said, pulling up a chair someone had brought down earlier, and made herself comfortable with a thick romance novel and a glass of wine. "Be careful."

"We will," Elyssa said with a faint smile.

Bella stepped through the portal and into the office. She motioned the others to follow. This particular office had no windows facing the interior of the hallway, making it the perfect place to open a portal since nobody in the hallway could see it. The only downside was its location on the top floor of the four-story building. The lower offices, filled with cubicles had presented too much of an opportunity for discovery.

Stacey opened the office door, and peered up and down its length. She gestured with her hand to signal the all-clear, and vanished down the hall. Elyssa removed two tiny spy-bots from her satchel, and sent them floating down the other corridors to monitor in case someone came.

"These floors are lightly warded," Bella said. "But things will change when we go downstairs."

Elyssa nodded. "It's time."

The two women went down the hallway after Stacey. The felycan had just finished removing a small vent grate about one square foot in diameter from the wall. The vent was far too small for a human to fit through. Stacey touched a symbol on the nightingale armor at her waist. The material retraced to a thin belt, revealing Stacey's naked form. She flexed her body, drew in a deep breath, and her body twisted, claws springing from her fingers, and fur rippling up her fair skin. Her face lengthened into a muzzle lined with sharp teeth while a tail grew from her backside. Within seconds, a black panther stood where Stacey had, its body shrinking even smaller until a small black cat remained. The thin belt of nightingale armor shrank to accommodate the new size.

The kitty looked up at Elyssa and Bella, one of its green eyes winking before it slid through the vent. Bella closed the grate behind the feline, and they moved down the hall to a thick diamond fiber door which led to the staircase. It was locked from the other side, though a rune reader on the wall allowed anyone with the proper access to pass.

"I hope it isn't locked from both sides," Elyssa said.

Bella examined the rune reader. "These look complicated, but you don't need much technical know-how to break them if you're good with deciphering runes."

"Are you good with runes?" Elyssa asked.

"Not particularly. I mean, I can do it, but I'll need a piece of paper and some time."

"Good thing Adam gave me a decryptor for my arcphone then," Elyssa said, chuckling despite the tension.

Bella sighed. "That's good, because rune decryption gives me a headache."

A faint clang sounded in the stairwell. A minute later, the door handle clicked, and the door swung inward. Stacey grinned at them, her body once again covered by the nightingale armor.

"It's a bloody maze in there," she said, retrieving the grate from the floor, and pressing it back into place.

The trio padded down the stairs, the nightingale armor muffling the sounds of their feet as they descended to the bottom floor of the three-story building. The Darkwater Arcsys datacenter likely lay in the basement, close to the large ley lines necessary to power it. At the first floor, the stairwell ended at a door and a blank wall.

Bella scanned the area with her wand. She muttered something in Spanish and tucked the wand away. "No hidden entrance to the basement. The Darkwater consultant told me there's a levitator down to the datacenter."

Stacey raised an eyebrow. "I hate it when they make things difficult. Did he show you where the lift is?"

She shook her head. "He said it he couldn't show it to anyone for security reasons."

Elyssa removed a small clamshell case from her satchel. "Stand back," she said, opening the stairwell door a crack and peering through it. The door opened into a clerical office. Cubicles provided ample cover for her and the others to slip through unnoticed, but they had to know where the entrance to the basement was first.

She opened the case. Red roaches scattered from within, their tiny forms racing across the floor in all directions. She closed the door and opened an app on her arcphone. As the roaches scattered, they mapped the surroundings, relaying it to the app.

"Disgusting but effective," Stacey murmured as she crouched next to Elyssa and watched the map appear.

Someone in the office beyond shrieked.

"Holy crap!" a man cried in panic followed by the sound of more screams and shouts of alarm.

Elyssa opened another app on her phone and directed the screen at her armor. A web of lights danced up and down the surface, and the black armor turned white, loosening until it resembled Arcane robes complete with a patch that read, "Magic Mike's Pest Control". She aimed the phone at the other two women, adjusting their armor to match hers.

"You Templars are sneaky people," Stacey said, regarding the loose-fitting robes. "I like sneaky people."

Elyssa checked the mapping app on her arcphone and saw the roach army had discovered two levitator shafts. One was located in a lobby just behind the front security desk. The other was tucked into the back corner of the first floor. "That's our destination," she said, pointing to the second lift.

"Brilliant," Bella replied. "Let's go."

Elyssa opened the door without attempting to be quiet. The traumatized eyes of the clerical people met hers. She walked up to a woman who'd climbed atop her desk, hair frazzled, and eyes wide with horror. "We're eradicating a roach infestation. You didn't happen to see any on this floor did you?"

"Hundreds of them!" a man said. "Please tell me they're not the flying ones." He shuddered. "They're the most terrifying thing in the world."

Elyssa felt certain the man had never ventured far from home if flying roaches topped his list of horrors. "Don't worry, we'll take care of them," she replied, making a show of aiming her arcphone at the floor, as if scanning for bug prints.

They walked down a hall, passing supply closets and other rooms with cubicles. Elyssa pretended to scan as they went. A man in black robes walked around the corner, his eyes narrowing at the sight of them. "Who the hell are you?" he asked, reaching for a staff at his side.

Elyssa blurred to him, striking him at the base of his neck with a quick chop. He dropped like a wet noodle. She caught him before he thudded to the floor, and carried him inside a nearby closet filled with magical cleaning potions. Elyssa poked him with a Lancer dart to keep him knocked out long enough for them to finish their business.

"Why didn't you let me try to sweet talk him?" Stacey asked.

The thought had popped into Elyssa's mind, but the expression on the man's face told her instantly he'd seen right through the deception. "I didn't want to take a chance, especially with a battle mage."

"Elyssa did the right thing," Bella said. "These men are trained to kill first and ask questions later."

Stacey shrugged. "I've often found a pair of these"—she cupped her breasts—"will get you past just about any man. Even if I have to knock them out while they're distracted."

"What matters," Elyssa said, "is that these disguises should work on anyone who isn't a supervisor or battle mage."

They crept down the hall, listening for the approach of anyone else, but Justin's ruse seemed to have cleared out most of the battle mages. Elyssa checked the time. Only fifteen minutes had passed since infiltration, but it felt like much longer. They had to hurry. And what if they couldn't find the transport schedule for Justin's mom? She pushed her doubts away. They could worry about that when they reached the objective.

"There's the office," Stacey said, pointing down the hall.

A placard on the wall read, *Arcsys Information Director*.

Elyssa peered into the office door. It was a large office, though cluttered with old arcterminals and other bits and pieces of equipment she didn't recognize. A young Asian man sat at the desk inside, his eyes glued to the monitor in front of him. She aimed a Lancer, and nailed him in the chest. With a startled grunt he slumped atop the touchscreen keyboard on the desk.

Bella slipped a lanyard from around the man's neck, and inspected it. "This is his access card," she said, putting it around her neck and tucking it beneath the robes.

Elyssa looked at the screen and saw the picture of a wet cat in a shower, its expression desperate. She pshawed. "Looks like he was working hard."

"That poor kitty," Stacey said, her lips pouting with empathy.

Elyssa tucked the slumbering man away behind a pile of parts so he couldn't be seen from the doorway. At least the clutter had some use. The Lancer dart would keep him asleep for a few hours.

While Bella kept watch on the hallway, Elyssa set her phone atop the touchscreen interface on the administrator's desk. The system looked like an advanced nom computer, though aether powered it instead of electricity and it used the aethernet instead of the internet. She activated the spell Adam had put on the phone, and waited.

*Searching...Arcsys node found.*

*Accessing...*

*Fail. Attempting root spell hack...success.*

Elyssa breathed with relief at the last word her phone screen. Files flashed past on the Arcsys terminal, presumably as Adam's script copied them to her arcphone. Even with her enhanced eyesight, the images moved too quickly to see what it was copying.

*Root access secured. Starting search \*Alice\*...no results found.*

*Starting search \*Alysea\*...no results found.*

"How much longer?" Bella asked, her body tense as she watched the hallway.

"I don't know," Elyssa said. "It's running searches, but it's not finding anything." She looked back at the screen.

*Starting search \*secure transport\*...results found. Accessing...*

The last word remained for so long, she wondered if the arcphone had frozen. "Come on," she said.

"Someone's coming," Bella hissed. "Oh, dear, it's a battle mage." She withdrew her staff, flicked it to full length, and aimed it down the length of the door.

"There's nowhere else to hide," Stacey said, eyes flicking around the room.

Elyssa ducked behind the desk, jerking Stacey down next to her. Bella backed away from the door too late. A man in a black robe appeared just outside the door and stared straight at Bella. Elyssa prepared to launch herself at the man the minute he moved toward the Arcane.

Instead, he merely grunted. "Where the hell is he?" he muttered to himself. "Lazy bastard always taking breaks." The man looked up and down the hallway. "Hey, Minh? I need you. My printer is broken again." He walked away.

Elyssa and Stacey blew out held breaths in unison.

"How the bloody hell?" Stacey whispered.

"I put up an illusion to make the office look empty," Bella said, wiping a bead of sweat from her forehead.

"Why didn't you do that the minute we came in here?" Stacey asked.

"I've been working on it all this time. It's not easy to make a convincing illusion of a complex scene."

Elyssa looked at her phone to see if the program had finished. Instead, large red letters flashed on the screen.

*Access Denied*

# Chapter 23

*Elyssa*

Fighting back the despair, Elyssa touched the phone screen. No response. Had they done all this for nothing? She flicked a finger across the screen again, but still nothing happened. Out of frustration, she rubbed her hand all across the screen.

*Please be patient while I work...*

Elyssa breathed a sigh of relief. At least the program hadn't broken her phone or frozen it.

*All attempts to access data have failed. Touch screen to continue.*

She did so.

*Account lacks permissions to access data node. If you receive this error, it means you'll have to access the Arcsys datacenter directly. Flick the screen to track the specific Arcsys node location.*

At least Adam had provided good instructions in case of an issue. She flicked the screen.

*Tracing...Arcsys node found. Populating map.*

A grid of hexagonal shapes filled her screen. Near the middle of the grid was a section highlighted in red and labeled *00 Access*. In the center of the highlighted section, a big blue "X" appeared on one of the nodes.

"Crap," she said. They'd hoped entering the basement wouldn't be necessary, but since the administrator lacked the credentials for the high-security files, it left them no choice. "It found the node, but we can't access the data from here," she told the others, showing them the map of the Arcsys datacenter.

Elyssa's phone vibrated. She flicked to a new text message from Christian Salazar. *Arcane Council is demanding we reopen the arch. I can't delay for more than fifteen minutes. Better hurry.*

"No, no, no!" Elyssa said, and showed the others the message.

"It bloody figures," Stacey said, shrugging as if they had all day. "I love a challenge."

Bella gritted her teeth and brandished the administrator's access card. "Let's do this, people. To the levitator."

Elyssa dispersed a couple more spy-bots down the corridor leading to the levitator and found the way clear. They hurried down the corridor to their objective. What looked like an empty security desk sat before it, but whoever was supposed to be stationed there had apparently left.

"Broken scroll printer," Bella said, pointing to a black printer with sheets of scroll parchment stacked next to it. Its touchscreen flashed the message, "Please clear jam."

"At least we got lucky on something," Stacey said. "Just hope he doesn't go into the admin's office while we're below."

"Nothing we can do about that," Elyssa said.

Bella swiped the access card across the reader on the outside of the levitator. The door dinged open almost immediately. Elyssa was about to step inside when Bella barred the way with her arm.

"What's wrong?" Elyssa asked.

The Arcane pointed to a silver pattern etched into the marble floor inside.

Elyssa had thought it was simply an aesthetic design. "What is it?"

"It's a ward. If we don't have the proper counter-ward, whatever that may be, we can't step inside there without it activating."

"What happens if it activates?" Stacey asked.

Bella grimaced. "I don't want to find out." She regarded it for a minute. "De-warding it is out of the question as well. I simply don't have time."

"Maybe the administrator has the counter-ward," Elyssa said. "Or maybe his access card is all we need."

Bella tapped her chin, staring at the pattern. "Actually, I think I recognize this pattern."

"You do?" Elyssa asked, daring to hope Bella could deactivate it.

"It identifies whoever steps on it. If you're not supposed to be there…" she trailed off peering at the pattern for a moment. "I think this ward will shock an intruder, and trigger an alarm."

"What if we put the administrator inside and stood on top of him?" Stacey asked.

"It'll still detect us," Bella said.

Stacey prowled the alcove. "Every levitator has another access point for servicing."

"What if I send a spy-bot down the lift with the administrator?" Elyssa said. "It could take a picture of the area below, and maybe we can use the portal to access it." She checked the time on her phone. "We have thirteen minutes before Christian has to reactivate the Obsidian Arch in La Casona."

Bella knelt, eyes tracing the pattern. "See what happens when you put one of your gadgets inside."

Hoping it wouldn't trigger an alert, Elyssa activated a spy-bot orb and let it float inside the lift. It sparked, plunked to the floor, obviously dead. She held her breath, expecting an alarm to wail at any minute.

"Interesting," Bella said, not attempting to retrieve the tiny sphere. "I think the ward disabled, but didn't destroy it. Perhaps it was designed such a way in case someone forgot a phone in their pocket."

"They're awfully protective of this place," Stacey said, eyes scanning the corridor. "If only we knew if this levitation shaft goes up to the roof or not. If it does, we might find an access door."

"Then we could lower ourselves down the shaft," Elyssa said. "But what if there's not enough room to slide past the levitator?"

"As with most magical levitation devices," Bella said, "there may be some slight give if we push it."

Elyssa hadn't dealt with a levitator quite as well protected as this one. "Do you think there's a chance the shaft will be warded?"

"I certainly hope not," Bella said.

Elyssa looked at the progress her army of magic roaches had made on the map and saw the second floor was nearly complete. She zoomed in on the section just above where they stood and noticed something missing. "There's no levitator shaft going to the second floor," she said.

"Bloody hell," Stacey growled.

Elyssa knelt and opened a smaller clamshell case with more of the little critters inside, aiming the opening toward the gap between the lift and the wall. The roaches swarmed the shaft. One went inside the lift and promptly went belly-up, proving the ward had no mercy on anything with eavesdropping spells. The map of the levitator shaft filled in, showing only a few extra feet of space above the levitation car where the shaft ended.

"The passage isn't warded," Bella said, watching the map. "Can your little minions take pictures?"

"I wish," Elyssa said. She noticed the map hadn't grown in a few seconds and realized why. "The doors below must be sealed tight because the roaches haven't mapped the area beyond."

"What a bloody conundrum," Stacey said, hand on hip.

Elyssa checked the status of her spy-bots and saw the hallway remained clear. The guy with the broken printer would probably be back at any minute. She looked at the map again, desperately searching for a vent or anything else that might lead down into the basement. The map outline showed a wide vent shaft angling straight down, but the map ended a few feet down—not far enough to be anywhere close to the bottom. It probably had a ward similar to the levitator killing the roaches before they made it very far.

Elyssa checked the time. *Ten minutes left.*

Her eyes wandered back to the map. A potential weakness caught her eye. "Follow me," she said, leading the others left, down the hallway, and to the door of a supply closet tucked into the back. The door was locked.

Elyssa jerked hard on the handle and felt the lock snap. She was sick of every little thing in this place blocking access.

"I know how you feel," Stacey said with a smirk.

The closet held a mishmash of items including boxes of blank parchment against the back wall. "Help me move those out of the way," Elyssa said.

"What exactly are we doing?" Bella asked.

"Getting into the shaft."

It took two minutes to clear the boxes. Elyssa tested the wall with her knuckles, rapping lightly. *Ordinary drywall.* "Can you cut this open, Bella?"

The other dhampyr nodded, withdrew her wand. A thin purple beam intersected the wall. She flicked her wrist in an approximation of a square, leaving a black line. With a jerk of her wand, the section of drywall fell to the floor. A concrete wall confronted them. Stacey stowed the sheet of drywall to the side.

"It appears to be normal concrete," Elyssa said, running a finger across it. "Reinforcing everything with diamond fiber would have been prohibitively expensive."

Bella dug into her satchel and withdrew several vials of liquid. She held up a pink one, shaking it. "I believe this potion will do the trick." After uncorking the vial, she screwed a nozzle to the top, and sprayed fluid all along the concrete. The surface bubbled. An odor not unlike burnt popcorn filled the supply closet.

"I hope that guard doesn't come back," Stacey said. "Because he'll smell this from a bloody mile away."

It took less than a minute for the concrete to sag into a soupy gray mess, revealing the back of the levitator car. On this side, however, a gap wide enough to squeeze through presented itself."That's not going eat through the floor, is it?" Stacey pointed at the puddle of concrete on the floor.

Bella poured a vial of blue liquid into it. "Not anymore." She produced another vial and sprayed the air with it. The popcorn odor faded. "Much better."

Elyssa looked down the shaft, flicking on her night vision. *Only seven more minutes.*

She couldn't see the bottom. A small glowball she dropped down the shaft fell for at least three stories before stopping. *Too far to jump.* The levitator had no cables to slide down. Wasting no more time, Elyssa withdrew a circular object about as big around as the palm of her hand from her satchel, and pressed it to the inside of the shaft. It sent a spike into the concrete with a distinct *thunk*, locking it in place. A hook protruded from a hole in the side of the device. She pulled on it, unspooling a foot or so of diamond fiber from within.

"I'll go first," Elyssa said. "Hopefully I can force the doors open at the bottom."

"How are we supposed to get down there after you?" Stacey asked.

"When I signal the all clear, just touch the button in the center," Elyssa said, pointing at it. "Or, if I can't get the doors open, it can pull me back up."

"Good luck," Bella said as Elyssa slid into the narrow gap between the shaft wall and the levitator car.

Some of the goopy concrete material got on her hands. She hoped it didn't melt her skin. Elyssa let go of the ledge and pushed out, feeling her hair brush the bottom of the lift. The rope played out, allowing her to rappel her way down the shaft wall until she reached the bottom. Once there, she inspected the doors.

*Sealed tight.* Reaching down, she unsheathed a thin dagger from her thigh, and jammed it into the seam. A quick jerk wedged the doors open a fraction. She quickly grabbed a very short but wide bar from her satchel, and placed it inside the opening, then pressed the center.

"Five minutes," Bella hissed from above.

The bar lengthened, pushing the doors open a little at a time. Each elapsed second felt like a winch tightening her nerves. *No time to waste.* She unhooked the rope and, using the glowball she'd tossed down earlier, flashed a signal to the other women. The rope retracted. Seconds later, Stacey dropped down beside her and signaled for Bella to follow.

By now, the wedge had opened the levitator doors most of the way, revealing a large room with black marble floors, walls, and ceiling. Hexagonal tiles spaced evenly in the floor drew Elyssa's attention. She looked at the diagram from Adam's program and realized they must be the nodes. But how was she supposed to interact with them if they were in the floor?

*Only three more minutes.*

Bella looked flummoxed. "Most of the heists Stacey and I pulled off were strictly low-tech," she said, looking around the room. "Perhaps I should devote a decade or two to educating myself."

"I wonder if those are the high-security nodes," Stacey said, pointing to a patch of gray hexagons near the center of the floor.

Elyssa looked at the map and judged the number of grids to be about right. "I'm a little leery about walking out there." What if the floor was warded?

Bella flourished her wand, winding it through a quick pattern. Purple butterflies popped into existence, fluttering across the room, painfully slow. Elyssa's stomach tensed. Could they do this? Or had they bitten off more than they could chew? The first butterfly reached the gray marble tile in the center. It popped like a bubble. The same thing happened to the others that entered the gray area, whereas the rest of them made it to the other side of the large room without incident.

"Bloody hell," Stacey said. "Now what?"

Elyssa ground her teeth in a very unladylike way. While she could appreciate stealth, sometimes it made her feel better just to beat the crap out of someone. She pulled out her arcphone and marched across the floor to the forbidden zone, tempted to find a good sledgehammer and smash it to bits.

Less than a minute remained before the Obsidian Arch reopened. It wouldn't take Kassus and crew more than five minutes to make it back to Darkwater headquarters from the way station. How could they possibly open this thing and hack it in such little time?

Bella caught up with her. "What are you going to do?"

"I don't know yet," Elyssa admitted.

"I wouldn't step on that part of the floor," she said, looking worriedly at the gray tiles not ten feet away.

"Not planning on it."

Bella stepped closer to the border of black and gray. A thin pedestal sprang from the floor in front of her. She yelped and jumped back a foot, pressing a hand to her chest. Her eyes narrowed as she looked at the device. "It's an access card reader," she said, and pulled the administrator's card from within her outfit.

"What if his card fails and triggers an alarm?" Stacey asked.

"We're running out of time," Elyssa said, unable to stop looking at the timer as it reached zero.

As if right on cue, a text message from Christian appeared on the screen. *Obsidian Arch is cycling on. Kassus and at least thirty mages are on the way back. I think they figured out this is a diversion. If you're still at their HQ you need to get out now!*

"No choice," Elyssa said. "Just do it."

"I agree," Bella said. "I feel distinctly inadequate for the technological side of this heist."

"I do feel a bit out of place," Stacey said with a sour look. "We've stolen more magical artifacts from museums than I can bloody count, but stealing something from a ruddy computer is more work than I thought it would be."

"We should have asked Adam to come," Bella said in a dejected tone. "But we were so eager to prove ourselves, I guess we just let pride get in the way."

Elyssa furrowed her brow. "Don't you dare tell the boys that, Bella, or I'll let Cutsauce pee on your bed. And you know how bad hellhound urine stinks."

Bella threw up her hands in a defensive gesture. "Don't be silly! I would never let Harry or any of them know we *needed* them for something."

Stacey laughed. "I say we go for it. If it fails, we run like bloody hell. If it works, we come out of this looking like superstars."

"Agreed," Bella said, looking to Elyssa. "Well, what do you say?"

"We're out of time and an army of angry battles mages might march in here at any minute." Elyssa felt a slow grin creep over her face. "Let's do this."

Bella took out the card and swiped it.

# Chapter 24

*Elyssa*

An alarm rang the instant the card touched the reader.

"Bloody hell!" Stacey yelled.

*"Madre de dios!"* Bella said, stamping her foot.

Elyssa flung a few choice expletives at the infernal device. If that didn't bring Kassus and crew running back at top speed, nothing would.

A crystalline structure with a touchscreen terminal popped from the floor, and the ringing noise abruptly stopped.

*Welcome, Administrator Minh Wan.*

"It—it worked?" Stacey said, staring incredulously at the screen. "But the alarm—"

"Maybe it was just a warning noise about the terminal popping from the floor," Bella said with a shrug. She looked up at Elyssa. "Let's break this puppy open."

Elyssa didn't waste a moment, laying her arcphone atop the touchscreen interface and running Adam's program.

The program went back through its same routine, until it began the search for secure transport. The search time ticked away in the upper corner of the screen, a nerve-wracking reminder of imminent discovery.

*Starting search \*secure transport\*...results found. Accessing...*

"Please work," Elyssa said as the timer hit the four minute mark, every second pressing harder against her chest like lead weights.

*Success! Copying results to file. Please wait.*

They cheered, high-fiving each other like a bunch of adolescent boys who'd just blown something up.

Elyssa's supernatural hearing picked up a ding from the levitator shaft. Her eyes went wide. "The lift is active!"

"How are we going to get out of here?" Stacey said.

"Take a picture of the node," Elyssa said, unable to do it with her phone since Adam's script was still copying files.

Bella snapped the picture. "I sent it to Meghan."

The sound of doors sliding shut echoed from up the levitator shaft. The sound of angry voices followed a second later.

"Ah, the blasted wedge," Stacey said, looking at the rod holding the levitator doors open. She blurred across the room and snatched it.

Elyssa looked at the display on her phone.

*Copy complete. Erasing access logs…please be patient.*

They didn't have time for this.

A portal sprang open next to Bella. Meghan stood in the mansion on the other side of the gateway.

"Get through," Elyssa said, motioning the other two women.

*Process complete.*

She snatched the phone from the node. "How do I make this thing go back down?" she asked frantically as the sound of the levitator thumping to a halt reached her ears. She heard a man yelling orders from within the lift.

Bella tossed the access card through the portal. Elyssa swiped it across the reader. The levitator dinged. The doors started to slide open. The terminal and card reader dropped into the floor. Elyssa dove through the portal. It winked off behind her.

"What happened?" Meghan asked, scanning them with her wand as if expecting to find serious injuries.

Elyssa's heart hammered against her chest. She took several deep breaths to calm herself. "I think we just pulled off a caper."

Bella whooped.

"We're bloody fabulous!" Stacey said, and the three women drew Meghan into a group hug.

After their brief celebration, Elyssa took out her phone, and called Justin.

"Are you okay, babe?" Justin asked, relief audible in his voice.

"Of course," Elyssa said. "Everything went according to plan." She winked at the others while they covered their mouths to keep from bursting into laughter.

192

"Oh, man, thank goodness," he said, as if she'd never faced a danger in her life.

Elyssa couldn't help but grin as her heart swelled with affection. He was so adorable when he worried about her. "It was pretty easy," she lied. "Are you guys okay?"

"I guess we're not as smooth as you," he said with a sigh. "We barely survived."

Elyssa went cold, her smile vanishing. The other women seemed to catch onto the sudden change in mood. She put the phone on speaker so the muffle spell wouldn't obstruct them from hearing.

"Now, don't freak out, because we made it out with all our arms and legs intact," Justin said.

"But not our sanity!" Shelton said loudly in the background.

"You're on speaker," Elyssa said. "Tell us what happened."

Justin summed up his activities with a tale that left the women exchanging concerned looks.

"Y-you saw women singing stone into an arch?" Elyssa said.

"I think we saw the people who actually created the arch system," Justin said. "I don't even think Mr. Gray knows who they are."

"Were they in our reality?" Elyssa asked.

"I don't think so," he replied. "I remember seeing two moons, so I'm pretty sure it was another realm." He blew out a breath. "We ended up back at my old house, and scared the crap out of some guy eating pizza."

"That would explain why the arch wasn't working earlier," Bella said.

Stacey arched an eyebrow. "Not to mention the screaming man with the pizza."

"Where are you now?" Elyssa asked Justin.

"We've been sitting in a coffee shop in Atlanta waiting to hear from you so we could use the omniarch to come back."

"Oh," Elyssa said, feeling a bit foolish for not thinking of that immediately and getting his story face-to-face. "Send me a picture, and we'll open the portal."

"Yeah, let us find someplace private," he said with a chuckle. "Don't want to make everyone in the coffee shop crap themselves."

"Why do men love to talk about people soiling their pants?" Stacey said with a sigh.

"Are you kidding me?" Justin said. "Anything to do with poop is funny."

"True," sounded a chorus of male voices through the speaker.

The women exchanged hopeless looks.

*Justin*

I led the guys to an alley, took a picture, and sent it to Elyssa. I had the jitters from too much caffeine and knotted nerves, unable to stop worrying about Elyssa while we'd waited. A portal opened a few seconds later, and we stepped from the alley in Atlanta back into the mansion in the Queens Gate pocket dimension. The first thing I did was give Elyssa a big hug and a kiss. I noticed the other guys doing the same thing with their significant others. We might have ended up in another dimension for all eternity, or been drained of light and turned into shadow people by the cherubs at the Grand Nexus. I felt lucky to be back home with the girl I loved in my arms.

I told her as much.

"I probably exaggerated how easy our mission was," Elyssa said in a sheepish tone.

"Hey, now, don't tell him how hard it was," Stacey said with a smirk as Ryland regarded her with a wolfish grin.

"Can I see your phone?" Adam asked Elyssa.

She handed it to him. He flicked through the screens. "Sweet, my search strings found a few things. I just hope it got the information we need."

We filed upstairs to the war room, and gathered inside. Adam copied the information to his arctablet and projected it above the table. As he scrolled through the data, I watched, trying to read everything. He stopped, mulling over what looked like invoices.

"This might be a problem," he said. "There are three separate invoices for secure transport trucks, all scheduled for the same date."

"Decoys," Shelton said.

Adam nodded.

"How are we going to know which is the right one?" I asked.

"Hang on," Adam said.

Shelton peered over his other shoulder. "Hey, what's that?"

Adam zoomed in on a map, and frowned. "Looks like a route."

194

"It's definitely a route," Shelton said, tracing a finger along it. "But if they're running decoys, where are the fake routes?" He closed the invoice file and looked at others, flipping through older invoices for transportation runs by Darkwater.

"They've been moving a lot of supers," Adam said. "I knew this work was outsourced, but this often?"

"Wait. Here are two more current route plans," Shelton said, opening a document with the same date as the other route. "Two trucks are going Kobol Prison."

"Kobol Prison?" Ryland said. "That place ain't been used in decades."

"Where is it?" I asked.

"It's out near Thunder Rock." Ryland shrugged. "They stopped using it because it was too close to the interdiction zone. Nobody wanted to work so close to a cursed granite quarry."

"Who could blame them?" I said with a shudder.

"I don't like this," Shelton said. "You remember how my dad had me rounding up political enemies?"

"Yeah," I said.

"What if they're doing the same thing now?"

We exchanged uneasy glances.

"Hey, I think I got it," Adam said, bringing up the three transportation routes side-by-side. "This," he said, stabbing a finger at the first one, "originates from that house you tracked the Conroys to. The others originate at the Grotto way station."

"They must be bringing prisoners in via arch," Elyssa said, tapping her chin and quirking her lips. "Unless they're rounding up supers in the Grotto and bringing them out. Seems if they were doing that to political prisoners it could be a little too visible."

"Let's forget these other mystery transports for now," I said. "The one coming from the Conroy house must be the one is carrying my mom. Let's concentrate on it and worry about Kobol Prison later."

"The one presumably carrying your mother isn't going to Kobol at least," Adam said. "It's going to an industrial warehouse owned by Darkwater."

"Now, why would Darkwater own a warehouse?" Shelton said, eyebrow rising. "That isn't the kind of business they run."

"Might be a special place they prepared to hold Justin's mom," Elyssa said.

"It would be better than having to relocate her every time they change houses," Bella added.

Shelton nodded. "Makes sense."

"We still need to nab her during transport," Adam said. "I don't have faith in our abilities to break open an astral prison."

The truth was, neither did I. "They're moving her tomorrow," I said. "Can we come up with a plan on short notice?"

"Bingo!" Adam said, startling me. "The person whose blood will be used to seal the truck is none other than Kassus himself."

"Talk about adding another difficulty level," Shelton grumbled. "You know he won't follow procedure and set aside a vial of his blood in case of emergency.

"I'd bet he won't be with the transport either," Ryland said. "He's the kind of man who uses people like cannon fodder."

"We'll get his blood somehow," I said. *Even if I have to storm Darkwater myself.*

The transport was moving out at noon the next day. That didn't leave a lot of time for planning. Thankfully, we had no shortage of individuals with dubious pasts. I found myself listening more than talking as they took turns tossing out ideas and either writing them down as possibilities or nixing them.

There were so many variables. What if Jeremiah Conroy or my sister went with the transport? Then we'd have a boss fight on our hands. The routing documents indicated the convoy would consist, at minimum, of two escorts, one in front, the other in back. That didn't mean Darkwater wouldn't bring more. We had to hope they were confident in the secrecy of their mission and the invulnerability of the transport truck.

Slowly but surely, a plan formed with enough flexibility to account for extenuating circumstances and unforeseen variables.

I called Thomas Borathen and asked for his help, though not in the way I'd first envisioned. He agreed, even going so far as to say it was a very sound decision. I almost blushed.

"What did he say?" Elyssa said.

"He's in."

"Sweet," Adam said. "I think this plan might actually work."

"Even I think it might work," Shelton said. "We make a damned fine team, if I do say so myself."

We examined the plan backward and forward, looking for weaknesses. The ones we found had no easy solutions, only contingencies we'd have to rely on. By the time we gave the stamp of approval to the final product, I wanted to crawl under the table and sleep.

"How do you feel about the plan?" I asked Elyssa as we walked upstairs to bed.

She offered me a smile. "It has a good chance to work, especially if we don't have to worry about the Conroys."

Later, I lay in bed, but of course I couldn't sleep. So much had happened today. We'd been to the Grand Nexus, crossed into another realm, possibly seen the arch builders, and disrupted one man's pizza night. If Mr. Gray didn't know who the builders were, the logical conclusion I drew was that the Seraphim also didn't know anything about them. Would these beings represent a future threat or were they just explorers?

I thought about my mom. I wondered how Ivy was doing. I felt my stomach tighten at the thought of Kassus and his men hunting for us. I thought back to the time Shelton, Stacey, Elyssa, and I had infiltrated Maximus's Atlanta lair and rescued my father. I'd been so new to my abilities then. Elyssa had almost died in my arms. Every time we found ourselves in another situation like this, it made me realize that our last day could be heartbeats away. I might lose Elyssa or a friend.

Accepting the mantle of leader was something I hadn't done easily. Thomas Borathen's words about my natural ability to lead made me feel reasonably better. But it seemed different to lead personal friends into a deadly conflict as opposed to leading a large army of people I didn't know.

I felt Elyssa's strong arms wrap around me. Felt her soft lips kiss mine. "Go to sleep, baby," she said, drawing me against her. "Everything will be all right."

I squeezed her back, relishing the feel of her curves against me. I kissed her deeper, ran my hand up her back and gripped a handful of her hair. I felt her lips smile as we kissed.

John Corwin

"I think I know how to help us sleep," I said in what I hoped was a seductive voice.

She nibbled my ear. "Just what the doctor ordered."

It wasn't hard to sleep after that, even knowing tomorrow we might die.

# Chapter 25

"The mailman cometh," Ryland told me on the phone.

"Does he have company?" I asked.

"Four dogs, two in front, two chasing."

Shelton must have seen the tension on my face as I disconnected the call. "Confirmed?" he said.

"Yes." My body trembled and I had trouble focusing.

Shelton snapped his fingers in front of my face. "Hey, set your timer."

I jerked, and flicked on the timer. Twenty minutes to go. I sent out a group text. *Confirmed and en route.*

We were thirty miles north of Atlanta near a wealthy subdivision in an area filled with farms, rednecks, and pockets of steep terrain. The road wound through a heavily wooded area, up a steep hill. On the left of the road, a steep slope descended into a cow pasture. On the right, a rock face climbed thirty feet to a small plateau.

My phone buzzed with a text from Adam. *Detour signs in place ahead. Traffic rerouted.*

*Fifteen minutes to go.*

Bella appeared from downslope. "Everything is ready."

Shelton looked over the map. "Everyone else is in place. Let's do this."

*Ten minutes left.*

I crossed the road, manifesting demonic claws as I did. At the rocky cliff, I leapt high, dug my claws into worn grooves in the stone, and climbed. When I reached the top, I turned to see Shelton and Bella duck behind an illusionary blind in the horse pasture. I lowered myself to my stomach. Took deep calming breaths to focus myself on the task ahead. Mom depended on me.

*Convoy passed*, said a text from Meghan. *Tight escort. Detour signs are in place.*

*Five more minutes.*

"This will be fun," Stacy purred next to me.

I stifled a yelp. "Holy butt nuggets! I didn't even hear you."

She smiled. "Still my little lamb at times. So adorable."

"This is not the time to scare the crap out of me," I said.

We both turned our heads at the same time as a truck engine rumbled in the distance. The wooded terrain hid the road past the bend before this stretch, so we waited, ears cocked as the bellow of a straining diesel engine grew closer and closer.

A black SUV nosed around the turn with another close behind it. The tractor trailer maintained a twenty-foot gap between the front escorts. I peeked over the lip of the ledge and saw the white slashes we'd marked on the road below. I took position, waiting for the last SUV to cross that mark. Stacey braced her back against a boulder and waited for my cue.

This was going to be a tight fit.

*Ten seconds.*

Stacey and I counted down on our fingers.

*Five, four, three, two*—She grinned, planted her feet in the ground and pushed. I braced my arms against the boulder I stood behind and, with a grunt of effort, pushed it over the ledge. Stacey's boulder hit a split second too late, crushing the front end of the lead SUV instead of landing in front and trapping it. Mine clipped the back bumper of the last escort.

Before the people in the SUVs could react, the earth trembled. Twin slivers of energy ran from the blind where Bella and Shelton waited. Each sliver split in two, cracking the ground and cleaving the road. One set sliced the road beneath the tires of the damaged SUV, and cut the asphalt just in front of the tractor trailer. The other set sectioned off the road with the last two vehicles.

The glow faded for an instant, and then a giant aftershock of light exploded from the ground. The earth beneath the road crumbled. The asphalt caved in, and all the SUVs except the one pinned by the boulder listed to the side before rolling down the slope and into the pasture. I winced at each roll, hoping we hadn't just killed everyone even if they were a bunch of murderous bastards.

"Justin," Stacey said, her voice serious for once. "It's time."

I touched the sleeves of my Nightingale armor. Gloves covered my hands. Then I leapt off the cliff. Landed atop the semi-trailer. I heard someone shouting and peered over the side of the truck in time to see four Darkwater people spill from the pinned SUV and take positions on solid ground. Two aimed their staffs at the boulder. Waves of energy shoved the heavy stone off the hood and down the hill. The crushed SUV slid into the ravine and rolled down the hill to join the other escorts. Two more Darkwater Arcanes waved their wands at the cliff face near the fissure in the road. The rock face crumbled, sending rubble to fill the gap.

The tractor trailer lurched forward over uneven ground. I lost my footing on the slick, diamond fiber surface, barely managing to grab the ledge and dangle above the road as the rig gained speed much faster than it should have. I saw dark-robed Arcanes hanging to the side rail on the truck cab, using the steps for footing as they worked their magic on the semi-truck.

One of them saw me, and shouted, aiming their staff. A bolt of yellow light singed the hair on my head. My hands nearly slipped from the trailer.

"Grips on," I said. The nightingale armor gloves emitted a sticky fluid. I felt my grip strengthen just as the truck crested the rise and rushed downhill. Wind whipped through my hair. A bug smacked into the side of my face as I struggled to swing myself atop the trailer.

The gloves helped but just barely. Another splash of heat warmed my back as an attack missed. The armor might protect me from a direct hit, but the impact nearly threw me off the truck.

My hands suddenly went sub-zero as the other Arcane sent a freeze bolt into my fingers. Ice formed on my gloves, and the last bit of purchase vanished. I fell. My feet hit the asphalt. My ankle twisted and snapped. I rolled off the road and smacked into a tree. I couldn't breathe. Couldn't move. Agony flashed up my spine. I felt broken shards in my ribs.

"Justin," cried a voice, and Stacey was there.

"Think I broke something," I wheezed.

"Bloody hell, you broke everything," she said. "I'm so sorry, Justin. I messed up everything." Tears welled in her eyes. "If I hadn't pinned that first car—"

"Agh!" I cried out, my voice deepening with demonic need. Hunger clawed at my insides as the healing process drained my reserves. Stacey's eyes went wide.

"Your irises are turning white, Justin," she said, looking more worried than I'd ever seen her.

I gritted my teeth against the pain. "Feed," I said, barely able to get the word out.

She leaned close. "Use me."

Stacey had never allowed me to feed from her before. Before I could reconsider, the demon pounced. My vision flickered into incubus mode. Stacey's halo shone like a brilliant star around her body. My tendril latched into it. She gasped, eyes widening, and moaned. I usually tried to neutralize my emotions before feeding, but pain consumed every ounce of control.

I felt my bones mending, my ribs springing back into place. My foot twisted from its awkward angle as my ankle snapped back together. The blinding pain receded and sanity returned. My gaze found a sea of lust in Stacey's eyes as she wavered in a trance-like state, her tongue running across her full lips, hungry gaze regarding me like a panther contemplating a steak. I withdrew the connection. The haze faded from her eyes. She scrambled backward, away from me, breathing heavily.

"Bloody hell," she said, rising unsteadily to her feet. "Why didn't I let you do that to me before you found a girlfriend?"

"The truck," I said, climbing to my feet and testing my ribs and ankle. I was still sore as hell. Supernatural healing or not, I'd taken a beating. "We have to catch the truck!" I retracted the gloves on the Nightingale armor, and fished in my pocket for my phone.

A black sedan screamed around the corner, and slid to a stop at the side of the road. Elyssa jumped out. "What happened?" she asked.

I pointed down the road where the truck had vanished. "We have to catch up to them!" I limped to the car and got in.

"I need to help the others subdue the remaining hostiles," Stacey said. "We'll catch up later."

Elyssa nodded. Jumped in the driver seat. Slammed the manual gearshift into first. "Buckle up," she said, and hit the gas.

The acceleration slammed my head into the headrest. She took a hairpin turn at a terrifying speed, the car hugging the road as though on rails. I felt my fingers digging into the armrest. I wasn't about to complain. Mom was just up the road and we had no time to lose.

My phone buzzed with a text from Adam. *Target just smashed through the detour and took the highway back toward Atlanta. Moving fast.*

I told Elyssa. "Why are they heading back into town?"

"Reinforcements," she said. "Probably have people coming from Atlanta to meet them."

"Great," I said. "If that boulder hadn't hit the hood of the lead SUV, this wouldn't be happening right now."

Elyssa didn't take her eyes off the road. "I was still coming from the first spotter position, so I didn't see what happened."

I told her.

"Crap happens," she said, maneuvering the snaking road with ease, trees and foliage to the sides a green blur. "That's why there's always a Plan B." She glanced at the GPS map. "Hopefully this shortcut will pan out, and we can catch up to them." She flicked the gearshift.

"Is this the Templar car you told me about?" I asked, my grip tightening as a pickup truck whizzed past in the opposite direction.

"Yep." We hit a straight stretch of road. Elyssa pointed toward an intersection ahead. "There they are."

I saw the tractor-truck roar past on the highway perpendicular to the road we were on. She gunned the accelerator.

"What's that big red button on top of the gear shift do?" I asked.

She ignored the question. "Get a sitrep from the others. We'll need them."

I took out my phone and called Shelton.

"We're all good here," he said. "Stacey and those giant cats of hers helped us round up the Darkwater people."

"Any casualties?" I asked.

"Just some scrapes and bruises on their part," he said. "The tumble down the hill disoriented most of them enough they couldn't walk straight, much less put up a fight."

I brought him up to speed on the pursuit. "We're headed straight back to Atlanta," I said as Elyssa screeched around the corner, putting us on the highway with the runaway semi-truck.

"Holy midgets on a go-kart." Shelton blew out a breath. "If that first SUV had fallen with the others, this would be over already."

"I know," I replied. "Nothing to be done now but catch them."

"Hang on," he said, speaking to someone else in an indistinct tone. "Good news. Plan B is here and we're on the way." He ended the call.

I just had to hope Plan B was enough.

Despite the magically enhanced engine in the tractor-truck, we were catching up. The Templar sedan was, of course, loaded with magical modifications. Our prey raced through another intersection just as the light turned red. Cars in front of us stopped, and traffic from the intersecting road began driving through.

"Why do they build highways and then clog them up with traffic lights?" Elyssa growled. "Hold on."

Before I could ask why, she flicked a switch on the center console. Gravity sucked my stomach down as the car lurched upward. The traffic lights grew large in the front view. I threw up my hands and shouted as we narrowly cleared the electrical cables. The ground rushed up to meet us on the other side. The chirp of rubber on asphalt indicated all four tires had just kissed the ground.

"Was that a turbo jump?" I asked, wondering if the car would start talking to me in a nerdy voice.

Elyssa snorted as she veered around a slow-moving car. "The car is a slider."

"Ah," I said. Sliders were essentially magical aircraft like flying carpets. I'd seen ones designed to look like helicopters so they'd blend into the normal world. It made sense to design some like cars. "Didn't you just break the rules by flying over those noms?" I asked, aiming a thumb toward the intersection behind us.

"I flicked on camouflage to hide us for a few seconds."

"So, instead of a flying car, they saw a car vanish and reappear on the other side of the intersection," I said.

"Maybe." She nodded toward the road. "There they are."

The semi-truck was quickly gaining on two cars inexplicably traveling the speed limit. One of the Arcanes on the side of the truck pointed toward us. I wondered if they'd use magic in front of the noms. They didn't, but the truck bumped one of the law-abiding cars, pushing it into a spin. Smoke boiled from the tires as it left the road and skidded to a halt in the wide grass median.

Something glittered in the road ahead. I peered closer.

"Caltrops," Elyssa said, pshawing. "They can't puncture these tires."

The nom cars ahead of us hit the sharp metal objects. Tires exploded. Cars spun out of control, colliding with each other. Glass showered the road. Bumpers and engine parts tore from vehicles.

"They don't need to pop our tires," I said, gripping the armrest tight.

An SUV smacked into the guardrail. Two more cars skidded to a stop, snarling traffic into an impassible barrier.

Elyssa flicked a switch. The car jolted. She swerved off the road and into the median, narrowly missing a car with steam billowing from beneath a warped hood. Despite the grass, the car never lost traction. A yell tore from my throat as we juked between two more vehicles spinning out of control across the median. The tires hit the road. I heard the hum of off-road treads beneath us. Elyssa flicked the switch again, and the sound faded.

I looked behind us at the carnage. "This car has all the options."

"No satellite radio though," she said, biting her lip as she avoided another wrecked car.

The semi-truck had widened its lead, but traffic was growing heavier as we neared Atlanta. Ahead, the highway terminated, turning into an interstate. That meant no traffic lights or intersections. It might work to our advantage unless more wrecked cars blocked our path. As if in answer, the semi-truck smashed into the side of another tractor-truck, sending it listing to the left. Cars swerved to avoid it. Brake lights lit up like Christmas trees.

Elyssa growled. "Screw this." She whipped onto the wide left shoulder of the road, said, "Hope this answers your question," and hit the big red button on top of the gear shifter.

The car made a whining noise like a jet engine spinning up. It roared. G-forces flattened my guts against my spine as we shot forward. Traffic blurred past. Within seconds, we pulled even with the tractor trailer. The Darkwater battle mages on the driver side of the truck regarded us with shocked looks for a split second. Then they whipped out pistols and opened fire.

205

Bullets pinged off the side of the car. I yelped and ducked.

"Bullet proof," Elyssa said.

Tires screeched. Cars swerved and careened like mad as civilians simultaneously crapped their pants and desperately tried to flee the erupting gun battle. Elyssa jerked hard to the right.

"Why are we getting closer to them?" I asked as guns and grim-faced shooters grew larger in my window.

Elyssa hit the brakes to avoid a yellow car. Downshifted, and swerved smoothly around it. "Slide open the armrest, and activate the touchscreen."

I did as asked and found a touchscreen interface inside. It presented the outline of the car.

"Touch the passenger door. When I give the go, hit the icon that looks like a white booger."

"Got it," I said.

She hit the gas. We pulled even with driver side door of the semi-truck. One of the Arcanes reached inside a compartment on the back of the cab and grabbed a big effin' gun. My video game street creds identified it as a six-round grenade launcher. A wicked grin crossed the Arcane's face as he aimed and—

"Now!" Elyssa said.

I touched the booger icon.

A white glob jetted from the side of the car, plastering the two Arcanes to the door of the semi-truck. The grenade launcher fired just as the glob pinned the attacker's arm. The round went straight up, hung in the air for an instant. I watched in horror as it hit the road and exploded. Luckily most drivers with good sense had abandoned the road behind, all except some guy in a pickup who seemed intent on videoing the chase with his phone. The pickup flipped and skidded on its roof.

I didn't have time to enjoy the fireworks.

The booger pinning the Darkwater thugs unfortunately also blocked access to the driver door. Somehow, I had to get inside the cab and hijack it. With two more adversaries on the other side, I had no idea how to do it without seriously injuring them or possibly myself. If I knocked them out, they'd hit the asphalt at a hundred miles an hour. There wouldn't be much left but red skid marks and spare teeth after that impact.

"Is the truck cab reinforced?" I asked. "Can I punch through the glass?"

"Yes, and I don't know," Elyssa said. "The specs Shelton showed us indicated it's the equivalent of an armored truck cab."

"Get me closer," I said.

It appeared she didn't have to worry about that, because the big-rig driver veered at us, trying to ram us off the road. Elyssa hit the red button and the car shot forward. The front end of the semi-truck clipped the trunk. The car's rear end spun sideways. Tires screamed. The world spun upside down as the car flipped.

# Chapter 26

I squeezed my eyes shut and waited for the sound of crunching metal as the car's roof smashed into the road. That sound never came. I felt the passenger door pound against my leg. I gasped in pain, and looked through my window. The upside-down view of the truck's front grill greeted me. The roof of the car hovered less than a foot above the ground.

"I activated the levitation spell," Elyssa said, fighting with the steering wheel, her hair a wild black mane as it dangled toward the roof. "But I can't get the car upright with that thing pushing us."

The semi-truck rammed us again. A spider web of cracks formed in the window. We shot forward, gliding as if on ice. I slammed the side of my fist against the window once, twice, three times. It broke apart, falling on the road. The truck grill smashed into us again, sending the car spinning like a leaf on a pond.

Elyssa cursed, desperately tugging on a red lever next to the parking brake, but whatever was supposed to happen, didn't happen. I unbuckled my seatbelt. My body thudded to the roof. As the car spun, I reached out the window and gripped the bottom of the car. I pulled myself out of the window. A diesel engine roared. I looked back as the truck rushed for me. My foot tangled in the seatbelt.

"Crap!" I shouted.

I felt a hand pull away the harness, freeing my leg. Heard Elyssa shout, "Go!"

With a desperate jerk, I pulled myself atop the bottom of the car just as the truck smashed into us again. The impact drove the car forward. I didn't have a grip and stumbled backward. In a last-ditch attempt to avoid becoming roadkill, I dove backwards. In mid-air, I twisted. My hands clawed open air.

# Dearest Mother of Mine

*I'm so dead.*

The truck grill surged to meet my face. My hands gripped the front end just in time to abort complimentary facial reconstruction. My feet found purchase on the front bumper. I peeked over the hood. Two glowing staffs on the passenger side aimed at my head. I ducked as beams of energy speared past. I didn't want to kill the murderous jackasses hanging onto the side of the cab, but they weren't giving me much choice.

*It sucks having a conscience.*

Since I was on the hood of the truck, the driver seemed a lot less concerned about Elyssa's car, and a lot more about me. He swerved left and right, as if that would dislodge me. I looked back and saw one side of the Templar car bounce, flipping it upright. The wheels floated about a foot off the ground an instant before the car straightened and dropped onto the road. White smoke billowed on impact. Cars ahead veered out of the way. My supernatural vision picked up wide eyes in rear-view mirrors as drivers realized their morning commute had just turned into a field day for traffic reporters. The semi-truck driver swerved left and right, as if possessed, in his desperate attempt to shake me loose.

His maniacal attempts offered a beneficial by-product. One of the Darkwater Arcanes dropped his staff as the big rig clipped a car. The other clung to the side rail for dear life. I peered over the hood at the driver and snarled. No more Mr. Nice Guy.

I let the demon out.

My hands grew large and thick as muscles bulged all over my body. The nightingale armor stretched to accommodate the growth, even covering the tail growing from my rear end. Pain spiked in my forehead as horns erupted from my skull, curving upward. I felt the senseless rage charging at me like a bull, and slammed the cage closed before the demon side of me took over completely. When I poked my head over the hood the next time, the driver's mouth opened in a rictus of horror.

I sprang atop the hood. Reared back my monstrous blue fist, and smashed the windshield. A single crack ran down the glass. I punched it again. A web-work of cracks splintered the window.

The driver panicked, swinging the wheel back and forth. My next strike punctured the glass. I gripped the edge of the windshield and

209

jerked hard, pulling it clear, and flinging it away. The driver screamed and pulled hard on the steering wheel. The turn was too much for the vehicle to handle. The trailer went sideways, jackknifing across the highway. I saw terror in the eyes of the Darkwater people stuck to the driver's side of the cab.

"Throw them on top!" Elyssa shouted, her car swerving next to the truck. I swung to the driver door, pulling at the sticky mass holding the Arcanes prisoner. It came loose with a sucking pop, though it still bound them together. I dropped the screaming Arcanes atop the roof of Elyssa's supercar where it held them fast.

I saw one of the two Arcanes on the passenger side cast a spell with his staff, and they jumped, rolling in a transparent ball of what looked like jelly. It bounced off the road and into the woods on the side. Only the driver remained as the trailer, tires smoking, listed to the side.

"Hit the brakes, you idiot!" I called out, my voice deep and guttural.

The man screamed and jammed his foot down.

The trailer jerked. The cab shuddered. The rig shifted left and hurtled into the grass median. A frightened roar burst from my mouth, joining the cries of the truck driver as we barreled across the median and into oncoming traffic. I saw two semi-trucks roaring toward us as we bounced over the shoulder and into the road.

Their tires locked. Rubber screeched. Tortured tires bounced and smoked. I grabbed the driver, saw he was buckled in, and snapped the belt off. I jerked him through the window and leapt. Thankfully, I landed in the grass in the median, skidding on my back with the hysterical driver on top of me.

Metal shrieked, clattered, and groaned as the goliath trucks smacked each other. With a flick of my wrist, I popped the driver in the back of head. His shouts cut off abruptly as he went to la-la land. Before anyone noticed my blue skin, horns, and demonic six-pack abs, I pushed my infernal essence back into its cave until my body returned to normal. I knew I shouldn't have manifested where noms could see me, but the truck driver had left me little choice.

The truck sat in the middle of the northbound lane with the other two big rigs pinned against the cab. The semi-trailer rested nearly perpendicular to the accident. I hoped Mom was okay in there. She was an angel, but this ride had been enough to make even the hardiest supernatural toss their lunch.

Traffic behind the accident snarled. Horns honked, and people sprang from their cars, phones recording the scene. The police would be here soon, and explaining a trailer that couldn't be opened would be impossible. I heard sirens in the distance and realized how little time remained.

I ran to the accident. The drivers of the other two trucks looked okay. They'd slowed enough to avoid more than front-end damage. I heard a thrumming noise to the east, and looked up to see a large black helicopter rise above the tree line. Racing behind the semi-truck cab, I found a box on the side of the trailer, and pulled the lever inside. Air hissed as the rear end of the truck sank from the hydraulics releasing air. I ran to the crank near the front of the trailer, jammed it into place, and spun it as fast as I could until the metal feet of the trailer touched the road. Reaching beneath the trailer toward the hitch, I disengaged the lock.

The truck cab wasn't going anywhere, meaning I had to do this the hard way. Bracing my feet against the trailer and my back against the cab, I pushed with all my might. I feared the cab might bend with the stress, but the reinforced frame held. I heard a click. A grinding noise. The trailer feet slammed onto the asphalt as the hitch came free.

"Holy crap did you see what that kid did?" someone yelled.

I looked down to see one of the other truck drivers staggering from his cab holding a hand to his bleeding forehead. The helicopter hovered overhead. A diamond fiber net harness unfolded from a hatch in the bottom, unfurling down both sides of the trailer. I pulled on the straps, sealing them beneath it. I crawled out, and gave a thumbs-up to the Templar pilot.

The slider—disguised as a military helicopter—strained upward, the extra weight of the trailer obviously dragging it down. I didn't know how much weight the levitation spell could bear, but somehow the slider managed to rise while bystanders gawked at the spectacle. It struggled to stay level and rose straight up until the trailer cleared the trees then glided away.

A thundering noise echoed in the south. The silhouettes of more aircraft appeared on the horizon. *Probably news choppers or cops.* I raced across the road where Elyssa waited. She'd popped a Lancer dart in each of the Darkwater Arcanes formerly glued to her roof, freed them from the sticky mass, and situated them on the median. I spotted the other Arcanes who'd abandoned ship before the crash pointing at us and running our way.

Elyssa hit them with darts, and they unceremoniously face-planted into the grass. "Let's go," she said, extending driving gloves from her nightingale armor as she slid into the driver seat. Elyssa pulled a U-turn, tires wailing against pavement, and shot off the road, down the embankment to avoid the traffic. We skidded on the grass. Elyssa flicked a switch and the tires found purchase, spinning up dirt and grass behind us.

We met the road, dodged between stopped cars, and jetted across the median to the northbound side, which was clear thanks to the accident. I looked through the rear window and saw two small black helicopters charging our way.

"I don't think those are police," I said.

"Must be Darkwater reinforcements," Elyssa muttered, looking in the rearview mirror and jamming the gearshift down.

I hoped our chopper had gotten away before they'd seen it. The other Darkwater Arcanes shouldn't have had time to report it. Traffic thickened ahead. Elyssa threaded through, but it cost us speed, and the choppers were closing. The touchscreen interface in the console blinked at me and dinged.

*Aether batteries low. Please connect to a charger.*

"Crap," Elyssa said through her teeth.

"If this things runs out, will we be dead in the water?"

She shook her head. "The engine runs on gasoline, but levitation and super boost rely on aether." She glanced at the GPS in the center of the dash. "We need to find cover. Look for a route with trees."

I flicked my fingers across the screen. Georgia had no shortage of roads with trees, and we were close to the northern lakes. "Take the next exit," I said. "Then turn left."

She swung across the lane, rode the shoulder, and steered up the exit ramp. Elyssa ran the red light, and narrowly missed colliding with two cars. We crossed an overpass. The road dipped and rose, crossing a lake.

I directed her through several more turns. "Into the park," I said, pointing out a state park entrance.

We zoomed past a parking permit booth and down a road covered by trees. We followed the winding asphalt for a distance. I heard the choppers thundering behind. The thrum of rotors abruptly stopped.

"They're running silent," Elyssa said.

Tension built in my chest. "They could be anywhere."

She pulled off the road and into a picnic area shaded by trees. Turned off the engine. Crickets chirped. A bird twittered nearby, and squirrels rustled in the leaves. I heard a whoosh of air as something swooped past overhead.

"They're here," she whispered.

"How do you charge the batteries on this thing?" I asked.

"We have aether stations for it," she said. "But an Arcane could do it, given enough time."

"How? Where?"

She popped the hood. We got out, and she pointed to a chunk of glowing crystal. "There."

I closed my eyes and flicked into incubus mode. When I opened them, I saw aether pulsing through tiny ley lines in the ground, and puffs of it floating in the air. I extended a tendril and, with a deep breath, drew it in. I touched the tendril to the crystal and willed it to push energy inside. Nothing seemed to happen. I heard the sound of feet crushing leaves nearby. The rustling seemed to come from several directions at once.

"Tracking this way," someone whispered from somewhere down the road.

*Fill it up!* A slight tug pulled at my insides. The crystal glowed a little brighter. *Faster!* I willed it with all my might. It didn't seem to help. In frustration, I pressed my bare hand to the crystal.

*Charge!*

I felt energy flow through my hand in a hot rush. The crystal flared bright as a star. I heard the console inside ding. Elyssa ducked into the car.

"It's full," she said, eyes glowing with pride. "You're a rock star, baby."

Two men in the black robes of the brotherhood appeared at the side of the road.

Elyssa shut her door as pulses of light splashed against it. I jumped in. Elyssa started the car, revved the engine, and peeled out, charging straight at the men. They leapt aside at the last minute.

Another group appeared ahead. She swung down a small dirt road. Ahead, I saw nothing but water.

"Hang on," Elyssa said as we hit the end of the road.

The car dropped like a rock. Just before we plunged into the lake, Elyssa flicked a switch. The vehicle lurched upward and glided just over the water, spraying a plume behind us. She hit the red button, and the car roared forward. We shot beneath a bridge. Following the bend of the lake, she threaded between two boats with startled fishermen, hooked a right, and shot up a boat ramp. The car dropped to the road, tires chirping. A squirrel racing across the road froze in our path.

"Ahh!" Elyssa shouted, hitting the levitation switch again.

I looked behind us to see the frightened rodent dash back into the woods.

"Stupid squirrels," Elyssa grumbled.

"It was just a squirrel," I said.

Leaving the levitation on, Elyssa activated camouflage. The hood of the car flickered, matching with the surrounding terrain. She pulled the steering wheel toward her chest like the control in an airplane; the car flew higher, narrowly clearing trees, and zooming over the green canopy of pine trees. I looked back and saw the choppers hovering over the bridge, but not moving to pursue.

"When I was first learning to drive, I took my brother Jack for a ride," Elyssa said. "I was so proud of myself. And then just when I was pulling into the driveway at the ranch, a squirrel ran across my path. I couldn't stop in time and hit it." She sighed. "I just sat there and cried while Jack tried to console me."

I touched her arm. "You're a ninja with a soft heart," I said.

She smiled. "I'm such a dork sometimes. I knew so many ways to hurt or even kill someone by the time I learned to drive, and yet, I cried over a squirrel."

"I love my beautiful dork," I said, and pecked her on the cheek.

She giggled.

214

We sped south toward the city with no signs of pursuit. Thirty minutes later, Elyssa landed on an empty stretch of road near the Templar compound as the console dinged with another low battery warning.

"Camouflage drains aether fast," she explained, steering down the long drive to the compound, her gaze sweeping the environs, presumably for squirrels. At the end of the driveway, she turned toward a large red barn. She drove through an illusionary stack of hay bales in the back and down the hidden ramp to a large underground garage. Rows of Custodian sedans like the one we rode in lined parking slots. Chopper-shaped sliders sat atop circular landing zones beneath large doors sliding doors allowing for quick deployment.

Ahead, I saw Shelton and the others waiting around the semi-trailer we'd liberated. I leapt from the car, ignoring the celebratory cheers, and ran to it. I pressed an ear to the side. "Mom? Are you in there?"

"We couldn't open it," Shelton said.

I pounded on the side. "Mom?"

I heard a faint voice. "Justin?"

Hot tears sprang into my eyes. She was in there. We'd done it. "We're going to get you out," I said.

Somehow, I would find a way.

# Chapter 27

"Justin, do you know the man whose blood sealed me in here?" Mom said.

"Maulin Kassus," I said, my voice low and angry. She remained silent for a moment, and I wondered if she was still ok.

"Don't go after him, Justin." She sounded so tired and weary. "He's too dangerous."

"Dangerous?" I heard myself laugh. "I've encountered nothing but danger since you left. Do you have any idea what we went through to get you here?"

"You've done too much already," she said. "Now that he knows you have me, it will be even harder."

For some reason, I felt annoyed and even angry at her warnings. "Too much?" I said in a scoffing tone. "*Maybe* if you hadn't abandoned me without explanation, or *maybe* if you'd informed me about your grand scheme, or maybe, just maybe, if you'd trusted me with the truth, you wouldn't be in this mess right now!" The last sentence came out in an angry yell.

Elyssa placed a hand on my shoulder. "You can't change the past, Justin."

"No, he's right," Mom said, her voice sounding hollow from within the container. "In the beginning, when I thought you had a chance at a normal life, it felt like the right decision. But once you came into your own powers, David and I should have told you more. There was a lot we couldn't tell you because the information was too important to fall into the wrong hands. We had nightmares about our enemies kidnapping and torturing you for information. When your father decided to return to House Slade, we thought you'd go with him."

216

"He's marrying another woman, Mom!" I took a deep breath to calm myself.

"Are you with people you can trust?" she said. "People who can know the truth?"

I looked around at the faces of people who'd been with me since the beginning, and those I'd accumulated along the way—Shelton, Bella, Adam, Meghan, Stacey, Ryland—I trusted each and every one with my life. "I'm with my family," I said, gripping Elyssa's hand. "Because, unlike my parents, they've stayed by my side."

I heard a faint sobbing noise from within. "I understand," Mom said. "I won't make excuses for myself or your father."

"Tell me the truth," I said. "No more vague evasions."

"Very well," she said. "My name is Alysea, and I was the first Seraphim to step foot on your world."

"I know," I said, the impact of hearing it from her own lips making my knees go weak. A part of me still couldn't believe the truth.

"How do you know?" she asked.

"It's not important," I said. "Are you one of the originals who ravaged our world?"

"No," she said. "But I am directly responsible, because I showed my best friend the way."

All of a sudden, I wasn't sure I wanted to hear the truth.

"The arches on our world had long been a mystery," Mom said. "Like this realm, we also have Obsidian Arches, and started using them even before I was born. But the Alabaster Arches were decreed too dangerous to use by our governing council." She paused. "I broke the decree and studied the Grand Nexus in secrecy. After decades, I discovered something quite startling. The Grand Nexus is like a tuning fork, Justin. If you adjust the pitch, it alters the destination."

"How long ago was this?" I asked, grasping at a timeline.

"Thousands of years ago."

I shivered at the thought. "Tell me more."

"The Cyrinthian Rune tunes the nexus, but it requires the user to attune the rune to themself. Previous attempts to use the nexus had nearly loosed horrific creatures from other realms on our world. But I had an edge others did not."

I held back a smart remark. "And that is?"

"I was a musical prodigy. I can hear perfect pitch. For some reason, this enabled me to feel the tuning of the Cyrinthian Rune. It allowed me to sense what lay on the other side of the portal if I allowed it to open. That was how I discovered the mortal realm."

I saw wonder on the faces of my companions, and felt it spread across my own as well. My mom had discovered the way to this realm. It sounded as if there were many more realms than the ones I'd heard about. "So, what happened?"

"I showed my best friend this amazing discovery," Mom said, her voice trembling. "We came through the Grand Nexus. When she discovered how weak the humans were, how she could feed from them, she began to toy with them, to exploit them. On our world, she had long sought power, but never attained it. In this world, she had more power than she could have ever dreamed."

I grimaced. "How in the hell could Daelissa be your best friend?"

"She wasn't always like this," Mom said. "She was once a leader for reform, but failure and disappointment jaded her. Turned her bitter."

"Why didn't you stop her?"

"I tried, Justin. I tried so hard." She sounded miserable. "At first I was just like her. I enjoyed the power and the way it made me feel. Then I realized these people were so much like us, but helpless against our abilities. By then, others knew about the mortal realm, even though I'd told her to keep it secret."

I thought back to my conversation with Mr. Gray. "What about your government? Why didn't they step in?"

"Feeding from humans gave us so much more power. Because the Grand Nexus was a secret very few of us knew about, Daelissa and the others were able to leverage this new power and overthrew our government. They invited allies to create their own kingdoms in the mortal realm."

"Like Methuselah?" I said.

"His real name is Fjoeruss," she said. "He used the name Methuselah in the mortal realm. Others used names you would find quite familiar as well."

*Mr. Gray is Fjoeruss?* "How did the war with the Darklings start?" I asked.

"Daelissa's twin sister," she said.

218

Despite the difference in hair color and skin tone, I already knew who that was as well. "Nightliss."

"Yes. The Darklings were oppressed, considered second-class citizens. I sought Nightliss's help. She saw the mortal realm as a new world for the Darklings to settle in. She wished to create peace."

"That didn't turn out so well," I said dryly.

"No. It sparked a civil war on our world and here."

"What part did you play in the war?" I asked.

"I still haven't rediscovered all of my memories, Justin, so I can't recall many details. Sometimes, I see flashes of memories. I remember leyworms appearing from the depths as we fought our way toward the Grand Nexus. I remember one of them sweeping Brightlings from our path. Daelissa and her people turned on the leviathan and killed it, though not before it took several of them with it. I remember Nightliss saving me from an attack. Our people closing in. An old man with a staff—ah, the leader of the Arcanes. I barely remember his name. Moses I think."

"Did you say Moses?" Bella asked, eyes wide.

Mom paused for a long moment. "The Cyrinthian Rune was there. I knew how to remove it."

"How?" I asked.

"Let her finish," Shelton said, his face captivated.

"Not by force, but by aligning the perfect pitch in my head with it," she said. "But before I could get there, someone else removed it by force." She gasped. "Moses knew something was wrong. He opened the portal to take us away. He led his people through, but Daelissa slipped through after him. Something happened and the portal closed. Nightliss and I were trapped along with many others." She cried out. "The memories hurt, Justin. I don't know if I can stand it another minute longer."

"It's okay," I said, pounding on the trailer. "Let it go!"

"The leyworm charged us. It was the largest one I've ever seen. It swept us into its maw before I could react. Somehow, I managed to hold onto one of the shards in its gullet. It sliced my hands, but still I held on, the glowing pit of aether threatening to consume me like it had Nightliss. And then there was a flash so bright I saw the skeleton of the beast highlighted all around me."

*The Grand Nexus.* It must have blown up at that moment.

Mom continued. "My insides felt as though they were being turned inside out. My skin blackened before my eyes. My grip faltered. The world faded." She whimpered. "My first remembrance of that time would not come for thousands of years."

"Holy angels in hades," Shelton breathed. "I hope somebody is writing this all down."

I was in shock. It sounded as though Mom had turned into a husk—a cherub. Had the leyworm protected her and Nightliss? "How did you come to be with the Conroys?" I asked.

"They raised me from childhood," she said. "I do not remember how they found me, or where they found me, but for some reason, I was an infant when they did."

I shared glances with Elyssa, Shelton, and the others. When she'd turned into a cherub, she must have fallen into the aether inside the leyworm and ended up as a cupid. Had the same thing happened to Nightliss? "When did you start remembering the past?" I asked. If she remembered her past, it meant the cupids would eventually remember. It also meant they might return to their evil ways.

"Bits and pieces have been with me since I reached my equivalent of your teenage years," she said. "I suffered recurring, violent dreams as I aged. The Conroys eventually told me they'd found me asleep in a preservation spell. I can't imagine how many centuries I must have been there, or who put me there in the first place."

"How did you meet Dad?"

There was a long pause. "I don't know if you want to know our story, Justin."

My stomach clenched. Hearing the truth had been harder than I'd expected so far. Could it get worse?

"Are you okay?" Elyssa said, concern in her eyes.

The rest of the group stood in a loose semi-circle around me and the trailer, almost as if trying not to crowd me despite the fountain of knowledge my mom represented. Shelton, Bella, Ryland, Stacey, Elyssa—my eyes caught on two other figures I hadn't noticed. Thomas Borathen and Nightliss stood a discreet distance away. I wondered how much of this Nightliss already knew. She and I would talk. I remembered my plans to take lessons from her. Those plans had obviously been washed away by the necessity of rescuing Mom.

I offered Elyssa a small smile. "I'm okay," I said, staring at the sealed back door of the trailer. Having this conversation under these circumstances sucked. I had wanted to see Mom's face when she told me the truth. I leaned my forehead against the trailer. "Tell me about Dad," I said.

I heard her sigh. "Let me first say there's a lot I can't tell you about him, Justin. He made me swear an oath. He'll have to tell you many of the details himself."

"What a load of crap," I said, drawing my head back, and glaring at the door as if she could see me.

"It's the truth," she replied. "We love each other, Justin. But we realized we had to make sacrifices for the greater good."

"You gave my sister to the Conroys when she was a baby!" I shouted. "How is that the greater good?"

"I couldn't stop them," she said, her voice a painful whisper even my supernatural hearing strained to discern.

"You're Seraphim. How could you not stop them?"

"Daelissa did something to me to keep me weak. She wanted me to believe I was a human Arcane. She wanted me to worship and love her so when she finally revealed my true powers, I would blindly follow her." The sound of quiet sobbing came from within the trailer. "I never wanted to lose Ivy or you. It drove a wedge between David and me. He had the power to take Ivy back by force, but he wouldn't do it. He refused to start a war over our daughter."

"How could Dad start a war?" I asked. "He was Castratae—the lowest of the low for Daemos—until he did all this Kassallandra crap to get back into favor."

"I can't say more," Mom said. "Daelissa did things to my mind to prevent me from hearing the truth. She did everything possible to indoctrinate me while I matured. I didn't even know what she was until I ran away with your father, and even then, it was hard for me to believe, thanks to what she'd done to my mind."

"How did you meet Dad?"

She remained silent for a moment. "I met and fell in love with your father twice, Justin. I can't tell you about the first time, but the second time, he came to me at great risk. He convinced me Daelissa was filling my head with lies. He rescued me, and I ran away with him."

I felt Elyssa's hand tighten on mine. Mom's story sounded so similar to ours, it sent a shock of pain at the memory. Daelissa had wiped Elyssa's mind. Made her forget me. Somehow, I'd made her fall in love with me all over again, thankfully without her killing me in the process.

"Why can't you tell me about the first time?" I asked in a gentler tone.

"The oath I swore to David. Please understand—"

"Fine," I said, taking a deep breath to bolster my patience. "What made you remember your past?"

"David helped me remember at first, but it was only bits and pieces, and even he didn't have all the answers."

I held my tongue despite the desire to ask how in the world Dad could help her remember, unless he'd known her a lot longer than she let on.

She continued. "When Daelissa put me under a preservation aegis inside the astral prison, it had an unexpected side effect. My mind healed. Memories returned. I helped Nightliss because I knew it was the right thing to do even if I didn't know why." She sniffled. "You don't know how hard it is when everything is so scrambled inside your own brain. When you don't know friend from foe. I haven't trusted myself for years, Justin. I know I've made terrible choices, and I refuse to make excuses for it. All I can do is swear by all the power I have to help you rid the world of Daelissa."

"I know exactly how it is when memories are scrambled," I said. "Because you did it to me." When I was little, she'd blurred memories from my mind to keep me from asking inconvenient questions.

"I'm sorry," she said simply.

I felt Elyssa press her cheek to mine, and closed my eyes as Mom's words sank in. I was still so angry with her. Just thinking about Dad flushed my face with hot fury. Why had he sworn Mom to silence? What secrets was he keeping from me? I thought back to the first time he'd told me what I was. How he'd taught me to feed, and told me about my kind—incubus, Daemos, demon spawn.

Maximus, the leader of a rogue vampire organization had captured him right after those revelations, hoping to use Dad's blood to increase the potency of his so he could turn humans into vampires. Elyssa and I had rescued Dad, but the next day we'd been chased from the home I'd grown up in by hellhounds, and pursued across Atlanta. Dad had, at some point, been marked for death by Underborn, the most notorious assassin in the Overworld, though I found out later the assassin had done it to draw me to him and test my mettle to see if I was the one mentioned in Foreseeance Forty-Three Eleven.

After that, I'd discovered Kassallandra was the one hunting my father because he'd run away with Mom instead of marrying her to unite the major houses of Slade and Assad. The next thing I knew, Dad had decided to marry the Daemas after all since Mom had left him and gone to the Conroys.

My mother and father were definitely down for the worst parents of the millennium award. If anything, I just wanted to punch Dad in the face the next time I saw him.

Despite Mom's explanations, there were too many things that didn't add up. They'd lied to me by omission, keeping me in the dark for most of my life. True, I hadn't manifested any abilities until I turned eighteen, but they had to have known something was changing inside me.

I remembered Underborn once telling me nothing was what it seemed. Even though an overused cliché, it was spot-on when it came to many of the people in my life. My parents largely remained enigmas. I'd discovered Mom was an Arcane during my talk with Dad, only to find out much later she was actually Seraphim. Dad had outright lied to me. Was he really just an incubus, or something more? Was he really just the outcast son, or was he playing everyone for fools?

I drew in a deep breath and let it out. My gut feeling told me Mom was being as honest as she could. One of these days I was going to lock me, Ivy, and our parents in a room and not let anyone out until they gave complete autobiographies.

"I believe you," I said finally.

"Thank you, son," Mom said, her voice broken and tired.

"You need to promise you won't hide anything from me again."

"So long as it doesn't conflict with previous oaths, I promise," she said.

I ground my teeth. Talk about giving herself wiggle room. "Teach me how to unlock my Seraphim abilities."

"That will be very difficult from in here," she said.

"Difficult but necessary," I said. "If I'm ever going to get you out of there, I need my magic to work." I told her about my experience with Darkwater and the ultraviolet light I'd shot from my hand.

"You were a late bloomer, inheriting more from your father's side," Mom said. "Ivy, however, quickly exhibited Seraphim abilities."

"Fine, so she's the star student," I said.

"The warmth you felt in your heart is normal. Our abilities are channeled through our hearts. Why a magical attack allowed you to access your abilities is something I don't understand."

"That's not what I want to hear," I said.

"Perhaps I can help him," said Nightliss, suddenly beside me.

"Is that you, my dear friend?" Mom said, her voice suddenly happier.

"I was your dear friend?" Nightliss said. "I fought with you?"

"You still don't remember," Mom said, the happiness fading to sadness in her voice. "Do you think you can teach him?"

"Perhaps the two of us can."

"I hate to break up the conversation," Thomas Borathen said, obviously not hating it at all. "But we need to think of practical matters first. The diamond fiber on this trailer is breathable, so it allows air in and out. However, there is no way to get food, water, or other sustenance to your mother, Justin."

He didn't need to say another word for me to understand his meaning. "How long can you last without food or water, Mom?" I asked.

She grew silent. "I can go longer than a human, even survive without food or water by putting myself into a deep sleep. But I cannot cast a preservation spell on myself or prevent my need for soul essence. Since diamond fiber repels magic, I can't even feed on aether."

"Does that make it worse?" I asked.

"Daelissa kept my reservoir very close to depleted," she said. "I was on the verge of starvation even as she put me under a preservation spell while in her astral prison. In other words, I'm on the brink of starvation."

"Are we talking days or weeks?" I asked.

## Dearest Mother of Mine

"If I do not feed within a few days," Mom said, the hopelessness plain in her voice, "I will likely die."

# Chapter 28

I would have gone after Kassus right then and there, but I was dead on my feet. Elyssa made me go inside the compound and eat, though all I could do was think about how miserable my mom was without any comforts inside the trailer. She was shackled and blindfolded. I knew how miserable it was to be restrained like that, thanks to Maximus. But even Maximus had given me food and water.

We'd left the portal open inside the Templar garage that morning before traveling to our ambush point. Elyssa and I stepped back through it to the mansion with the others. Despite my worries and concerns, I fell asleep instantly.

My phone woke me up mere hours later.

"Cinder?" I asked in a croaking half-asleep voice. The fact that we'd kind of forgotten the poor guy at El Dorado all this time penetrated my fog-addled brain.

"Justin, I believe we have a problem."

I blinked the sleep out of my eyes. "What is it now? Do we need titanium diapers for the little tykes?"

"I saw other people here earlier," Cinder said. "I am not positive, but I believe they belong to Darkwater."

His words jolted me awake. "What? How?"

"A sizeable force of them came through a smaller arch in the control room. I believe they came prepared to combat cherubs."

"What makes you think that?" I asked.

"Perhaps it's best if you come here. I'll show you what they've done. I suggest you open the portal in the back corner of the control room where it will be out of sight." He disconnected and sent me a picture of the location.

I checked the time. It was five in the morning. At least I'd gotten a little rest. I considered letting Elyssa sleep, but valued my life enough to prod her awake and tell her where I was going.

She was up and dressed in two minutes, and made me wear a fresh set of nightingale armor. The thing looked like a black unitard, but at least it didn't bunch up in the crotch. I retracted the armor to a thin black belt and wore shorts and a T-shirt over it. We grabbed some food from the pantry and left a note on the fridge so people would know where we'd gone.

Cutsauce yipped and ran after us, apparently eager to be off on a new adventure, but I told him to stay behind as usual. I didn't know what a cherub might do to a hellhound, and didn't want to find out. He gave us a dejected look as we left him sitting in the den with a chew toy.

"Your mom really laid a load on you, didn't she?" Elyssa said as we descended to the cellar.

"I felt pretty crappy about it at first, you know?" I shrugged. "But when I put it into perspective, I guess it's not much worse than everything else we've been through."

"Isn't it weird knowing she was the first angel to come here? And how old that makes her?" Elyssa blew out a breath. "I'm still having trouble with that one."

I chuckled. "I guess my mom is vintage, huh?"

"Totes," she said with a wink. "I'm dying to know what she won't tell us about your dad."

"You and me both," I said, trying not to dwell on the matter.

We took the portal to El Dorado, emerging in the far back of the control room where an alcove hid the portal from view. As we walked down the center aisle we gasped in unison.

Cherubs were all over the control room. On the bright side, they were all in clear cube cages as opposed to running free, greedy to suck us dry.

Cinder appeared from behind one of the containers. "Hello, Justin and Elyssa."

"Is this what Darkwater was doing?" I said, feeling a little rude for not saying "Hi" first.

"Yes. They came with devices one might use to capture rabid animals, and in their simplicity, worked brilliantly." Cinder walked to

227

the containers. "Unfortunately, they also witnessed a live angel birth while they were here."

"Oh, crap," I said.

"Very much oh, crap," Cinder said, nodding. "Slitheren and several of his companions were not here to prevent this from happening. I hid and observed, calling you the moment they left."

"With news like that, it won't be long before there's an army of them down here," I said.

"We should leave this instant," Elyssa said. "They could be here any minute." She turned to Cinder. "How long ago were they here?"

"Not more than an hour ago."

"Did they see how the leyworms eat the husks?" she asked.

"I do not believe they made that connection," he replied. "They wanted to investigate, but since the leyworms have become better about depositing the cupids in more orderly fashion, the Darkwater people didn't wish to go any closer to the two leviathans guarding the infants."

I looked around. "Where are Slitheren and his gang?"

"I believe they went to gather other cherubs scattered throughout the caves." Cinder glanced back at the huge leyworms coiled around the nursery.

An arch activation hummed from the center of the control room. We exchanged startled glances and ran into the main cavern, ducking into a dark corner which gave us a clear view of the leviathan leyworms and the control room door. I counted at least twenty dark-robed people emerging from the door, Kassus at the lead. He looked furious, but I couldn't make out his words as he slashed his hands through the air at the people following him. I could only imagine his rage pertained to the truck hijacking.

Two of the lead men walked to the front center area, pointing out the long trench the leyworms had carved, and then toward the glow in the center of the cave where the ginormous dragons perked their heads above scaly coils. I didn't think they could actually see the nursery from that location. One of the men flicked a shiny orb in the air. It darted above the leyworms, bypassing them for an overhead view.

"An all-seeing eye," Elyssa said. "They're going to see everything."

The ASE returned to the sender a moment later, and projected an image large enough for everyone to see, including us. Clearly nestled in between the two leyworms were the angel babies in cribs. One burst into tears. Gray amorphous wings puffed into existence for an instant before fading.

A round of surprised noises emanated from the crowd. Kassus let out an astounded curse.

"This is not good," I said.

"Why are they rounding up cherubs in the first place?" Elyssa asked. "Obviously they didn't know about making cupids, so what are they doing?"

"Clearing the relics," Cinder said. "If they plan to reactivate the Grand Nexus, they probably wish to make them safe for new arrivals."

"Makes sense," Elyssa said.

Kassus made motions with his hands as if indicating he wanted to build something, or maybe set something in place, and jabbed a finger at the leyworms. Three men hesitantly approached the beasts, staffs at the ready. As they closed in, the leyworms raised their heads and made low, rumbling hisses that turned my bowels to water even though they weren't directed at me. The men aimed their staffs at one of the creatures and fired solid beams at it. The energy refracted from the dragon scales, apparently not even irritating the leviathan. The dragon lowered its head, opening its razor-lined maw wide. A pulsating glow grew within.

The men turned tail and ran.

"Morons," Elyssa said.

Kassus shouted at them, but his words failed to convince the men to resume their attacks. They weren't complete idiots. I hoped Kassus tried something. All I needed was a drop of his blood. He backed up a step and stumbled over a sharp-looking piece of rubble. His hand went out to catch himself. I held my breath, hoping, praying he would cut himself. One of the other men caught him before he fell. Kassus shook off the helping hand and glared at the leyworms.

He snapped his fingers. Motioned to one of the other men, and made him stand apart from the others. A woman stepped forward, and waved her staff at the man. Bit by bit, his body vanished from view until only a slight distortion remained visible.

229

"Camouflage," Elyssa said, grimacing.

I stared hard at the slight shimmer in the air as the figure made its way toward the leyworms. The red dragon sniffed the air, its parietal eyes blinking, and then lowered its head. As the shimmer closed to within a few feet, the giant bellowed a roar that seemed to shake the cavern.

I saw the shimmer in the air beat a hasty retreat.

"Hah," Elyssa said in a low whisper. "I like these dragons. They're smart."

"They're going to keep trying until they figure something out," I said. "We need to move the babies, pronto."

"I don't know if the leyworms will allow it," Cinder said. "They've been rather reluctant on that point."

"We need to make them see it's for the best."

"Where in the world would we keep them?" Elyssa said. "They aren't like normal babies."

"The mansion," I said. "Plenty of space."

"They'll need to feed," Elyssa said. "The leyworms provide essence for them."

I face-palmed as an obvious resource occurred to me. "We need to ask my mom how to care for the babies. Maybe her memory is better than Nightliss's."

"Perhaps we could convince the leyworms to let us move the babies to another relic," Cinder said. "One with powerful ley lines, but no Alabaster Arch."

"Where are Slitheren and his pals?" I said, dropping into a sitting position with my back against the stalagmite. "They could chase these bozos off so we could have a little discussion with Gigantor and Lulu."

"Let me guess, the purple one is Lulu?" Elyssa asked.

I returned a wan smile. "I suppose I could have gone with Violet."

"I really don't know where you come up with the names you give animals." She joined me in the sitting position.

"I believe I have a solution," Cinder said, still peering at Kassus and his minions.

I slipped an arm around Elyssa and squeezed her tight. Nothing like spending time with my girl while the man who wanted to kill me stood only a few hundred yards away. "Okay, let's hear it."

"The dungeons beneath Arcane University are large enough to accommodate the leyworms, and the ley lines there should be powerful enough to sustain feeding."

Elyssa peered around our hiding spot at the ginormous creatures. "I don't think the dungeons are nearly tall enough," she said. "The dragons are massive."

I joined her gaze, measuring with my eyes, and something occurred to me. "You know how tall and wide the Obsidian Arches are?" I said. "You could fit a jumbo jet through one of them."

"Maybe without the wings," Elyssa said.

I pursed my lips, trying to imagine the size of the arch. "Why are the arches so large? The people I saw building an arch weren't any larger than a normal human, so why would they need the arches to be so big?"

Cinder tilted his head slightly. "It is an interesting question. The arches in the control room are human sized."

"The Grand Nexus—assuming that's the big Alabaster Arch we saw—was as large as an Obsidian Arch," I said. "Even as big as the leyworms are, they could comfortably fit through those arches."

"Are you saying the leyworms built the arches?" Elyssa said. "Why bother to build the small ones then?"

I shook my head. "No, that's not what I'm saying. What I'm saying is maybe the arches were built to accommodate something the size of a leyworm."

"Perhaps the leyworms came from the world of the builders," Cinder said. "They do have a relationship with the ley lines we don't understand, and the arches are powered by ley lines."

I thought back to how Dash Armstrong had wired Slitheren into his mad scientist lab, using the poor leyworm to power a smaller arch. "What if the dragons are like portable ley lines?"

"They're leaving," Elyssa said, turning back onto her knees to peer around the stalagmite.

I watched Kassus heading toward the control room. I was so tempted to blur up to him, maybe nick his neck with a sharp stone, and steal some of his blood. I could probably do it, I realized, if I took

231

him by surprise. Before they could even react, I'd be gone. I felt a hand tighten around my bicep.

"Don't even think about it," Elyssa whispered.

"I can do it," I said. "Just a scratch. It's all I need."

Her violet eyes smoldered. "I will knock you out before you get a foot away from me."

"Don't you have a Templar gadget that could get his blood?" I asked.

Her stony stare told me the answer.

We sneaked back to the control room and peered inside. Kassus and his men were nowhere to be seen. I jogged back to the giant leyworms.

"I know you don't want to hear this," I told them, "but we really need to move the babies. Those men will be back. They won't give up until they get what they want."

The dragons simply regarded me, occasionally blinking their eyes, and poking their forked tongues out.

"Do you understand me?" I asked.

Gigantor let out a hiss.

"Do they know how to nod and shake their heads?" I asked Cinder.

"I believe they do, but they have never communicated with me in such a way." A bell dinged, and the golem walked toward the nursery. "It is feeding time."

The poor guy had obviously been trapped down here too long. "In case you didn't realize it," I said, "Kassus is coming back. We need to move the babies now. No time for bottle feeding."

"Their diapers also require changing," he said. "Otherwise you might experience an unpleasant odor when trying to move them."

"Where are we taking them?" Elyssa asked. "The dungeons are too tight, and I really don't think it's a good idea for them to burrow out extra space with the university campus overhead."

I imagined the caverns collapsing beneath the weight of the school, dropping students to certain death in the bowels of the earth. It reminded me of our last major challenge involving the Cyrinthian Rune. "I don't know," I admitted after thinking it through. "We need big ley lines and isolation." I realized Elyssa and I had followed Cinder into the nursery where the golem picked up a bottle and held it

232

to the mouth of an infant. "We don't have time," I said in exasperation.

"I agree," Elyssa said. "For the time being, let's move them to the mansion." She picked one of the babies up, wrinkled her nose. "Ugh. I think I just experienced one of those unpleasant odors."

I grabbed a baby, too, wondering if I should double-fist it and try to take one in my other arm. Elyssa walked for the gap between the giant serpents, but the dragons shifted, blocking her from leaving. The red one lowered its head to glare at us from one eye.

"We have to move them," I said. "Don't you understand?"

It hissed, opening its mouth to display teeth taller than me. I backed away. "I'm putting the baby in the crib," I said, and did so.

Elyssa set hers down. "Why are they so protective? Do they have some use for the babies we don't know about?"

Whether they did or not, I knew if we didn't move them, it was only a matter of time before Kassus figured a way to steal them.

# Chapter 29

"Perhaps you should plan to fortify our position here," Cinder said, powdering the bum of a cooing cupid as he changed its diaper. "It does not appear likely their protectors will allow us to move them."

I almost shot back a smart-assed response, but he was right. "I guess we'll head home and let the others know," I said. Elyssa and I were taking one last look at the nursery when part of the answer to our dilemma hit me. I didn't dare mention it in front of the dragons though.

We headed back to the control room. Elyssa snagged a couple spy-bots she'd left monitoring the place to review the footage of the Darkwater people, and sent out two more to monitor the area outside in case the people came back in our absence. After stepping through the portal and closing it behind us, I turned to her.

"We can use the portal to sneak the babies out," I said. "All I have to do is open it in the nursery, and we can wheel the cribs through before the leyworms can stop us."

She quirked her mouth and nodded. "It is a good idea, but I don't think it's the right one."

"Why isn't it right?"

"Because we need the leyworms. They're the only ones who can feed the cupids without us resorting to offering ourselves or others to do the job." She sighed. "Until we have a better place to move them, we'll have to hope the leyworms are up to the task."

I had a feeling once Slitheren and the younger leyworms returned, their defenses would be quite a bit stronger. Maybe Kassus wouldn't be able to get past the leviathans. In any case, his presence would be a golden opportunity for me to get his blood and free my mom.

I had lunch with Elyssa, and then travelled via the portal to see Mom. She didn't respond when I knocked on the side of the trailer. I knocked again, my stomach feeling sick with worry. What if she'd miscalculated about how long she could last?

"Mom?" I said, knocking again.

"I'm here," said an exhausted voice.

I blew out a sigh of relief. "How are you feeling?"

"Tired," she said. "I considered putting myself in a light preservation spell, but the effort might cost too much of my dwindling reserves."

I should have taken the chance with Kassus earlier, I thought. *Damn it, why didn't I try?*

"I'm sure my health isn't the only reason you've come, son. What do you need?"

I pushed aside the anger and took deep breaths to center myself on the task at hand. Then I told her about the cupids.

Her incredulous gasp echoed from within the container. "They live again? How is this possible?"

"I think it's the same thing that happened to you," I said, referring to the last thing she remembered at the destruction of the Grand Nexus. "It's why you were raised as a child by the Conroys."

"It's unbelievable, but it makes sense," she said, wonder still in her voice.

"Yeah, as if anything about life makes sense," I said. "Well, Kassus found out about them. Apparently, he and the Darkwater people are going to the relics with Alabaster Arches and clearing them of cherubs. That's how they stumbled across the cupid nursery. We may need to move the babies, but we're not sure how to feed them soul essence without the leyworms."

"They're consuming soul essence at this age?" Mom said. "They shouldn't require that for the first few years, at least not until they learn to channel."

"Channel?" I said.

"Yes, that's what we call it when we use our magic."

"Isn't it all channeling?" I pulled out my staff and imagined how Shelton and the others did it. "Arcanes channel through staffs and wands."

"That's actually casting," Mom said. "Believe me, I learned how to do Arcane magic, and there are many differences. The source remains the same, but the method is much different."

"Explain," I said.

"Arcanes use an internal well to hold their aether. When they use magic, they draw upon that well, focusing their will through a staff, wand, or other instrument to enact the spell. Our kind have the ability to channel aether directly from the source."

"But we have an internal well," I said.

"We do, yes, and it's much larger than an Arcane's. On the downside, we don't utilize it as efficiently as Arcanes do, possibly because they've had centuries to perfect casting from smaller reservoirs."

I still wasn't too clear on the difference between channeling and casting, except for how we utilized the aether. I could appreciate the strength we had, namely being able to draw directly from a ley line and into a spell. But we were off subject.

"Back to the cupids—you say they shouldn't be feeding off soul essence yet. Why do you think these are?"

"Perhaps they are different since they've been reborn. They are not normal Seraphim children, I can tell you that."

We talked a little longer, but she didn't have much more to tell me other than most normal angel infants breastfed like humans. Our brief conversation only raised more questions, which I didn't ask since Mom sounded so tired.

I pressed my hand to the side of the trailer, wishing more than anything I could touch her hand, or bring her comfort. "I love you, Mom."

My supernatural hearing picked up the faint sounds of crying from within. "I love you, too, son. I'm sorry for all I've put you through."

I leaned my forehead against the side, squeezing my eyes shut to dam up the tears. "It's okay," I said, my voice hoarse. When I was younger, Friday night was family night. Dad would buy pizza, and we would all watch a movie or play board games. As I'd grown older, I'd

236

wanted to hang out with my nerd friends or play computer games instead of sitting with the parents.

*What I wouldn't give to have that back right now.*

Had my childhood been a sham? Had family nights been faked by my parents to make us seem normal, or had they really wanted to be that way? A part of me burned to question Mom about every aspect, but she needed rest and I needed to spend my time tracking Kassus and drawing his blood.

I knew where Kassus would be again soon. That was a huge advantage. All I had to do was figure out how to capitalize on it. I called a meeting when I returned home. Many in our gang already knew since Elyssa had told them.

"Let me get this straight," Shelton said. "You want to ambush a squad of elite battle mages?"

"We don't have to ambush them," I said. "All we need is Kassus."

"Even if we all pitch in, that ain't an easy task," Shelton said. "Those people are used to fighting. They're conditioned to respond to surprises with deadly force."

"What about a drain ward?" I asked, looking at Bella. "You know how to make them. Why don't we rig the cavern with them?"

She pressed her lips together. "Sure, we could try. It might take me a couple of days to make one, though."

*We don't have a couple of days.*

"How about stealth tactics?" I said. "Can we separate Kassus and knock him out?"

Elyssa answered. "Separating him would be the tricky part. If I can get him alone, I'll just dart him and knock him out."

"How about we shoot all of them with Lancer darts?" I asked. "If we all fired at once, they'd never have a chance to respond."

She moved her head side-to-side as if considering the proposal. "It might work."

"Hold on," Shelton said holding up his hands palms out. "If these guys are worth their salt—and I know for a fact they are—their robes are warded with armor and magic resistance spells. To stand a chance at knocking them out, we'd have to hit every one of them on naked skin. That would mean neck, head, or hands."

I considered the odds of us nailing twenty-plus people with such precision. It didn't seem likely. If even a handful remained conscious, they could still put up a hell of a fight. And what if Kassus brought in even more battle mages his next visit?

"We have some pretty important unanswered questions," Adam said, rescuing us from silence. "The first is what do the leyworms want with the cupids? If we know the answer to that, we'll probably know why they don't want us moving the babies. And next, does Kassus have even the remotest chance of stealing a baby right out from under the leyworms, especially once the younger ones return from wherever they went?"

"Good questions," I said. "But that's not the matter at hand. We need Kassus's blood. Since we can't move the babies, we might as well use the situation to our advantage."

"I just feel like it might be a big risk not moving the babies," Adam said. "Using them as bait doesn't feel right."

"We're not using them," I said. "The leyworms won't let us move them, so we're making do with the situation."

"I don't think directly attacking these men is the answer," Meghan said. "While we each have our strengths, they have the manpower and firepower to kill us all."

"I'm not advocating attacking them," I said, frustration starting to rise within me. "We don't have time to sit around and hope Kassus makes a mistake. We need his blood *now*."

"We want to help you any way we can," Adam said. "None of us here wants your mother to die."

"If we go about this the wrong way, a lot more than your mom stand to die," Ryland said. "Maybe we should have a talk with Commander Borathen. He might spare a squad to help."

"I already talked with him," Elyssa said.

I huffed. "And the answer is no," I said. "Shouldn't even bother asking him. It's not like he helped rescue my mom." I knew I was being unfair. He'd left the decision in my hands and I'd decided the political consequences would be too severe, opting only for auxiliary help.

Lips pressed tight, she raised an eyebrow at me. "He said yes." I could tell from the tension in her voice she wasn't happy with me right then.

"Oh," I said.

She sighed and shook her head. "He had to reposition assets thanks to the Synod moving their own troops into my father's territory, but he agreed to provide us with his best special ops squad to resolve the situation."

"Whoa, why didn't you mention this earlier?" Shelton said.

"I just got the text from him a few seconds ago," she said. "He told me Alysea is too valuable to let die, and that, so long as the operation could be done in a way to minimize exposure, he would provide support."

"Does he know about the cupids?" Adam asked.

"No, but we'll have to tell him," Elyssa said. She gave me a cross look. "Happy?"

I looked away. "Yes."

"I'm happy you're happy," she said in a tone indicating she was anything but. "This opens up several options, including the one Justin mentioned earlier about simply knocking them all unconscious. We have other crowd-control options that might work, depending on what sort of defenses Kassus's people have."

"I'd like to know what his people are doing with the cherubs," Adam said.

I wanted to know the answers to a lot of things, but right then, nothing else mattered but blood. "Let's get these Templars here," I said, trying to ignore Elyssa's baleful glare. "If we set up a trap and nail them with Lancers all at once, maybe we can do this thing."

I dismissed the meeting. Elyssa stormed from the room. I followed her up to the bedroom, and shut the door. "Why are you so mad?" I asked.

"My father hasn't helped?" she said in a rhetorical tone. "Really? After providing a pilot and a slider to retrieve the trailer? After providing a place to keep your mother? After providing the car you and I used in the operation? After leaving the decision for his intervention in your hands?"

"I didn't mean it like that," I said. "He just wouldn't get involved—"

"And he had a very good reason for not showing his hand," Elyssa said. "You can't just plow into everything, heedless of consequences, Justin. Sometimes you have to use tact and tactics."

"Fine," I said, throwing up my hands. "I'm sorry I insulted your father. That wasn't my intention."

She sank onto the bed, tears welling in her eyes. I looked at her, completely confused. Why was she having such an overreaction? I thought back to what I'd said, but aside from some whining, I couldn't think of anything to bring Elyssa to tears. As usual, seeing her cry made me feel like a complete villain. I sat beside her, wrapping my arms around her shoulders and hugging her.

"I'm sorry, baby. I was a complete ass. Please forgive me."

She turned and buried her face in my shoulder. "It's not you," she said. "It's everything going on with the Synod and the Templars." Elyssa looked up at me, her face beautiful despite the red blotches from crying. "They tried to murder my father, Justin. They tried to kill you and everyone in a leadership position. What are they going to do next? How can we stop them if they try?" She drew in a shuddering breath. "I don't know what to do."

Her reaction suddenly made sense. I knew exactly where she was coming from. She felt powerless to stop the Synod from killing her father and other people she cared about. It was one thing to fight an army, but another thing entirely to stop one man or a group of them on a suicide mission. If Ivy hadn't warned us, there would have been so much blood spilled that day, including my own.

I kissed her on the forehead. "I understand. If we can get my mom out of that box, she'll be one more layer of protection." I hated referring to my mom like that, but it was true.

"Then that's what we have to do," Elyssa said. "Save your mom so we can save everyone else."

"How do you think we should do it?" I asked.

She wiped tears from her face. "I think your plan could work. It's simple, straightforward, and not as complicated as most of the stuff you come up with."

"It's just stupid simple," I said, offering her a grin. "You can say it."

She laughed, her hands absentmindedly picking a piece of lint from my shirt and flicking it away. "Those plans are usually the best." She surprised me with a kiss. "You always know how to cheer me up."

I wished I knew exactly what I'd said to clear the air, but just smiled as if I had everything covered. "I like seeing you smile."

She took out her phone and dialed. "Let's get this party started."

# Chapter 30

Twenty-five Templars outfitted with Lancers and bearing satchels full of other crowd-control items stepped through the portal and into the main cavern outside the El Dorado control room. Thanks to our omniarch, they'd arrived a little over an hour after Elyssa's request.

I'd called ahead and spoken with Cinder to make sure the coast remained clear before coming, even though we opened the portal farther back into the main cave for easy insertion and escape should that become necessary.

"We'll set up the perimeter," said the leader of the elite Templar squad, a man named Hutchins.

The group of dark-clad Templars dispersed, placing what looked like rocks in a loose circle around the area where the Darkwater people had stood the last time.

"Those are stun mines," Elyssa explained. "We can trigger them to blind and disorient a group. Once they go off, we'll knock them out with Lancer darts and secure them."

"This is the kind of equipment I'm talking about," I said, feeling immeasurably better about our success. We spent the next thirty minutes watching the men set up. Shelton and the others remained on standby, but I didn't think we'd need their help with the pros on our team. Once everything was set up, Hutchins and his men hid behind other boulders and debris they'd moved into strategic positions and waited. Elyssa and I picked our own hiding spot with a good view. We both had Lancers equipped and ready. I figured with this many people firing darts, we stood a good chance of hitting most of the people Kassus brought through.

The dragons, for their part, merely watched, their huge heads swiveling around the cavern as the men worked, apparently unconcerned so long as nobody tried to violate the boundary of their giant coiled bodies.

The wait dragged on and on.

"What's taking Kassus so long?" I asked Elyssa.

She leaned back against the rock. "Tackling two leviathan dragons isn't an easy task. I'm sure he's taking his time with preparations."

I sighed and sat down, trying to calm my anxiety. My mind kept playing through scenarios, each one ending with me drawing Kassus's blood with a small brass-enclosed vial Meghan had given me. It didn't have a needle. All I had to do was put it against the man's bare skin, activate it with a button, and it would draw and store blood.

Time slogged forward. I thought about my mom and how weak she was becoming. I thought about letting her feed off me the minute I burst inside and rescued her. I wondered how Kassus planned to get past the dragons. Would he use brute force, or try something sneaky like the camouflaged man earlier? He seemed like a violent person, but I knew he wasn't stupid. Nobody earned a reputation like his by being a fool.

Finally, I heard a faint hum from the control room. A light flashed three times from a position near the door.

*They're here.*

My stomach twisted. My shoulder muscles pinched. This was it.

*Go time.*

The Darkwater people filed in, each one bearing large satchels. I strained my eyes to pick out the features of each one, but didn't see Kassus's bald head in the mix. The black-robed people unpacked machine guns and began setting them up on tripods in a line across the front. I noted they all stood within the perimeter of stun mines.

"Are those nom weapons?" I asked Elyssa.

She peered out at them, her eyes darting from one weapon to the next. "Looks like it," she whispered back.

"What do they expect to accomplish with those?"

"I need to see the ammo, but even I can't make out the details from here." She took out a pair of black binoculars and gazed through them for a moment. When she slid back behind the barrier, she looked concerned. "Those bullets are tipped with diamond fiber," she said. "I don't think I've seen anything like it before."

"What does that mean?"

Her eyes looked lost in concentration for a moment, and snapped wide. "The dragons are magic resistant, but if you think about what they are, they're like aether sponges. Maybe it has to do with their relationship to aether. But diamond fiber repels magic, and ordinary bullets use scientific properties to work. Kassus must think this ammo will penetrate their scales."

"But the bullets are so small," I said. "Even if they do punch through scales, how could they hurt something that size?"

She shook her head slowly. "I don't know. It'd be like mosquito bites. But if enough mosquitos bite you, it's seriously annoying and painful."

"So their brilliant plan is to piss the giant dragons off," I said. "We won't need to do anything. They're gonna get themselves killed."

"There's something we're missing," she said. "Even if they provoke the dragons, what do they hope to gain?"

"I still don't see Kassus," I said, using her binoculars to survey the invaders. "What if he doesn't show?"

Her forehead pinched. "We can't let them go through with their plan."

"But we'll give away our advantage." I dropped back behind cover. "Kassus will know that someone else is aware of this place."

We both watched in silence as the men finished setting up. A dark figure appeared from the shadows, nearly giving me a heart attack.

"Target is not present," Hutchins said. "What are your orders?"

Elyssa looked from me and back to the man. "We apprehend them as planned."

"No," I said. "Just wait. Maybe Kassus will show up. Maybe he's on the way right now."

Hutchins's eyes narrowed. "We need to act now before they start firing."

"Please, wait," I said, gripping Elyssa's hand. "Just a little longer."

Hutchins turned to me. "I respect what you've done, Slade. I saw you in action the day the Synod tried to assassinate Commander

Borathen and the others. You're quick, decisive, and from what I've heard, you've earned the respect of those you work with." His lips pressed together for an instant. "But this is a tightly controlled operation. Cadet Borathen and I have the experience and the knowledge necessary for success. I understand the primary target isn't here, and if Elyssa tells us to stand down, we will. But given what's at stake"—he nodded his head toward the nursery—"I don't see it as an option to let these people potentially destroy what could be a valuable asset to us in the future."

"There might not be a future if we don't capture Kassus," I said. "My mother can help us *now* when we need it the most."

He nodded. "I understand."

"Justin, we can't let the battle mages attack," Elyssa said. "We'll find another way to capture Kassus."

I clenched my fists, trying to keep my anger down. How could Elyssa do this to me? To my mom? Didn't she see what was at stake?

Hutchins's gaze intensified as he seemed to notice something in the front of the room.

I followed his gaze to see a blue-tinged bubble surrounding the Darkwater people. The muzzles of the machine guns poked through it.

"A shield to block magic attacks," he said. "The bullets and machine guns can go through it, but the mines can't," he said. "They're not powerful enough to punch through."

"We waited too long," Elyssa said. Her troubled eyes met mine. "Now we'll be lucky if we can do anything to stop them."

Her words stung me even if she said them without malice. I still didn't believe attacking these men was the right thing to do. Not because I didn't want to protect the leyworms or the babies, but because Kassus was the whole reason we set up this operation. It seemed short-sighted to go through with it otherwise because we'd lose the element of surprise. With Kassus and his men, that might be the only thing preventing us from ending up dead. Elyssa might have the right to give the commands, but I couldn't be afraid to let her know I disagreed.

"Stand down," I said. "We wait for Kassus."

Elyssa arched an eyebrow. "Since when are you authorized to give commands to these men?"

"Maybe I'm not," I said. "But I called together this operation. I came up with the plan. Maybe I don't know what the hell I'm talking about, but Kassus is the goal, not protecting the leyworms or the nursery." I motioned my head toward the monsters. "Do you really think machine guns and fancy bullets are going to kill them? The minute they open fire, the leyworms will slaughter them."

"I don't—" Elyssa began.

I interrupted her. "Answer me this: If we go ahead with the operation while they have a shield up, what are the odds of achieving our goals?" I glanced at Hutchins.

"Substantially reduced," he said. "The mines will only faze those at the outer edges. Those in the center will be more protected. Some of the mines were moved by the Darkwater people when they cleared out the place to set their guns, which will also result in reduced impact."

"Do you agree?" I asked Elyssa.

She looked at me as if puzzled by my behavior. "Yes."

"Then we stand down and wait."

Hutchins looked to Elyssa.

She regarded me for a long moment before nodding. "Stand down."

I turned back toward the Darkwater men in the front as they made final preparations, loading the machine guns with bullet belts. One of them set up another tripod that looked a lot like a mortar launcher while another opened a case and removed a rocket launcher. A few choice curses escaped my lips. Kassus obviously believed in all or nothing. I didn't know if a hail of bullets could kill the leyworms, or possibly the cupids, but the man was an evil son of a bitch for taking this path.

I scanned the cavern and decided on a different plan. "Hutchins, see the cluster of stalactites above the attackers?"

"We call them OPFOR," he said. "Opposing force."

"Whatever," I said, waving away his jargon. "Can you get a charge up there?"

He regarded it for a moment. Nodded. "We have a flying carpet we could use. The ceiling is high enough the OPFORs won't see us."

"Do it," I said. "If they open fire, we'll bring down the roof on their heads."

"Yes, sir," he said, not even bothering to check with Elyssa, and vanished into the shadows.

"We're going to have a talk after this," Elyssa said.

I realized I wasn't angry with her for her earlier decision. I also realized I wasn't particularly concerned if she was mad at me now. There was something about taking responsibility for all these lives that weighed heavily on my shoulders in some ways, while lightening the burden in others. Maybe I'd gone a little cold, or maybe I'd just accepted that a natural part of leadership was accepting loss.

I simply nodded in reply to her statement. Even though the stalactites above the Darkwater people were barely visible from the floor, I couldn't actually see the roof of the cave. My supernatural night vision wouldn't reach that far. I thought I noticed a shadowy shape moving far above, but couldn't be sure.

"How will you feel about killing those people?" Elyssa said.

My head turned sharply toward her, surprised by the question. The answer came to me without thinking about it. "Probably sick to my stomach," I said, especially considering how gruesome it would be. "But Kassus might think it was an accident with their explosive weapons instead of an outright attack."

She nodded. "I wasn't accusing you of anything. I wanted you to think this through as opposed to a non-lethal strike."

"Considering the circumstances now, I don't think non-lethal is a possibility." I spared another glance above, anxious to know the explosives were ready. "If we fail to incapacitate them, we'll have a full-scale battle on our hands with Templars versus battle mages." In my head, it sounded geek-tastic, at least if it were on a movie screen. In real life, it would be messy as hell.

"I agree," Elyssa said. "But only because we waited."

"I thought we were going to talk about this later," I said without turning my gaze from the ceiling.

She made a very unladylike growl. "Yes, we are."

Somehow, I managed not to gulp.

Hutchins appeared. "Charges are set. We have two options. One will blow off the entire group of stalactites, in effect increasing the odds of killing nearly all OPFORs. The second option will only bring down a few select stalactites and offer incapacitation with minimal deaths. My man also arranged the charges to match the explosion signature of a mortar launcher so it won't look as if a third party engineered it."

*He read my mind.* It was obvious why Hutchins was on special ops. "Excellent. We'll need to wait until they start firing."

"Just tell me if you want lethal or non-lethal."

"We'll try non-lethal first. Maybe that will send them packing for the day and bring Kassus back to do the job right."

"Yes, sir," he said.

I was beginning to like being in charge.

Someone with Darkwater shouted orders. I glanced at them to see people manning the machine guns. The mortar and rocket launchers were out of sight. I wasn't sure if they planned to use them for the first salvo or not.

"Aim!" shouted the Darkwater person.

A dozen machineguns swiveled toward the leyworms.

"Fire!"

The cavern exploded with noise. Tracers lanced through the air as bullets whizzed past. The dragons bellowed. Twisted. Gigantor loosed a terrific scream of pain.

A shock of white light exploded in the cavern, blinding me temporarily. "Stop!" cried a voice so loud it rang in my ears.

The guns stopped firing. I blinked my eyes, waiting for the bright afterimages to fade. When they finally readjusted, I looked to the front to see Darkwater people rubbing their eyes, looking dazed and confused. The shield had vanished, and the machine guns hung limp, smoke rising from the ends of the barrels.

I spotted a man in a top hat, wearing a white suit and a light blue bowtie. A gray goatee and a long white staff identified the man readily enough.

Jeremiah Conroy.

# Chapter 31

"You will leave," he said in a voice loud enough to wake the dead, pointing his staff toward the door.

The men wasted no time packing their equipment and hightailing it out of there while Elyssa and I exchanged confused looks. Hutchins watched Jeremiah like an eagle, never taking his eye off the man.

"What's going on?" Elyssa whispered.

I shrugged, confused as she was. Why had Jeremiah called off the attack? Didn't he own Darkwater? Hadn't Kassus told him about his plans to engage gargantuan dragons in open warfare? On the other hand, I felt immensely relieved I wouldn't have to bring the roof down.

After the last Darkwater person left, Jeremiah walked toward the dragons. My heart raced with fear. I knew what this man was capable of. On the other hand, we now had him surrounded by Templars and could probably knock him out and take him prisoner. He could order Kassus to unseal the truck.

*Bam! Good guys win.*

Before I could give the command, the red dragon came forward, lowering its giant head next to Jeremiah. Its snout stood nearly twice as tall as the Arcane. Jeremiah patted the snout, almost as one might pet a dog. The dragon made a snuffling noise and rumbled. Jeremiah raised an eyebrow, and I saw a shield flicker around his body. Then he bowed to the leyworm, backed away, and left.

The command to apprehend died on my lips. Had the leyworm warned him somehow? And why in the hell had it let Jeremiah Conroy pet it?

"What the hell is going on?" Hutchins said, his stoic exterior faltering.

"I really need to have a talk with those dragons," I said. "Gigantor acted like he and Jeremiah are best buddies."

"Well, now we know why he stopped the Darkwater idiots from hurting them," Elyssa said. "He's *friends* with them."

Hutchins looked at a device on his wrist. "Area is clear of OPFOR."

I stood and stretched as questions raced through my head. "There's a lot about Jeremiah Conroy that doesn't make sense."

"Like how he knew about the Cyrinthian Rune, and how to disable the shield around it, for one thing," Elyssa said.

"Or why he apparently hasn't given Daelissa the rune yet," I said, "assuming Mr. Gray and Lornicus told me the truth."

"He's definitely not a Seraphim?" Elyssa said.

"I don't think so." I tapped a finger against my chin. "According to Ivy, he was against the assassination attempts on your father and the others. He's had multiple chances to kill me—"

"Don't forget he nearly killed you in Maximus's stronghold," Elyssa said. "And he told Ivy to let you die before she saved you."

I shuddered at the memory of having my breath cut off. Of being held helpless with no hope of surviving until my mom had miraculously showed up and saved me. "He told Ivy not to save me, but he didn't interfere with her either."

Unfortunately, I had a lot on the stove that was more important than digging into Jeremiah's psyche. Part of me felt crushed, defeated. We hadn't even had an opportunity to capture Kassus. But wondering about Jeremiah also brought to mind resources I hadn't considered using. One in particular might be the answer.

"What are your orders?" Hutchins said, looking at Elyssa.

She raised an eyebrow, looking my way as if daring me to say something. "Remain on standby. Take your men back through the portal, but leave a scout. The minute you see activity, I want to know about it. If Kassus shows up, notify me and get in position. I showed the Arcane in your squad how to use the omniarch so you can get back here in an instant, if need be."

He saluted. "Yes, sir." Hutchins made a circle in the air with his finger, and shadowy forms of Templars appeared around him like—well—magic.

Elyssa took me by the arm and directed me toward the portal. "So, *Almighty Commander*," she said, putting particular emphasis on the last word. "Do you have any orders for me?"

We walked through the portal. Shelton and the others were crowded around the omniarch, eyes confused.

"What the hell just happened?" he asked.

I shook my head. "Your guess is as good as mine. I'm going to eat."

Elyssa and I walked up the stairs. I felt her expectant eyes on me, waiting for the talk. I wouldn't blame her if she was mad at me, but I felt justified in what I'd done. I was disappointed in the outcome, but that had been out of our control. If she'd taken the action she'd wanted to, it could have compromised everything else. I was angriest at myself. The minute Jeremiah had been alone, I should've ordered him knocked out. Then again, how the hell was I supposed to foresee the dragon warning him?

We reached the kitchen, empty of people since just about everyone else was still downstairs. Elyssa opened her mouth to say something. I gripped her shoulder and pinned her against the wall with one hand in a blur of speed.

Her eyes flared with surprise.

"You may not agree with my decisions, Elyssa, but they're my decisions to make. This was my operation, and I should have insisted the Templars be under my control before the start. Not establishing the proper chain of command was my mistake." I paused, seeing if she'd respond, but her violet eyes stared at me, smoldering with intensity. I had the distinct feeling she might actually kick my ass after this. I continued anyway.

"If you don't agree the Templars in my operations should be under my control, then we won't use them. I feel I made the best decisions under the circumstances, and if you don't agree, I'm sorry." I took in a deep breath. "I love you, but I refuse to be treated like a non-combatant after everything I've been through. I've earned your respect, and the respect of the others, just as you all have earned my respect."

Her jaw tightened. I tensed, waiting for her to punch me. She shook her head, her gaze never leaving mine. "*You*," she said in a rough voice, "are so"—she narrowed her eyes—"sexy when you take control like that."

She pushed me atop the kitchen table and straddled me, pressing her lips hard to mine. We rolled off the table and thudded on the floor, still kissing, as blood turned to fire in my veins. I felt my shirt rip off. Felt her fangs sting my neck. I grabbed her hair, pulling her head back and saw the fangs beneath red lips. I nipped her neck. Heard her moan. Felt her hands press to my chest.

I heard a little growl and a yip followed by a human yelp of surprise.

"For crying out loud, people, get a room!"

We looked up, panting, into Shelton's disturbed gaze. Cutsauce stood near his feet, wagging his tail.

"This is a kitchen, not a damned bordello," he said, throwing up his hands and slamming the door shut behind him.

Elyssa and I burst into laughter. Then we gathered our things and ran upstairs to finish what we'd started.

After eating and recovering some energy from the day's activities, I called Lornicus.

"You never call, you never write," he said.

"I've been busy."

"Indeed," the golem said. "You successfully retrieved your mother, or so I've heard."

"Almost." I'd considered how much to tell him, especially with regards to the possible discovery of the arch creators. Unfortunately, I already knew what his price would be for my next request. "I need Maulin Kassus's blood."

"Ah, I can see how that might be a problem."

I told him about Kassus discovering the babies, and tossed in Jeremiah's strange behavior as a bonus. "You have spies everywhere. Can you help me get the blood?"

"Indeed I can," Lornicus said. "I can have it for you tomorrow."

My mouth fell open. "You can?"

"Yes. But there is my price."

My teeth clacked together. *I knew it!* "I thought we were partners."

"We are, Mr. Slade," Lornicus said. "But, as with the cost of rescuing your mother, this is a bit above simple information sharing."

252

"Skip to the point," I said, exhibiting the part of me I'd learned from Shelton. "What do you want?" I already knew the answer, but with luck, he might have something less distasteful than baby-snatching.

"Very simple," he said. "As I stated before, I would like one of the cupids."

My hand clenched around my phone. "You want to trade blood for a baby angel. That's not a fair trade."

"It's immensely fair," he said. "You're receiving a grown angel who also happens to be your mother, and I'm receiving an angel that will require a great deal of care, changes of diapers, and all sorts of other things I can only imagine." He sniffed. "Really now, you'll have several more cupids all to yourself."

"That's not the only issue," I said, trying not to grind my teeth. "The leyworms won't let us take one. Maybe you don't remember our earlier conversation, but they won't even let us move them to keep them safe from the likes of Darkwater."

"I believe you're intentionally forgetting something which could prove indispensable in such an endeavor," he said. "Namely, your omniarch."

*Damn it. This golem thinks of every angle.* "And once you have the angel, you'll indoctrinate it and turn it into a terror."

"No sense in being melodramatic, Mr. Slade." A smug note sounded in Lornicus's voice.

I still didn't see any possible way I could rationalize kidnapping an infant, no matter how much I wanted to save Mom. Giving a child to a complete stranger, not to mention a golem, was just plain wrong. *It's just one angel. I can rescue Mom!* "You realize these babies aren't fresh out of the oven. They're different. I think the same thing happened to my mom when the Grand Nexus was destroyed. Her memories returned as she aged. What makes you think you'll be able to control whoever I give you?"

"There are no guarantees," Lornicus replied. "But I must try and hope for the best. It is better than extinction."

"Extinction?" I said. "What are you talking about?"

"Will you do it or not?" he asked in a brisk tone.

"I need to think about it." I should have just flat-out told him no, but didn't want to burn the bridge just yet.

"The clock is ticking, Mr. Slade. Your mother may not last much longer."

I choked back a nasty response. "I guess you have no conscience about it one way or the other. After all, you're just a soulless golem." I disconnected. *Son of a bitch!* I hissed an angry breath between my teeth. I had to find an alternative.

In the war room, I found a tray with spherical indentions designed to hold ASEs, and sorted through them until I found the one with the invoices for the supernatural transportation trucks. After flicking through the files for a few minutes, I located the routes for the trucks, and traced the one from the Conroy's house to the industrial park they'd planned to take Mom. I took out my phone and marked the spot on my map for future reference. I scanned through more and more documents, hoping to find what I needed.

I lost track of time until Elyssa showed up, a concerned look on her face. "Why didn't you answer my texts?"

Glancing at my phone, I saw two missed texts from her and one from Shelton. "Sorry, I guess I didn't hear it."

"More like you filtered everything out," she said, pulling up a chair next to me, a mug of steaming liquid in her hand. "Why are you going through this stuff again?"

I told her about Lornicus's demand.

"It's no different than before," she growled. "What do you want to do?"

My eyebrows arched. "I want to get my mom back, but I can't just hand over a helpless baby."

"That doesn't answer why you're going through the information we stole from Darkwater."

I told her what I was looking for and why.

She took a sip from her mug, eyes never leaving mine. "I guess it could work."

"Gee, don't encourage me too much." I sighed and flicked to another page, scanning the dates.

"I'll help."

"You don't have to."

She punched me in the shoulder. "Stop feeling sorry for yourself, punk."

I grabbed another ASE with a copy of the information and gave it to her. "Is that coffee?"

"It's tea."

"I need coffee. All this reading is about to put me to sleep."

Her lips curled into a smile. "Shelton just made a fresh pot."

"Maybe I can ask him to help."

Her smile turned amused. "I don't think you want to disturb him right now."

I felt my eyebrow arch. "Why?"

She snickered. "Let's just say there's probably a tie hanging from the doorknob to his bedroom right now."

"Oh," I said, dragging out the vowel. "I wonder how he handles Bella without supernatural strength."

Elyssa shuddered. "Gross, Justin! TMI."

I laughed, left the room to get some coffee. Cutsauce yipped and raced ahead of me, stopping in my path and growling as if he wanted me to follow. I did so, and found something dead and furry in the hallway. It looked like a rat. My hellhound barked and sat next to it, tail wagging.

"Great job," I told him, petting him on the head. "You're keeping us all safe, big fella."

He growled, prodding it with his nose.

I really didn't want to touch the nasty thing. "Uh, why don't you take it outside," I said.

Cutsauce pushed the rat over with his nose so I could see how the skull was crushed.

"Jeez, did you do that?" Apparently, the little hellhound was stronger than I thought. I considered going to the kitchen and finding a stick to pick it up with when I realized something very strange about the corpse. The floor around it was unstained by blood. The fur was clean. With a crushed skull, there should have been brains and gunk all over the place.

Overcoming my distaste, I knelt down and looked at the skull. It wasn't made of bone, but wood. The fur felt strange, like polyester or something similar. The flesh beneath the fur was actually rubber or foam. To outward appearances, this thing looked exactly like a rat. On closer inspection, I realized it was a golem.

# Chapter 32

I picked up the fake rat by the tail and took it back inside the war room, dropping it unceremoniously on the table. Elyssa shrieked and leapt several feet into the air.

"Why the hell are you putting a dead rat on the table?" she asked, her surprise turning to anger.

"It's not a dead rat," I said, and explained the fake corpse.

"You think Lornicus has these things spying on us?" she asked.

"Most likely."

Elyssa turned it over in her hands. "What crushed its skull?"

"I think maybe Cutsauce bit it."

"Strong puppy."

"He might be cute and tiny, but he is a hellhound." I wondered if Lornicus had sent these inside the house as part of the bargain for keeping me safe from the Black Robe Brotherhood, or if they'd been here longer. It also explained how he seemed to know things before I told him. If so, why did he deal with me at all? The only reason I could think of was his desire for a cupid.

I called Stacey. She and Ryland were staying in the mansion, but the place was so large it saved time just to phone. Plus, I didn't want to risk finding a tie on their doorknob.

"Yes, darling?" she purred.

"We have a rat problem." I gave her the details.

"How very fortunate I am your friend." She let out a throaty laugh. "I'll take care of it."

"I don't think your friends will like the way these taste."

"It is of no matter," she said. "The hunt is the fun part."

I dropped into a seat at the table. "I hope the muffle wards on this room kept those damned things from hearing our conversations."

"We'll just have to assume Lornicus knows everything," she said, looking around the room.

The room was barren of anything but the table, which would make it difficult for a rat to have slipped in unnoticed. I had to admit using rodents was pretty ingenious. I wondered if they were in the walls, too. A place like this had to be riddled with secret passages even if the walls seemed solid.

"Templars use golem roaches," Elyssa said. "They're useless for recording intel because of limited storage, but they're great for mapping."

"I haven't seen many bugs around this place, not since the golem butler cleaned it up." I picked up Cutsauce and scratched behind his ears. "You're awesome," I said. "You're the bestest little hellhound in the whole world."

He growled, probably at the term "little" but still licked my nose with his black tongue. His sulfurous breath didn't smell too awful to me, though I had to wonder if that had something to do with my infernal nature. I made a second trip to the kitchen, this time procuring coffee and some snacks, and went back to the war room where Elyssa and I pored over documents. We discovered all sorts of interesting things, keeping conversation limited and typing or writing notes to each other instead of saying anything important in case rat spies hid in the walls.

We discovered more transport jobs to the warehouse Darkwater had been planning to keep my mom in, and dozens of transports out to Kobol Prison. How many people were they locking up?

*We can't let this stand,* Elyssa wrote on an arctablet, making another notation about a transportation route to the prison. *We have to find out who they're keeping there and save them.*

*Yes, but first Mom,* I wrote back.

She smiled. "I know, I know."

Adam's program had downloaded a lot of other information from the Darkwater node, including other business dealings the organization had. They ran all sorts of dirty little rackets, including quite a number in the mortal world. They had gambling clubs, strip clubs, and a variety of other rackets involving organized crime. Shelton had been right about them being the equivalent of the Overworld mafia. We found personnel files. It seemed the vast majority of Darkwater employees were also with the brotherhood, aside from clerical workers. Nearly every Arcane had notations which indicated whether they'd be a good prospect for brotherhood membership or not.

On the other hand, they still employed a large number of Arcanes who apparently knew nothing about the true nature of the business. They tended to be less skilled battle mages and were sent to do simple security jobs for clients.

It was on one of the personnel dossiers I finally found the information I'd been looking for. "Eureka!" I shouted.

Elyssa shot me a dirty look. "If you startle me like that one more time tonight—"

"Look," I said, not wanting her to finish that thought. I pointed to the image of an able-bodied young man assigned to bodyguard duty. I saw the initials "BRB" on his sheet, indicating he was in the Black Robe Brotherhood. There was a brief description beneath his picture.

*Assigned to Conroy residence until further notice. Note new address.*

There was a long list of addresses beneath. The second from the top matched the old address we'd tracked the Conroy limo to. That meant the first one had to be where they lived now.

"How are we going to do this?" Elyssa asked.

"Just me and you," I said. "We'll tell the others, maybe have Shelton standing by at the arch in case."

"How are we going to get inside?"

"Remember my idea for leap-frogging the portal across the yard and into the house?"

She nodded. "I just hope opening the portal doesn't trigger an alarm."

"Why would it?" I shrugged. "I don't see another choice."

Elyssa checked the time. "It's two in the morning."

"Best time to act," I said.

"What makes you say that?"

I took out my phone and scrolled to the address on my map. "Something I read in a thriller about an ex-military cop who wanders aimlessly around the country beating the crap out of bad guys."

"So, I guess it must be right then," she said, grinning. "You're such a dork sometimes."

I gave her a smirk. "Sometimes? Baby, I make dork cool." I slid the phone across to her. "Looks like they've moved to Buckhead. We can probably portal into the Grotto and drive from there. I'll send Shelton a picture and have him open another portal then we'll try my leapfrog plan."

"Sounds good," she said, taking my hand and squeezing it. "Do you think Ivy will help?"

"Of course she will. It's her mom, too."

"She can be...unpredictable."

I kissed Elyssa's hand and stood up. "Yeah, but this is a no-brainer. Plus, I think she'll be happy Mom is free."

"I sure hope she sees it that way, instead of thinking of us as kidnappers."

I went upstairs and knocked on Shelton's room. Bella answered the door.

"Is something the matter?" she asked.

I told her our plan.

"Well, I suppose it's too important to wait until morning," she said. "I'll help you. Harry will only be cranky if I wake him up."

"What the hell is going on now?" Shelton said, appearing at the door. He raised an eyebrow. "Oh, you. I guess you need our help."

"How did you ever guess?" I asked.

He mumbled something rude, and went back inside the room.

"We'll be out in a jiffy," Bella said.

They joined us a few minutes later.

"Risky," Shelton said, after I described Lornicus's request and our alternate plan. "But Ivy sounds like a better choice than giving that heartless thing a baby."

"Why, Harry, you do care," Bella said, pinching his cheek.

He growled. "And I ain't happy about those damned rats you mentioned either. I guess a felycan has her uses after all."

"Why don't you go give her that back-handed compliment to her face?" I said with an amused grin.

"Just keeping my wits in true form," he said. "If I don't act like an ass, people are gonna know something's wrong."

As we walked down to the arch, Bella asked me a question. "Why are you taking the portal to the Grotto instead of going straight to the front of the house?"

"Uh, we don't know what it looks like," I said.

"Not even with street view?"

"Street view?" I face-palmed. How had Bella, the least technologically proficient person I knew come up with that when the rest of us hadn't?

"I amaze even myself sometimes," she said smugly.

I zoomed into street view in the maps app on my arcphone, and saw a blurry image. I had to go back a couple of houses for a crisp picture. I concentrated on the image, and opened the portal just in front of the sidewalk. Black iron gates guarded the driveway beyond. Elyssa and I stepped through.

"Leave it open. We'll take some pictures and try again."

The houses on the street were massive, each one boasting a stout fence, privacy hedge, and a driveway stretching across a long property. Thanks to the landscaping, I couldn't see into the Conroy's yard very well. Thick hedges and trees blocked the line of sight. We jogged to the neighbor's house, and encountered a similar problem.

"Maybe if you open the portal as far into the property as possible, we'll be able to see more from there," Elyssa said.

Unlike the other yards, I couldn't even see the Conroys' house from the road. "I guess it's our only choice."

Unwilling to risk even a step onto the driveway, I took a picture through the gate, using the zoom on the camera. We went back to the portal, and reopened it. A sawgrass bush blocked the view ahead. I poked my head through the portal and looked to the left where the driveway curved beneath a curtain of branches from a willow tree.

"These people are paranoid," I said, taking another picture so we could get closer to the branches, hoping they weren't booby-trapped to electrocute intruders.

Elyssa procured a long wooden rod and tied a small digital camera to the end while I opened the portal closer to the willow tree. She set the timer on the camera, and pushed it through the willow branches. She pulled it back, and we looked at the picture.

Something out of a nightmare grinned back at us, razor sharp teeth gleaming in the flash of the camera. It stood about four feet tall with a huge head full of bristling hair, and a mouth big enough to swallow Cutsauce whole.

"Holy shi—" I closed the portal. "What the hell is that thing?"

"Looks like a troll," Shelton said with a low whistle. "Haven't seen one of those in a long time."

"So they don't just exist on the internet," I said.

"Old man Conroy doesn't play around," he said. "Trolls don't just work for anyone."

I groaned. "We need to find another way in."

"Through those trees where the driveway curves?" Elyssa said.

I shrugged. "Might as well try."

I opened the portal well away from the willow tree and poked the camera into the dense stand of saplings. Something jerked hard on the pole. I tugged on it. The next yank nearly dragged me through the omniarch. I gave it one more hard tug, and fell over backward as the pole came loose. The camera was gone, only the well-chewed end of the pole left.

"I don't think this idea is working," Elyssa said.

I pounded the floor. Flung the pole against the back wall. "That old bastard won't stop me." I paced the floor for a minute, mind running through scenarios before I decided I needed to see the outside of the house again. Elyssa and I stepped through the portal onto the sidewalk in front of the house. We walked up and down the road, peering through fences, but the landscaping in the Conroy yard blocked vision from street level. I looked for a tree to climb. Though the yards boasted custom landscapes, everything from a desert theme with an adobe-styled Spanish house, to yards filled with fruit trees or hedges, none had a really tall tree in position to overlook the Conroy residence.

"Can I knock out a troll with a Lancer?" I asked Elyssa.

"Maybe with a hundred darts," she said. "They're built like tanks."

"Are they all so short?"

She shook her head. "I think that one is young. Then again, I haven't seen many trolls, either. The last one I saw was in the Cho'kai."

"How did you deal with it?"

Elyssa chuckled. "I ran."

If something made my ninja girlfriend run, I knew it had to be bad. I'd seen her climb the back of a tragon—half tyrannosaurus rex, half dragon—and knock it unconscious with Lancer darts.

I stopped in front of the tall black iron fence guarding the neighbor's yard. The tips ended in sharp-looking points. I could see this house from the road thanks to the wide green lawn with little in the way of bushes. The fence bordering it and the Conroys' was just as tall, and thick cedar trees ran interference with sight from ground level. I took a couple of steps back, ran, and jumped, narrowly clearing the top.

Elyssa followed suit, adding a neat flip at the apex of her leap, hitting the ground in a roll, and stopping in a three-point stance like something out of a movie.

"Showoff," I said.

She stuck out her tongue.

We ran, following the fence until we reached the house, and cut across the lawn. I heard growling, and a Doberman appeared from the dark, racing toward us. I grinned at it, let loose a little of my inner demon, and growled. The Doberman whined, turning tail so fast its hind legs spun out on the grass.

"Meanie," Elyssa said.

We climbed up a gutter downspout, reaching a lower part of the roof, and made our way to the highest peak. From there, I saw more of the Conroys' yard. The driveway snaked beneath multiple willows with dense stands of other trees all along it. The landscaping was a mish-mash of vegetation, only making sense in the context of hiding guardian terrors.

I wondered what would happen should a hapless door-to-door salesman somehow slip inside the gate, hoping to sell a few vacuum cleaners. Would the trolls kill anyone, or simply knock them out and toss them on the street? With that kind of firepower at their disposal, why did the Conroys even need Black Robe Brotherhood thugs to stand guard?

Then again, they couldn't exactly take trolls out shopping with them. It stood to reason they needed humans—or reasonable facsimiles thereof—to guard them in the normal world. Since my night vision couldn't take in all the details I needed from this distance, we used a pair of Templar binoculars to scout the best place to open a portal.

Light shined from within a window on the third floor. I went prone on my belly and used my camera to take a picture. I sent a picture of our current location to Shelton. He opened the portal, and we stepped through back to the mansion cellar. I reopened the portal using the picture I'd just taken. Through the window I saw a long carpeted hallway devoid of decorations or furniture.

"Doesn't look like anyone uses that floor," Shelton said. "You sure they live there?"

"Why else would they have trolls in the front yard?" I asked. "This must be the place." I took a picture of the hallway, closed the portal, and reopened it inside the house. Taking a deep breath, I stepped through.

Nothing exploded or tried to bite my head off.

I blew out a sigh of relief.

*We're in.*

# Chapter 33

Elyssa stepped through after me. We stood in silence, listening for signs of life on the floor. Sconces with a candlestick design offered dim light to see by. Most of the doors hung open to bare rooms. Even the bathroom lacked towels or toilet paper. Considering the size of their household, it wasn't too surprising they'd not furnished every room unless there were a lot more Conroys than I knew about. Only the last room on the left had furniture—a single wooden rocking chair, and a small round table with an unlit candle on it. Moonlight filtered through the round window. I shuddered.

*Creepy.*

For some reason, the scene reminded me of a horror movie I'd seen years ago. Thankfully there wasn't an old woman or a corpse in the chair, or I probably would have run screaming.

We crept down the hall to a set of hardwood stairs leading down. Our nightingale armor muffled our footsteps, though I winced at each step, wary of the creak of wood which might give us away. I hoped they hadn't warded the place yet, though with guards wandering the house, it seemed motion detection might be overkill unless they had a way of separating intruders from the people who belonged here.

As an added bonus, we didn't have blueprints, or any idea about the layout of the house. For all we knew, human sentries might wait around any given corner. The stairs led to yet another carpeted hallway lined with doors. This one showed a little more panache, boasting a table with candles, and a painting or two hanging in ornate frames.

Elyssa held up a closed fist, motioning me to stop. She turned and mouthed, "Ivy's bedroom is probably on this floor. More secure."

I nodded. It made sense. The master bedroom was probably here somewhere as well. It also meant Jeremiah or Eliza Conroy could be chilling in a room nearby, probably curled up with a good book and a glass of wine if not actively plotting world domination. I wondered if Daelissa called this place home, or if she slept hanging upside down in a cave, dreaming of enslaving the human race.

Since Elyssa had ninja training, I let her check and clear the rooms. Most were as empty as the floor above. Ahead, I saw a large staircase dividing the house into two wings. A long chain hung from the domed ceiling above, connected to a chandelier which shined dimly, though presumably not at full strength since it was well past bedtime. A door at the far end was closed. It might be the master bedroom. Would Ivy's room be on that side?

We cleared the rooms one-by-one until the central staircase loomed close by. I heard a man speaking in low tones from somewhere below but couldn't make out his words. He didn't sound like Jeremiah, so I figured he might be one of the Darkwater men. We hadn't checked to see if there were more than the one we'd found assigned here. Elyssa peeked over the balustrade. Motioned me over. I looked down and saw a well-appointed den. Flames flickered in a large fireplace on the far side. Ornate plush chairs with end tables next to them sat atop an Oriental area rug.

Continuing on, we crept low next to the railing. Once on the opposite side of the stairs, I caught sight of a man in a black robe talking to another identically-clothed man. The second's face matched the picture in the dossier. I didn't recognize the other one. It looked as though a kitchen lay through an entryway down a hallway behind them. It remained brightly lit. One of the men raised a mug to his lips, nodding at whatever the other man was saying, and they shared a hushed laugh.

Elyssa went prone, peering through the marble columns on the balustrade. We remained there, my gaze flicking behind and to the sides, paranoia making each second creep by. The feeling someone was sneaking up on us toyed with my senses. I was dying to ask Elyssa why we'd stopped, but fought the urge. She finally backed away from the railing on her stomach, stood, and moved to a corner with a table and painting. She snapped a picture. It turned out okay despite the low light. She texted it to Shelton with a message telling him to be ready to open a portal in case we needed a fast escape.

The next room on the right contained a bed with white comforter and dresser, but no occupant or other signs of habitation. Four more doors remained, including the closed one at the very end. The room across from the first looked much the same, as did the next room on the right. Two more rooms to go. My heart pounded. The thudding sounded in my ears.

*Jeremiah Conroy might be right behind that door. Ivy might not even be here.*

I took a slow quiet breath to calm myself. If Jeremiah caught us snooping around his crib, I had no hope of leniency from him. I tapped out an emergency escape text on my phone for Shelton, ready to hit "send" in an instant should it be necessary so he could open the portal.

I heard a change in the tone of conversation from below. A third voice joined them. Elyssa grimaced. Motioned back toward the stairs. We crept to the balustrade and saw a third man. If the number if wrinkles on his forehead were any measure of stress, this man was near the breaking point. Unlike the others, he spoke just loud enough for us to understand.

"You need to let us know if the old man is going anywhere," he said.

"Are you crazy?" the man from the dossier—I remembered his name was Bob— hissed. "He said we weren't supposed to—"

The new man waved him off. "Kassus said he's senile. Doesn't know what he's doing."

"How does he plan to do it?" the second man asked. "I don't think guns are going to work."

The third man shrugged. "Says he has a plan. Your part is simple. Let us know if the old man goes anywhere. We'll take care of the rest."

"Not good," Bob said. "I'm scared of him."

The third man poked him in the chest. "You should be more afraid of Kassus."

"Are you kidding me?" His face widened with fear. "Jeremiah Conroy is way scarier."

"Just do it. Kassus is convinced he can get past those monsters." The third man sighed, as if he wasn't all that happy with the plan despite his outward bravado. "Anyway, I got to go. Do your job, or Kassus will have your head."

Elyssa and I shared concerned expressions. The only thing those men could be talking about were the cupids. Kassus was going against Jeremiah and doing his own thing.

"When?" asked the second man.

"Not tonight, but soon," the third man replied in a harsh whisper. "I'll let you know." He turned and walked down the hallway, toward where I imagined the kitchen was located.

We listened to the two men for a while, but they failed to offer any other useful nuggets of information, aside from how they were terrified of pissing off either of the powerful men they found themselves caught between. I sure didn't envy them. We were just about to turn away, when one of the men mentioned something about a break-in. I touched Elyssa's shoulder. She stopped her backward momentum.

"They think it was the Slade kid," Bob said. "That's how he figured out the route for the package."

"Makes sense," the other man said. "They know he's in Queens Gate. Only a matter of time before we get him."

"Do we really want to mess with this Slade guy?" Bob gave the other man a concerned look.

"Don't worry. There's a lot of us and only one of him."

"Only one? I heard he has Templar support, man." Bob shuddered. "They disabled four escorts, hijacked a special transport, and air-lifted it away."

"Doesn't matter how strong or protected he is." the other man shrugged. "You can kill anyone if you surprise them at the right moment."

"Slade killed Victor, and I'd say the kid was more surprised than we were." Bob slashed a finger across his throat. "Victor was nearly as badass as Maulin and the kid beat him in a fair fight."

The other man chuckled. "Wasn't all that fair. We had Slade outnumbered—" He broke off and blinked a couple of times. "You know, maybe you're right. If that kid took out Victor in one shot, maybe we should leave him be."

Bob nodded encouragingly. "I'm with you."

"If only we had a choice."

The men exchanged dejected looks before going their separate ways, one out the front door, and the other toward the kitchen. I presumed they were making their rounds.

Elyssa backed away, smoothly pushing herself from prone to standing with a single pushup. It looked cool, so I did the same, and nearly fell backward into a table with a vase. She caught my arm to steady me and gave me an admonishing look with a raised eyebrow, somehow managing an amused smirk at the same time. I didn't know how she stayed so calm.

As for the conversation, it was clear Kassus's men now had a healthy respect for my abilities. On the downside, it also meant they wouldn't be half-assed about trying to kill me. Being underestimated had its advantages.

We crept back to the last door on the left. It and the door at the end were the only two closed. In my mind, that meant they had to be occupied. Still, we'd followed protocol to the letter, clearing the open rooms because it would have really sucked if someone who was scared of closing their door at night saw us creeping past.

Elyssa touched the knob. Slowly twisted it. The latch made a click, which would have been faint to normal ears but sounded quite loud to me. She eased open the door. From the dim light of the chandelier in the central stairwell, I made out a pink wall. As the door opened further, the light fell onto a king-sized four-poster bed straight out of a fairy tale. Stuffed animals adorned the shelves. A huge fluffy dragon sat atop the bed. Pink and purple dominated.

*Definitely Ivy's room.*

Except Ivy wasn't there.

The bed looked as though someone had been in it, but unless she could turn herself invisible, or had hidden herself because she heard us coming in, I didn't think my sister was around. We went inside and closed the door anyway. Ivy had quite a bag of tricks, and we had to be sure the room was empty.

I turned on a lamp sitting on a table next to a stuffed bunny. The room was as large as the others we'd seen, but cluttered by comparison. A bookshelf sat against one wall, filled with fairy tale books and several classics by Mark Twain.

Elyssa's eyes went soft as she pulled a yellow book from the shelf and showed me the title: *Being A Good Sister For Dummies.*

I smiled. Maybe I needed the corollary book for brothers.

We spent the next few minutes combing the room but failed to turn up my sister. The windows in the room were closed, the locks engaged. I had little doubt window locks would prove much of an obstacle for Ivy, especially since she could presumably blink through a closed window so long as she had line of sight. Elyssa directed me out of the room, and eased the door closed behind us. She pointed toward the last door and gave two sharp shakes of her head.

*Don't have to convince me.*

Going into the master bedroom would be like hopping into an alligator pond with chicken strapped to our faces. Creeping back down the hallway, we made our way to the stairs. Elyssa made a fist, indicating I should remain. She flipped over the balustrade, hanging upside down by her legs so her head hung just below the ceiling on the first floor. She dropped, flipping and landing on her feet without a sound, thanks to the Nightingale armor. She vanished, returning a few seconds later, and gave me the signal to proceed.

Since I wasn't nearly as smooth as her, I hurried down the stairs, grateful for the stealth armor. White marble tiled the hallway below. The sound of shoes tapping on the hard floor reached our ears. Elyssa pressed her back to the wall behind a table in the middle of the hall. I flattened myself beside her. The footsteps drew closer. I felt a bead of sweat trickle down my face. Whoever it was would only have to glance to the side to see us.

Then again, if it was one of the human guards, one dart should take care of them. Elyssa touched her collar. A black mask spread from her neck up, covering her head. I did the same with mine. The material was so light, I hardly noticed as it covered my face. Despite the outward appearance of a solid black mask, I could see through it as though nothing covered my eyes.

The footsteps stopped. I heard a man talking to himself in a low whisper. "Maude, I may be a battle mage, but you're the real magic in my life. Will you marry me?" The voice sounded like Bob's. "Good, but not good enough," he said after repeating it once more. A pause. "Maude, you set my loins on fire. I want to light you up for the rest of my life."

I wondered if Elyssa wore a grimace like the one I felt contorting my face. We had to knock this guy out if for no other reason than to prevent another atrocious marriage proposal escaping his mouth.

The footsteps resumed and faded. Elyssa peeked around the table. She blurred to the corner where another hallway intersected this one, and looked down it. She crooked her elbow at ninety degrees, holding up a fist. Her hand flicked open, fingers waggling forward, indicating I should follow. I was really starting to feel like a secret agent, if not an outright ninja with the way she led.

I poked my head around the corner and saw Bob standing a little way down the hall from us, looking into one of the ornate mirrors hanging on the wall. His lips moved, but I intentionally tuned him out to avoid a brain hemorrhage. Elyssa's head remained turned toward the man, though the mask prevented me from making out her expression. She finally pointed down the hallway we were in, apparently deciding not to put Bob out of our misery.

*Maude, whoever you are, I feel bad for you, girl.*

We slinked down the hall. Bob's partner abruptly walked around the corner. He had just enough time to make a frightened face before a silver dart sprouted from his neck. He fell into Elyssa's arms. She motioned toward a closed door a few feet down from us. I opened it to reveal a small library. A moment later, I found a closet inside the library and opened it. Elyssa deposited the man in a sitting position against the back wall of the closet, and concealed him with a dust cover I found on a shelf.

"How did we not hear him?" I whispered.

She inspected the man's shoes. "Rubber soles."

I wondered why Bob hadn't worn quieter shoes, but figured if his ideas for good marriage proposals were any indication, he wasn't the kind of guy who even thought about that sort of thing.

After creeping around the various hallways for a while, we found a door concealing stairs leading down into a lit area. Elyssa descended without hesitation. At the bottom, we found what looked like a gauntlet room—a practice area where Arcanes could cut loose without worry of killing anyone or damaging personal property. A couch sat against the wall near the stairs. I heard quiet sobbing and saw a petite figure lying on the cushions, face buried in a fluffy pink unicorn.

## Dearest Mother of Mine

It was my sister, Ivy.

# Chapter 34

I lowered my mask. Elyssa did the same, revealing a sad look. I paused, not wanting to frighten Ivy, mainly because I wanted to avoid the possibility of a deadly reaction on her part. Seeing no other option but to signal our presence, I said, "Ivy," in a hushed tone.

She bolted to her feet, showing a blotchy red face and wide tear-stained eyes. For a long moment she stood there, pink orbs of deadly energy coalesced in the palms of her hands. The energy whiffed out, and she ran to me, gripping me in a tight hug.

"Justin," she said, shuddering. "What are you doing here? I'm so happy to see you."

I hugged her back, feeling my shirt grow damp as she unloaded fresh tears into it. "What's wrong?" I asked.

"They took Mom away without even telling me," she sobbed. "They said they were moving her to a better place until Daelissa decided what to do with her."

I directed her back to the couch, and sat beside her. Elyssa remained near the staircase, acting as a sentry.

"Ivy, I have Mom," I said. "We rescued her."

Her blue eyes went wide, and a smile broke out on her face. "You did?" she said in a loud voice. She covered her mouth, face contrite, and lowered her voice. "You did? How?"

"I can't explain everything," I said. "But it was a lot of hard work, and very dangerous."

"I don't like the people Bigdaddy uses," she said, frowning. "He says they're necessary." Her forehead pinched into a confused look. "How did you find us? Did you sneak in here to tell me Mom was okay so I wouldn't worry?" She smiled and continued before I could get in a word edgewise. "You did, didn't you?" She hugged me again. "I love you, big brother."

"I love you too, Ivy," I said, feeling my eyes mist. "But, that's only part of the reason I came."

Ivy released me, big eyes looking into mine. "Oh?"

I nodded. "One of those men Jeremiah uses"—I refused to use the word "Bigdaddy" anymore—"his name is Maulin Kassus. Do you know him?"

Her eyes narrowed. "I don't know their names because Bigmomma won't let me near them, but I have seen a few of them."

I took out my phone and displayed an image of Kassus.

"Oh, I've seen him," she said, nodding. "He looks mean and acts like a real poop-head."

"He's a poop-head all right," I said with an involuntary grin. "Even though I rescued Mom, I have a huge problem."

"Did that man do something to Mom?" she asked.

"Sort of," I said. "He's the one who sealed the doors on her prison. It's diamond fiber, so I can't break in—"

"He blood-sealed her prison," Ivy said, her lips pressing tight together. "And you want his blood."

I repressed a shudder, thinking how that trailer would become Mom's coffin before much longer. "Yes, but I've had a lot of trouble getting it."

Her lips curled back into a snarl. "The next time he comes here, I'll get his blood."

I saw Elyssa grimace.

My little sister could be scary.

"The only problem is, he doesn't come here very much, and my grandparents won't let me out of the house." Ivy sighed. "I sneak out, but it's harder and harder to do it without them finding out."

"Why are you down here?" I asked.

"I didn't want them to hear my crying," she said. "It's kind of embarrassing, because Mom did something bad, and I guess I'm not supposed to be sad that Daelissa locked her away."

"Maybe you should tell them you don't like what they did to her," I said.

She shook her head. "Daelissa scares me. She's so strong."

"Why don't you come with us?" I said. "You can live with us, and once we rescue Mom—"

"You need me here to get Kassus's blood and save Mom," she said. "Afterward, I totally want to come live with you." Her eyes sparkled. "I'll miss my grandparents, but they've been acting so weird lately, I hate being around. I hate being told what to do all the time, and they still haven't taken me to the zoo!"

"We'll go to the zoo first thing," I said. Hesitated. "Look, we can find another way to get Kassus's blood if you really want to come now." I was definitely concerned for her if Daelissa got wind of our plans.

She shook her head vehemently. "No way, Justin. I got this."

"Where is Daelissa now?" I asked.

"I don't know. She came by a couple of weeks ago to give me some lessons and told me I would rule the world by her side." Ivy shrugged. "She says crazy things sometimes. Bigdaddy says it's because she hasn't been home in too long."

"It's because she's not a good person," I said.

Ivy nodded. "After she tried to kill all those Templar people and you, I started thinking you might be right about her. I mean, she might be just a little crazy now, but a visit back home would clear everything right up."

I sometimes marveled at Ivy's naiveté. Jeremiah and the others had done a good job preserving her innocence—or possibly ignorance—so they could better use her. I quelled a burst of righteous anger and forced a smile. "We can let her figure out how to get home all by herself. Speaking of which, what did Jeremiah do with the Cyrinthian Rune?"

"You mean the little orb we took from you a while back?" she said, raising an eyebrow. "I don't know what he did with it."

"Did he say anything about giving it to Daelissa?"

She shook her head. "Oh, no. Bigdaddy said we had to keep it a secret from her." Her lips quirked. "I think he doesn't like Daelissa as much as he pretends to."

"You're growing up. You're starting to think for yourself, and realizing not everything is what it seems." I hated to quote Underborn, but the assassin had a point. My sister had been brainwashed from birth. It was a testament to her inner strength that she was already starting to see through the lies. "Do you know what the rune does?"

She nodded. "It's supposed to open the Alabaster Arch back to Seraphina."

"Is that the name of the angel world?"

"Yep. At least that's what Daelissa calls it."

"Do you have a phone or any way for me to contact you?" I asked.

She produced a slim pink arcphone from within the folds of her blue dress. "I stole it. I'm not supposed to have it. Bigmomma say they rot people's brains and turn them to zombies."

"She might have a point," I said, thinking of how much time I spent idly looking at mine or playing puzzle games when I wasn't out preventing the apocalypse. "Give me the number." I punched it into my phone as she recited it. I considered telling her about the omniarch but didn't know if she might slip up and mention it to Jeremiah. Our best course would be to leave the way we came without her tagging along. Something else occurred to me. "I have powers similar to yours."

Her eyes brightened. "Like Seraphim?" She clapped her hands together and hopped once. "That's great, Justin. I don't like your demon side very well."

"Daemos aren't all bad," I said. "Do you have any idea how to control angel powers?" I gave her a brief version of my run-in with Darkwater and how I'd used the power without telling her about the kill shot on Victor.

Her forehead scrunched. "Well, you feel warm in the heart like you said, and then you channel it into forms."

"But how do you get the warm feeling?" I asked.

"Hmm." She looked up as if thinking. "I just pull on the aether around me and channel it through, or if I need a lot, I store it inside." She tapped her chest. "You can channel it out of your feet like this"—she levitated off the floor a few inches, then landed—"or collect it in your hands." Pink orbs blossomed in her palms, growing larger before shrinking. "If I don't use it, I just let it go, or absorb it, though you have to be careful or you can overheat your heart, and Daelissa said that could hurt me."

I focused on my heart. Heard it thumping in a steady beat. Tried to imagine aether flowing through it. As usual, nothing happened. "It doesn't seem to work like that for me."

She pursed her lips. Pressed a hand to my chest. "I can feel something in there. Feels like it's sputtering. Kinda like a candle in a breeze." She shrugged without removing her hand. "Daelissa said I was like that when I started to figure it out."

"When you first started channeling, did it just happen?" I asked.

She nodded. "Daelissa would hurt me sometimes." A sad look flashed across her face. "She said it was the only way to learn. One day, I got so mad when she hit me with a bolt, I felt a fire light up inside me, and I hit her back." She giggled. "I scorched the front of her dress."

"Sounds like what happened to you," Elyssa said, eyes glued to the stairwell.

"Let's see if this works," Ivy said. Light flashed between her hand and my chest.

Breath exploded from my lungs. I staggered backward. Heat flared in my chest, coursed down my arm, and an ultraviolet orb swirled malevolently in my palm. I cupped my hand before my face and marveled at the beautiful but deadly magic. I willed it to grow, pushing more heat from my chest into my hand. It *whooshed* and doubled in size. I flinched, lost my concentration, and the heat faded. The sphere flickered and puffed away into sparkling purple mist.

Ivy looked at me with wide-eyed wonder. "That was dark light."

"Is that a good thing?" I asked.

"Well, technically it's a little evil, but since I don't think you're evil anymore, it's probably okay."

I felt my eyebrows rise. "I thought you didn't like Darklings."

Ivy looked at the floor, pressing her bare toe into the carpet. "I think maybe they're not so bad. I kinda liked Nightliss."

Relief warmed me. *She's thinking for herself.* "Why is your magical energy pink?"

"Oh, I can change colors, but that doesn't mean anything, really." She held up a hand, displaying a white energy orb. "I can make it ultraviolet, but that doesn't mean it's dark light."

"What's the difference?"

A shrug. "I'm not sure. Daelissa just told me it was bad." She inspected my hand. "Can you do it again?"

I sighed. "No, the heat went away and I can't turn it back on."

"Want me to light it again?" She gave me a mischievous grin.

I backed away. "Uh, maybe not right now." Even though I really wanted my angel powers to work, now wasn't the time to knock myself silly trying to accomplish miracles.

Ivy reached up and patted my shoulder. "It's okay. You're not a failure."

"Thanks, sis." I couldn't hide the grin. It felt so good to know my sister didn't think I was evil anymore.

"We should probably go," Elyssa said. "We had to knock out a guard. It means Jeremiah will know someone was here."

"Where did you put him?" Ivy asked, concern stitching her brow.

"In a closet in the library."

"I can make him forget." My sister smirked. "I'm not very good at blanking, but since you just did it, it shouldn't be a problem. Can you put him somewhere else so he won't wonder why he's in a closet when he wakes up?"

"Yeah," I said. "Better do it now."

The three of us crept back upstairs to the library. Bob was nowhere to be seen, probably off perfecting his proposal, I hoped. We moved the unconscious man to a chair at a desk.

"I'll make him forget," she said. "You'd better go. And watch out for trolls in the yard." She grimaced. "They're gross."

I hugged my sister, and kissed her on the forehead. "Be careful when you get Kassus's blood," I said. "Please don't put yourself in danger."

"Don't worry about me," she said, flashing an innocent grin. "I can be devious."

*How well I know that.*

We crept back to the stairs. The foyer looked clear, so we went up the stairs, and made our way to the stairs leading up to the third floor. We straightened from our crouches, stretching, and happy to be almost out of this place as we walked toward the third-story hallway. I opened my mouth to say something when Elyssa's eyes went wide with horror. Her hand clamped over my mouth, and she stopped dead.

I followed her gaze and saw a silhouette in the first room on the right. The room with the rocking chair. My night vision flickered on.

Jeremiah Conroy sat inside.

# Chapter 35

My bowels and bladder attempted mutiny. It was all I could do to keep my wobbly knees from dropping me to the floor. I felt Elyssa's arm on my chest, pushing me gently backward. We backed up to the edge of the door, hidden from sight.

The Arcane sat in a rocking chair with his profile to us. A candle flickered on the small round table next to him. I remembered how creepy this setup had seemed to me upon entering the house. Seeing the old man there alone multiplied the creep factor by about a zillion. His gaze rested on something in his hands. I peered at the object, and realized it looked like the statuette of a woman carved from rock. The paint looked faded, though it was impossible to judge the age based on such a thing since a preservation spell might protect it.

Jeremiah produced a clay flagon from his right, took a long draw from it. A trickle of red liquid down the corner of his mouth looked like red wine. Surely it wasn't blood. I was wondering why a man with such wealth would use a clay container for his wine when I noticed his clothing. He wore the rugged robes I might picture on someone from the Middle East. His goatee was no longer gray, but black, and his skin looked olive by the dim candlelight.

I rubbed my eyes. The man looked just like Jeremiah Conroy, but much younger and of a different nationality. I felt a pinch on my arm, and looked to Elyssa. She mouthed, "Who is that?" to me.

"Jeremiah," I mouthed back.

She shook her head slowly with disbelief.

I texted Shelton, and told him to open the portal in the hallway. A second later, it blinked into existence. I was immensely grateful it didn't put off more light than the sconces on the walls. Shelton peered in from the other side of the portal. I put a finger to my lip, eyes wide with urgency.

He nodded and remained still.

Before we made a run for the gateway, temporary insanity gripped me. I took out my phone and set it to a low light option, praying I had the flash set to off. Then I snapped several pictures of Jeremiah and his strange statue. There was something very odd about this man, and I intended to get to the bottom of it.

Just as we took a step, the man moaned, and said something in a foreign language. He pressed the statuette to his lips, and murmured, "Thesha."

Elyssa pinched me again, probably because we'd frozen in plain view of the doorway. I suppressed a gasp and quickly stepped out of sight. I heard the scrape of the rocking chair against the hardwood floors and wondered if Jeremiah was standing. Elyssa and I ran for the portal. My entire body felt weak, as if I were trying to scramble out of a swimming pool while being chased by a shark.

We leapt through the portal. I looked at Shelton, and slashed a hand across my neck. The portal winked off.

Elyssa and I let out long gasps at the same time. Her face looked as white as mine felt. That had been a close one. Then we burst out laughing.

"Oh my god, I thought I was gonna crap my pants," I said.

"You should have seen your face," Elyssa said, tears of mirth gathering in the corners of her eyes. "I can't believe you didn't faint."

"I wanted to," I said. "But we made it!" I held up a hand, and Elyssa gave me a high-five.

"Hell yeah, we did," she said.

"Whoa, people," Shelton interrupted. "What happened?"

"I'd like to hear as well," Bella said, looking up from a Scrabble board on a table.

I told them about our close and very bizarre encounter with Jeremiah.

"No wonder you two looked so scared," he said, chuckling. "I knew something had to be in that room the way you were looking at it."

"We also contacted Ivy." I recounted the conversation.

"Nice," he said. "Now we're on easy street, right? Just gotta sit back and wait for the sister to deliver?"

"This is good news, Justin," Bella said.

I felt my light mood fade into heavy sobriety. "No, there's the chance she won't see Kassus for a while."

"She gave me the impression she doesn't see him often," Elyssa said. "Which means we need to plan for Option B."

"Giving a baby to Lornicus?" Shelton said.

"I already know how to take one baby," I said, feeling my lip curl in disgust at the idea. "Just snag it with the portal. But the leyworms would never trust me again."

"I don't want that to happen," Elyssa said. "You'd be compromising what you believe in. You might never forgive yourself."

"It would be hard to make myself do it," I said.

"Well, it's a good thing you have me." She grinned. "Because I know another way."

Hope lifted my spirits. "Really?"

"Remember what we heard those guards talking about? Kassus isn't done. He's going back to steal an angel even against Jeremiah's orders."

"Do you think he'll put in a personal appearance?"

"I would almost guarantee it," Elyssa said. "If he ordered his men to disobey Jeremiah and didn't show up himself to oversee it, they'd think he was a spineless coward."

"That moron is really gonna try for another baby?" Shelton said with a snort. "Oh, man. If Jeremiah finds out, he's dog food."

Elyssa tapped something on her phone. "I told Hutchins to be on guard. We can have the special ops squad deployed in minutes if need be."

"Then all we gotta do is wait," Shelton said. "Easy money."

I had the feeling it wouldn't be that easy. A yawn nailed me out of the blue. I checked the time and saw it was past four in the morning. It was hard to believe our sojourn into enemy territory had taken only a couple of hours. "I need some sleep," I said, as another yawn attacked my jaw.

"I agree," Elyssa said.

"Damned straight," Shelton said. "Besides, Bella was kicking my ass at Scrabble again."

We woke up late the next morning around ten. I leapt from bed, as if by hurrying, I could somehow make Kassus show his ugly face. Unfortunately, the world didn't work that way.

"Hutchins told me his men are in position and will notify us the second anyone shows up in the nursery," Elyssa said.

"And Ivy will tell me if anything happens on her end," I said. I sighed. "I hope this isn't all for nothing. I just keep thinking…"

"About what, baby?" Elyssa kissed me on the cheek.

"I realized that if it comes down to choosing between a cupid and my mom, I'll choose her every time." I looked into my girlfriend's eyes. "Does that make me a bad person?"

A sad smile graced her face. "No. It makes you normal. For what it's worth, I'd do the same thing even if I had trouble living with it afterward."

"Would you?" I asked. "Could you live with it?"

Her eyes seemed to focus inward. She nodded. "Yeah, I think I could. These Seraphim, they invaded our world. They killed our people. Just because they're reborn doesn't mean they're not the same people who committed atrocities in the first place."

"Some of them are Darklings, though," I said. "Some of them were on our side."

"You can't tell the difference though, can you?" she said.

"At this age, it's hard." I'd looked at the cupid's wings when they manifested. I knew from experience Nightliss's were ultraviolet since she was a darkling, and Daelissa's were white. But the babies' wings looked shades of gray. "I don't think the Darkling or Brightling aspects emerge until the angels are a little older."

"Somehow, I would convince myself the baby I was taking was a Brightling," she said. "Deluding yourself is the easiest way to rationalize an impossible situation."

"This doesn't even come close to an impossible situation," I said. "I mean, it hurts and disgusts me to have to make the choice, but I realize if I knew Mom was close to death, I'd do it in a heartbeat. In fact, if Kassus doesn't show tonight, I'll do it."

She touched my shoulder. "You sure?"

"Yeah." I patted her hand. "I'll feel worse about the leyworms hating me than I will the baby."

Elyssa wrapped her arms around me, and pressed her face to my chest. We stood like that for some time, simply reveling in the moment. I felt the moment coming to an end and kissed her on the top of the head. She gazed up at me, violet eyes dark with emotion. Her soft lips found mine, lingered for a moment. "Whatever you do, I will always love you, Justin."

"Even if I kick a puppy?"

She laughed. "Shut up." Her hand gripped mine. "Let's eat breakfast. You've done all you can do right now. Ivy said she'd call if she got anything, and Hutchins will notify us when it's go time. And if neither one pans out, we'll resort to baby snatching."

Elyssa's summary made me realize I really didn't have anything else to do until Kassus showed his face somewhere. We made breakfast—pancakes, bacon, and eggs—and sat on the upstairs deck, enjoying the cool morning weather. Even though it was almost Christmas in the normal world, the weather in the pocket dimensions didn't always match up. It suddenly reminded me of my original mission before all this mess had started.

"I wonder if everyone got the invitations to our Christmas party," I said.

Elyssa giggled. "What made you think of that?"

I shrugged. "The weather, I guess."

"We haven't even bought party favors or planned what we're going to cook."

"Wouldn't it be absolutely amazing if I had Ivy and Mom here for Christmas?" I felt moisture building behind my eyes just at the thought of it, and choked up.

"I think you will," she said, hugging me tight. "We're going to make it happen."

"Let's do turkey and dressing," I said. "Oh, and deviled eggs."

Elyssa made a face. "Deviled eggs are gross."

"You know us demon spawn, we like our eggs filled with yellow stuff."

She laughed. "My mom makes really good asparagus casserole. I'll ask her to bring some."

I raised my eyebrows. "You think your parents would really come?"

She cracked her knuckles. "Oh, they'll come all right."

"Bella said she could make arepas and empanadas," I said.

"Never would have thought to have those for Christmas dinner," Elyssa said. "But she is a pretty good cook."

We talked about the dinner, about possible gifts to buy people, and had a few good laughs imagining ridiculous gifts we could buy for Shelton. I wanted to get him a pair of buttless chaps but make out the card so it appeared to be a gift from Bella. Elyssa wanted to buy him a pair of fluffy bunny slippers to wear around the mansion. We were laughing so hard as we one-upped each other with ridiculous gift ideas, I almost didn't hear my phone ring.

I answered when I saw who it was. "Hey, Stacey."

"Hello, my lamb," she said. "Are you in the house somewhere?"

"On the upper porch."

"Ah. Perhaps you would like to see what my friends have accomplished."

I stood up. "Definitely. We'll be right down."

"I'm in the large storage room in the west wing," she said. "I assumed you wouldn't want a mess in the living quarters." She ended the call.

I gobbled down my remaining bacon and wiped my mouth. "Stacey wants to show us something," I told Elyssa.

She picked up her mug of tea and followed. When we reached the storage room, I felt my mouth drop open. A hundred or more cats prowled the room, meowing, stretching, napping, and rubbing against each other. Countless golem rat corpses lay in a pile in the center. Stacey stood near the pile stroking the head of a white cat who curled around her shoulders.

"Ah, there you are," she said, slinking over to us with the grace and sexuality of a panther. "My friends say the house is now clean of vermin." She spat the last word. "I have asked them to remain and keep watch should more of these false creatures attempt subterfuge. Many have agreed. There are plenty of real vermin to eat on the premises, especially in the dungeons."

"Wow, thanks," I said. I scratched the ears of the kitty on her shoulders. "And thank you, too."

The cat meowed, regarding me as royalty might regard a peasant.

"They also kept some alive for your study," she said, pointing to a cage where several of the golem rats wandered in circles as they encountered the cage walls.

"Good thinking," I said, wondering if we could actually glean useful information from them.

I texted Shelton and Bella. Cinder might have been good to ask, but he was still playing babysitter in the nursery.

"I can hack into one of their sparks," Shelton said, making a disgusted face when he saw the pile of fake rat corpses in the room.

Bella reached inside the cage. The rats inside didn't squeak or try to bite, though they sensed the open door and made a break for it. Cats pounced on them before they got far, and returned them to the cage. The dhampyr held up a single squirming rat, her face screwed into a grimace.

"It certainly feels real."

Shelton manned up and took the rat from his girlfriend. We followed him into the war room where he secured the golem rodent to the table with strips of diamond fiber. He took his arcphone, flicked his finger across it a few times, and grunted. "Here's the app." He put the phone next to the rat, and activated the program. "It's gonna take a while, depending on the complexity of the spark."

"As in, let's wait here, or come back in a few hours?" I asked.

He glanced at the readout. "Give me two minutes, and I'll know how complex the spark is."

"I guess it's impossible to know what the 'dead' rats know," I said, making air quotes.

"No spark, no info," Shelton said. "If Lornicus controlled these things with an arcphone like he claims to do with the gray men, then he probably got his information remotely. At least Stacey's pets purged the place."

"They are not pets," she said, eyes flaring.

Shelton waved her off. "Fine, our good and dear feline friends."

The felycan pursed her lips. "Perhaps you'd like some real rats deposited in your bed while you sleep."

Bella made a face. "Maybe I should go back to my room for a few nights."

Stacey burst into laughter.

"Got it," Shelton said a moment later. I peered over his shoulder as he scrolled through a wall of text. "These are pretty simple sparks. Doesn't look like a lot of scripted movements besides evasion and detection."

"Are they remotely controlled?" I asked.

He shook his head. "No, these look automatic. They're programmed to return to a specific location where their information is transferred to an ASE."

"So it's not a live feed?"

"Nope, record and upload." He mapped out the coordinates where they went to upload their data, displaying a location in the wooded area outside the mansion.

"I'll dispatch my friends to take a look," Stacey said, and whispered something to the cat around her neck. It meowed, promptly leapt to the floor, and dashed away.

"Looks like I can tap into the video," Shelton said, projecting an image on his phone above the table so the rest of us could see it. We watched a first-person account of the rat's journey as it ran from the woods, and through a small crack in the house foundation, letting it inside. It ran through a dark area for a while before entering a lit room that looked like the hall outside the kitchen.

Muffled voices sounded. The rat's view turned back and forth, as if searching for the source. It dashed beneath the crack between the floor and the bottom of the door, and into the kitchen.

"Maybe I should get some whipped cream," said the slightly distorted sound of Shelton's voice from the video. "I'll show you how much fun—"

Shelton's face went red. He turned off the projected image picked up the phone. "Pretend you didn't hear that."

Bella burst into laughter.

"How was the whipped cream?" Stacey asked in a sultry voice.

"Not another word," Shelton said. He sighed, put the phone on the table, and projected the image again. "Damned rats."

"I thought that was a kitchen, not a bordello," I said with a snicker.

He gave me a dirty look.

The video resumed, showing a rat's-eye view of the house. The golem rodent tried to enter the war room, but every time it did, it bounced back from the threshold.

"Ah, the repel wards kept it out," Bella said. "Those wards are designed to keep active all-seeing eyes and spy-bots out. I guess the rat's spells were similar enough that it repelled it as well."

"Good news," I said, feeling a profound sense of relief settle over me. "At least this room wasn't compromised."

Shelton rewound the video, showing the rat's day in reverse. When it hit the beginning, I saw a flash of what looked like a face before the video went black. "Wait a minute," I said. "What was that?"

He advanced it a frame at a time until the image of the forest bordered the black. As the rat's view shifted, it angled up for a brief instant, showing a face. I didn't recognize the man whose face it was, but I most definitely recognized his attire.

"That's not a gray man or Lornicus," I said.

"Holy crap," Shelton added.

Lornicus hadn't sent these rats. The Black Robe Brotherhood had.

John Corwin

# Chapter 36

"They found us," Elyssa said.

A tremendous boom sounded and the floor shook. Glass rattled and the table jumped, sending ASEs scattering like marbles. Everyone exchanged shocked looks before running into the hallway and into the den. I saw three-clawed foot attached to a flaming leg slam the ground outside. Looking up through the windows in the vaulted ceiling I saw something out of nightmares open its mouth and roar. Two horns the size and shape of mammoth tusks jutted from the sides of the creature's reptilian head. Its arm swung forward and a colossal fist smashed into the window.

"Holy infernal bat crap, it's a demon!" Shelton shouted.

The window bent inward, stretched and repelled the thrust. The creature roared again and slammed the side of the house. Chandeliers clattered, and a bookshelf teetered precariously before falling over with a crash.

I stood stunned, unable to move at the sight of the monster. What in the hell could we do against something like that? It looked at least as tall as the mansion, flames licking from between the cracks in its rocky volcanic flesh. I'd seen a demon when I was little. Scary as it was, it had looked nothing like this. A crude iron chain encircled the monster's neck, the end hanging loose across its chest.

"What do we do against that thing?" Shelton said.

I had no answer.

Another thud rocked the house. The place had to be enchanted to hold up against the pounding, because I didn't think for a minute a normal house would remain standing from such a beating. The house had once belonged to Ezzek Moore and the Arcane Council long ago.

288

They must have prepared it to withstand attacks, but against something like this?

I looked at Elyssa. She looked as out of ideas as I was.

*You're part demon. Think of something!*

Demons didn't just come knocking. They had to be summoned. That meant there must be a summoning rune nearby. When I'd seen a demon as a child, I'd somehow spoken to it. That one had been summoned using a piece of plywood studded with nails and patterned with wire. An aether generator had activated it. Turning off the power had closed the summoning portal and sent it home. I doubted the brotherhood used such a thing. They'd probably spent time crafting the rune, maybe in the earth outside. If we could close it, we could banish the demon. But how could we accomplish that with battle mages waiting outside?

I took a quick headcount as the floor shook again. We didn't have nearly enough people to handle this thing. The best bet would be a hasty retreat through the portal downstairs. I sucked in a breath as an idea came to me.

"Elyssa, how fast can your father assemble a team?"

"Immediately," she said.

"Shelton, open the portal to the Templar compound. Elyssa, call your father. Tell him we need reinforcements. Bring them through the portal to the mansion then open the portal behind the attackers so the Templars can flank them."

Elyssa whipped out her phone and dialed. Shelton gave me a look as if he thought I was out of my mind. I probably was, but this place was home now, dammit, and I wasn't going to stand for this.

"Go!" I roared at Shelton.

He and Elyssa booked it out of there, heading to the cellar stairs.

I turned to Stacey. "Do you think we could get some moggies to help us?" She could turn ordinary felines into monstrous cats, but I didn't know how long it would take.

"I already have several here in the wine cellar," she said. "I thought they might be useful considering how much trouble you attract."

"How many?"

"A dozen. I can ask for volunteers, and morph perhaps two or three more, but it will take at least twenty minutes for each one, and all my effort." Her gaze settled on me. "I will be unable to fight."

"Do it. Ask your moggies to clear the area behind the mansion first."

Woods surrounded the house, and I had no doubt the battle mages were waiting for us to emerge. Dusk loomed outside, making the monstrosity slamming the house glow like a bonfire.

Stacey blurred from the room, taking the other staircase down to the wine cellar beneath the kitchen.

"Bella, if I wipe out the summoning rune, will that banish the demon?"

"No, it will unleash the demon from its controllers. You need the name to banish it." She bit her lip, apparently thinking hard. "However, a demon like this won't be able to keep its corporeal form for long before returning back to the demon realm. It requires the summoners to constantly fuel it with aether to remain. If we disrupt them, it will only be a matter of time before its body disintegrates, and its spirit returns."

"Does the summoning rune need to be near the demon?"

"It must be close. They probably used an area nearby in the woods. The demon is chained to its proximity."

"A tether?"

She nodded.

I flicked into incubus sight, extending my senses. Against my better judgment, I went closer to the window, and saw aether pouring into the giant creature. I followed the funnel of energy with my eyes, spotting an area behind splintered trees where the ground glowed a sullen red. *The summoning rune.*

My phone rang. I answered.

"Justin, we have a squad of thirty arriving in five minutes," Elyssa said. "My father said he has demon specialists on the way, but it could be ten minutes or more."

"Get the first wave through, and send them into flanking positions outside," I said.

"Got it." She disconnected.

How had Kassus gotten beneath our guard? What had happened with Lornicus's early warning system? There was no time to think about it. I had to do something. Reaching inside, I lowered the barrier between me and the demon half of my soul. It rushed out. I felt its senses perk and alight on the creature outside. A feeling of sheer rage suffused me.

*How dare you invade!*

Apparently, my demon half wasn't pleased at all. For once, I agreed. My body surged, muscles coiling around my arms and legs. My jeans stretched and tore. I felt my tail lash behind me like a whip, and horns burst from my forehead. My t-shirt ripped as chest and back muscles swelled. The ground fell beneath me, beast mode stretching my frame over a foot taller. My body stabilized. By the reflection of a broken wall mirror, I saw blue flames ignite in my eyes.

*Kick ass.*

I might not be as big as the thing outside, but I might be able to distract it. Turning, I dashed upstairs, simultaneously slamming shut the barrier between me and my demonic side, preventing it from consuming my remaining control. Even in such an emergency, I didn't want that to happen. I would grow even larger, berserk, and attack friend and enemy alike.

I ran out to the balcony where Elyssa and I had enjoyed our breakfast, and stood nearly eye-to-eye with the infernal beast. Unfamiliar words tore from my throat in the guttural language of the demons. I understood them, even if I couldn't repeat them. *You face your destroyer!*

That got the demon's attention. Eyes like burning meteors focused on me. A giant, clawed fist the size of my body raked at me. I blurred to the side. The patio furniture splintered. A wave of heat rushed past my face. I picked up a large potted tree in the corner and flung it at the demon. The clay pot shattered. Dirt rained down the creature's face. The poor tree burst into flame and fell to the ground.

It struck again. I dodged to the side. Heat washed against my body, singing my clothes, but not affecting my skin. Out of the corner of my eye, I saw a second set of claws sweep toward me from the left. I tried to jump too late. The impact crushed the air from my lungs. I flew sideways. I felt branches raking my body. My hand snatched the top of a pine tree. The thin bough cracked and broke from the strain.

John Corwin

My clawed toenails dug into the trunk, and my tail wrapped around the tree on pure instinct. I sucked in a breath. The odor of brimstone filled my nostrils. The creature lumbered toward me, straining before jerking to a halt at the edge of the house and roaring displeasure. Its claws splintered nearby trees, narrowly missing me. The thing must have reached the end of its tether.

"Suck it!" I yelled in my deep demon voice.

A bolt of light speared past, narrowly missing my shoulder. I looked down to see a battle mage aiming his staff. Something swift, large, and studded with bony spines leapt from the shadows. The man screamed as a moggie the size of a grizzly bear took him in the throat, the cat's jaws crunching on flesh and bone.

I winced.

I felt another wave of heat as the demon swiped at me again. I had it distracted for now, but would it be long enough? I looked at the ground for more danger and spotted two men in an area of the woods cleared of brush. A complex pattern glowed against the bedrock. The men held up staffs, slammed them into the ground. The pattern burst into blue flame. A basso roar detonated the air. I slammed hands over my ears as the sound assaulted my super hearing.

A brilliant light flashed, and a creature spun in a vortex from the ground, icy blue fire flickering like lightning. Its torso looked almost human but everything below the waist swirled like a tornado. Icy claws gleamed. Heavily muscled arms tensed. Three glowing eyes regarded me from an otherwise perfectly smooth and featureless face.

*I am so screwed.*

My demon half seemed to agree.

The monster made a sound like a deep sad sigh. Its hands rushed together to crush me between them. I leaned back hard, pulling the limber tree back away as the hands clapped together. The shockwave propelled the tree toward the house. I leapt just as the fire demon surged for me. Its talons grazed my leg and I spun out of control, crashing hard on the roof, skidding along the top and to the crest.

My claws scraped the surface and caught on the peak of the house. The ice demon loosed a deep undulating sigh at its fiery sibling and slashed at it. I saw the summoners struggling, eyes squeezed shut as they seemed to pull on an invisible chain. The ice demon flinched, bellowed at the sky. I had to stop those men. Against

292

one demon, it was all I could do to evade death. Against two—well I had better odds beating Bella at Scrabble.

I stood and saw a shimmer as a portal opened just beyond the trees on the road. Black-clad Templars poured from within, spreading out, and running until I lost sight of them in the tree line. I heard a whoosh. Something slammed into my back. I smelled burning cloth as I slid face-first down the roof straight toward the gaping maw of the fire demon. The ice creature lunged for me. I pushed my hands against the roof, flinging myself in the air at the last minute, flipping upside down. Time seemed to slow. I saw the ice demon's claw swiping for me. Saw the fire demon's gaping maw opening to swallow me. The sky came into view. My back slammed onto something hard, and time flickered back to normal. Searing heat crackled into my flesh. My hand caught on a fiery horn just before I slid off the head of the fire demon. I twisted, trying to ignore the furnace boiling against my skin, and gained my feet.

A roar ripped from my throat. I gripped the horn and jerked. The volcanic flesh around the base cracked. My tail wrapped around the other horn. Ignoring the sizzling of my own flesh, I bellowed and jerked on the first horn with both hands. The horn tore loose, blood like lava dripping from the root. The fire demon screamed and swiped at me. Jerking hard, my tail instinctually whisked me backward. The creature's fist slammed its own head. My feet lost purchase, and I dangled upside down by my tail. I saw the ice demon's blank face. It lunged for me, claws whistling through the air. Somehow, I pushed off the fire demon's face with one hand, swinging away just in time. The ice monster's blow caught its sibling in the top of the head. Rocky flesh crumbled away, revealing glowing orange lava beneath.

Still hanging on with my tail, I planted my feet against the fire demon's head and swung myself around the remaining horn. At the peak, I jumped, reversed the grip on the uprooted horn, and drove the point into his left eye. Orange fluid jetted from the burst orb. In my peripheral vision, I saw blue claws swinging toward me. Gripping the fire demon's remaining horn with both hands, I jerked hard, baring the monster's face.

Icy blue claws gouged chunks from its face.

The fire demon had apparently had enough. Ceasing its attempts to grab me, it gripped its fellow monster by the throat and slammed it against the side of the mansion. Steam hissed as ice and fire came into contact. The mansion's stone façade could take no more and cracked. As the demons fought, I leapt to the deck, my feet crushing a table beneath me.

Remembering the effort the demon summoners had put into keeping the ice demon from beating on its comrade, I knew the fire demon controllers must be struggling with their monster right about now. I climbed to the roof and raced along it. At the far end, I leapt to a tree, dug my claws into the wood, and slid down, shedding bark and drawing deep gouges. I hit the ground in front of a startled battle mage. He fired a stream of blue orbs at me. I ducked and rolled beneath. Came up beneath the man and hit him with an uppercut.

Bones crunched and his body flew up about twenty feet before thudding back to earth in a lifeless heap. I had no time to feel guilt as a beam of light splintered a nearby tree. A moggie streaked past me, taking the attacker down in a flurry of claws, fangs, and a spray of blood. A wave of screaming energy from an unseen attacker ripped into the giant cat, shredding its flesh like moldy cloth. Dark blood spurted from the feline as the death wave ripped through it. The moggie made a horrific mewling sound before collapsing.

*Pro tip: Stay out of the way of those death waves.*

I dodged through trees, found another man hiding, and bashed his head against a stump. Ahead, I saw the demon summoners, teeth clenched, eyes squeezed shut as they fought to regain control. I picked up a nearby log a few feet in length, and hurled it at the man on the left. It slammed into his chest, knocking him backward into the brush. The other man's eyes flashed wide, and he screamed. A ring of energy from the summoning rune pulsed outward, cleaving trees, and slicing the man in half like deli ham.

Flicking into incubus sight, I watched as the glowing tether crackled with energy. The rune might hold the demon from wandering far, but no one controlled it now. A bellow rose from the direction of the house. I looked in time to see the two demons clawing at each other with raw abandon, everything else forgotten. Lightning flashed from the vortex beneath the ice demon, spraying shards of volcanic flesh from the fire demon through the air.

Templars appeared from the trees, lancers and swords at the ready. They saw me, but thankfully seemed to know I wasn't a threat—just a demon boy in the most ragged jeans a designer could ever hope to fashion. A beefy figure appeared and touched his neck. The mask peeled down his face, vanishing to reveal the square jaw and piercing violet eyes of Michael Borathen.

"We incapacitated the summoners on the other side," he said. "We have to hope the demons engage each other until their power runs out and banishes them."

"Sir," said a female voice from one of the Templars, her face hidden behind the mask. "Exorcists are on the way. They should be able to control the demons until they expire."

Michael nodded, sparing words as usual.

My shoulders sagged with relief. I suddenly felt so very tired. But I also felt safe enough to push back my own demon, shrinking down to my relatively diminutive six feet. Michael tossed me a black belt from within his pack. I secured it around my waist with one hand, and touched the hem. Nightingale armor flowed down my legs beneath the jeans, and I tore off the ragged remains with a grunt, letting them fall to the ground after retrieving my phone from a pocket. Maybe they'd be useful in a Paris fashion show, but I was done with them.

"Where are the captured mages?" I asked, my mind suddenly flicking to the mastermind behind this assault. "Is Maulin Kassus here?"

"I don't know," Michael said. "The OPFORs fled when we engaged. Some escaped."

"No, he's got to be here," I said. "He's got to!"

I raced through the woods, looking at the scattered bodies of brotherhood members. I found a gaggle of bound and unconscious battle mages in a makeshift Templar holding area. It only took me a minute to realize Kassus wasn't among them.

Exorcists—apparently a division of the Templars designated to counter demon threats—appeared moments later. They contained the raging demons by draining the power from the runes until the monsters howled and collapsed, their bodies crumbling to elemental forms, as their demon spirits were sucked back into the demon realm.

Despite my exhaustion, I combed the woods, looking and hoping to find the man responsible. Elyssa found me, took me by the arm, and directed me back to the house. I was too weak to resist her. As night settled in, Michael came inside and reported.

"Maulin Kassus isn't here," he said. "He must have escaped."

"No, no, no," I groaned, feebly attempting to pound the table. The world blurred, and I slumped, fatigue weighing heavy in every inch of my body.

"Justin, you need to feed," Elyssa said. "Please."

Fighting back useless anger, I nodded. It was over. We had won.

But we had also lost.

# Chapter 37

It took all my effort not to drain Elyssa. Her shoulders shuddered as she fought the sexual urges caused by my voracious feeding. Despite the still-clawing hunger, I stopped, afraid I would hurt her.

"Are you better?" she asked, panting, tears glistening in the corners of her eyes.

I managed a nod, and must have fallen asleep right after.

I jerked awake. Looked wildly around the room, and found Elyssa sleeping next to me. Daylight streamed through the window. I was famished in more ways than one, my stomach growling for food, and my demon snapping for sustenance. I didn't dare feed from Elyssa. Her face looked too pale for her fair skin. She must have been exhausted when she offered herself to me last night. I'd drained her too much. My stomach knotted as I kissed her forehead.

She moaned and continued to sleep. Ordinarily, she would have sprung awake. She needed blood. I ran downstairs, fetched some blood packs and boiled eggs from the refrigerator. Upstairs, I sat next to Elyssa, nomming on eggs and waiting. She stirred. Blinked sleep from her eyes.

"Justin?" she asked in a weak voice.

I pulled the tab on a blood pack to heat it up. Propping her up with my hand, I held it to her mouth. Her nostrils flared. Fangs protruded from behind her lips. She grabbed the pack and drained it. I opened the other one and handed it to her. This one she sucked on in a more controlled manner.

"You know how to make a girl feel good," she said with a smile, licking blood from her full lips. "I was too tired to move last night."

"It's my fault," I said. "I took too much from you."

297

She smiled, caressing my jaw with her hand. "Anything for you, my hero."

"Are you bound by an oath not to feed from people?" I asked. She usually refused when I tried to return the favor.

Her eyes went distant. "I used to think it was evil. Then again, I used to think a lot of things were evil before I met you." A smile graced her face.

"Now that you know real evil, will you please feel comfortable taking blood from me? I hate seeing you so tired. You've told me before blood packs don't taste very good."

She nodded slowly. "We'll see."

I leaned back and groaned, rubbing my face. "I can't believe we went through so much and still lost Kassus last night."

Elyssa lay her head on my chest. "He probably left the minute he saw things spin out of control."

"I'm going after him," I said. "Today. Even if I have to march down to Darkwater headquarters and take him by force."

"You'll do no such thing," Elyssa said, turning hard eyes on me. "My father now believes the Templars have jurisdiction to go after him. They'll arrest him and bring him in."

"Really?" I asked. "But won't Kassus claim it's an internal Arcane matter?"

"He and his men attacked supers who aren't Arcanes, including you," she said. "Kassus crossed the line."

"He's attacked me before. Why didn't your father arrest him then?"

"Because it wasn't in public. This time, there were plenty of witnesses. It's a slam dunk." She raised an eyebrow. "I say we sit back and relax while he does his job. You'll have Kassus's blood by this afternoon."

The anger vanished. I felt a grin split my lips. "Have I mentioned I love you?"

"Maybe once or twice." She pecked my lips with a kiss. "I'm feeling so much better." Her eyes narrowed as she looked into mine. "You're still hungry, aren't you?"

I sighed, nodded. "I'm not feeding off you. I took too much already."

"Let's go into town. Maybe you can feed off the locals without inciting an orgy."

I laughed, my mood lightening at the promise of Thomas Borathen arresting Kassus today. "Let's do it."

We had brunch in town. I chowed down pancakes while simultaneously feeding incubus-style from several nearby patrons. As ten a.m. approached, I found myself checking the time like a nervous tic.

"Any idea when your father plans to go after Kassus?" I asked.

"Should be any time now," Elyssa said. "I can't imagine why he'd wait too long." She dug in her purse. "Where's my phone?"

"When was the last time you used?" I asked.

"Last night when I talked to Dad." She huffed. "Can I use yours? I'll text him."

"Sure. Just make sure, if you act bossy, he knows the message is from you, not me."

Her lips curved into a smile. "Maybe." She tapped in a message. A moment later, my phone dinged with a reply. Elyssa glanced at it, her grin fading to concern. "We need to go right now."

I dropped some tinsel on the table to pay for the meal as my guts tightened. "What's wrong?"

"Dad sent me a message earlier, but I didn't see it because my phone is probably down in the arch room somewhere. He needs you to present the accusation." She shook her head. "That's the archaic way of doing it. I didn't think anyone did it anymore."

"I have to present the accusation?" I said. "What do I do, tell everyone what a jerk this guy is?"

"Something like that. Let's go."

We took a flying carpet up the cliff and back to the mansion, ran downstairs to the arch room. Elyssa's phone sat on a table near the arch. She snatched it, and checked it. "Yep, here's his message from this morning. Crap." She typed something on her phone. It dinged, and she held up the picture of a room. "We're going there. It's a Templar safe house in the Grotto. We can catch the trolley to Darkwater from there."

I opened the portal to a plain white room. On the wall hung a portrait of a woman dancing in a field of flowers. We ran out of the front door, and hopped aboard a passing trolley. It took us to an area

299

near Darkwater, so we ran the rest of the way. We were unprepared for the sight awaiting us.

Thomas Borathen stood on one side of the street, about twenty Templars lined up beside him. Across the road stood another fifty or so Templars, their backs to the black iron gates guarding the Darkwater building. The three-story complex boasted panes of rippling liquid glass, and piano-black marble framing. It managed to look classic and foreboding all at the same time.

A squat two-story building sat on our side of the road, its windows boarded up, and signs posted to the side indicating its imminent renovation for some other Arcane company to take over. It didn't look nearly as impressive as the Darkwater building.

"I'm sorry, Commander," Elyssa said, snapping a salute to her father. "Why does Justin need to testify?"

"Kassus demanded it," he said.

I suddenly felt very vulnerable. What if the crazy battle mage planned to assassinate me while I stood on the sidewalk and shouted at him? At least Thomas had brought a lot of Templars. I looked across the road at the other complement, and did a double-take when I recognized a tall man with a long red cape flowing behind him.

"Isn't that—"

"Artemis Coronus," Thomas finished. "Seneschal to the Grand Master of the Templar Synod."

"Oh, no," Elyssa said.

"Why is he here?" I asked.

"Maulin Kassus requested them. Artemis is the one demanding a testimony from the accuser." Thomas raised an eyebrow. "I don't expect it will make a difference one way or the other."

Artemis had also demanded my arrest during the Maximus incident. He'd tried to remove Thomas from command of his Templar legion and demanded they stand down instead of attacking the vampire compound. Thankfully, nobody had followed his orders.

"Who do I present testimony to?" I asked.

"You'll need to announce it to everyone present," Thomas said. "Check your phone. I sent a list of accusations." He then stepped into the street. "By the rule of Overworld law, I hereby call the accused, Maulin Kassus to stand forth and hear the voice of the accuser, such that he may declare yea or nay to the charges, such that we, the designated enforcers of the law may determine if such charges warrant his arrest and trial."

"Hear, hear!" shouted the Templars assembled near Thomas.

Artemis regarded me with narrowed eyes as I stepped into the street. He spat on the ground. "With such a witness as this, perhaps you're best calling this a day, Borathen." Some of the men behind the Templar knight laughed, as if it was the best joke they'd heard in ages.

Maulin Kassus walked from the front of this building, his body phasing through the liquid glass. He held eye contact with me, smirking, as he walked outside the gate and to the sidewalk. "I am here," he said, lip curling into a sneer as he looked me up and down.

I glanced at the text from Thomas. *Short, concise, to the point. No surprise there.* Stepping into the street, I read the text in a loud voice. "I, Justin Slade, hereby present accusations against one Maulin Kassus for injuries suffered against me and persons under my care. Principally, I accuse him of demonic summons, attempted murder, destruction of property, and trespass. I swear by my blood, my kith and kin that this statement is true."

"The accused may state his case," Thomas said.

"The accused has no case against me," Kassus shouted. He held up a scroll of parchment, and unrolled it. "This document is a signed order for demolition for an abandoned house on Greek Row on property owned by Arcane University. The house was determined empty by a team of Arcane engineers, and subcontracted to Darkwater for demolition." He jabbed a finger at me. "Little did we know this demon spawn and his comrades had taken over the house, illegally squatting inside. Little did we know he used his infernal abilities to plant demonic traps outside the building. My men were attacked by his demons. Had we not been so experienced, and taken control of the beasts, they might have killed us."

"You're lying!" I shouted.

Kassus grinned. "This spawn is the liar. He is the one illegally summoning demons and destroying property. I demand his arrest and execution for attempted murder by demonic summons."

"I have witnesses," I said.

"Oh, you mean the other squatters? A felycan? A dhampyr?" He strutted before Artemis and the Synod Templars, hands spread as

301

though regaling them with wondrous tales. "This spawn's 'friends'"—
he formed air quotes, giving me a dubious look—"killed my men.
The felycan used moggies to murder people I knew and cared about."
His face turned sad. "They were hard-working men and women with
families." He stabbed his finger at me. "This spawn and his vagabond
trash should be rounded up and executed."

"We believe the stronger case lies with this man," Artemis said,
placing a hand on Kassus's shoulder. "Spawn are well-known for
manipulating the facts to suit their own needs. It is also true that
felycans are anti-social, murderous folk who care nothing for the rule
of law." The Templar knight pointed at me. "By the authority of the
Templar Synod, you, Justin Slade, are under arrest."

"He's a liar," I said, backing away as Synod Templars encroached
on me.

Kassus flicked my accusation away and smiled. "I'm an
upstanding Overworld citizen, *spawn*. Maybe they'll let you say
goodbye to your mommy before they take you in."

Rage exploded, and the world flashed red. I lunged at the man.
"You filthy, lying piece of trash!"

Strong hands gripped my shoulders. Another set of arms
tightened around my arms. I struggled to free myself. All I had to do
was scratch the asshole. Maybe nick his jugular in the process. A drop
of blood. That was all I needed!

"Justin, no!" Elyssa said.

The red faded, and I realized she was the one holding me from
behind. "He's going to get away with it," I said.

"Right now, we have no choice," Thomas said, his face set in
grim lines. "You're a disgrace to the Templars, Coronus," he said,
eyeing the Templar Knight with disdain. "If you continue to interfere,
you'll start a war."

"A war you can't hope to win," Artemis said. "With the Divinity
and sheer numbers on our side, there's little you can do but accept the
inevitable."

"I am anything but accepting of idiocy," Thomas said, his voice
still calm. "You were once a good man. A hero. But power has
corrupted you. Blinded you to the truth."

"Cease your heresy, Borathen; I will hear no more of it." Artemis
motioned with his hand. "Take the boy."

Thomas motioned, and his people stepped forward, forming a barrier between me and the larger force of Templars. "Not today, Coronus."

"If you wish a battle, I think you'll find we are more than ready," the Templar knight said. "Templars, engage anyone who does not immediately lay down their arms."

Swords sang as they slid from the sheaths of the Synod Templars. I noticed none of the Templars under Thomas's command so much as moved for their sword, still standing in a neat orderly row, hands crossed behind their backs. I felt my stomach drop at the impending battle. I saw Kassus back away through the black-clad soldiers, and make his way back into the Darkwater building. Anger seethed in my chest. I wanted to race after him, but knew it would be pointless with so many soldiers in the way.

Elyssa seemed to notice the lack of action on Thomas's people, but gave nothing away with her expression, instead, assuming a position similar to the others.

"I have video proof of the demon summoning," Thomas said. "The entire area was observed by ASEs." He flicked a silvery sphere to Artemis.

The other man caught it. "I'm sure this is fabricated."

"You can't fake Templar ASE footage, Coronus, and you know it."

The Templar knight scoffed, and threw the all-seeing eye into the gutter along the road. "I won't believe your lies, spawn lover."

Thomas sighed. "I had to be sure we couldn't reason with you before I slaughtered you and your men," he said.

"In case you hadn't noticed, we have you outnumbered two to one," Artemis said. "The only slaughter today will be yours."

Thomas turned his head, and nodded to his people.

The Templars under his command slid red bands on their biceps. Since both sides wore identical nightingale armor, it made sense to differentiate themselves. As one, they slid swords from sheaths, and assumed a uniform fighting stance, perfect in order and alignment.

Thomas looked back to Artemis. "Numbers mean nothing without discipline," he said in a calm voice. "You told me that long ago when I first joined the Templars. I looked up to you then as a friend and a mentor." He shook his head, his stony expression saddening for an instant. "I regret what centuries of power have turned you into, Artemis. I regret what you are about to make me do."

"You're stalling, Borathen," Coronus said. "And it is you who have lost your way."

Thomas sighed. "You chose your men for blind, unreasoning loyalty. I can tell from their reactions, they care nothing for the rule of law. Let us see if they at least care for their own lives."

Some of the as-yet unmasked people in the Synod squad looked uneasily at each other. I wondered if they'd thought Thomas would back down, considering the odds. Now that he seemed determined, I could tell they didn't relish the idea of battle.

Artemis Coronus's face turned scarlet, his lips peeled back with rage. "To arms, men! Kill anyone who does not surrender." He looked at the hesitant line of his soldiers. Jabbed a finger toward us. "Attack!"

The enemy line surged across the road.

The Templars were at war.

# Chapter 38

I wore no sword, though I'd had foresight enough to put on nightingale armor before leaving the house. For me, the apparel was becoming as necessary as underwear. I felt useless. How many of Thomas's people would die? How could I have prevented this?"

Thomas roared a command.

The first wave of opponents attacked.

Swords clanged. Thomas's sword blurred in a silvery arc, taking off one man's sword arm. He ducked beneath a swing from another attacker and plunged his sword through the man's chest. The Nightingale armor was apparently no protection against Templar steel. Thomas kicked the dead man away, sliding his sword free, and met another attacker's down-stroke. Elyssa's sai swords caught an incoming katana inches from cleaving her face.

In a blur, she swung the enemy steel away. The tips of her sais plunged into the man's neck. Blood gouted, and he went down with a gurgling scream. A sickened look crossed my girlfriend's face, quickly replaced by resolve as another enemy appeared.

I felt useless, having brought no weapons with me. I found a sword in a puddle of blood, a dismembered hand still clinging to it. With a shudder, I pried the lukewarm, dead fingers away and gripped the blood-slicked handle. I looked over the scene. Pure chaos reigned from the Synod men while Thomas's men maintained a neat line and methodically cut down their enemies.

Twitching corpses and body parts littered the street. Elyssa ducked beneath a stroke aimed at taking off her head. She sliced the enemy's hamstring. Another man came from behind her, sword raised. Thomas caught the killing blow on his sword, gripped the attacker's wrist, and broke his arm. Instead of killing him, he slammed the butt of his sword on the crown of the man's head. Elyssa dispatched her assailant and met her father's eyes. He nodded.

I saw Artemis's apoplectic face as he roared commands, all but impossible to hear over the fray. Thomas strode toward the Templar Knight. Elyssa intercepted a Synod Templar before he could reach her father. She caught his sword on the prong of her sai, twisted hard, and flung the sword from his grasp, sending it plunging through the back of his comrade. She flipped backward, her foot slamming so hard against the man's chin I heard the crack and saw teeth jettison from his mouth. Elyssa landed lightly on her feet, swords at the ready. Her opponent hit the ground and didn't move.

The sounds of battle dwindled. I looked around and saw why. Scores of dead and wounded Synod Templars littered the street. Only a couple of Thomas's men even seemed wounded.

Purple infused Artemis's face.

"How dare you!" he shouted. "We will slaughter you in your homes, Borathen! We will hunt you to the ends of the earth!" He flung back his cape and rushed Thomas.

Commander Borathen's sword flicked aside the first thrust. Artemis's long, straight sword blurred. Thomas ducked, feinted a strike. The Templar Knight spun away from the feint and caught Thomas's true attack just before it removed his head. Their attacks became so quick they were blurs to my supernatural vision.

Artemis blocked a blow, slammed his shoulder against Thomas's chest, and drove a dagger toward his heart. Thomas flinched, taking a deep cut on his sword arm. Blood sprayed through the cut in the Nightingale armor. I gasped and moved to help.

Elyssa's arm barred the way. "This is his battle to win or lose."

"He's your father," I said.

Her jaw tightened. "I know."

Artemis backed off, a smile curling his face. "You can't win, Borathen. In case you've forgotten, I never once lost the Templar Sword Tourney."

"That's because I never competed in it," Thomas said, a rare grin touching the corners of his lips.

"Brave words from a man who's about to die," Artemis said. "You can't hope to win, traitor. Especially with an injured sword arm."

306

A steady rain of blood trickled from the long slice in Thomas's arm. He snorted. "I suppose it's a good thing I'm left handed." He tossed the sword to his other hand.

A laugh burst from Artemis's lips. "I've never liked you, Borathen. You were stiff and frightened as a pig being led to slaughter when I first met you. How you rose from being a peasant to commander boggles my mind even to this day."

"I once respected you, Coronus. I used to think you embodied all that it meant to be a Templar Knight." Thomas's eyes went hard. "But now I think it will be a pleasure to end the miserable creature you've become."

Artemis blurred forward, a sword in one hand, dagger in the other. Thomas ducked beneath Artemis's sword arm, pivoted, and sliced the man's arm off at the elbow. The Templar Knight screamed as blood spurted from the stump. Despite the wound, his other arm flicked forward. Thomas's back foot slipped in a puddle of blood, and the dagger caught him in the chest. He went down hard, scarlet fluid splashing.

Elyssa cried out. One of Thomas's men grabbed her before she could rush to her father's aid.

Sensing a victory, Artemis bent down, grabbed the sword from his severed hand, and strode to where Thomas lay gasping. He raised the sword high. I looked at the grim faces of the Templars on our side. Was nobody going to stop this madness?

*You're not a Templar.*

Their rules didn't apply to me.

Artemis's sword plunged point-down toward Thomas. Drawing on my magic, I flung strands of energy toward the Templar Knight, intending to jerk the sword off course. Before they reached it, Thomas rolled. He swept Artemis's legs from beneath him while gaining his own feet, despite the blood streaming down the front of his armor.

"Borathen!" Artemis roared as he rose on his hand, stump, and knees.

A silver flash cut off his shout. His head dropped into the pond of blood with a splash, mouth open in a rictus of fury and maybe just little bit of surprise.

*Having your head cut off will do that.*

307

I felt a hotdog from three days ago threaten to make a return trip up my throat.

Thomas wiped his sword clean of blood on Artemis's own cloak before the headless body hit the ground. He looked at his daughter. Staggered, and went down on his knees.

Elyssa streaked toward him. "I need a healer!"

One of the other Templars knelt next to Thomas and began working on him.

"Why did you kill Coronus?" she asked. "You could have arrested him."

Thomas grimaced as the healer removed the dagger. "He was corrupt beyond repair. To arrest him would have invited more political upheaval. I, for one, am sick of the politics." The healer did something to stanch the bleeding and helped Thomas to his feet. The commander gave a hand signal, and several horse-drawn wagons approached, driven by Custodians, the Templar cleanup and cover-up crews.

I snapped out of my funk, as my mind returned to another vital matter. "Kassus is inside. I need his blood." It seemed a trite thing to say in the face of a street already flowing scarlet, the coppery scent assaulting my nose.

"Apprehend Maulin Kassus," Thomas said to his soldiers as the healer helped him to one of the wagons.

The unwounded Templars wasted no time marching on the Darkwater building and entering.

*Finally!*

I couldn't wait to see the look on that bastard's face when they dragged him outside. I was going to enjoy drawing his blood.

It didn't take long to discover how premature my plans were.

"We've secured the building," one of Thomas's people reported fifteen minutes later. "The target was seen fleeing into their underground data room. We found a hidden tunnel that leads to the sewers. It appears Kassus exfiltrated that way."

"Are you freaking kidding me?" I roared. I felt eyes lock onto me, but I didn't care. Kassus had escaped right under our damned noses again. And now there was no telling where he was going. I slammed my fists against the boarded windows of the building next to us, splintering wood, and bellowing with fury.

"Throwing a temper tantrum won't solve anything," Elyssa said, grabbing my arm and spinning me to face her. "So, stop it right now before I smack the crap out of you."

I stood, seething with rage, panting from my exertions. It didn't take long for my rage to melt into helpless frustration. "I don't know what to do," I said.

"Just think about it instead of acting like a child," she said.

"My mother is going to die if I don't catch him."

She threw up her hands. "Yeah, and shouting like a maniac is going to solve it, right?"

I looked down. "No."

"Exactly." She huffed a breath. "Just think about it for a minute. Think about how much effort Kassus put into trying to kill you."

I nodded. "A lot."

"He went to extreme measures. He's not done with you." She snapped her fingers. "There's only one way out of the Grotto."

I sucked in a breath. "The way station."

"Let's go." Elyssa ran to one of the carts, and pulled a carpet from one. She tossed it on the ground.

I hopped on behind her. The carpet levitated above the crowd of Templars and shot down the road. We sped through winding streets, over the heads of people going about their daily lives, unaware of the merciless bloodletting not far from them. We reached the doors to the way station and disembarked from the carpet. I snatched it off the ground and hurried through the doors after Elyssa.

A line of travelers stretched from the yellow-and-black-striped circle around the towering Obsidian Arch in the center of the cavern. We ran down the line, examining faces. Kassus wasn't there.

"The control room," I said, motioning Elyssa to follow. We ran to the left of the arch toward the stables. The scent of dung, hay, and animals hung heavy in the air. We circled behind to the alley between the stable and the cave wall. I ran my hand along the stone until it touched the door, hidden behind illusion. I opened it and peered inside.

Two arch operators with disgruntled looks stood on the platform in front of the world map arrayed along the wall, animatedly talking. Seeing no army of waiting brotherhood members, I jogged over to the two men. "Has Maulin Kassus been here?" I asked without preamble.

"Hey, aren't you the kid who was in here the other day?" asked a familiar-looking Arcane.

"Yes." I fought to stay calm. "Please answer my question. He's a fugitive, and we're here to arrest him."

Elyssa narrowed her eyes at the man, giving him her no-nonsense look. The blood spattered on her face from the recent battle made her look scary as hell.

He gulped. "Yes, he was just here. He ran back to the arches over there." He pointed to the alcove of omniarches. "We've never used those. I don't even know how they work."

"He used one?" I asked.

"Yes, somehow he did." The Arcane shrugged. "Where he went, I have no idea."

"Show me the exact one."

The man led us to the closest one. If Kassus had opened a portal, he hadn't left it open behind him. I cursed under my breath.

"Thanks," I said, barely able to make myself show common courtesy as frustration and anger roiled in my stomach.

Elyssa and I left the control room, and stood in the alley.

"How does Kassus know about the omniarches if the arch operators were clueless?" I asked.

"I don't know." She pursed her lips. "Unless the spy rats—"

"Oh, crap," I said. "I'll bet one of those little bastards saw us using our arch."

"If he knows how to use one, he can go anywhere. He probably took it to another control room somewhere."

I closed my eyes and thought furiously. If I was on the run, where would I go? "Darkwater has been clearing cherubs from relics with Alabaster Arches," I said. "If he didn't want to be seen by anyone, he would probably go to one that's empty of danger."

"El Dorado was clear of danger so far as he knows and also has something he wants," Elyssa said. "The cupids."

"I think you're right," I said. Another thought hit me. "What if he comes to the same idea I had about stealing one?"

"You mean open a portal right next to it? But I don't think he knows what the nursery looks like with the leyworms surrounding it."

"Yeah, but they got an overhead view with the ASE, remember?"

"Oh, no. You're right." Elyssa took out her phone and called Cinder. Shook her head. "No answer."

"That's not like him." I ran for the control room door. "That's where we have to go."

"Through an untested omniarch from the control room?" she asked with a surprised look.

"No choice."

We ran back inside, startling the arch operators yet again. I ignored them, running past and to the omniarch Kassus had used. I pressed my thumb to the silver circle on the floor around it, closing the circuit, and concentrating on the part of the cave beneath El Dorado we'd used to covertly enter the place while waiting to ambush Kassus. It flickered into view. We stepped from the portal and into pandemonium. Streaks of deadly energy flew past, shattering stalagmites. Silver Lancer darts whistled through the air.

The ambient lightning in the cavern seemed to be at full brightness, illuminating the cavern like the sun. Elyssa shoved me behind an outcropping of rock as a bolt of blue energy plowed into the floor, spraying shards of stony shrapnel. Gigantor and Lulu encircled the nursery, their huge, lean muzzles bellowing roars at a group of black-robed invaders taking cover behind a shield and rock formations near the front of the cave as they attacked. I saw the prone forms of Templars and brotherhood members scattered about the cavern. Whether they were dead or merely unconscious, I couldn't tell.

Elyssa looked at her arcphone and cursed. "The signal is jammed."

A figure in nightingale armor blurred toward us, rolling to duck beneath a death ray, and pressed its back to the wall. The mask peeled away to reveal Hutchins. "We tried to contact you, but one of the OPFORs accidentally set off a stun mine we'd placed while they were positioning equipment. The rest of their group threw up a powered shield and turned on an aethernet jammer to keep us from communicating with anyone outside."

"Sitrep?" Elyssa asked.

"Eight casualties, at least three fatalities on our side. We've incapacitated over a dozen OPFORs with Lancers." Despite the staggering losses, Hutchins's faced remained stoic as he reviewed the

311

situation. "The OPFORs arrived a couple of hours ago. We don't know what their original plan was. They set off the mine before they executed."

"Any sign of Kassus?" I asked.

He shook his head. "Just his men."

Kassus must have set this plan in motion before attempting to murder me in my own home. If he knew he'd have people in place here, why hadn't he shown?

"Oh, crap," Elyssa said, her eyes locked on the cave roof above the nursery.

I flicked my gaze in that direction in time to see a flying carpet dropping rapidly through a portal far above. I caught a glimpse of Kassus as he dropped directly into the nursery in the middle of the coiled leyworms. The leyworms were too preoccupied with the attackers outside to notice the man sneaking into their midst.

I threw the carpet Elyssa and I had ridden on the ground, and jumped on, feeling my feet magically bond to the carpet. Elyssa's arms wrapped around my waist. I willed the carpet toward the nursery just as Kassus's carpet shot straight up. I saw a cupid in his arms. He noticed me and leered.

"I'll kill you, Slade," he shouted. "It's only a matter of time." With that, he vanished into the portal.

The giant leyworms rotated their heads toward the noise.

"No!" I shouted as my carpet raced for the rift.

The portal winked out.

One of the leyworms roared. A pulse of energy the size of the thing's body lanced into the air where the portal had been. A tremendous boom echoed in the cavern, and the portal ripped wide open. I shot through the new hole, riding the carpet like a surfboard as Elyssa held on tight. We swooped into another control room, location unknown. The orientation abruptly shifted since the portal had been oriented up while the opening here was to the side.

"Something's wrong with the omniarch," Elyssa said.

I executed a hockey stop with the carpet, looking around the control room for a sign of Kassus. Sparing a glance back at the entry, I felt my eyes widen with horror. The portal was huge. The omniarch warped around it, much like walls and other solid objects did when the portal opened inside them. But that wasn't what terrified me.

## Dearest Mother of Mine

Gigantor had launched itself toward the portal and was coming straight at us, maw gaping wide.

# Chapter 39

My muscles froze at the sight of the red-scaled leviathan streaking toward us, an angry roar bursting from its throat. Gigantor might be after Kassus, but I was between it and its prey. What if it caught up to the Arcane and swallowed him whole? I'd never get the man's blood.

Steeling myself, I swept the rug around, riding it like a surfboard ripping a wave, and shot toward where I thought the control room exit might lie. We flashed past an Alabaster Arch, up toward the map platform. I heard the loud crack of rock behind. Flicked my gaze back as the giant leyworm slithered into the control room behind us. It plowed straight down into the floor, vanishing beneath the rock.

"Justin, watch out!" Elyssa shouted.

I swung my gaze forward, ducking just in time to swoop through the control room door and into a cavernous way station. An Obsidian Arch loomed large in the center, apparently intact. Yellow light suffused the cavern much like the others I'd seen. I spotted movement across the way and saw Kassus making for a wide, sloping tunnel. Urging the carpet on, we flashed across the cavern just a few feet above the polished floor. The tunnel curved, reminding me of the one at the Grotto way station, the bend keeping Kassus from sight. We reached a straightaway. Sunlight streamed through an opening ahead. I saw vines and other undergrowth blocking part of the exit, though much appeared to have been cleared away.

The carpet jetted from the opening. I had to veer sharply to avoid a huge tree, twisting my feet, and bringing the carpet to a halt. Trees and vines blocked every direction, granting very little room to maneuver. Hot humid air pressed against my skin. The sound of insects and other animals echoed through the dense forest. All these sensations flicked through my mind in an instant before my brain grasped the obvious. Kassus wasn't threading his way through the trees.

I directed the carpet straight up. We rose above the tree line. Steep canyon walls bordered a jungle valley on all sides. I wondered if we were in Africa, or lost in the jungles of South America.

"There!" Elyssa said, pointing to a receding form on a carpet several hundred yards away.

I swung the carpet around and willed it forward. Wind whistled past my ears, drawing tears from my eyes. This carpet's magical wind barrier didn't seem to be working. I dropped to my knees, pulling Elyssa down with me. Despite the wind, the magical bond holding us to the carpet felt firm. I hoped by ducking low, we'd be more aerodynamic.

Either it worked, or Kassus had a slower carpet. He grew closer in the distance.

Elyssa's grip tightened around my arm. "Look behind us."

I did and immediately regretted it. Trees bent and broke like twigs as something humongous plowed through them. Startled birds took flight in a riot of colors as a dragon obliterated their perches. A bellowing roar shook the air. Within an instant, it seemed every bird in the vicinity took flight with a cacophony of shrieks and squawks of alarm.

A wave of black bats flapped past us, bodies slamming against us as we jetted through the swarm. Elyssa and I ducked closer to the carpet as the air came to life with flapping bodies and high-pitched cries. I sputtered as a hairy body smacked into my face, its claws gripping my skin. I pulled away a frightened looking bat. I flung it away, spitting out hair, and felt my own spittle smack me in the face as the wind flung it right back at me.

*Smooth move, Einstein.*

The air cleared as the flying creatures gained altitude above us. I spotted Kassus fighting through a wave of white fowl. His staff threw out waves of energy ahead of him, turning the birds to blackened, smoking forms that fell back into the green canopy.

He turned to look at us, a fierce scowl radiating fury. He aimed his staff at us, but a stray bird conked him in the head. His aim shifted and a shaft of light scorched a score of birds nearby instead of us. A

315

white blanket fluttered from the cradle of his other arm where he held the cupid.

He fired another shot. I veered left, easily dodging his attacks at this range. Kassus gave up his attempts, and angled up a cliff face. We followed. As we leveled off, even with a small plateau, I saw moving forms, a metal railing, and realized with horror Kassus was leading us straight toward what looked like a place where tourists viewed the magnificent sights behind us.

We were no more than fifty yards behind the Arcane. I saw people on the plateau pointing at us. Kassus aimed his staff at the railing where a man leaned on it, a large camera to his face. A narrow beam sliced the rails away. The man screamed as he fell forward into open air.

"Bastard!" I shouted, and took the carpet into a steep dive.

Elyssa gripped the man's hand just feet above the trees. The extra weight dragged on the carpet, pulling it toward the jungle. I gritted my teeth, straining, and willing the rug to rise. Its velocity slowed. Then it shot straight up while Elyssa swung the terrified man to the carpet.

"What the hell is this thing?" he cried out, falling to his knees and gripping the sides of the carpet.

"Where are we?" I asked.

His wide eyes stared blankly at me for a moment.

I snapped my fingers in his face. "Where are we?"

He blinked. "The Three Sisters."

"What country?"

He peered over the edge of the rug, and his face blanched. "Australia," he said through chattering teeth.

We crested the ledge, glided a foot off the ground as wide-eyed, dumbfounded people stared. Elyssa pried the man's hands from the edge of the carpet and guided him off. He stumbled, dropped to his knees, disbelieving eyes following us. I swung my gaze around the area, scanning for Kassus.

A piercing roar shattered the air and the entire ledge rumbled.

The dragon was coming. I spun the carpet back over the ledge and saw trees bursting from the ground in the monster's wake. Did it intend to come up here? The attention of the tourists shifted. Someone pointed over the railing and screamed as the dragon's glowing maw rose above the trees.

"Run!" I shouted. "Get out of here!"

Apparently, people had no problems taking advice from a man on a flying carpet, because they scattered, screaming. Anyone who didn't speak English seemed to take the cue from the panic of fellow humans and bolted toward a parking lot.

The ledge rattled. Chunks broke off, sending the rest of the railing and pay-per-use telescopes tumbling into the abyss. Elyssa gripped my arm, and pointed at a figure rising over a tree-topped hill before vanishing on the other side. I swung the carpet in pursuit, pulling into a steep climb. Tree tops brushed the bottom of the carpet as we raced along. At the peak, I spotted Kassus diving down the slope above the switchback road below and toward a plain dotted with scrubby bushes and rocks. A herd of kangaroos scattered as he swooped over them and toward a small town in the distance.

I angled to follow, kneeling to give us more speed. Just as Kassus reached the outskirts of the town, his carpet dropped a foot. He pounded a fist against it, but something seemed wrong with his ride.

Our carpet shuddered and slowed. My feet lost cohesion for a split second, and I gripped the side of the rug for support.

"The magical charge is running out," Elyssa said, her grip on my waist tightening.

"Looks like Kassus isn't having any better luck," I said.

The Arcane's carpet landed. Kassus stumbled off it and onto the road. A red car skidded to a halt just in time to miss the man. Our carpet lost more altitude. Kassus jerked the driver from the car, and got in. Tires screeched as the car raced into town.

I looked frantically for another car while the carpet slowed, drifting toward the ground. We might be able to catch Kassus on foot, but it would be much harder. How the hell did someone charge a magic carpet? I didn't see anywhere to plug it into an outlet. I thought back to the flying car and how I'd powered it. Planting my hand against the carpet, I closed my eyes, and willed aether to flow from me and into it. The fabric went limp and we dropped like rocks.

Elyssa cursed.

I looked down. Saw the ground rushing to meet us. This was going to effing hurt.

*Power on, you stupid carpet!*

I drew in a breath and blew out, willing power into the carpet. *Energize!* It went stiff. Caught the air. Shot forward just feet above the ground. I kept my hand on the carpet, pushing aether into it, unsure how to tell when it had a full charge.

A terrific rumbling sounded behind us. I whipped my head around to see the road churning behind us as if a mole the size of an airplane was tunneling beneath it. The upheaval shoved cars off the road, sent power poles leaning at crazy angles, and left a trench where the road used to be.

Kassus's car screeched around a corner. I shot above houses, aiming diagonally across the town. The leyworm changed course.

"How does that thing know where the baby is?" I asked Elyssa.

She shook her head, fear and wonder in her eyes. "Maybe the same way those things tracked that portable arch we used to escape from El Dorado."

I couldn't stop watching as a house literally bounced in the air in the leyworm's wake, breaking the structure in half when it landed. I looked for signs of life, praying nobody had been inside. More houses broke apart, collapsing as the earth bubbled then collapsed just as suddenly, shattering foundations and leaving nothing but rubble behind.

Kassus had to know he had nowhere to run, especially if the leyworm could follow him anywhere. His car emerged from the other side of the small town. I heard the motor roaring as he pressed the pedal to the floor. Slowly but surely, the car began to pull away. I willed more power into the carpet. It surged forward. Wind tore at my face, blurring my vision with tears. I pressed my lips tight and leaned into it.

*Where is he going?*

I looked back and saw the leyworm falling behind. It must be tiring. I couldn't imagine the amount of energy it took to move that much mass. The rippling earth receded, vanished. Had it given up?

Despite our extra speed, we weren't gaining on Kassus. I clenched my teeth, frustration building, rage simmering in my chest. He couldn't get away this time.

*Get him!*

My chest flared like an inferno. Heat blazed down my arm. The carpet shot forward. The scenery blurred for an instant, and we closed in on the car like it was standing still.

"Justin!" Elyssa shouted.

I didn't dare turn my head for fear of losing my concentration. I felt the fragile connection with my angel powers waver. The odor of burning rug reached my nose, and I knew we had to reach Kassus now or never.

"We're burning up!" Elyssa said, fear in her voice.

Not a lot of things frightened my ninja girlfriend that much, so I knew the situation had just hit code red. But I couldn't stop. Not now. The car was just twenty yards ahead.

I felt heat on my back. Felt the carpet going limp beneath us. I turned my head and saw blue flames sputtering in the wind. Nearly half the carpet was blackened or turned to ash and scattered in the wind. It lost power, and I knew this time I wouldn't be able to stop us from hitting the ground at horrific speed. Elyssa slapped her hands against my ribs. The nightingale armor grew webbing beneath my arms and between my legs.

"Hold your arms and legs out!" she said, an instant before spreading hers. The air caught in the webbing, and she glided away.

I did the same. The air slammed into me. Hot flames flashed past as the carpet plummeted to the ground. I slowed. For an instant, it felt like I was flying. Then I dropped. I tried to execute a roll when I hit the ground, instead landing awkwardly on a rock and twisting my ankle. I cried out with pain. Elyssa glided like a flying squirrel, ducked into a roll, and managed to miss the plentiful rocks before springing to her feet gracefully.

I stood, limping, and watched the car race away. "Son of a bitch! He's getting away again!" I tried to run, but my ankle was having none of it. I felt my face turning red hot. Felt my fists clench tight enough to crack my knuckles. Maybe if I manifested I could catch him. Maybe if—

The ground ahead of the car exploded upward in a rain of earth and rock. Gigantor bellowed loud enough to vibrate the air. Before Kassus could stop the speeding vehicle, the leyworm swallowed it whole. I heard the horn honk twice before the creature submerged into the ground and vanished.

"Oh, no," I said. "Please, no." My voice sounded weak. My knees gave way, and I dropped to the ground. Kassus was gone. Mom was going to die.

# Chapter 40

I heard Elyssa speaking with someone. "Dispatch Custodians to these coordinates," she said. "Major cleanup." I heard her snap a picture. Felt her arms embrace me. "I'm so sorry, Justin. I'm so, so sorry."

I found the strength to look up from the ground and saw tears in her eyes. "Me too," I said. "Me too."

"I sent Shelton a picture so we can go home."

"Home to what?" I mumbled as my heart constricted with pain.

The portal opened a few minutes later. Shelton saw us and shook his head. "Why do I get the feeling there's a long story behind you two being in Australia?"

I couldn't muster a response. Defeat overwhelmed my will to do anything but mope as I rose to my feet and stepped through the portal and back into the mansion with Elyssa.

My phone rang. It was Cinder. I didn't feel like talking to him or anyone else for that matter. It rang until it went to voicemail. The portal winked out behind us.

"Are you okay?" Shelton said. "What happened to him, Elyssa?"

"We lost Kassus again," she said. "A leyworm ate him."

"Holy crab cakes in a public toilet," Shelton said. "Oh, man, I'm sorry."

"Mom's going to die," I said, and would have dropped to the floor if Elyssa hadn't held me up.

Another phone rang. Shelton pulled his out. "Yeah?" he answered. His eyes flashed wide. "Be right there." He gripped my arm. "Get back inside the omniarch circle," he said, indicating the silver ring on the floor.

I didn't have the will to resist.

"What's going on?" Elyssa asked.

Shelton grunted. An image of the El Dorado cave flickered into existence within the omniarch. I sighed, sucked in a breath, and walked forward.

*It's over. I need to tell Mom goodbye.*

Tears welled in my eyes at the thought. I reached deep down inside for the strength I knew was there. We'd done everything superhumanly possible to save her. After all was said and done, we'd lost the fight. I would miss Mom with all my heart. Hot moisture dripped down my cheeks as we walked deeper into the cavern. She'd put me through hell these past few months. She'd done the unforgiveable and abandoned her own child. But she'd done it to atone for letting her daughter be taken from her. Her actions had wounded me deeply, placing everyone I loved in mortal danger. Through it all, I knew she'd loved me. Maybe I was stupid for thinking so, but she'd made a choice no mother should have to make.

Despite everything, I knew one thing for certain.

*I forgive you, Mom.*

I could only hope she was still alive for me to tell her that.

I felt Elyssa's hands stiffen on me. "Oh my god," she said.

Looking up, I felt my own eyes grow wide. A crushed car sat before the two giant leyworms. The portal in the cave roof was gone, and Gigantor was back, coiled around the nursery next to Lulu.

Without thought, I raced to the car. I saw a black-robed form inside, pinned between the roof and the driver seat. On the passenger side, I saw a cupid wriggling. Kassus's eyes blinked open. He tried to move and couldn't. The bent door held his arm and leg from one side while the car roof pressed his body to the seat. Kassus screamed like a little girl.

"Let me out of here! Let me out!"

I leaned in, feeling an evil grin peel my teeth from my lips as I saw blood seeping from a wound in the man's head. I found one of Meghan's blood vials in the utility pack at my waist. Pressed it to Kassus's head and watched as the glass filled with crimson liquid. Elyssa wrenched the other door open, and took the cooing cupid back into the nursery as the leyworms, heads resting on the cave floor, watched.

"How does it feel to be trapped, Kassus?" I said in a low whisper. "How does it feel knowing nobody's going to set you free, that you're going to die in here?"

"C'mon, Slade, please. You've got to let me out. I-I can't stand tight spaces." A tear trickled from the corner of his eyes.

"I don't think so," I said, knowing full well I wouldn't let him die like this no matter how much I hated the bastard. "Enjoy your stay, you piece of crap."

"Let me out!" he screamed over and over until his raw voice faded into a whimper.

Elyssa and I were already running back through the portal. I closed it, reopened it in the Templar garage. Stepped through and ran for the container. Two Templar guards watched as I blurred toward the tractor trailer. I pressed the button on the vial and trailed blood down my finger, swiped it across the door seam. The doors swung open.

I saw the small form of my mother in a kneeling position on the floor, her arms and head secured in what looked like a medieval torture device, a black cloth over her eyes. I opened them with Kassus's blood, and tore off the blindfold. She sagged into my arms, her blonde hair spilling across her face.

"Mom," I said. "Please be alive. Please!"

Elyssa pressed her ear to Mom's mouth. She looked up at me, eyes heavy with regret, and shook her head.

I gingerly laid Mom's head on my lap, smoothed hair from her face.

*Ivy looks so much like her.*

Tears burned my eyes. Ivy wasn't going to lose her mom. *We* weren't going to lose her. I drew in a deep breath, feeling for the one thing I knew could save her. Flicking open my incubus senses, I saw the dim halo of light fading to a dull orange around Mom's still form. I latched onto it with my tendrils, reached down deep inside me and did what I had done so long ago for someone else I loved. I pushed essence through my tendrils and into her.

My efforts hit a wall. Black spots danced before my eyes. Was I tired, or was something in Mom blocking me? I redoubled my efforts. Still nothing. Thinking back to the feeling I'd had when energizing the carpet, I focused on my heart.

*I love you, Mom.*

I felt a flicker of heat. Essence pulsed along my tendrils.

Everything went black.

Unfamiliar faces flashed through my mind. Words, shouts, all incomprehensible, assaulted me. Emotions, thoughts, odors, all too fleeting to be anything but impressions washed over me in a confusing wave.

I hovered above a sea of bodies in a land of twilight. Humans in primitive leather armor surged toward an oncoming army. The front lines crashed together. Bodies flew through the air. My vision focused on the enemy charge. Fangs flashed, blood sprayed, and the human line melted under the onslaught of vampires and a variety of horrors I'd never seen.

Someone shouted words in a language I didn't recognize. Clouds in the gray sky opened and brilliant white light rained down on the vampires, splashing like molten liquid. I heard their screams even above the din of battle.

More images flickered past. People dying. Vampires leaping twenty feet through the air, pouncing their prey and killing them with vicious precision. Leviathan leyworms charging a line of Seraphim. The scenes ran faster until they were nothing but a blur. And then, a brilliant flash of light followed by absolute darkness.

I sucked in a breath.

I was back in the trailer, Mom cradled in my lap. Her eyes flashed open, revealing black orbs. She gasped, and her hands locked around my throat. I felt energy flood from me in a torrent. Felt my muscles go limp. Watched as brilliant light burst from my mouth. Before I could say or think anything else, consciousness winked into oblivion.

"Justin," said a calm, female voice. I felt a hand smooth my hair back. "It's Mom, sweetie. I'm here, and everything will be okay."

"Mommy," I said, snuggling into warm folds of fabric.

*Mom?*

I jerked awake. A curtain of blond hair hung above me. I saw Mom looking down at me, blue eyes smiling back.

"You're alive," I said, pushing up from the hard floor of the trailer. I hugged her as tears filled my vision. "I can't believe it."

"I'm sorry," she said, rocking back and forth in our embrace. "What I've put you through—" her voice broke.

"I forgive you," I said. "I was angry for a long time. But I have to believe you did it for a reason."

"I don't deserve your forgiveness," she said in a soft voice. "Your father and I put you and Ivy through too much. No matter the reason, no one should do that to their children."

Questions rose to my lips, but I pushed them away. The time for answers would come, but now was not the time or the place. Pushing myself to wobbly knees, I pulled Mom up. Elyssa stood nearby, her own eyes welling with tears. She smiled. Nodded. Everything was good.

For now.

# Chapter 41

"Here's to the master of disaster!" Shelton said, raising a champagne glass in toast. "May he one day calm the hell down so we can lead ordinary lives."

"Hear, hear!" went up shouts around the long table in the mansion's dining hall.

I grinned, gripped Elyssa's hand, and fought down a wave of hopeless optimism. Friends and family crowded around the table. The Borathens had come, even Michael, who sat to his father's right. Nightliss and Katie grinned from across the table. Felicia and her boyfriend Larry sat next to Meghan and Adam. Stacey giggled as Ryland bit into a giant turkey leg while Cutsauce ran around the table yipping and begging for scraps.

Bruce's nephew, Darren, sat near Shelton. Apparently, Bruce had sent a picture of the Russian prison cell to Shelton. According to Shelton, rescuing the young man had been pretty simple, aside from finding him in the middle of using the toilet and the awkward situation of running through the portal before he had a chance to use toilet paper. I was happy I hadn't had to witness the scene and glad Shelton had held up his bargain with the surly Overworld Transportation Authority employee.

Adam pulled me aside after dinner. Shelton joined us.

"Thought you might be interested to know we figured out how to use the Alabaster Arch to get to the Grand Nexus," Adam said.

I felt my eyes widen. "You did?"

He nodded. "My program downloaded a lot of information on the research Darkwater and arch operators were doing on the arches. Apparently, there's a pattern you trace on the modulus, and it'll rejigger the Alabaster Arch's coordinates."

326

I remembered what the arch operator had tried to tell me the day we'd first run into Kassus and his men. "What's the pattern?"

"Remember when we accidentally appeared in the Grand Nexus?" Shelton said.

"How could I forget that?" I asked, my mouth going dry at the thought of control room full of cherubs.

"Yeah, well we noticed a symbol that looked a lot like the Cyrinthian character for zero, except instead of just the circle with the upside-down "V" in it, it also has a horizontal line across the center." Shelton took out his arcphone and displayed it for me. "Darkwater discovered this is the pattern you have to trace on the modulus before activating the Alabaster Arch."

"Why haven't they cleared it of cherubs then?" I asked.

Adam chuckled. "Did you see how many are in there? It'd be impossible without some serious manpower."

"Yeah," Shelton said with a nod. "No way we're going there until we figure out how to handle that horde."

I blew out a breath. "At least we know Daelissa can't get to it."

"Yet," Shelton said.

"Yeah." I grinned. "Awesome work, guys. We'll figure this out."

Shelton groaned. "Maybe we shouldn't have told him."

Adam laughed.

The Christmas party ran on into the night. I kept things casual, doing my best not to wonder about the dubious future which lay ahead. I went outside by myself, enjoying the cool breeze as it cleared my senses. The front door opened, and I turned to see Mom. She sat on the front stairs next to me, and pecked a kiss on my forehead.

"I'm amazed at what you've accomplished, Justin," she said, shaking her head slowly. "You've surrounded yourself with so many good people. Pulled them together despite their differences." She took a sip of wine. "I tried to do what I could on my own, but Daelissa always seems a step ahead."

"Ivy wants to come live with us," I said. "She was going to try to get Kassus's blood." Thomas Borathen had taken the Arcane into custody, locking him away in the specially built cells beneath the Templar compound.

Mom smiled. "I want to bring her here as soon as possible." She raised an eyebrow. "If that's okay with you."

"Yeah," I said with a grin. "I'd like that." A sigh escaped my lips as thoughts turned to someone else. "What about Dad?"

Her smile faded. "There's a lot you don't know about him. So much I swore an oath not to tell."

"Is he really an evil mastermind?" I asked. "Why would he suddenly decide marrying Kassallandra is a good idea?" Supposedly, he'd been betrothed to the red-headed Daemas before he met Mom. I wasn't so sure anymore it was the truth.

She took a sip of wine, and looked into the dark. "He wasn't entirely truthful to you about a lot of things. He's far more capable than he lets on."

"Can you elaborate?" I asked, tired of the word games that passed for answers.

"It's better if you ask him yourself."

Considering his wedding was close on the horizon, I wanted to confront him soon.

*Confront, or ask?*

I bit my lip. A lot would depend on him. Another question pestered me. "What does Jeremiah Conroy want, and why hasn't he given the Cyrinthian rune to Daelissa?"

"Ah," Mom said, a wan smile teasing her lips. "He *is* an enigma. There's something about him I feel I should know. My memory of the past is still so fuzzy and faint in many ways. I'm not sure if that's due to Daelissa's mind tricks, or simply due to the Desecration. I know the answer to who he really is must be locked in there somewhere if I could only break through the haze." She sighed, shook her head. "I don't know how you've managed so far. David and I kept you in the dark about so much, and yet, you've overcome obstacle after obstacle."

*Not all of them.*

Mom rose, stretched, and yawned. "I promised Nightliss I would talk with her. Perhaps we can help each other remember our past."

I stood and took her hand, looking her in the eyes. "Are you being honest with me right now? Or are you throwing up more barriers? It wouldn't make me very happy to find out later that you're intentionally hiding things from me."

"Aside from the subject of your father, I am telling you all I know," she said, squeezing my hand. "You can trust me, Justin."

I nodded. "I want to. You can understand if I'm a little leery, though."

She returned a sad smile. "I do understand." Mom kissed me on the forehead. "We'll talk later, son."

"Tell me the moment anything comes out of that noggin of yours," I said, and hugged her.

After the door closed behind her, my phone buzzed with a text message. *Please come to the road.* The message was from Lornicus.

I paused. *Talk about creepy.* I texted Elyssa. She joined me a moment later.

"I let Shelton know to charge out with the army if he doesn't hear from us," she said. A shudder passed through her shoulders. "I don't trust this golem."

"That makes two of us," I said.

We made our way down the long drive to the road. A lone figure stood silhouetted beneath a flickering gas lamp. Lornicus saw the two of us and smiled.

"Ah, Miss Borathen. So pleased to make your acquaintance," he said, offering a hand.

She looked at it suspiciously, not offering her own in return. "What do you want?"

"Ah, yes," he said, withdrawing his hand. "I can see you're uneasy about me, but I assure you, Justin and I have an agreement. I present no threat to him."

"Considering how you kidnapped him, you'll forgive me if I don't agree."

He smiled. "Understood." His gaze turned to me. "I'm happy to see you accomplished your goal without my help."

"I doubt that," I said. "You didn't get your own pet cupid."

A shrug. "It would have been fascinating to acquire one, but I am not displeased with you by any stretch of the imagination."

"What about Mr. Gray?" I said. "Did I screw up his master plan again?"

"He considers your accomplishments quite troubling, I will admit, though, at present, I believe he intends to leave you be." The golem folded his arms behind his back. "I have other offerings of information you may find useful, however."

I raised an eyebrow. "Oh? And what would you want for this information?"

"I'm sure you can guess," he said.

I snorted.

"Before you make any hasty decisions, Mr. Slade, let me give you a sample."

"Fine," I said, waving a hand dismissively. I wouldn't entrust the golem with a pet chipmunk, much less a baby angel. "Let's hear it."

"For one, I can offer you the truth behind Jeremiah Conroy."

"Interesting, but I think we'll figure that one out on our own."

"I also have fascinating insight into your father's past." He smiled.

"The truth or just conjecture?" I asked, feeling my curiosity pique.

His lips pressed into an amused smirk, as if he'd just found the weak spot in my armor. "The truth, of course. Mr. Gray knows quite a bit about David Slade."

*Just walk away.* My gut feeling agreed with my brain for once. "No deal," I said. "Is there anything else besides a cupid you'd be interested in?"

"For such a valuable piece of information, I'm afraid not, Mr. Slade." He sighed. "I don't understand why you're so reluctant to give me one Seraphim infant. The leyworms have their own plans for them, you know. I don't think you'd like what they have in mind."

"Enlighten me," I said, wondering what in the world the leyworms could want with the cupids. True, they were intelligent beings, and they obviously had no intention of letting anyone steal their strange brood. But were the creatures truly planning something bad?

"They are not of this realm," he said. "While I don't know their true origins, I'm certain they were put here by a greater power."

"What, to terrorize spelunkers?" I said in a scoffing tone. "They seem pretty content to stick to the caves."

Lornicus shrugged. "Mr. Gray believes they were put here by whomever created the arches. He believes they are the ones who sowed this realm with ley lines, giving rise to magic in preparation for them to create the arches."

"Great. Are you telling me there's another invasion besides the Seraphim we have to worry about?" I asked. What he said fit with the little I knew about the creatures. They had an affinity with ley lines and aether I couldn't explain.

"I do not know, Mr. Slade." The golem gave an apologetic smile. "Please consider what I've said. Allowing the leyworms to keep the cupids, as you so quaintly call them, could be a terrible mistake."

"And giving them to you would be just as bad," I said.

"Hmm, I don't agree with your assessment." He shrugged. "I suppose time will have to tell, won't it?"

"I guess so," I said.

"Until next time," Lornicus said, and walked away.

Elyssa shook her head as she watched the receding form. "That *thing* gives me the creeps. Never give in to his demand."

"Not if I can help it," I said.

"It acts as if a person is just something you can give away." She scowled. "I just hope what he said about the leyworms isn't true."

I took Elyssa's hand, and smiled. "Let's not worry about it right now. It's almost Christmas. Maybe we can convince jolly Saint Nick to lend us a helping hand."

She laughed. "I can only imagine us fighting side-by-side with elves." She quirked an eyebrow. "You realize we have unfinished business, right?"

"Well yeah, there's my dad, Daelissa—"

"No, silly." She poked my nose and grinned. "We never finished our little match."

My brain rewound the past few days before what she meant hit me. "Oh, our wrestling match."

"It's not wrestling." She tugged my hand. "Let's go finish this. I want to kick your butt and be done with it."

"Not gonna happen," I said, following her.

We trashed talked all the way down to the gauntlet room. Elyssa wore a tight sweater and skirt which came to mid-thigh. I had on jeans and a T-shirt, neither of which I wanted to rip to shreds by manifesting. I had a feeling she would beat me handily unless I came up with something. I swung my arms in circles, did some stretches.

"Stop stalling," Elyssa said, hands on hips.

"Your legs are really distracting," I said. Not to mention the way the sweater hugged her curves.

"All's fair in war," she said with a wicked grin, hiking her skirt to show a little more leg. She flashed across the room.

I had time for a startled yelp before she was on me. I twisted to the side, barely keeping my feet as she tried to sweep them from beneath me. We gripped each other's shoulders, our arms tensing to throw the other off balance. Elyssa jerked. I felt her foot against my stomach as she flipped me over while lying on her back. Using the momentum, I finished the flip, landing on my feet, and turned to pin her. She was already up, her foot sweeping low. I jumped. Landed. She finished the spin, her other foot flashing out. I dove forward, off-balance, and landed atop her. We both fell to the floor tangled in each other's arms, laughing.

As we lay on our sides, laughter dying away, I pushed a lock of raven hair behind her ear. "Guess it's a tie."

She nodded. "Probably better this way."

"Better?" I said with a grin. "It's the best. I love you. Thanks for always being there for me."

"As if anyone or anything could stop me." She smothered me with a kiss. "I love you."

I was happy. My family was growing by leaps and bounds. Mom was here. I'd soon bring Ivy here. I felt nearly complete.

*Watch out, Dad. You're next.*

####

# Section A
## MEET THE AUTHOR

John Corwin has been making stuff up all his life. As a child he would tell his sisters he was an alien clone of himself and would eat tree bark to prove it.

In middle school, John started writing for realz. He wrote short stories about Fargo McGronsky, a young boy with anger management issues whose dog, Noodles, had been hit by a car. The violent stories were met with loud acclaim from classmates and a great gnashing of teeth by his English teacher.

Years later, after college and successful stints as a plastic food wrap repairman and a toe model for GQ, John once again decided to put his overactive imagination to paper for the world to share and became an author.

Connect with John Corwin online:
Facebook: http://www.facebook.com/johnhcorwinauthor
Blog http://johncorwin.blogspot.com/
Twitter: http://twitter.com/#!/John_Corwin